Emma Fraser is an ex-nurse and she completed her training in Edinburgh. After writing several medical romances under the name Anne Fraser, her research into medical training in the early twentieth century inspired her to write about strong Scottish nurses and female doctors during World War I and her first novel as Emma Fraser, *When the Dawn Breaks*, was the result. *When the Dawn Breaks* was shortlisted for the Epic Romantic Novel RoNA Award in 2014. Emma lives with her husband and two children in Glasgow.

Also by Emma Fraser

When the Dawn Breaks

WE SHALL REMEMBER

Emma Fraser

sphere

SPHERE

First published in Great Britain in 2014 by Sphere

A CIP catalogue record for this book
is available from the British Library.

Hardback ISBN 978-0-7515-5123-5

Printed and bound in Great Britain by
Clays Ltd, St Ives plc

Papers used by Sphere are from well-managed forests
and other responsible sources.

MIX
Paper from
responsible sources
FSC® C104740

Sphere
An imprint of
Little, Brown Book Group
100 Victoria Embankment
London EC4Y 0DY

An Hachette UK Company
www.hachette.co.uk

www.littlebrown.co.uk

To Hanka Kościa and all those who, like her, risked or lost their lives during World War Two.

Acknowledgements

As always, I owe so many people thanks for their help with this book. Firstly my daughter Katherine for alerting me to the true story of Dr Eugene Lazowski and Dr Stanislaw Matulewicz, who created a fake typhus epidemic that saved many Poles from German labour and death camps. Reading about them inspired me to write this story.

Huge thanks also to my friend Karen and my daughter Rachel for accompanying me on my trips to Poland; to my sisters Flora and Mairi for your support and encouragement during the writing of this book and your valuable insights; to Dr Maria Graham for showing me the collection of memorabilia from the Polish hospital in Edinburgh; to Thalia Proctor, Manpreet Grewal and their team for their patience and insights; to my agent Judith Murdoch and to Hanka Kościa, who joined the Home Army as a cadet when she was sixteen and who shared her incredible story with me – you are amazing.

And last, but not least, to my husband Stewart for giving me the time and space to write this story – I know it's not always easy living with a writer!

Books I found particularly helpful while writing this book and that readers might find interesting were: *The Eagle Unbowed* by Halik Kochanski, *We Were Young and at War* by Sarah Wallis and Svetlana Palmer, *Station 43: Audley End House and SOE's Polish Section* by Ian Valentine and *The Spy Who Loved: The secrets and lives of Christine Granville, Britain's first agent of WWII* by Clare Mulley. Any errors are, of course, mine.

When you go home tell them of us and say
for your tomorrow we gave our today
Attributed to John Maxwell Edmonds (1875 – 1958)

They shall grow not old, as we that are left grow old:
Age shall not weary them, nor the years condemn.
At the going down of the sun and in the morning,
We will remember them.
From 'For the Fallen' by Laurence Binyon

Chapter 1

Warsaw, Poland
1 September 1939

Irena cowered under the chassis of the car, pressing her face into the road so hard it hurt. Bullets ripped into the metal only inches away from her, and as spurts of dirt from the side of the road bit into her skin, she covered her head with her hands and screamed.

The drone of the plane receded and she risked a look to her left. A man staggered to his feet, his arm hanging limply by his side, and took a few uncertain steps towards her before falling to his knees. He reached out a bloody hand, his pleading eyes fixed on her.

She was about to scramble out from under the car to help him when she heard it: the whine of the returning plane.

Using his uninjured elbow to propel himself forward, the man inched towards her, in a desperate, floppy movement.

'Hurry,' she urged. She wasn't sure if she'd spoken the words or merely thought them. If he could make it to the car he'd be safe – at least, as safe as she was. Under the car she ran the risk of death; out there in the open, it was almost a certainty.

Please. Help me, he mouthed. His eyes were wide pools of terror.

She wanted to, God, she wanted to, but she couldn't make her body move.

The screeching of the plane grew louder, and as it descended, Irena could clearly make out the swastikas on the wings. It opened fire again; a staccato of bullets slashing the ground. The man jerked a few times and lay still.

Just when she thought the Luftwaffe pilot was going to make another sweep, a Polish plane dropped down from the clouds. Immediately the German turned his attention to his attacker, and within moments both planes had disappeared from the sky. Irena curled into a ball. Only a few hours ago she'd been sleeping, dreaming of Piotr. Now she was in the middle of a nightmare.

Her father was wrong. Everyone had been wrong. This wasn't war. This was murder.

Yesterday, she and Magdalena, like so many other Varsovians, had been making the most of the last day of the summer holidays. It had been gloriously warm so they'd spent the morning in the park, sitting on a bench chatting, stopping now and again to watch the children as they played close to their mothers and nannies. As an elderly couple strolled past with their arms linked, Irena and Magdalena exchanged an envious look. Like most young Polish men, their fiancés had been with their units for well over a month.

'Just think! In a few months we will truly be sisters,' Magdalena smiled. She was to marry Irena's brother Aleksy at Christmas. She tucked her arm into Irena's. 'You and Piotr will be next.'

'Not for another two years. Not until I have qualified.'

'I couldn't wait that long. I can hardly wait three months!'

'Piotr and I have all the time in the world to be married,' Irena replied. Even as she said the words she wondered if that were true. There had been talk of war with Germany for some time, and since the invasion of Czechoslovakia and the increasingly strident demands from Hitler for a corridor from the Reich to East

Prussia, the prospect had seemed almost inevitable. But then Britain and France had signed a treaty and everyone had relaxed. Germany wouldn't do anything now, they told each other, and if there was a war it would be short lived. With Britain and France on their side they'd teach Hitler a lesson he wouldn't forget.

No one was truly concerned about the possibility of war. If anything, most people, especially the younger ones, were excited by it and there was almost a carnival air about the city. All the same, Irena couldn't help but worry. With her brother in the air force and her fiancé in the army, it would be stupid not to.

'When do you think we'll see Aleksy and Piotr again?' Magdalena asked.

'Soon, I hope.' Irena squeezed her friend's hand, shaking away the feeling of unease. There was no point in worrying about something that might not happen. 'Come on, Madzia, let's find somewhere to eat. I'm ravenous and if we still want to go to the concert and make it home before dark we should get on.' As she often did out of term time, Irena was spending the night at her friend's home a few miles out of Warsaw.

But in the early hours of the morning, Irena was woken by the sound of rumbling. Assuming it was a summer storm, she'd thrown back her bed covers and gone to close the window she'd left open to allow some night coolness into the room. At first she thought the flashes in the sky were lightning, but then realisation dawned. This was no storm. It was the sound of cannon coming from the east.

She ran to wake Magdalena and they stood at the bedroom window, holding hands, listening to the dull thud of explosions and watching in stunned silence as the sky filled with planes.

'Perhaps it's a training exercise,' Magdalena whispered.

Irena didn't think so. 'Come on, we should listen to the news.' On the landing they met Magdalena's mother, Elżbieta. The usually unruffled aristocrat looked pale and frightened. Her hair was coming loose from its plait and she was wearing a robe hastily pulled over her nightdress. 'What's happening?'

'We're going to find out,' Irena replied. 'There's bound be an announcement on the radio.'

They hurried downstairs to the drawing room where Elżbieta switched on the wireless.

'Poland is under attack. We are at war with Germany, but Polish forces will resist. Stay calm.' The terse announcement was repeated and followed, a few minutes later, by the national anthem and Chopin's Polonaise in A major. As they listened they were joined by the two maids and the cook, all in their nightclothes.

'Dear God,' Magdalena's mother murmured, crossing herself. 'I didn't think they would really do it.'

As the strains of the Chopin's Polonaise faded, the announcer came back on. 'Danzig and Krakow are being bombarded. We urge residents to stay calm and wait for further announcements.'

'Where's Tata?' Magdalena cried. 'And Piotr and Aleksy!'

Magdalena's father, Colonel Łaski, was Piotr's commanding officer in the Uhlan and Aleksy, Irena's brother and Magdalena's fiance, was a pilot with the Polish Pursuit Brigade.

When Magdalena started to cry, Irena gathered her into her arms. 'They'll be all right, Madzia. You'll see. Our army is strong. Besides, now that the Germans have attacked, the British and French will come to help us.'

Despite her words, Irena wasn't sure. They would come, but would they come in time? And what about *her* father? Thank God he had come to meet with a colleague at the Warsaw medical school, otherwise he'd be in Krakow.

'I must go,' Irena said. 'Knowing Tata, he'll have gone straight to the hospital. I have to go there, too. It's what he'll expect me to do.'

Her friend raised her tear-stained face. 'You can't. It's too dangerous. Stay here with us. Tell her, Mama.'

Irena drew away. 'I have to go, Madzia.'

Magdalena clutched her arm. 'Have you lost your mind? You can't go out there. At least wait a while. Perhaps the Germans will leave us alone. Maybe they're just making a point.'

Her friend had always been a dreamer. All her life she'd been protected from the harsher realities by parents who treated her as if she were too young to make decisions for herself. Irena loved her friend but sometimes Magdalena's unwillingness to see what was in front of her nose exasperated her. 'Anyway, you aren't a doctor,' Magdalena continued, 'only a medical student. What can you do?'

'I don't know.' Irena shrugged. 'Something. Anything. I just have to be there.'

Elżbieta added her protests to her daughter's. 'It's not safe. Your father would never forgive me if I let anything happen to you.'

'Nothing will happen to me!' Oddly, she wasn't at all frightened. She wanted to be in the thick of things. Nothing this exciting had ever happened before. It might soon be over and she didn't want to miss her chance to be part of it. Gently she removed Magdalena's hand from her arm. 'I won't be a moment.' She ran upstairs and into the guest room, pulled her dress on over her slip and started gathering together the rest of her belongings.

'Don't leave, Renia. Please.' Irena turned to find that Magdalena had followed her upstairs. 'I couldn't bear it if anything happened to you.'

Irena gripped her friend by the elbows. 'You mustn't worry about me. Warsaw is the best defended of our cities. It's probably safer there than here. You should come with me.'

'Mama won't leave, you know that.'

Irena lifted her valise. 'If there's any danger take shelter in the cellar and don't come out until you're sure it's safe.'

By the time they went back downstairs, the anti-aircraft guns were in action and the sky had cleared.

'Perhaps it is over,' Magdalena said.

Irena thought it unlikely. Aleksy had told her that fighter planes had only enough fuel to remain in the sky for short periods. The German aircraft would have had further to travel and so would need to refuel sooner. No doubt after they refuelled they'd be back. If she were going to go, it had to be now.

Elżbieta tried again to stop her from leaving but when she saw that Irena was determined to have her way, she grasped her hand. 'Take the car,' she said. 'It will be quicker than the train – supposing they're still running.' While Irena had been upstairs, Elżbieta had dressed and done her hair. She still looked less than her usual immaculate self, but she'd regained the bearing and courage befitting a Polish officer's wife.

'Won't you need it?' Irena asked.

'You know neither Magdalena nor I can drive. And with no chauffeur . . .' She frowned as if the inconvenience of being without a driver was more of an irritation than the war. 'Besides, we won't be going anywhere. Not until we hear from the colonel. He'll let us know when it's safe.'

'Phone me,' Magdalena pleaded, as a maid opened the front door, 'as soon as you have any news.'

'Of course,' Irena promised, kissing her one more time. 'Now go back inside.'

She drove as fast as she dared but outside the city she was forced to slow to a crawl. The road was blocked by a tide of people, travelling in both directions: those with cars – the richer Varsovians – heading out of the city, suitcases tied to their roofs; and the country folk – carts piled high with chairs, beds, suitcases and even livestock, the sick, the old and the very young clinging precariously to whatever they could hold onto – heading towards the city. Those without transport walked, clutching suitcases with one hand and their children with the other. Directly in front of Irena was a family, the mother holding onto her two children by the hands while the father, almost bent double under the weight of several suitcases, led the way.

She tooted the car horn, but it made little difference. It would have been quicker to walk – or to take a train, which, she could see, were still running.

It was then that the German plane had swooped down and opened fire on the train. Irena watched in horror as bullets punctured the metal and windows exploded in a hail of glass.

The plane climbed sharply, and panic-stricken passengers spilled from the train, scattering in all directions.

But the plane circled and came back, losing height rapidly. As people threw themselves into ditches or under carts, it opened fire again.

Irena scrambled out of the car and rolled under the chassis, covering her ears in a vain attempt to blot out the screams of terror and the relentless sound of machine-gunfire.

Now, as the sound of their engines faded, the air was filled with the terrible cries of the injured and the dying. Slowly, those who could lurched to their feet while others sat in shocked silence as if they didn't know where they were.

Irena forced herself to crawl out from under the car and staggered to her feet. As she took in the scene, bile rushed to her throat. She'd never seen anything like the carnage in front of her. Everywhere she looked there were torn and mutilated bodies, their belongings scattered across the field. Her body shaking uncontrollably, Irena moved towards the inert form of the man who had been reaching towards her and, although she knew it was pointless, felt for his pulse. Nothing. Her chest tightened. If only she'd been braver, he might still be alive.

Near him, a woman was on her knees, her body folded towards the ground as if in prayer, the back of her head caved in. Next to her corpse, a man cradled a bloodied youth in his lap. Despair washed over Irena. There were so many. What could she do? Where should she start?

On legs that felt boneless, she stumbled over to a man desperately calling for help. His wife had been hit in the shoulder and was pale and clammy, but conscious.

'It's okay,' Irena murmured. 'You'll be okay.'

She tore away the shredded cloth from the woman's shoulder and within seconds, dark gelatinous blood covered her fingers. The exit hole was about the size of a baby's fist. If the bleeding couldn't be stopped, the woman would die.

Irena ripped a strip from her dress and stuffed it in the wound. Almost immediately her temporary bandage was saturated with blood.

The woman needed surgery. She needed a proper doctor. Someone who knew what they were doing. As panic threatened to overwhelm her, Irena forced herself to take a deep breath. *Think.*

She grabbed the husband's hand and placed it on top of the dressing. 'We need to get her to hospital.' She pointed to the car. The man nodded and scooped his wife into his arms.

'Put her in the back seat. Press down on her wound as hard as you can and keep pressing, no matter what happens.' Irena prayed the German planes would stay away a little longer.

As they hurried towards the vehicle Irena caught sight of the family who'd been walking in front of her car just minutes before. The father was face down, a few feet away from his wife and children. His blond-haired son, who couldn't have been more than five, held his cap in the fingers of one hand while the other stretched out towards his mother as if he were reaching for her. She lay beside him, her body covering her little girl. Irena turned to the man next to her. 'I'll be back as soon as I can.'

With her heart beating a sickening tattoo in her throat, Irena ran towards the family. She stopped by the father and felt for a pulse. Nothing. Then she knelt by the little boy's broken body. His bony legs protruded from his too-big shorts and he had a scrape on his knee that was beginning to form a scab. He must have fallen a few days earlier. His green eyes, wide with surprise, stared sightlessly at the sky.

Bullet holes had riddled his small body, almost cutting him in two. Blood had soaked through both his shirt and his neatly buttoned grey jacket and pooled in an untidy circle around his body.

She drew in a long, shuddering breath and turned her attention to the mother and daughter.

As she'd suspected, the mother was dead too, her head almost severed from her torso by the force of the bullets. The little girl, however, had been shielded by her mother. It was just possible she was still alive.

Mustering all her strength, Irena dragged the woman off her child. As the mother's body sprawled on the ground, her neck lolling to the side at an unnatural angle, bile rose once more in Irena's throat, making her gag.

The girl was covered in blood and Irena's hands shook as she felt for a pulse. It was there, thank God, rapid and weak, but there nevertheless. The blood must be her mother's.

Irena ran her hands across the child's body before lifting her dress. It was difficult to be sure with so much blood everywhere but she couldn't see any bullet wounds. But then as the child moaned, she saw it: a small hole, the size of the tip of Irena's thumb, right at the top of the child's leg.

She reached into her pocket, yanked out a handkerchief and folded it into a small square before placing it on top of the wound. Then she tugged off her scarf and tied it tightly around the child's thigh. If she could get her to hospital the little girl might have a chance.

She picked her up, carried her back to the car and laid her gently on the front passenger seat.

She looked around. There were still so many injured. So many who would die without immediate help. But if she stopped to help them, the two in her car would die. She ran around to the driver's seat, clambered in, and cranked the starter motor. Relieved it caught first time, she looked over her shoulder at the couple. The husband's face was almost as pale as his wife's.

'How is she?'

'She's bad. What took you so long? She needs to get to hospital.'

'Just keep pressure on the bandage.' Irena laid one of her hands on the temporary dressing covering the child's leg and pressed down. She manoeuvred the car between the victims, her blood-covered fingers slipping on the steering wheel, but she knew she couldn't stop, even to wipe them.

If the German planes came back now they'd be sitting ducks.

It seemed to take forever to reach the hospital. Irena had to nego-tiate her way through more fleeing people and with every minute that passed, her injured passengers' chances of survival were decreasing. She kept glancing at the sky, but there was no sign of the German planes. Every so often, she asked the husband for an update on his wife's condition. She was still bleeding and along the way had lost consciousness. He kept murmuring to her, telling her she was going to be all right, if only she would hold on. In the passenger seat beside Irena, the child's breathing had become laboured and she looked pale and clammy. If the wound didn't kill her, shock might.

At last, the hospital appeared in front of her. It had been hit too. Large chunks of the perimeter wall were missing and the doctors' quarters to the left of the main building were on fire. She drove into the forecourt and yanked on the handbrake.

It was almost as chaotic here as it had been on the roads. Horse-led carts and ambulances with injured men, women and children streamed in through the gates. Nurses and doctors scurried around, examining the injured briefly, before calling out orders to stretcher-bearers. The Polish Red Cross were there too, rushing towards each ambulance as it arrived.

Irena leaped out of the car and lifted the little girl into her arms. A nurse hurried over to her.

'What's wrong with her?'

'She has a bullet wound to her groin. I'm not sure if the femoral artery is damaged but just in case I applied a tourniquet. There's another casualty in the back – a woman. She took a bullet in her shoulder. Her husband is keeping pressure to the wound. There are many more casualties out there. About five miles away. On the main road west. A lot of them are dead, but there are others who need medical attention.'

'I'll take her.' The nurse gestured to a man on the steps to come forward. 'Get someone to deal with the woman in the back, then send some ambulances towards Wesola. See if you can find a nurse to go with them. If you can't, someone from the Red Cross will do.'

'They need a doctor,' Irena protested. 'And more than one. The planes might have come back.'

'All the doctors are busy, but I'll see who I can find.' As she talked, the nurse placed the child on the stretcher and signalled to the stretcher-bearers. 'Take her inside. I'll come in a minute and check her wound before I decide what needs to be done.' She glanced at Irena. 'I don't want to take the bandage off until I'm certain we can control the bleeding.'

At least the nurse knew what she was doing. She had to be a year or two younger than Irena, but, outwardly at least, she was calm and confident.

'I could go with the ambulance,' Irena offered. 'I'm a medical student.'

The nurse shook her head. 'You don't look in any state to help.' Her voice softened. 'You've done well so far and we're going to need all the help we can get later.' She wiped a blood-stained hand across her forehead and, for a moment, Irena saw the fear in her eyes. But just as quickly it was gone and the professional mask was back in place. 'You're covered in blood, you know. If you plan to stay and help you should wash first – and get changed. We don't want to terrify the patients any more than they are already.'

As she turned away, Irena grabbed her arm. 'I'm all right. Just tell me what you want me to do.' Her teeth were chattering so much she could barely speak.

The nurse gently removed Irena's hand, placed her arm around her shoulder and led her across to a bench. 'It's going to be a long day and an even longer night. Take a few minutes to pull yourself together. Then, if you really want to help, report to Sister Radwanska. She'll tell you what to do.'

Irena started to protest, but without warning tears blurred her vision. She wanted to follow the nurse inside, she wanted to help, but she no longer trusted her legs to support her. Instead, she buried her head in her hands and wept.

Chapter 2

Edinburgh, 1989

'There has to be some mistake,' Sarah said. 'I don't know a Lord Glendale. Never even heard of him.'

She studied the man across the desk. Alan Bailey had a spot on his chin and had cut himself shaving. If indeed he even shaved. He looked barely old enough to be out of school let alone a partner in a firm of posh Charlotte Square solicitors. He was wearing a suit that must have cost a fortune, a pinstripe shirt and a ridiculously flamboyant bowtie. The office was empty apart from the over-large desk and three chairs. It was quiet, almost unnaturally so, given the proximity of Princes Street.

When she'd opened the letter asking her mother to make an appointment to see one of the partners at Hardcourt & Bailey, Sarah had phoned to tell them her mother was in hospital.

'I'm sorry to hear that,' Alan Bailey had said smoothly, but without the slightest hint that he meant it. He'd paused. 'Will she be discharged soon?'

'No. Not in the immediate future.' Not that it was any of his business. 'Look, perhaps you should tell me what this is about?'

'It's really a matter best dealt with in person,' Bailey muttered.

'In that case,' Sarah suggested, 'can I come instead of my mother?'

'Would you mind holding the line for a moment?' There was the sound of someone covering the receiver with a hand and then the muffled voices of two people. While she waited, Sarah added milk and wine to her shopping list on the hall table.

'Sorry to keep you, Miss Davidson, but I needed to have a word with my senior partner. He thinks we should speak to Mrs Davidson in person.'

Sarah's jaw tightened. 'My mother can't talk and can only walk with support, so it's unlikely she'll be able to come to your office any time soon. She's in the rehabilitation ward of Astley Ainslie Hospital, if you'd like to check with her doctors.'

'Perhaps we could visit her at the hospital.'

'Only immediate family are allowed to visit at the moment.' Sarah wasn't sure if this were true. It hadn't come up in conversation with the nursing staff as Sarah was the only visitor her mother ever had. But Mum was in no condition to be bothered by solicitors. Come to think of it, Sarah was in no condition to be bothered by solicitors. On top of the twice-daily trips to the hospital – and the visits to her mother's house in the Borders to check for mail and to see everything was all right – there was work to think about, too. Her boss had been sympathetic about Sarah taking time off at first and had given her a week's compassionate leave, but over the last few weeks he'd become increasingly fed up with her frequent absences from the office. If it weren't for the fact her curiosity had been piqued by the solicitor's letter, she would have been tempted to tell the firm of Hardcourt & Bailey – and Alan Bailey in particular – to take a jump.

Even then Alan Bailey had hummed and hawed about it being irregular but, if she were indeed Lily Davidson's daughter, and could prove her identity by bringing her passport along, he supposed it would be all right.

But the last thing she'd expected when the time of the appointment finally arrived was this. A complete stranger had left two properties to her mother, should the solicitors fail to locate a woman called Magdalena Drobnik.

'There is no mistake. Lord Glendale also asked that your mother be given this.' Bailey handed her an A3 envelope.

Sarah turned it over in her hands. It was made of thick, good quality paper and had Mum's name on it, written with a fountain pen in a neat, decisive handwriting. Perhaps inside was a letter explaining the strange bequest? But she should get Mum's permission before she opened it. Dealing with her mother's business correspondence was one thing, personal letters quite another.

'And as for Magdalena Drobnik? Who is she?'

Alan Bailey sighed. 'We were rather hoping your mother would be able to help us with that.'

'I can't recall her ever mentioning her.'

He leaned back in his chair and studied her as if he were a teacher and she a schoolgirl he'd caught smoking behind the bicycle shed. 'As I told you, your mother will only inherit should we not be able to find Miss Drobnik or if she's deceased. We've started looking for her but so far have drawn a blank.'

'And if you don't find her, Mum will inherit Lord Glendale's Edinburgh house and another in Skye. I still don't understand. Why my mother?'

'I'm afraid I couldn't tell you even if I knew.'

'Didn't whoever made out the will ask Lord Glendale? One of the senior partners perhaps?'

'My father made out the will. Sadly he died last year. Even if he were still alive, he might not have been able to shed any more light than I can. Our job as solicitors is to draw up wills, not to question their contents.' He sat upright, picked up a pen and twirled it between his fingers. 'Lord Glendale's instructions were straightforward. Apart from the bequest, on his death, your mother was to be handed the envelope I have just given you.' He cleared his throat before continuing. 'The estate includes a house in Charlotte Square – just across from here, actually – as well as one in Skye. It may well be that the house in Skye will have to be sold to cover the inheritance tax that will be due prior to the estate being settled. Or, should your mother go on to inherit, she could choose to keep it and sell the Charlotte Square house, although I would advise against it. The Edinburgh property is more likely to keep its value. In the meantime, your mother has been appointed joint executor along with us. We hold a set of keys to both properties should you require access.'

Why on earth would Lord Glendale have named her mother in his will? Could they have been lovers? It was entirely possible that her mother had had a life Sarah knew nothing about. The thought of her mother having a secret lover both depressed and warmed her. It would be good to think she'd found love, even late on in life. She'd never even known her mother to have a friend. However, if they'd had a relationship, surely Sarah would have met him?

'When did Lord Glendale die?' she asked.

'A month ago. He was diagnosed with a fast-growing brain tumour a few months before that.'

Which would explain why he hadn't visited her mother in hospital. 'This has come as a bit of a shock. I still can't help but think some mistake has been made.'

'As I said, if you are the daughter of Lily Davidson, last residing at Cliff Top near St Abbs, and it certainly seems you are, then there has been no mistake. Naturally, as a reputable firm we have carried out the necessary background checks.' He closed the folder and set it to one side of his otherwise clear desk. 'And I do have to emphasise your mother only inherits as a "whom failing". We will, of course, make every effort to locate Miss Drobnik but that could take years.'

'Drobnik is an Eastern European name, isn't it?'

'Polish, actually.'

'Have you thought about looking for Miss Drobnik there?'

'Of course,' he said, looking as if he'd sucked on a lemon. 'Unfortunately the Polish government, for all the talk of perestroika, isn't too helpful when it comes to assisting the West with information regarding their residents, although now that democracy looks a real possibility we may have more success in accessing information.'

As there seemed little else Bailey was able to tell her, Sarah returned her passport to her handbag and stood. 'I'll take a set of keys for the houses. I should check on the one in Charlotte Square. It may have sprung a leak or something . . . ' She tailed off. There was no need to justify herself. He'd already said he was happy to give her keys.

Alan Bailey opened the drawer of his sleekly modern oak desk and tipped the contents of an envelope onto the table. 'A member of the firm has already carried out an inventory.'

Sarah stiffened. Did he think she was going clear the house and flog Lord Glendale's possessions on a street corner? 'I can assure you, Lord Glendale's belongings are safe with me.'

His cheeks reddened. 'It's standard practice. I'm sure you aren't planning to remove anything from either of the properties until such time as we are certain that Miss Drobnik can't be located.'

His obvious embarrassment softened her irritation. She took the keys from him. 'You will let me know as soon as you find Miss Drobnik, won't you?'

Back on the street she paused outside the entrance to Hardcourt & Bailey. She checked her watch: two thirty. Afternoon visiting was from two to four and the Astley Ainslie – or the Ghastly

Astley, as she secretly called it — was a good half-hour walk from here. But given that Lord Glendale's Edinburgh home was only on the other side of the square, she couldn't resist a quick look.

Situated between Rose Street and George Street, with their designer shops, cafes and bars, and only a stone's throw from Princes Street, Charlotte Square was one of the most expensive places to live in the capital. Unlike many of the grand town-houses elsewhere in Edinburgh, most of these hadn't been subdivided into flats and were therefore highly sought after.

She found number nineteen and stepped back to look at it. Lord Glendale's home — a three-storey, neo-classic sandstone building — had to be worth a small fortune. If Mum did inherit it, she could sell it and there would be money for her to buy a ground-floor flat with a garden near Sarah and if necessary, God forbid, as much private care as she could possibly require. It seemed that fate had stepped in just when they needed it most.

Although she was itching to see inside, her mother was expecting her at the hospital and after that, she really had to get back to the office.

She hitched her handbag onto her shoulder and hailed a pass-ing taxi. There was no point in getting too excited; there was still the matter of Magdalena Drobnik to consider. If she were still alive then her mother would get nothing. But who the hell was Lord Glendale and why had her mother been named in his will?

A short while later, Sarah paused at the door of ward 18 where her mother had been a patient for the last four weeks. Mum had only recently turned fifty. According to the doctors, it was unusual but not unheard of to have a stroke at that age. It could, they said, have been caused by any number of reasons, most likely a small bleed. It was possible that her mother would make a good recovery, but equally possible that she would continue to have small bleeds and if this happened her mother might lose what movement she still had.

After a couple of weeks in a medical ward, Mum had been transferred here for rehab. At least that's what it was supposed to be. In reality it was filled with old people with dementia, a few like her mother who were post stroke, and, heartbreakingly, a young girl who'd come off the back of her boyfriend's motorbike and who spent most of the time curled up in her bed, her day punctuated only by visits from the physios and her anxious family.

Sarah took a deep breath and walked in, wincing at the faint but unmistakable smell of urine. When she saw Mrs Liversage bearing down on her, she was tempted to hide. Not today of all days. An encounter with the old lady was rarely short and sweet. But too late – she'd already been spotted.

'Is Mother waiting for me?' Mrs Liversage, clutching the frame of her Zimmer, stopped in front of her, peering past Sarah to the ward entrance. She always asked the same thing. 'School's just finished, and I mustn't keep her. Mother so hates to be kept waiting.'

'I didn't see her,' Sarah said evasively. 'Perhaps you should ask the nurses?'

'Nurses? What nurses?' Mrs Liversage frowned. 'Don't be silly. There's only teachers here.'

Sarah bent to whisper in the elderly patient's ear. 'Don't tell everyone, but I think there's cake for tea.'

Mrs Liversage perked up. 'Tea? And cake!' She allowed Sarah to turn her around and guide her to the day-room. When she was seated, Sarah poured her some tea from the thermos she'd brought and after scrabbling around in her bag, gave her a slice of the pre-packaged ginger cake she'd intended for Mum.

Leaving a pacified Mrs Liversage munching, Sarah hurried

down the ward, past the nurses' station and to her mother's bay. Her heart squeezed painfully as she caught sight of her mother. As usual she was in the high-backed chair next to her bed, but the pillows that normally propped up the side that had been affected by the stroke had fallen to the floor and without their support her mother was tipped over to the right. She was dressed in a green cardigan that didn't belong to her and blue polyester trousers with an elasticated waist. No one had applied her lipstick for her or found the time to comb her hair. Sarah groaned. Before the stroke, Mum would have died rather than let anyone see her like this.

'Hello, Mum,' she said, dropping a kiss on her cheek.

Her news would have to wait until she'd seen to her mother. She laid the pile of clean laundry on the bed and pulled the screens. 'Okay, Mum, let's get you sorted. What would you like me to do first? Help you with your lunch or change that cardigan?'

Her mother smiled lopsidedly but said nothing. The stroke that had robbed her of movement on her right side had also affected her speech.

Sarah pushed aside the plate of congealed blended mince and mashed potato that the hospital optimistically called lunch. Luckily, as well as the cake, she'd also brought a yogurt and a plastic spoon with her. The last few weeks had taught her to come prepared.

She peeled off the lid and sat down on the bed. 'Try some of this, Mum. It's your favourite.' But when Sarah lifted the spoon, her mother pressed her lips together.

'Please, Mum, you have to eat something. You must keep your strength up.' Since the stroke her mother had lost weight from her already slim frame. Sarah tried again, but her mother turned her head away.

'How will you get better if you don't eat?'

Her mother pointed to her stick, which was propped up against the wall, and Sarah placed it in her good hand. It had become her mother's preferred way of communicating. Two taps meant no and one, yes.

'Do you need the bathroom?'

One tap. *Yes.*

'I'll go and get a nurse, shall I?'

Another tap.

Sarah could have taken her mother to the toilet herself, but something inside her shrank away from such an intimate act. Mum would hate it too.

She pushed the screens aside and avoiding Sister Haggerty, who quite frankly terrified her, found a staff nurse writing up some notes in the duty room. To her relief it was Linda. Sarah rapped softly on the door. 'Excuse me, Linda, but I'm afraid my mother needs to go to the bathroom.'

'Oh, hello, Sarah. How are you?'

'I'd be happier if Mum had had lunch and was wearing her own clothes.' She did her best to keep the exasperation from her voice. She didn't want to risk the nurses taking against her – or more importantly – her mother.

'We've been a little short-staffed today,' Linda said. 'Nurse Gillespie called in sick this morning. Sister tried to get the powers-that-be to send us a replacement from one of the other wards but no joy. Short-staffed all over, apparently. Surprise, surprise.'

The beginning of a headache tugged at Sarah's scalp. 'Does the ward ever have its full complement of staff?'

'Sometimes. I can't remember the last time, though.' Linda placed her pen in the top pocket of her uniform and stood. 'I'll take Lily to the loo.'

It was something else Sarah disliked about the ward; her

mother would hate to be called by her first name. She'd pointed this out to the nursing staff several times but she might as well talk to a brick wall.

'How is my mother doing?' Sarah asked. 'I don't see much improvement.'

'You have to be patient. It can take months for a patient to recover as much as they are going to. In the meantime, we're carrying on with physio and speech and language therapy.' Linda paused and squeezed Sarah's shoulder. 'I know it's hard and that you don't see much difference, but she has some movement in her right side now. You're doing all the right things – coming in to see her, helping with the passive movements, talking to her.'

It didn't feel like enough. Her mother had never been one for socialising and to be stuck here with people she had nothing in common with had to be hellish. But what could Sarah do? Mum needed more care than Sarah could give her. Which was why, if the houses did come to Mum, it would be a godsend. Although she wished this Magdalena Drobnik no ill, it wasn't as if she knew her and if she was dead, the sooner it was confirmed, the better. Then she could move Mum to a private facility while they sorted out a long-term solution.

By the time Linda had taken her mother to the toilet, a laboriously slow process, Sarah was seething with impatience. She'd tidied Mum's locker, returned the tray of uneaten food to the metal food trolley, poured her mother a cup of tea from the thermos and replaced her mother's soiled clothes with the clean ones she'd brought with her.

After Linda had settled her mother back in the chair, she helped Sarah change her mother's cardigan. 'Always work from the affected side,' Linda said. 'You'll need to get adept at this for when Lily comes home.'

'Surely she isn't ready quite yet?'

'Oh, I'm not talking about right now, but in a few weeks' time perhaps,' Linda said. 'You'd like that, wouldn't you, Lily? Back in your own home with all your things around you.'

Mum rapped the stick again and her eyes blazed as she held Sarah's gaze.

'Oh, Mum, I know you want to go home but you heard what Linda said – it won't be long now.'

Linda folded a rug over her mother's legs. 'Right. I'll leave you two in peace.'

At long last, they were alone. Sarah crouched by the side of her mother's chair.

'Remember I told you yesterday that I had an appointment with the solicitor today?' she said. Her mother lifted her good shoulder in an almost imperceptible shrug.

Sarah moved in front of her mother so she could see her better. 'They had something very interesting to say. Mum, did you know a Lord Glendale?'

Her mother frowned and shook her head slightly.

Sarah sat back on her heels. 'Well, that's weird because he's named you in his will.' When her mother continued to stare blankly at her, Sarah took the envelope from her bag. 'The solicitor also gave me this. It's for you. From Lord Glendale.'

When her mother still didn't respond, Sarah continued. 'Would you like me to open it?'

Her mother nodded.

To Sarah's surprise, all the envelope contained was two photographs. She'd been so sure there would be a note explaining the will. She double checked to make certain there was nothing else before turning back to the photos. The first was of a woman in a skirt and blouse standing next to a man in a Second World War uniform. Sarah was just able to make out the wings of the RAF insignia on his chest. He was very good-looking and judging by his easy smile and confident stance, knew it. Could he be a young Lord Glendale? In that case he was a lot older than she'd assumed. Certainly too old to have been her mother's lover.

The woman next to him was beautiful, with high cheekbones and almond-shaped eyes. She was standing awkwardly, her body turned slightly away from the man at her side, almost as if she didn't want to be in the picture. One thing was for sure: neither was Sarah's grandparent. Although she'd never met them – they'd died before she was born – there were several photographs of them in her mother's house.

Sarah looked past the figures to the building in front of which the couple were standing. Only the steps and pillars were visible. It could be any building in any city.

She placed the photo in her mother's good hand. 'Do you recognise them?'

While her mother was looking at it she picked up the second one. It was of a little girl, four – possibly five – years old. The length and style of her smocked dress and velvet-trimmed coat as well as the lace-up boots suggested a bygone era; the forties maybe. A chain with a tear-drop pendant hung around her neck. Sarah studied the child more closely. There was something in the set of the mouth, the steady, almost angry stare that was familiar.

'Is this you, Mum?' Sarah leaned over to show her. 'It is, isn't it? Look, she's wearing the same necklace you have. When was it taken? How come Lord Glendale had it?'

But her mother was still staring at the picture of the couple, tears sliding down her cheeks and into her mouth, her thin shoulders shaking.

Sarah stared at her aghast. She'd never seen her mother cry.

She knelt beside her and dabbed her wet cheeks with her hanky. 'Oh, Mum, what is it?'

Her mother raised her head. 'Mm . . . Ma . . . '

Sarah could see the frustration in her eyes. 'God, sorry, Mum.' She'd forgotten it was no good asking Mum questions that she couldn't give yes or no responses to. Sarah grabbed the stick and placed it in her mother's hand.

'Okay, let's start again. Do you recognise the man?'

Two taps. *No*.

'What about the woman? Do you recognise her?'

One tap. *Yes*.

'Is she Magdalena Drobnik?'

A firm tap. Yes. Her face crumpled and she clutched Sarah's hand. 'Ma . . . Ma . . . elp. Nu . . . '

'What is it, Mum? Do you need a nurse?'

Once more a series of taps. 'Huh . . . ' She managed.

'I'm sorry, Mum. I don't understand.'

'Ho . . . Ho . . . ' Her mother blinked and waved her stick at the door again.

'Home? You want to go home?'

One tap.

A lump lodged in Sarah's throat and she took her mother's hand, rubbing her cold fingers. 'Oh, Mum. You can't. Not yet. You have to be here so they can continue with the speech therapy and the physio. You know that – although Linda and I are hoping it will be soon.'

At that moment Sister Haggerty came over. 'Now, Lily, what's upsetting you?' She pinned Sarah with a look. 'You know it's not good for your mother's blood pressure if she gets agitated.' She whipped the screens around the bed. 'What your mother needs is peace and quiet. Perhaps you should come back later. When Lily is calmer.'

Sarah reluctantly got to her feet. She placed the photograph of the little girl back in the envelope but when she tried to retrieve the one of the couple from her mother, she curled her fingers around it and pressed it to her chest.

Sarah bent and kissed the top of her mother's head. 'It's okay, Mum, you keep it. I'll see you this evening.'

As Sarah walked to the door, her head was spinning. So the woman in the photograph was Magdalena Drobnik. But how did her mother know her and why did her photo distress her so much? One way or another, she was going to find out.

Chapter 3

Warsaw, 1939

Irena wiped the sweat from her brow. It was hot inside the hospital and she'd been on her feet for almost fifteen hours. Yesterday, as soon she'd regained control of herself, she'd fled to the bathroom. She'd hardly recognised the woman in the mirror. Her dress was ripped and covered in blood; her face, hands and arms equally bloodstained. Pulling off her dress, she'd stood in her underwear and scrubbed her skin until it burned. She'd found a hospital gown and, thankful it covered her from neck to shin, redressed. Then she'd gone in search of Sister Radwanska who'd immediately put her to work.

Throughout the day rumours had circulated: the Germans had entered Warsaw; the Germans had been beaten back. Krakow was obliterated; Krakow was fighting back.

It was impossible to know what was true and what wasn't. Whenever she thought about Aleksy and Piotr, her chest tightened.

Were they still alive? As the vice-grip around her chest increased she pushed the thoughts away. She mustn't think of anything except what she had to do here. Sister Radwanska had allocated her to the surgical ward and instructed her to keep an eye on the post-operative patients. All the doctors and most of the nurses were in theatre or in the reception area dealing with the casualties that had flooded in.

During a lull she'd grabbed an opportunity to slip away to

check up on the child she'd brought in yesterday. Luckily the bullet had gone all the way through the leg, narrowly missing the femoral artery, and the doctors had successfully stopped the bleeding in theatre. But she wasn't out of danger yet: she'd lost a great deal of blood and sepsis was a real possibility. No one knew her name and, as yet, no relative had come to claim her. Hopefully someone would soon.

Irena reached for the little girl's hand. Her fingers were soft and limp, the nails bitten to the quick. She had the same blond hair as her dead brother, still streaked with blood, and although she was as pale as the cream hospital walls, she was pretty.

If she and Piotr ever had a daughter, she might look like this.

She closed her eyes as the image of the last time she'd seen Piotr played in her head. They'd been spending the weekend with other guests at his parents' house in the country. After a day spent picnicking, they'd changed into evening dress and danced to a five-piece band. Piotr, in his officer's uniform, his sword at his waist, looked noble and handsome and she'd ached with love for him.

'You are so beautiful, my love,' he whispered in her ear as he twirled her around. 'When we are married I'm going to keep you all to myself for at least a month. Preferably permanently in my bed.'

She'd smiled up at him. 'Only a month? Shame on me for not making you want me more.'

'Let's not wait,' he said, no longer smiling. 'We could get married tomorrow. I'll find a priest and persuade him to marry us. With the tip of my sabre if I have to.'

'But we agreed to wait until I've finished my studies.'

'Two years, Irena. I'm not sure I can wait that long. It's different now. I think there will be a war and we're not as well prepared as everyone says we are. We should get married now. We don't have to tell anyone except my parents and your father.

I can support you. And when I'm away you can live with Mama and Tata. They love you almost as much as I do.'

Why hadn't she said yes? If she'd known that less than a month later she could be facing a life without him, she would have.

A hand fell on her shoulder, rousing her from her reverie.

'My dear, I've been looking for you.' It was her father, his face slack with fatigue. She'd known he'd eventually find his way to the hospital – and to her. Seeing him brought the tears perilously close. She took a deep breath and blinked them away. Even in these circumstances, Tata wouldn't like it if she became emotional in front of patients. He squeezed her shoulder. 'Why are you still here?'

'The nurses told me you were in theatre. I couldn't leave. Not until I had seen you.'

'They let me know you were here but we've been so busy I couldn't come before now.' His face tightened. 'So many terrible injuries. How can they do this to children?'

Irena used her free hand to cover his. When they'd spoken about the possibility of war in the past, her father had been calm. 'I was in Warsaw during the last occupation,' he'd said. 'If they come again – if they occupy us again, God forbid – they will be arrogant and aggressive. There will be killing and they will take everything we have, but they are Europeans. They will act like an occupying army but they will behave with restraint.'

No one could believe it now. The German pilot who had killed the girl's family must have known they were civilians. Yet he had shot them anyway. And throughout the hours there had been similar reports. Other trains had been targeted and many more civilians killed as they tried to flee from the wreckage. There were whispers of mounds of bodies piled high by the side of the roads. She wished she could tell her father what she'd witnessed but she knew she would break down if she did.

'Any word of Aleksy or Piotr?' she asked instead.

'No. And we mustn't expect to hear anything for a while. It will take time for news to get through to us. Don't give up hope.' He pulled up a chair and sat down next to her, taking his glasses off to rub the lenses. 'Now, Irena, I want you to listen to me. You must leave Poland.'

'Leave?'

He leaned closer and lowered his voice. 'I have an address. The Baron, your godfather, gave it to me last year when we met in Austria. Remember the medical convention I attended?'

Irena nodded. She'd only met her godfather once, when he'd come to visit them in Krakow. She'd been a child then, no more than ten, but she remembered a tall man with blond hair and blue eyes who'd treated her as if she were a young lady instead of a little girl still in short dresses.

'It's the address of someone he knows well – a man of importance who lives in England and who will help you. Maximilian must have suspected something might happen to Poland. Perhaps he knew more than he let on?' He shrugged. 'Who knows? Things have been tense between our two countries for so long I think we Poles have been guilty of ignoring what was inevitable. We should have taken it as a warning when the Reich invaded Czechoslovakia and no one raised even a whisper of protest.' He shook his head. 'But that is in the past. We must look to the future now. I have no doubt that the Nazis will enter Warsaw. Perhaps not this month, or the next, but they will come. Our army is too small, too poor and too ill-equipped to hold them back for ever.'

'But the British and the French! They will come to our aid. They promised and once they come, the Germans will be beaten back.'

Although her father smiled, his eyes stayed bleak. 'I hope you're right. In which case, as soon as the Germans are no longer a threat, you could return.'

'My place is here, Tata – with you and Piotr and Aleksy and everyone else! I can't – I won't – run away.'

'It is what your mother would have wanted. It is what I want.'

She looked around the ward. The beds, most of which had two patients in them arranged head to toe, had been pushed together to make room for more. Even the space in the centre of the ward had been utilised. Still there weren't enough beds for everyone and many patients had to make do with a mattress on the floor. It was worse in the corridors outside. There the injured lay, in pain, confused, bloodied and unwashed, waiting for the doctors to operate or for a bed to become vacant.

A nurse, grey with fatigue and shock, moved between the beds, stepping over patients, checking bandages and taking temperatures and pulses. Some of nurses had been about to go off night duty when the attack had started, but they were still here.

'I can't go, Tata. I'm needed here. There aren't enough doctors and nurses to care for the injured as it is.' She held up her hand as he started to protest. 'I know I'm only a student but I can be useful.' She made herself smile. 'Besides, who will make sure you rest if I am not around to keep an eye on you?'

Her father rose to his feet, stifling a groan as his stiff legs complained. 'You take after your mother. She was stubborn too.' He held out an envelope. 'Here's the address. Hide it but never lose it. I have also written the details of my bank account in case you ever need money. Perhaps you are right and the English and French will help us put an end to this. But I still think you should go now. If the Germans occupy our country you will not find it so easy to leave then. Now go home and get some rest and we will talk again tomorrow.'

The little orphan girl's eyes fluttered and she moaned softly. Irena squeezed her hand. 'You go, Tata. I'll stay a little longer.'

Chapter 4

'Britain and France have declared war on Germany!' Januz, one of Irena's fellow medical students, rushed into the ward with a huge grin on his face. 'We're saved!'

'Not soon enough to help him,' Irena said softly. She closed the eyes of her patient, a middle-aged man with terrible burns, who had been admitted yesterday to the hopeless ward. She'd given him as much morphine as she'd dared, but he'd moaned in pain almost right to the last. At least his suffering was at an end now.

'Aren't you happy?' Januz said when she didn't reply.

She was relieved, of course, but happy? She doubted she'd ever be able to get the images of what she'd seen these last days out of her head. 'I'm pleased if it means that this war will be over soon.' Especially if it meant that Piotr and Aleksy would be coming back to her.

Through the opened window they heard the sound of cheering and went across to look.

The street in front of the hospital was filled with people – more than Irena had seen in one place since the Germans had first attacked. Some were attempting to sing 'God Save the King', even though it was clear they didn't know the words, others 'La Marseillaise'. As people danced in the street, cars trundled by, joyously tooting their horns. In the hospital forecourt, nurses and doctors paused to hug each other.

Irena closed her eyes and murmured a prayer: 'Mother Mary, let it be over. Please send Piotr and Aleksy home.'

But three days after Britain and France declared war on Germany, there was still no sign of them coming to their aid. Krakow had been occupied and, if anything, the sound of gunfire had intensified. Irena was at home and getting ready for bed when her father called up to her.

'Renia, come quickly.'

She rushed downstairs and her heart almost stopped beating when she saw Piotr standing in the hall. Her prayers had been answered. She ran over to him and flung herself into his arms. 'You're alive!' She was crying and laughing at the same time. 'Are you all right? You're not hurt, are you?'

'I'm fine, my love,' Piotr said, holding her tight. He smelled of smoke and sweat and blood. 'We're passing through Warsaw on our way east. We're moving out at first light but I had to see you.'

'Come and sit. Are you hungry? Tata, could you ask Krystiana to bring some bread and soup?' Krystiana came in once a day to see to Irena's apartment. Although she had boys of her own in the Polish army, and had to be desperately worried about them, she'd told Irena she'd go mad with nothing to do at home but wait for news of her sons.

'Is it going badly?' she asked when Piotr was seated.

'It could be better. We keep waiting for the British or French to attack the Germans but so far they haven't. Perhaps tomorrow.'

'Have you seen Aleksy?'

'No, I'm afraid not, but I've heard he's all right.'

'Thank God,' Irena whispered. 'We've been so worried.'

He leaned across and took her hand. 'Sweetheart, it doesn't

look good. Our regiments don't seem to know what the others are doing. We've lost almost three-quarters of our planes and we are running out of petrol to fly the ones we have left. What little remains of the Pursuit Brigade is being sent to Lublin in case what's left of our air force is destroyed by the Luftwaffe. If help doesn't come soon then we'll be in real trouble. Our pilots may have to get out – most likely to France where they can regroup.' His voice was dull. 'Try not to worry too much if you don't hear from Aleksy for a while.'

'Do we have a chance?' Irena whispered.

He squeezed her hand. 'Of course. We're not ready to give up.'

It was difficult to absorb what he was telling her. He sounded defeated.

Piotr rubbed a hand across his face. His usually immaculate fingernails were encrusted with dirt. 'I used to think there was glory in war. I was wrong. And it's not just the Germans who are doing the killing. A mob of Poles set upon a village of ethnic Germans and massacred them. These people were their neighbours, their friends. It's madness.'

'My God, Piotr! What is happening to us?' Only a week ago she would have found it impossible to believe.

At that moment Irena's father came in carrying a tray, Krystiana following close on his heels. 'You should let me carry that, Doctor,' she scolded. When she saw Piotr a smile spread across her wrinkled cheeks and she went to hug him.

'Krystiana, you've no idea how I've longed for a bowl of your soup,' Piotr said, taking the tray from Irena's father. As she watched him eat, Irena noticed how thin he looked. Wasn't the army able to feed its soldiers?

When he'd finished, Krystiana took the tray from him and headed back out of the room. At the door she turned. 'Come back when you can. In the meantime, I shall pray for you and all our young men.'

'I have to get back to the hospital, so I'll leave you two alone,' Tata said. He held out his hand. 'May God bless and protect you, son.'

Irena wanted to hold back time. She had a sick feeling that this might well be the last time she saw Piotr. She wanted to beg him not to rejoin his regiment, to stay here with her, but Piotr would hate that. So she would behave with the dignity and courage expected of her.

'Don't cry, sweetheart,' the man she'd hoped to spend the rest of her life with said, rubbing the pad of his thumb gently across her cheek. She hadn't even realised she was crying.

'We should have married when we could,' she whispered. 'We should have been together as man and wife. I should have lain in your arms and let you make love to me.'

'Irena!' Piotr pretended to be scandalised. 'Ladies don't talk of such things.'

'This lady does. I only wish we had time now.'

He pulled her into his arms and held her so tightly she could barely breathe. 'I don't have to be back until dawn,' he murmured.

She could feel his heart beating against hers. She knew what he was asking and how could she refuse? Tata had left and Krystiana would be returning to her small flat once she'd finished tidying the kitchen. Even if she hadn't been, Irena wouldn't have cared.

She took Piotr by the hand and led him to her bedroom. Her heart was pumping so hard she thought it might burst.

She closed the door and turned to face him.

'Are you sure, my love?' he asked.

She was. These could be the last hours they had together and she wanted to spend every moment as close to him as she could get. She wanted to feel his hands on her body, his naked skin against hers. She wanted to know what it was to be loved by him, something she had imagined several times but always thought they would have years and years to experience.

Her fingers were trembling as she started to undo the buttons of his tunic. 'I have never been so sure of anything. But you will have to show me what to do. I don't want to make a mistake.' She dipped her head as colour rushed to her cheeks.

'And you a doctor?' he teased. He lifted her chin until she was looking him in the eyes. 'This is not how I imagined it. I wanted it to be perfect.'

She had come to the last button and opened his shirt, feeling for his skin under the vest he wore. He sucked in a breath as her fingers skimmed over his stomach. She stepped away from him and his eyes glittered in the light from the moon as she slipped her dress over her head. Next she undid her bra and unclipped her stockings from her suspenders, acutely aware of him watching her every movement. When at last she stood naked in front of him she raised her chin. Although she was tempted to cover her nakedness with her hands she wanted no shame or embarrassment to spoil this first time.

'My beautiful love,' he murmured. He moved towards her and picked her up in his arms, holding her against him for a moment before lowering her gently onto the bed. He undressed quickly; his trousers and vest joining his shirt in an untidy heap on the floor. All the time he kept his eyes fixed on hers. The bed sagged under his weight as he lay down beside her. He placed his hand on her hip and turned her towards him, running his hand along her side, and hot flames shot through her body. He cupped her face and when he kissed her she let the feel of his mouth and hands wipe away the terror of the last few days.

*

Later, as he slept, she raised herself on her elbow and looked down at him. So that was what all the fuss was about? No wonder. It had hurt a little but he had been so gentle, almost too much, so that she had wrapped her legs around his hips and pulled him close. She hadn't wanted gentleness, that would come later, she had wanted to be possessed, she had wanted to obliterate the past and future, and making love with him had done that.

The clock on her mantelpiece ticked away the minutes. She would have given anything to stop time. All she wanted was here in this room. If only they could stay here for ever, wrapped in each other's arms. If only they could sleep knowing that they had a thousand tomorrows – knowing that there would be children, that they would grow old together.

And she supposed there might still be children. They hadn't used protection. Even if the church allowed it, Irena had never thought of acquiring it. Why would she? She hadn't expected to make love with Piotr until they were married. But if she did have his child, she wouldn't regret it.

She traced his face with her fingertips, trying to imprint every line and contour into her memory. He looked more vulnerable asleep, almost like a young boy. She kissed the small furrow between his brows. Then his hands were on her waist and she felt herself lifted until she was lying on top of him.

'I dreamed you were in my bed,' he moaned. 'And I woke to find you here. Is it true?'

She smiled. 'You need to rest.'

'You think I want to sleep when I can look at you?'

'It will be dawn in less than three hours.' Her throat was tight, but she wouldn't allow herself to cry.

His hands travelled up her back, sending heat rushing to her pelvis. 'In that case we mustn't waste a minute.'

An hour before dawn she filled a bath with water from the

stove for him. When he was in, she soaped her hands and rubbed them across his back and chest.

'You are practising to be a good wife,' he said with a grin.

'Will I do?'

His hands reached out and suddenly she was in his lap, the water splashing onto the floor. 'You are perfect. All a man could ever want.' He traced the curve of her mouth with his thumb. 'I love you. When this war is over, when we have defeated the Germans, we will marry straight away. If I could find a priest, I would marry you now.' His eyes filled with shadows. 'If I don't return—' She made to protest but he stopped her words with a finger to her lips. 'If I don't return, you mustn't mourn me too long. You must live your life.'

'I will never love anyone else. If I can't marry you, I will marry no one.'

'You were meant to be a mother. You were meant to be loved. You have a great heart, Irena.'

'And it is all yours. Please, Piotr, don't speak to me of a life without you in it. It is not a life I would want to live.'

'You must. It is what will make this all this worthwhile. Never give up, Irena. I can do anything – survive anything – as long as I know I am fighting for the life you will yet have.'

Now was not the time to argue. Instead, she raised her face to his and let her lips give him her promise.

A short while later he stood in front of her. He had shaved while she'd done her best to remove the dust and bloodstains from his uniform. Her heart hurt so much she thought it might shatter into a thousand pieces.

'Come home to me, my love,' she whispered.

He threaded his hands into her hair, pulling at the pins so that it tumbled around her shoulders. He buried his face in her neck and breathed deeply. 'You smell so good. You feel so good. No matter what happens this is how I will always remember you.'

'Don't. Don't say that ... It sounds as if you think we will never be together again.'

He tipped her face so that she was staring into his eyes. 'I will come back, I promise. You must take care of yourself for me. Get out if you can. If we don't stop the Germans, do whatever you need to survive. Whatever it takes, whatever you have to do, stay alive. Live the life God meant you to lead. Now it's your turn to promise me.'

'I promise.' She forced a smile, blinking away the tears that burned her eyes. 'Now, aren't you going to kiss me, dearest one?'

Chapter 5

Irena picked her way through rubble-strewn streets, thick with smoke from the hundreds of buildings that still burned, and squeezed her way past several carts piled high with pots and pans, even wardrobes and beds. Two days after Piotr left, the Germans had surrounded Warsaw and, shortly after, started bombing it. And continued bombing hour after hour, day after day. There was hardly a building in Warsaw that wasn't damaged.

Almost more terrifying than the explosions was the awful screaming sound the German Stukas made as they dived from the sky, before dropping their bombs on top of the buildings and the fleeing civilians. Now Irena was needed more than ever at the hospital and so she made her way there each day, darting from building to building, trying to avoid the explosions and falling debris. Even if her help hadn't been required, there was no point in staying at home. A bomb was just as likely to fall on her there as on the street. Besides, she would go crazy with only her thoughts to keep her company.

The hospital was in chaos, as it had been since the day the war started. Hundreds of people lined up in the corridors waiting to be seen, the staff singling out those who they could help and those destined for the hopeless ward.

She spotted her father bending over a mother and child as they sat against the wall in the corridor. The mother held her little boy tightly as Tata listened to his chest. He smiled at them and said a few words, before pinning a white label onto the child's shirt.

When the mother smiled back it was clear that she didn't have a clue that Tata had just condemned her son to death.

'Renia! Thank God!' her father said when he looked up and saw her.

The stretcher-bearers came forward and carried the child away, the mother trotting at his side, smiling. Was it fair to give her hope? Wouldn't it have been better to tell her that her child was about to die so she could hold and comfort him in his last hours? Irena didn't know any more.

'I am fine, Tata. I brought you some bread. Have you eaten?' She hoped he'd found a bed somewhere to put his head down for a few hours. He wasn't getting any younger and had had pneumonia last year. He needed his rest.

'Yes, yes. Some soup. You mustn't worry about me. The nurses see that the doctors eat.' He paused. 'Any news of our allies? I haven't had time to listen to the wireless.'

She shook her head. No word of her brother, no word of Piotr or of the West coming to their aid. 'There could be an announcement any time, Tata. Perhaps they were taken by surprise?'

But it had been over two weeks since the Germans had attacked and still the British and French did nothing.

'We mustn't give up hope,' he replied, repeating the words everyone said to each other but with less and less conviction.

She could tell he didn't really believe what he was saying. 'Of course, Tata. We must never give up hope.'

The next day, Russia invaded Poland from the east.

Chapter 6

Edinburgh, 1989

Feeling like an intruder, Sarah unlocked the large front door of number 19 Charlotte Square. She picked up the post from the floor and placed it on the hall table. Despite the warmth of the late-summer sun outside, the house was cold and smelled musty.

The hall, which still had the original mosaic tiles, was almost as big as her entire flat. There were oil paintings on the wall and a small ornately carved table with a Bakelite telephone. A mahogany and wrought-iron staircase led upstairs.

She opened a door to her left and entered. It was a sitting room, pretty much as it must have been in Victorian times, right down to the heavy damask curtains hanging on the full-length windows that overlooked the residents' gardens in the square. The only nod to modernity was a gas fire.

Across from the sitting room was a dining room, furnished in a similar style but with a large, heavily polished mahogany table and chairs. The fireplace in this room had a bucket of coal and kindling next to it. In front of the window was a desk and she wondered if Lord Glendale used this room as an office.

Upstairs, the largest of the numerous bedrooms had obviously been Lord Glendale's. The room was tidy, the bed neatly made, although his jacket, a dark blue and purple tweed, still hung over the back of an armchair. It smelled vaguely, but not unpleasantly, of tobacco smoke. But it was the painting above the fireplace that drew her attention. It was of the woman in the photo. She was wearing a cream blouse with little mother-of-pearl buttons. She sat on a rock with her knees drawn up to her chin, her woollen skirt pulled over her knees. The sea was behind her and in the distance, cliffs. Her blond hair was blowing across her face, wisps caught in the corner of her mouth. Unlike her wary expression in the photograph Lord Glendale had left for her mother, she was laughing, as if caught in a moment of perfect happiness.

On the mantelpiece, directly below the painting and next to a neat row of pipes, was a silver-framed black-and-white photograph of the same woman, this time wearing a man's shirt over a black one-piece bathing suit. She was towelling her hair as if she'd just come out of the sea. Magdalena Drobnik had clearly meant a great deal to Lord Glendale.

It felt intrusive to be in his bedroom so Sarah continued with her exploration of the first floor.

As well as the bedrooms, there was a bathroom with a Victorian steel claw-foot bath and, as she peeped around the door at the end of the hall, a large, elegant drawing room.

Another flight of stairs took her up to three small attic rooms. This, she imagined, would have been where the servants lived in the days when people still had them. Now the rooms were used for storage. There were several cardboard boxes and old-fashioned trunks lined up neatly against the wall.

She retraced her steps to the drawing room on the first floor. Light flooded in through the large floor-to-ceiling sash windows, which, like the sitting room below, looked out to the residents' gardens in the centre of Charlotte Square. A faded Persian carpet covered most of the polished wooden floor and oil paintings – originals, Sarah suspected – hung from picture rails. Tall, dark-wood bookcases lined the walls and Sarah ran her fingers over the spines. Interspersed between leather-bound first editions were a few paperbacks, mainly thrillers, but also the odd crime novel.

Above the fireplace, an oversized gilt mirror reflected a group of paintings that made her gasp and whirl around. She hadn't noticed them when she'd first stepped into the room as they had been hidden by the door. They were landscapes – or more precisely seascapes – painted in bold, sure strokes and the artist had captured the sea in motion so well, Sarah could almost smell the salt air, feel the spray on her face.

She knew the artist. It was Mum.

The memory of their last holiday rushed back, bringing with it a sickening sense of grief and loss.

It was a summer afternoon, and Sarah had been between her junior and senior honour years. She'd returned from her waitressing job hot, sticky and irritated, to find her mother in the back garden, her shoes kicked off and drinking a glass of wine. Her mother was always immaculately groomed – except for the oil-paint under her fingernails when she was working on a canvas. She never went barefoot and she certainly never sprawled. One of these facts was unusual, taken together they filled Sarah with something she couldn't quite define. Unease? Sadness? Most of all, she felt a terrible longing. She stood at the back door and watched her for a moment. Her mother's eyes were closed, her face tilted slightly towards the sun, her toes pressing into the lawn. She looked almost *abandoned*; that was the word that came to mind.

Tentatively Sarah stepped towards her, the soft grass muting her approach. She looked down on the woman who was her mother but whom she had never felt to be her friend.

As if sensing her, her mother's eyes opened and she smiled – another rarity. It lit her face and made her seem younger. More like the mother Sarah remembered before her father had left her – left them both.

'Oh, hello, Sarah. I didn't expect you back so soon.' She waved her glass. 'Would you be a love and get me a refill? And why don't you join me?'

Sarah's unease grew. Mum never drank and disapproved of Sarah drinking. Before Sarah left for a night out, her mother always gave her a list of warnings: never let anyone allow you to become separated from your friends; don't go anywhere with anyone you don't know – especially if it's a man; put a jacket on or you'll freeze to death; take a pair of sensible shoes with you; make sure you have enough money to get a taxi home – you never know who is on these late night buses . . . And so the list went on. If her mother had her way, Sarah would spend every evening at home watching TV drinking nothing stronger than cocoa. So for her to be drinking and to ask Sarah to join her was, well, unheard of.

But nice. Perhaps now that she was almost twenty-one her mother had decided she was adult enough to be trusted to look after herself. Whatever the reason, Sarah was intrigued by this new side of her.

She poured her mother a fresh glass of wine from the fridge, noting that half the bottle was already gone.

'Here you are,' she said, passing her mother the glass before sitting down on the lawn. Her mother didn't even insist on her getting a blanket in case she spoiled her clothes.

'Here's to summer.' Her mother raised her glass for Sarah to chink. The wine was good, much better than anything Sarah had drank at university – of course, despite her mother's warnings, she had had her fair share of tipsy evenings.

'Is that what we're celebrating?' Sarah asked.

Her mother waved her hand in the air and a little wine

splashed on the ground. 'I've sold a painting! My first one! Can you believe it? And the gallery wants more. Lots more.'

'That's wonderful, Mum.'

'We should take a trip,' her mother said, 'to celebrate my sale and your twenty-first. Where would you like to go?' She leaned forward and fixed her brown eyes on her daughter. 'If you could choose anywhere – anywhere at all – where would it be? Imagine the world was your oyster.'

Go on holiday? They never went on holiday. Her mother barely left the house. Sarah would have loved to have gone backpacking in Europe or volunteer in Africa the same as Gilly, but Mum had made it clear that that was out of the question. Trips, especially to third-world countries, were filled with dangers, both specific and unimaginable. So what could she suggest? Where would her mother like to go?

'What about Italy? We could go on the train as far as Dover and take a ferry from there and then another train.'

'Abroad,' her mother said doubtfully.

So much for the world being her oyster. It was getting smaller by the minute. Sarah searched frantically for an alternative. 'The west coast of Scotland, then? Or Dorset or Devon?' The idea took hold. 'We could go and see our old house. The one with the apple tree in the back garden.'

Another shadow crossed her mother's face. Clearly the thought of revisiting Devon, where they'd lived when Sarah was a little girl and her parents still together held little appeal. 'Dorset then?'

Mum set her glass on the grass and clapped her hands together. 'Dorset, it is. I'll find us a little cottage somewhere we can see the sea. We could go next week.'

Sarah had been planning to visit Matthew in London but she held her tongue. This trip could mean a new start for her and

Mum – a chance to get to know one another. She couldn't let it slip away. 'Dorset would be great.'

Now five years on she wondered if one of these paintings was the one they'd celebrated? If so, Lord Glendale's buying it had made Mum happier than Sarah had ever seen her. It had also been the start of her mother's success as an artist. So who was he? He'd bought a number of her paintings, left her properties in his will, yet Mum had been emphatic about not knowing him.

As a clock chimed, she glanced at her watch. Damn, it was four. Gilly was coming for an early supper and Sarah hadn't been to the shops yet. In addition, she had to drop into the office with the proofs she'd been working on at home. As long as she'd been working as a copy editor she'd never missed a deadline and she didn't want to start now.

But she needed to know more about Lord Glendale and the mysterious, beautiful woman in the photograph. And she had an idea where she could start.

Chapter 7
Warsaw, 1939

Irena watched from the balcony of her apartment as the German army marched into Warsaw. There was no longer anyone to stop them. Poland had finally admitted defeat and surrendered.

With Russia against them too and without the Allies coming to their aid, their situation was hopeless. Yesterday what was left of the Polish army had turned in their weapons before being rounded up and marched off to prisoner-of-war camps, although it was whispered that many had managed to evade capture and were heading for France via Romania. She prayed that Piotr and Aleksy were amongst them.

She was proud of her countrymen and women. They'd held out as long as they could. Hundreds, perhaps even thousands, of people had answered the call to defend Warsaw – digging ditches and building walls in a desperate attempt to keep the enemy out. And all this while they'd been slowly starving. Before the German attack, the Polish government had urged Varsovians not to hoard food and in the last couple of weeks Warsaw had been without food, water or electricity. At the hospital, they'd been forced to carry out operations and treat the sick and dying by candlelight and with limited medical supplies and no anaesthetic. It'd been clear they couldn't carry on for much longer so it was almost a relief when the Germans had arrived.

Perhaps now the worst had happened they could get back to

some sort of normality? At least the incessant bombing and artillery fire had stopped, although large swathes of Warsaw lay in ruins and almost every inch of the parks was taken up with makeshift graves.

The drumming of German boots and the sounds of their tanks and armoured cars was almost deafening. There were so many of them. Row upon endless row of fresh-faced soldiers goose-stepped behind their mounted officers who rode at the head of the column. Unbelievably, some of those watching cheered – and not just cheered but threw flowers in the path of the soldiers. Did they think a few flowers would make the Germans treat them better? Or were these the Poles of German descent? She recalled what Piotr had told her about the ethnic Germans that had been massacred by a group of Polish civilians. She still couldn't bear to think it was true. Despite the repeated partitioning of Poland, the ever-changing boundaries, German and Pole had lived in peace and harmony for years. Some of their German neighbours even had sons, husbands and brothers in the Polish army.

She was about to turn away in disgust when a girl, perhaps a year or two younger than her, broke free from the line bordering the street and ran into the path of the marching soldiers and screamed at them. Irena couldn't make out the words, but judging by the twisted expression of hate on the girl's face, this was no welcoming greeting.

A man about the same age rushed towards her and, grabbing her arm, tried to lead her away. But she wasn't having it. Irena was proud of her; she was doing what most of them, the cheering masses excepted, wanted to do – tell the Germans what they thought of them and their conquering army. But the girl should be careful. The soldiers might arrest her.

Her companion was clearly trying to reason with the

Germans, his arms held open as if to say, *She's upset, you can imagine, she's lost her brother, her father, she's not well. I'll take care of her, she won't bother you again.*

The marching soldiers halted. It was obvious no one knew what to do.

At the front of the column, a motor car with two officers stopped and the driver looked back.

'Go,' Irena whispered as if the girl could hear her. 'You've made your point.'

The motor car turned and drove back along the line of soldiers until it reached the couple. The German officer in the passenger seat stood up and said something to the girl. But she shook her head and let loose a stream of what was clearly invective.

Her friend looked horrified. He pulled her to the side, almost lifting her from her feet. She was pretty, with a turned-up nose and full red lips.

Without warning the officer raised his arm and shot the man in the forehead.

He crumpled to the ground. The girl gaped at him, her face frozen.

Almost in slow motion she lifted her gaze to the officer, her mouth opening and closing like a fish.

'Run!' Although Irena screamed the words, there was no chance the girl could hear her. The watching bystanders stepped back as if to say *they have nothing to do with us.* Some turned their heads. The shouts had turned to a low, fearful murmuring.

The girl looked around, as if expecting someone from the crowd to do something. Then the officer, a small smile on his face, lifted his arm again and pointed the gun at her forehead. Irena wanted to close her eyes, wanted to turn away, but she couldn't. The officer's arm jerked once and the girl folded.

The officer holstered his pistol and said a few words to the soldiers who were watching impassively. Two detached themselves from the column and dragged the girl to the side. Then they picked up the man and threw him on top of her. He landed on his back, his arms and legs splayed wide as if in surrender.

Then, still in perfect lines, the soldiers continued to march.

Chapter 8

The execution of the young couple was only a foretaste of what life under occupation was to be like for Warsaw – one of oppression and fear. A Nazi-controlled Central Government was formed and soon after that posters appeared on every wall, telling the citizens of Warsaw what they could and could not do. Anyone failing to adhere to the laws would be punished by immediate execution. Yesterday Irena had seen an execution notice naming a fifteen-year-old girl. Her crime? She had ripped a German poster from the wall.

Her death had not gone unavenged. Four German soldiers were mown down in the street. The Nazis had been swift to react, rounding up and executing a hundred civilians in return. Although Irena hated everything about the Nazis and was glad the Poles were fighting back, she couldn't accept that killing one German was worth the death of so many innocent people.

Refugees flooded in from territories occupied by the Germans and the areas annexed by the Russians. Many who came to the hospital seeking treatment told stories of being ordered to leave their homes with only the clothes on their backs. Everyone walked around with a stunned look on their faces. How could this have happened? How could this have happened so quickly? The universities and schools remained closed and they'd introduced rationing to below subsistence level – a mere 600 calories a day.

The Jews' situation was worse. Their food rations were half that of the other Poles. They weren't permitted to enter shops and had to register their businesses and homes with the German authorities. Notices appeared on the gates of all the parks forbidding Jews from entering them and they were even forbidden to sit on benches or walk on the pavement. Wehrmacht soldiers often stopped the orthodox Jews and made them stand while they snipped off their side locks, the small act of needless cruelty amusing their tormentors greatly. Adding to their humiliation, every Jewish man, woman and child over the age of ten had to wear a white armband with a blue Star of David.

But despite everything, daily life was slowly returning to a semblance of normality. People shopped, or at least queued, for what little food was available. Electricity had been restored, the hospitals continued to function and the trains and trams were running again. Irena's father had been summoned by the professors of the Jagiellonian University in Krakow for a meeting. He'd left yesterday, promising to return as soon as he could.

Now she was on her own. Krystiana hadn't come in the last few days and, with Tata away, Irena missed her comforting presence. Krystiana had sent a note saying that she'd be back as soon as she could, but in the meantime Irena wasn't to worry. But she did. She worried all the time. She was *scared* all the time. Scared for herself, for Piotr, for Aleksy, for everyone she loved – and for Poland. It was as if she had a permanent band of steel around her chest. But almost stronger than her fear was her growing hatred for the Nazis, which no amount of praying lessened. Since the brutal slaying of the young couple she was filled with a restlessness as well as a burning need for revenge that left a sour taste in her mouth.

She hadn't heard from Magdalena since the occupation and constantly worried about her friend. If something had happened to her during the bombardment of Warsaw, she couldn't bear it. It was a waste of time to try to telephone as most of the lines were still down, so at the first opportunity, Irena took a day off from the hospital to visit Magdalena and her mother. Luckily she still had the car Elżbieta had lent her and it had just enough petrol left in it to make the journey.

As soon as she turned into the driveway, foreboding washed over her. The once immaculate grounds were overgrown with weeds and a shutter was hanging loose from one of the upstairs windows.

Her dismay deepened as her friend, hair tangled around a face devoid of make-up, hurried out to meet her. Magdalena never left her bedroom until she was perfectly groomed but it wasn't just her disarray that alarmed Irena – no doubt most of them took less care with their dress than they had before the war – it was the Star of David armband she was wearing.

'Any word of Aleksy?' they said together, after they'd kissed and hugged then, realising that neither could have news, they linked arms and started walking towards the house.

'What about Piotr? Have you heard from him?' Magdalena asked.

Irena shook her head. 'I'm praying he was one of the soldiers who managed to escape over the border.'

'Do you really think they both could have made it?'

She didn't, but there was nothing to be gained by sharing her doubts with her friend. 'If anyone could it would be them. What about your father?'

'We haven't heard anything. Mama keeps looking out for him as if he'll just come striding up to the front door one day.' She lowered her voice. 'I'm so scared, Irena – so scared for all of us.'

Irena pulled Magdalena closer and for a moment they stood

holding each other. She was frightened too. And even more so now she'd seen the star on Magdalena's arm.

'Why on earth are you wearing that?' she asked, pointing to it. 'You're not Jewish.'

'It's ridiculous,' Magdalena said, frowning. 'You know how we all had to register so we could be issued with ration books?'

Irena nodded.

'Mother and I went along and they asked her all sorts of questions. They kept referring to some documents they had in front of them. They demanded to know about Mama's parents. I didn't know but Mama's mother was born a Jewess and according to the Germans that makes Mama and me Jewish.'

'Did you try to argue?'

'Of course. I told them we were Roman Catholics and if our crucifixes couldn't convince them, our priest would. That neither me nor Mama had ever so much as stepped inside a synagogue, never mind celebrated Jewish holidays. Heavens, we don't even know when they are! But they wouldn't listen. One of them hinted that if Mama kept on complaining he'd arrest her. Isn't it crazy?'

It was more than crazy, it was terrifying. Given the way the Jews in Warsaw were being treated, to be classified as one was dangerous.

'There is talk that they are taking the best houses for themselves. A group of Germans have already been here to look at ours. I think they liked it.'

Dear God.

'Where are the servants?' Irena asked.

Magdalena twisted a lock of hair between her fingers. 'Oh, they left. Ages ago.'

'All of them?'

'Yes.'

Magdalena's mother came down the steps and tilted her cheek for Irena to kiss.

'Magdalena tells me you haven't heard from the colonel,' Irena said, after Elżbieta had asked about Aleksy and Piotr.

Elżbieta shook her head. 'No. We hope he's safe somewhere. We hear that the Russians have taken many of our officers to camps in Siberia.' She plucked at her cardigan and shivered. 'It's so cold here, how will they manage there where it is so much colder? He only has his greatcoat to keep him warm. Do you think they'll supply them with something warmer? If he would write and let me know where he is, I could send him some things, a food parcel perhaps.'

Magdalena glanced at her mother. 'And where, Mama, would you get the food to send him?'

She turned to Irena. 'Luckily we're still getting some eggs from our chickens. I'll give you some to take with you when you go. We're living on eggs and jars of pickled cucumber these days.'

Distracted, Irena nodded. Magdalena and her mother weren't coping well. The family was too used to having servants to cater for their every whim. Without them, or the colonel, they seemed lost, smaller almost. 'Maybe you should hide the car in a barn or something?' she suggested. 'You might have it taken if you don't.'

Elżbieta shrugged. 'Even if we could drive, we have no petrol. You might as well keep it.'

'You could sell it. I've heard that people are bartering cars for carts and food. Perhaps you could do the same. In fact, you should hide any valuables or money that you have, while you can.'

Yet another of the decrees forbade Poles – and in particular the Polish Jews – from keeping more than a few zloty. The rest, they were told, should be deposited in German banks. How stupid did they think they were?

'I'll wait until Colonel Łaski comes home,' Magdalena's mother said. 'He'll know what to do for the best.'

Irena glanced at Magdalena and raised her eyebrows but her friend just returned her look with a sad smile. She waited until her mother had gone into the house before saying, 'She won't accept that Tata might never return. She can't believe that all this won't be over soon. I find it best to humour her. Maybe if we stay here quietly, mind our own business, give the Germans everything they want, they will leave us alone.'

'I don't think they'll do that,' Irena said urgently. 'They're rounding up people at random in Warsaw and taking them to God knows where. Don't you have anyone who can help you get out of Poland?'

'Mama won't leave as long as she believes Tata might return and I won't go without Aleksy.'

Irena grabbed her friend's arm, acutely aware as she felt the bone through the flesh of how painfully thin her friend had become.

'People are saying that large numbers of our pilots escaped to France and are continuing the fight there. We must believe Aleksy is amongst them. If he is, he'll want you to do whatever you can to survive.'

Magdalena smiled faintly. 'We'll be safe if we stay here quietly and don't draw attention to ourselves. Now why don't you come and have some lunch with us?'

'Sweet Mary in Heaven, Madzia, remember Kristallnacht! The same thing could happen here. There must be a reason the Nazis are singling out the Jews. They're making even the old people work – making them dig pointless ditches. They've forbidden them to use the parks or benches or trams. The Nazis hate the Jews. You should leave. Today! Now! You can stay with me. My apartment is small but we'll manage.' She drew a shuddering breath. 'If your mama won't, you must.'

Magdalena lifted her chin. 'Leave Mama? On her own? It's out of the question.'

'You have money – use it to get away. Go to France, Hungary, anywhere where you'll be safe.'

Magdalena raised her hand towards the house. 'Can you imagine Mama anywhere but here? It's her home. We are landowners, Irena. We have responsibilities. We don't run away.'

'But what if they take your lands and home for themselves?'

'They can have the lands. We'll get them back when they leave. And what will anyone do with a house this size? I am certain they'll allow Mama and me to remain in one of the wings.'

Irena shook her head. She could see it was hopeless. Magdalena had always been stubborn in her own quiet way.

She spent the rest of the afternoon with them, trying to convince them to go into hiding, but both Magdalena and her mother were adamant that they wouldn't be going anywhere. The worst was over, Elżbieta kept insisting. However, Irena couldn't shake the sense of foreboding she'd felt when she'd first arrived. There had to be a reason that the Nazis were singling out the Jews. Didn't Elżbieta and Magdalena realise that the Jews in Berlin had been executed just because they were Jews? Who was to say that the same wouldn't happen here? But she shook the thought away. Why would the Nazis do the same to the Jews of Poland? It was inconceivable. There were too many for a start and what would they gain by it? They already had what they wanted. No, perhaps Magdalena was right. Maybe it was safer here than in Warsaw. As long as everyone kept their heads down and out of the way of the Nazis, they would be all right.

Chapter 9

However, life under occupation only got worse. The Germans tried to tempt the Poles, with promises of increased rations, to work for the Reich in their factories, but news came back about the terrible working conditions and soon there were no more volunteers.

So the Nazis took to forcing them; selecting people at random. In one day alone they rounded up almost twenty thousand Poles, herded them into trucks at the point of a gun, and drove them away. They'd heard that the men had been sent to forced-labour camps and the women – most of them between the ages of seventeen and twenty-five – to East Prussia as agricultural labour.

Irena returned to Magdalena's home once more, hoping to make her friend understand that the situation was getting ever more desperate.

This time there was no Magdalena or her mother rushing to greet her. Instead, a large, unfamiliar car was parked in the driveway.

Filled with dread, Irena ran up the steps and banged on the door. It was opened by a corpulent, moustached German police officer.

'Yes?'

'I'm looking for Madam Łaski and her daughter.'

'They're no longer here.' The man made to close the door in her face but Irena jammed in a foot to stop him.

'What do you mean they are no longer here? This is their home. They wouldn't just give it up.'

He shrugged. 'I have no idea where they are, nor do I care. This house is no longer theirs. Houses such as these aren't needed by Jews.'

She bit down on the retort that rose to her lips. It was too dangerous to antagonise anyone allied to the Reich.

This time he did close the door in her face. Slowly Irena turned away. Perhaps Magdalena and her mother had taken her advice and gone into hiding, or, even better, found some way to leave Poland altogether. In that case why hadn't they let her know? Maybe they'd had to go quickly and there hadn't been time.

But the feeling of dread wouldn't go away.

Chapter 10

The first days of November brought snow and bitter cold. Despite the posters on every wall, the swastikas flying from most buildings and the presence of soldiers on every street, everyday life settled into a rhythm: people continued to go to work, still shopped in the open-air markets and gathered in the cafes and bars. Irena went to the hospital every day to do what she could. The little girl she'd helped had been discharged to the care of her aunt who'd come from one of the outlying villages in search of her family when they didn't arrive as planned. She had been distraught to discover that her brother, sister-in-law and nephew were dead, but finding little Maria alive seemed to give her the strength to put her own grief aside.

So many people had been displaced it was difficult to know who was where.

Since the occupation the number of casualties with traumatic injuries had slowed to a trickle, but admissions, particularly of children and old people suffering the effects of cold and malnutrition, had increased sharply. The nurses and doctors worked tirelessly, teaching the medical students while they toiled alongside them. However, it was a different kind of medicine and a different type of teaching than before the war. The medication they once had ready access to no longer existed, equipment had been damaged and either was in short supply or kept breaking down and so they often had to compromise and innovate when it came to treating the patients. Although Irena had learned more in the last few weeks than she had during the whole of her training, she and her fellow students looked forward to the university reopening in the near future. The Germans were repairing the railway tracks and telephone lines and although neither worked as well as they had before the invasion, it was possible to use the trains and, sporadically, make a phone call.

However, there was still no word from her father and Irena was becoming frantic. Every day she went to a cafe to use their phone to call him at their Krakow apartment, but either it didn't ring or it wasn't answered.

She was cleaning the septic wound of a patient when Dr Czatoryski, one of the senior doctors who knew her father well, asked her to come to his office.

The way he looked at her chilled her.

Dr Czatoryski lit a cigarette and waited until she was seated before he spoke. 'I have news of your father. It's not good.'

Irena's heart thumped sickeningly. 'Is he hurt?'

'He's alive. At least he was yesterday.'

Only when her breath came out in a long, shuddering sigh, did she realise she'd been holding it.

'What's happened?'

'The professors of the Jagiellonian University were called to a meeting allegedly to discuss the reopening of the university.' He pushed a glass of water towards her and she took a sip, glad of something to moisten her dry mouth.

'I'm sorry to have to tell you,' Dr Czatoryski continued, 'but the Germans arrested all of them, including your father. They assaulted the rector. They even shot a student who tried to protest.'

Irena gripped the arms of her chair as a wave of dizziness made her head spin. 'Why? What did they do wrong?'

He put his thumb and forefinger to his mouth and removed a flake of tobacco. 'Nothing! What does anyone need to do these days?' He leaned towards her. 'They claim the professors had attempted to reopen the university without obtaining permission. But that's only an excuse. We suspect the Nazis want to remove the Polish intelligentsia, and keeping universities and schools closed is only the first step. We have good information they have lists of professors, lawyers and doctors and that they plan to arrest them all.'

Irena shivered and threaded her fingers together to stop them shaking. It was hard to believe that the Germans would keep a bunch of old men prisoner just because they lectured at a university. But then only a few weeks ago she would never have believed anything she'd witnessed since the start of the war. 'Where did they take them?'

'They've imprisoned them in an old Polish military barracks in Krakow. We must hope that they'll release them soon.'

'And if they don't?'

The doctor ground out his cigarette in the ashtray. 'I don't know.'

'We have to do something. My father's not strong.'

'We will try to protest. It's all we can do.' He rubbed his neck with the back of his hand and stood. 'I'll let you know as soon as we find out the Germans' intentions as far as your father and the other professors are concerned.'

'I must go there. I must try to see him.'

He sighed. 'I would advise against it. I doubt they'll let you past the front gate. And perhaps it's best if you don't draw attention to yourself. They shot one of the students, remember?'

Still, she couldn't stay here and do nothing. Whatever Dr Czatoryski said, she wasn't going to stay in Warsaw, not when her father was in prison in Krakow. She had to, at the very least, make an attempt to see him.

It took several days for Irena to secure a train ticket to Krakow. The railway station, one of the few buildings undamaged during the fighting, was always crowded and chaotic.

The unheated carriage was freezing and Irena was glad of the body heat from her fellow travellers – a woman with her two children, an older man travelling with his wife and two elderly women, their thin faces pinched with cold. Apart from a quick nod to each other, no one maintained eye contact or spoke. These days it was impossible to know who to trust.

They were almost at Krakow when the train lurched to a halt. It wasn't unusual; the trains often stopped at random, sometimes to let soldiers on to check identity papers, sometimes because the track was damaged, and sometimes for no obvious reason. People had become accustomed to long delays and random searches, or at least resigned to them. It didn't mean they'd lost their fear, however; the searches often resulted in summary executions and arrests.

Irena wiped the condensation and ice from the inside of her window. Seven men, their bodies slowly revolving in the wind, their faces mottled black and blue, were swinging from gallows on the other side of the railway line. Sour-tasting bile rushed into her throat and she covered her mouth with her hand. Hearing an anguished cry behind her, she reached for the blind and snapped it closed, blocking out the sickening sight.

The old woman sobbed into her handkerchief, while the mother, her children pressed into her side, rocked back and forth. The older couple looked away, the man lifting his paper and hiding behind it.

The train jerked and continued on its way.

It took another two hours to reach Krakow, a journey that should have taken less than half the time, and all the while Irena's thoughts never strayed far from the dead men. Would that be Tata's fate?

She left the train and hurried towards the prison in Montelupich Street. Unlike Warsaw, Krakow was relatively undamaged, the Germans having decided to make it their base from which to control Poland. It was more like a German city now with its military bands marching along the street and the well-dressed and well-fed wives of the German officers.

But despite pleading and an eight-hour wait at the prison gates, they refused to let her see her father.

She had no choice but to return to Warsaw – and wait.

Chapter 11
Edinburgh, 1989

'How exciting!' Gilly said as she opened a bottle of wine. She held up a glass and raised an eyebrow, but Sarah shook her head. She still had copy-edits to work on tonight.

She'd run out of time to go shopping so had been forced to conjure up a pasta dish from some past-its-best mince, and despite her best efforts, it didn't look quite right. 'I'm afraid it's not very appetising,' she apologised. 'Let's hope it tastes better than it looks.'

Gilly added a liberal dose of red wine to the pan. 'Never found anything that couldn't be improved with a slug of alcohol.' She tasted it. 'Yummy. But come on, surely you must know Lord Glendale? Fancy you being connected to aristocracy.'

While Sarah had been making supper she'd filled her friend in on the day's events.

'I doubt very much that I am connected to him, although my grandparents might have known him.'

It was another possibility she'd thought of and an increasingly likely one. From the little her mother had told her about her grandparents they'd been wealthy at one time. 'That could explain why he had a photograph of my mother in his possession. Perhaps he just wanted to return it to its rightful owner.'

'Returning a photo is one thing, making your mother a legatee is quite another. Doesn't he have family?'

'I thought about that too so I looked him up in Debrett's at the office.'

'Debrett's?'

'It's the *Who's Who* of aristocracy. It lists all sorts of information about British aristocrats: antecedents, living and deceased relatives, schools, universities . . . all sorts of stuff. Anyway, I found him easily enough. He was the only son of the third Earl and Countess of Glendale, Simon and Isabel Maxwell, so until he inherited the title he would have been Lord Richard Maxwell. He was born in nineteen fifteen, educated at Fettes in Edinburgh, studied law at Cambridge and joined the RAF in nineteen thirty-nine. I'm pretty sure it's him in the photo.'

'Or a friend of his?'

'Possibly – but I'm going to go with my instinct that it's him.'

'What else did it say?'

'He never married and there are no children listed. His parents are both dead as are two uncles – one in the First World War, and the other, the original heir to the title, in nineteen twelve. It doesn't give a cause of death but he was pretty young. There's also an aunt listed – a Lady Dorothea – who was pretty impressive. She served in both wars and was called to the bar in nineteen twenty-four – one of the first women to do so. She retired in nineteen fifty-five. Although there's no date of death next to her name, it's unlikely she's still alive. She probably died after the edition I looked at was published.'

Gilly set two plates on the table and held out her hand. 'Can I see the photo?'

Sarah shook her head. 'Mum wouldn't let me have it back.'

'She knew him, then?'

'She claims not. But she recognised the woman as Magdalena. I wish I did have the photo to show you. She was stunning. He was bloody gorgeous too.'

'Wonder why he never married, then? Might have been gay, of course. They kept that sort of thing pretty quiet in those days.'

'Trust me, he wasn't gay. He had a painting and a couple of photos of Magdalena in his bedroom. If you'd seen them you would know he had to have been besotted with her. And he had a few of Mum's paintings.' She explained about the seascapes on his drawing-room wall.

'How intriguing! Maybe being single he had some sort of godparent role?'

'Perhaps, but in that case why has he never been part of her life until now?' She tipped the pasta into a bowl before setting it in the centre of the table. She grinned. 'God, this takes me back.'

'Me too.'

They'd met the first day Sarah moved into Halls. She'd been sitting on her bed, feeling a little sorry for herself, when a redhead, with the curliest hair she'd ever seen, burst through her door. 'Thank God,' she'd said. 'I've been going crazy waiting for someone to show up.'

From that moment on she'd been dragged along in Gilly's wake, her new friend insisting they attend virtually every event in Freshers' week and signing them up for every male-dominated society and club. After first year, they'd shared a series of crummy flats until they'd graduated, after which they'd gone their separate ways – Gilly moving in with Tim, and Sarah to London. But they'd always kept in touch and, since Sarah had moved back to Scotland, they saw each other at least once a month. Except for Gilly's appearance – the wild red curls had been cut into a Princess Di style and coloured blond – her friend hadn't changed. She was still a live wire, still the same restless, risk-taking Gilly. Sarah wished she could be more like her.

'So what next?' Gilly asked, winding a strand of spaghetti around her fork.

'I'm not sure.'

'What does your dad say?'

Sarah pushed her plate away. She didn't seem to have much of an appetite these days. 'I haven't spoken to him yet.'

Gilly raised an eyebrow. 'But you're going to, right? He might have all the answers – or some of them.'

Sarah shifted uneasily in her chair. 'I plan to phone him later.'

'I'm amazed you didn't call him straight away. I know you two don't get on but, Christ, Sarah, if anyone can clear up this mystery . . .'

Not getting on was one way of putting it. Since his marriage to the woman he'd left her mother for and their subsequent move to South Africa, she and Dad had virtually lost touch, although, of course, she'd phoned him to tell him about Mum's stroke. Foolishly, she'd allowed herself to believe that, just this once, he'd remember he had another daughter apart from the one he had with his second wife, but if she'd expected him to jump on the next plane to come and see them, she'd been disappointed.

'Yes, well. As I said, I'll call him later. In the meantime, Gilly, Lord Glendale is the obvious link. Seeing as he can't tell me anything, I wondered if one of the surviving family members might know something. Lady Dorothea, his aunt, has a son listed in Debrett's and apparently he still lives in London so I phoned Directory Enquiries for the number. Unfortunately, it's unlisted.' Sarah picked up their plates and put them in the sink.

'Why don't you just go and see him? Isn't it time you saw Matthew anyway?' Gilly said.

Sarah ignored the last comment. She didn't want to talk about Matthew.

'I can't just turn up at a stranger's door. What if they're furious about the will? What if there was a falling-out? I'd hardly be welcome on their doorstep.'

Gilly laughed. 'Oh, Sarah, don't go all Chicken Licken on me.'

Sarah bristled. 'Don't you think it's time you stopped calling me that?' Whenever Gilly had lost patience with Sarah's reluctance to go on one of her mad-cap escapades – and throughout their time at university there had been several – she'd taunted her with Chicken Licken who'd been so terrified that the sky would fall on his head, he'd persuaded Ducky Lucky and Henny Penny to be scared too. Then they'd run into sly Foxy Loxy and he'd convinced them to come to his den where they'd be safe. Needless to say, Chicken Licken, Henny Penny, and Ducky Lucky never made it out again. Which, Sarah had told Gilly, proved that *her* way of thinking was the right one.

Admittedly, in this case, Gilly had a point. What was the worst that could happen? They could turn her away, or refuse to speak to her – so at the most she'd be embarrassed.

'I could go, I suppose. There's only one problem, though: I don't like to leave Mum.'

Gilly raised an eyebrow. 'You could fly down to London in the morning and be back the same evening. Or better still, stay the night with Matthew. I'll pop in to see your mum and tell her you'll be in as soon as you return.'

It *was* about time she visited Matthew. Since her mother had become ill they'd seen little of each other. And bugger Gilly and her 'Chicken Licken'; she'd do whatever it took to find out who the Glendales were.

'Okay, then. If Dad can't clear up the mystery, I'll try to get a flight to London tomorrow. If I do, I'd appreciate it if you could look in on Mum while I'm gone – you're a sweetie for offering. But I should be the one to tell her I'll be away. She'll fret otherwise.' She glanced at her watch. 'Aren't you supposed to be meeting Tim in the pub, like twenty minutes ago?'

Gilly leaped to her feet, almost sending her glass of wine flying. 'Christ. I'd forgotten.' She picked up her handbag and dropped a kiss on Sarah's head. 'You know there could be a story in this. Personally I can't wait to find out what it is.'

After Gilly left, Sarah washed and put away the dishes, wiped the working tops, swept the floor and even contemplated mopping it. But if she were to catch her father before he went to bed, she couldn't put the phone call off any longer. As she waited for him to pick up she tapped her fingers on the hall table.

As soon as the stilted small talk was over and he'd asked about her mother, she told him about her visit to Hardcourt & Bailey.

'So do you know who Lord Glendale was?' she asked.

'Your grandparents were the only toffs I ever met. They might have known him, I suppose. You say he's left Lily a house?'

'Not exactly. And there are two.' She explained the terms of the will.

He whistled. 'The pair of you have fallen on your feet, haven't you?'

That wasn't quite how she'd describe her, or Mum's, life right now, but she bit back the retort. 'I don't suppose the name Magdalena Drobnik means anything to you either?'

'Not a dicky.'

Bugger. She'd hoped he'd be able to tell her something. 'Lord Glendale also left Mum a photograph of herself as a little girl. Do you have any idea why he might have had it?'

'A photo of your mother, you say? Now that's interesting.'

'Why?'

'It's not really up to me to tell you. It's your mother you should be asking.'

Sarah gritted her teeth. 'She can't exactly talk for herself at the moment, Dad. Just tell me what you know. Please.'

The line crackled and for a moment she thought they'd been disconnected. Her father's sigh came over the line. 'Right. Fine. Did you know your mother was adopted when she was a child?'

Sarah almost dropped the phone. 'No!'

'I guess she still hasn't told you then?'

Sarah swallowed hard. 'No.' It was so like Mum that she hadn't. But still hurtful.

'Sorry, love, I thought she would have by now, although it wasn't something she liked to talk about. She only told *me* when we needed a copy of her birth certificate to get married.'

Sarah's head was spinning. Was it possible Mum was Magdalena Drobnik's child? And if Magdalena was Mum's mother, was Lord Glendale her father? It would explain the photo and the bequest – and Mum's reaction to the woman in the photo. Perhaps she hadn't being trying to say Magdalena. Perhaps she'd been trying to say *mother*?

'You say she was a little girl when she was adopted. Did she tell you who her natural parents were?'

'Apparently they died when she was very young. That's all she told me.'

'Died? Are you sure? Both of them?'

'That's what she said. In the war.'

If Mum's natural parents had died during the war, then Lord Glendale and Magdalena Drobnik couldn't be her parents. Unless Mum had lied to Dad. She wouldn't be the first person to smudge the truth. Better to be adopted because your parents had died than because they'd given you away.

'She must have told you something else!'

'I did try to ask, but Lily said she'd spent her life trying to forget what happened to her when she was a child – that people who thought talking about the past was cathartic didn't have a clue what they were on about. I'd never seen her in such a tizz. And that was that. It was never mentioned again.'

'I can't believe I never knew any of this! She must have said how they died!'

'I know it was something to do with the war, that's all. You know, Sarah, loads of children were orphaned at the time and sent all over the country – particularly out of London.'

Mum had been born in 1939. Dad was right. It was perfectly possible that her parents had been killed during the war.

'Hold on a sec, Dad – their names – at least Mum's mother's name – must have been on the birth certificate.'

'That's the thing. She never did find it – all she managed to find was an adoption paper with your grandparents' names on it.'

So what was the connection with Lord Glendale? Unless Mum's natural parents had been close friends of his. His family had owned a home in London and the capital had been badly bombed during the war. In which case why hadn't he ever made himself known to Mum? To leave two properties to a woman on slight acquaintance seemed unlikely. And Mum *had* known Magdalena. How?

'Sarah, are you still there? I need to go. Mirinda wants me for something.'

Mirinda could wait for once. 'How old was Mum when she was adopted?'

'I'm not sure. Five or six, I think. As I said, she didn't like to talk about it.'

'In that case she would have been old enough to remember her parents. What if Magdalena was Mum's mother? Perhaps she was a refugee and she and this Lord Glendale had an affair and she fell pregnant? Maybe Magdalena couldn't keep her baby. She might have been Catholic, many Poles were.' Sarah had once copy-edited a book by a woman who had been forced to give up her baby in the forties. Perhaps the same thing had happened to Magdalena? But if that had been the case, then Mum would have been given up for adoption when she was a baby. Unless Magdalena had died and that was why Mum had been adopted. But that didn't work. No one would bequeath properties to a dead woman. There had to be another explanation.

'Look, Sarah, this is all very interesting but I really have to go.'

After hanging up on her father, she took the photo of Mum as a child into her study, and held it next to the framed picture of her and her mother she always kept on her desk. Sarah had been about six at the time and was clinging to her mother's hand, looking up at her. Her mother was staring straight ahead, although Sarah vividly remembered the almost painful pressure of her fingers biting into her palm. *Could* Mum be Magdalena and Richard's child? She tried to visualise the woman in the photo and the painting. If Magdalena and Mum looked alike, it hadn't been obvious to Sarah – but then she hadn't been looking for a family resemblance. Magdalena had blue-green eyes and blond hair and Mum had brown eyes and dark hair and Lord Glendale had been tall and blond. That didn't necessarily mean they couldn't be related. She wasn't good at seeing similar features, even when friends with babies insisted they looked exactly like Aunt Geraldine or Uncle Fred.

She lifted the photo of her and Mum and peered at it. There was little resemblance between mother and daughter; where Sarah's hair tended to curl if she didn't dry it straight, her mother's fell in a sleek, natural curtain. Their eyes were different too; Mum's were almond shaped and dark brown whereas Sarah's had a touch of green from her father's side. Sarah's mouth was fuller too and while Mum had always been slim, Sarah had to work to keep off the pounds. The one thing they did share was their small slightly turned-up noses. But what struck Sarah most was that the eyes of both the child and the adult versions of her mother had the same fearful expression.

What was Mum anxious about that day? Were they near a road and she was frightened Sarah might run into it? Certainly Mum was always worried something would happen to her only child. Sarah had been in her first year at high school before Mum, after a furious argument, had allowed her to walk to school on her own. Even then, one day during lunch break, Sarah had looked over to find her mother watching her from the school's perimeter fence. That had resulted in another blazing row, but at least it had stopped her mother's absurd, and mortifying, behaviour.

If she'd lost her parents as a small child, no wonder she'd been frightened something would happen to Sarah.

How come she knew so little about her mother? As a spasm of grief and regret gripped her, she traced the outline of her mother's face with her fingertip. She'd never understood how Mum could be so over-protective yet so distant. She'd resented her so often – always hoping that Mum would talk to her, really talk to her, like Gilly and her mother did. But apart from once, it had never happened. Perhaps it wasn't too late to get to know her now?

She could start with finding out what had happened to Mum's birth parents and to do that she needed to find out more about Magdalena Drobnik and Richard Maxwell.

Chapter 12

At visiting the following afternoon, Sarah was surprised to find her mother more alert than she'd been since the stroke. She was sitting up in her chair, propped up correctly with her hair neatly combed.

'Hello, Mum. You're looking better.'

Sarah appropriated a plastic chair from a patient without visitors and sat down next to her mother. It was only then that she noticed she still had the photo of the couple clutched in her hands.

Linda stopped at the foot of the bed. 'Excuse me a moment, ladies, but I need to take Lily's blood pressure.'

'I was just telling Mum how much better she looks,' Sarah said.

'She's done well today. She managed a good bit of her breakfast and a little of her lunch too.' Linda slipped the ends of the stethoscope into her ears and held up a finger before pumping up the cuff on Sarah's mother's arm. She listened for a while and frowned.

'What's the matter?' Sarah asked.

'Her BP is a little raised. Nothing to be concerned about.' She wrapped the stethoscope around her neck and marked her mother's chart before leaving them alone.

Sarah reached forward and placed her hand over her mother's.

'Please don't be annoyed but I spoke to Dad last night. I told him about the photos and Lord Glendale's bequest.'

Her mother's eyes blazed. She pulled her hand away and tapped her stick twice on the floor. Sarah's parents hadn't spoken since they'd divorced and whenever Sarah so much as mentioned Dad's name her mother became tight-lipped.

Sarah knotted her fingers together and took a deep breath. 'He told me you were adopted, Mum. I wish I'd known. I wish you'd felt able to tell me.'

The fire in her mother's eyes dimmed. 'S . . . Sad.'

'Oh, Mum, you could have told me.' Sarah swallowed. 'Is that how you know Magdalena?'

One tap – *yes*.

'Was she your birth mother?'

Her mother's face crumpled. Two taps. *No*.

'Are you certain? You know you can tell me—'

Her mother looked at Sarah with imploring eyes and jabbed the stick on the floor. One tap. Pause. One tap. She stared at Sarah as if willing her to understand.

'It's okay, Mum. I'm just trying to work out how you know Magdalena and why her picture upsets you.'

Her mother looked at her, her brown eyes burning with frustration.

'Okay, I'll rephrase that, does her picture upset you?'

Two taps. *No*.

'Does something about her upset you?'

One tap. *Yes*. 'N . . . N . . . ' Her mother was getting agitated. She waved her stick in the general direction of the ward and Sarah swivelled in her chair. Most of the beds had visitors, except Mrs Liversage who was wandering up and down the middle of the ward, crying and calling for her mother and father. A nurse took her by the arm and led her towards the day-room.

'Has Mrs Liversage been upsetting you?' Sarah asked.

Two taps. *No.*

'Someone else in the ward?'

One tap. Then after a pause. Two taps. *Yes and no?*

Sarah shook her head. She didn't know who was more frustrated, her or Mum. 'Is it being in hospital?'

One tap.

So her distress was less to do with the photographs than being in hospital. 'I know you hate it here but it's where you need to be – for the time being at least – but I'll speak to Staff Nurse after visiting and see if she has an idea of when you might be discharged.'

Her mother smiled lopsidedly. ''ome. Plis.' It was the most she'd said since her stroke. The doctors had said that she might regain her speech in time and possibly most of the movement in her right side. Perhaps now wasn't the best time to be considering taking her home. Not when she finally seemed to be making progress.

'I'm going to London to see Matthew, Mum, and while I'm there, I'm going to see if I can find out anything about Lord Glendale. I'll only be away for a night. Is that all right?'

Her mother nodded.

The bell rang to signal the end of visiting. As Sarah bent to lift her bag her mother gripped her wrist with a surprising strength. 'Ma . . . ' She took a deep breath 'Eena. F–F–Eena.'

'You want me to find Magdalena?'

One tap.

Magdalena might not be Mum's mother, but whoever she was, she clearly meant something to her.

'I'd like to see the doctor about a date when I might be able to take my mother home,' Sarah said to Linda before leaving.

'Sarah, as I said yesterday, Lily still needs a great deal of nursing and therapy.'

'I could employ someone privately.' Although she didn't know how. By the end of the month she'd barely enough money in the bank to live on, let alone pay for a nurse. But she could sell her car or take out a loan. One way or another, she'd manage.

Linda was looking at her as if wondering whether to say something. The sympathy in her eyes was like a shock of ice along Sarah's spine. 'What is it?'

'Your mother's blood pressure isn't coming down despite the medication we're giving her. You know that someone who has already had a stroke has an increased risk of having another. It's possible she might never be able to go home.'

'But you said—'

'That she'd be going home soon. I only said that to keep her fighting. If Lily thinks she'll never leave here she might give up.'

'Mum will never stop fighting – not as long as she still has me – and I won't let her.' Sarah's throat was so tight with the need to cry, she could barely speak. 'Don't *you* dare give up on her.'

'Oh, Sarah, we won't. I promise. I just wanted you to be prepared.'

She would never be prepared for Mum dying.

She sat in her car in the hospital car park for a long time, close to tears. She'd promised Mum she'd find Magdalena so that was what she was going to do. She turned the ignition. She might not be able to do anything else for Mum, but if Magdalena was alive she was bloody well going to find her.

Chapter 13
Warsaw, 1940

Most of the time Irena managed to push what was happening in Poland from her mind, but too often she was confronted with terrifying and heart-breaking reminders. Almost every day men and women were rounded up at gunpoint and made to stand with their hands against a wall while the soldiers searched them. Some were released, others shot. Nobody knew what they'd done – if they'd done anything – and nobody intervened. But as soon as the soldiers had left, people would hurry to remove the bodies, leaving lit candles in their place.

When she wasn't sleeping or queuing for food, she was at the hospital, studying or attending lectures. The only light in the endlessly grey, terrifying days was that the university had started underground teaching. She never discovered until the day before, where and what time the classes would be held and it was often changed at the last moment.

Today, she'd come back from one such lecture to find a letter waiting for her. With no fuel to heat her apartment, it was as cold inside as it was outside. She wrapped herself in a blanket and sank into a chair, tucking her legs underneath her.

She didn't recognise the handwriting on the envelope but when she opened it, a note and two more envelopes, one addressed to her and one to Aleksy, were folded in half inside. This time she did recognise the handwriting. It was Magdalena's.

Magdalena was alive. Thank God. She tore open the envelope and started to read.

My dear friend,

I am not sure whether this will ever reach you or my darling Aleksander. A nurse here has offered to post them and I pray that she will do as she promises.

I don't even know if either of you are alive but I have to believe that you are. If you have been to our old home you will have learned that Mama and I were forced to leave it. Mama wanted to go east as she was certain that we would find Tata there. Instead, we were taken by the Russians and put behind barbed wire. My dear, I will save you the particulars, except to say that I do not expect to survive. Sadly, Mama has already passed away. She was forced to sell her coat and shoes for food and as you know she wasn't strong. I do not think it will be long before I join her. I am so cold, so hungry, I can't bear to stay alive.

If you find Aleksy, please give him the letter I enclose with this one. My only regret is that I could not see you both, even one more time.

May God bless and protect you, my sister.
Your loving friend,
Madzia

Irena's fingers were shaking as she opened the note. She cried out as she read the words.

I am sorry to have to tell you that your friend passed away shortly after writing these letters. She seemed peaceful at the end. I told her I would try to get them to you and I have done my best.

The letter wasn't signed.

She cried for a long time. She cried until she could cry no longer. It was too much. Magdalena was dead and in all likelihood Aleksy and Piotr were too. Her father was in prison and might never be released. She'd survived being fired upon, she'd survived the bombing of Warsaw, she'd done her best to be strong, but this was too much.

This bloody, bloody war. Damn the Russians. Damn the Germans.

Chapter 14

Irena was in her apartment thumbing through a medical text-book when there was a knock on the door. She and Krystiana, who'd reappeared one day, murmuring something about being ill, looked at each other in horror. Frequently in the night they were woken by the sound of hob-nail boots running up the stairs, followed by gruff commands and cries as people were forced from their homes at gunpoint. But if it were the Nazis, they'd be pounding on the door, shouting at them to get out.

Her heart beating so fast she was having difficulty breathing, she opened the door to find her father standing there. When he saw her he sagged against the door jamb. 'Irena, my dear. I didn't know if you'd be here. I couldn't be sure.'

'Tata! Thank God! I've been so worried. Hurry, come inside.' She did her best to hide her shock. Gone was the upright, well-groomed father she'd always known. In his place stood an old man, the gold metal of his glasses held together at the bridge by a piece of tape, one of the lenses cracked. He'd lost so much weight that his collarbones jutted out and his shirt looked as if it had been made for someone much larger.

Krystiana hurried over and they each took one of his arms and led him over to a chair. 'I will fetch coffee and something to eat,' Krystiana said and left them.

'Tata – what did they do to you?'

He patted her hand. 'I'm all right. I'm alive. And now I know you are too, I am even better.'

Krystiana returned with some bread and a pot of what passed for coffee these days and Irena poured her father a cup, folding her hands over his to stop them from shaking. She waited until he'd drunk a little. 'Take some bread, Tata,' she said. 'I'll warm up some beetroot soup to have with it. I wish I had something else to give you.'

'Keep it,' he said. 'My stomach has become unaccustomed to food.'

'You must try to eat something, Tata. You're so thin.'

'Perhaps later.'

'Did you escape?' she asked.

His mouth twisted. 'Escape? There was never any chance of that. No, my child, they let some of us go. The older ones.'

'Tell me everything. Start at the beginning.'

He stared at the floor, his hands hanging between his knees. 'They called us to a meeting,' he said. 'We thought they were going to confirm that we could reopen the university. But instead SS Sturmbannführer Bruno Muller read out a speech. He said we had tried to resume our research and organise exams without permission and that was an act of malice and hostility towards the third Reich. Yes, those were the words. *An act of malice and hostility*. Can you believe it?'

She could believe anything the Nazis did.

'We were told we were under arrest and would be taken to a prisoner-of-war camp. Imagine! One hundred and eighty-three of us. Some weren't even employed by the university. They just happened to be in the wrong place at the wrong time. A student, a hot head, protested and they put a bullet in him.'

He covered his face with his hands. Irena had never seen her father look so defeated and it frightened her. All her life he'd been this strong man she'd looked up to, her immutable rock.

'Don't talk any more, Tata. It can wait. You should rest.'

He took a shuddering breath and raised his head. 'I have had enough time for rest. I need to tell you what happened. We have to find a way of telling the world what is going on here. I heard that the outside world put pressure on the Nazis to release us, and in the end – but only after they'd almost killed us – they agreed to let some of us go. Those of us over forty.' A smile flitted across his face. 'They must believe we are too old to be a threat to the new fascist world they envisage.' He grasped her hand. 'It is the young they want to get rid of most. It is why you must protect yourself.'

'Tata—'

'Remember when I said that the Germans were decent people. That we shouldn't worry? I was wrong. This isn't the same army as in the last war. These aren't the same people.' He leaned forward, his blue eyes blazing. 'I must tell you what they did if only to make you understand why you must leave.' His lips were taking on a blue tinge and Irena felt for his pulse with her fingertips. It was rapid and weak.

'Tata, it can wait. You need to rest, to get your strength back.'

He pushed her hand away. 'There's no time, Irena. You have to listen.

'They took us to the prison on Montelupich Street. After a few days we were transferred to the old barracks of the Polish twentieth Infantry regiment. They have a sense of humour at least. Then we were moved again. Our new prison was Schutzhaftlager Sachsenhausen near Berlin – at least that was the sign we read on the gate. We were ordered into a barrack and told to take off our clothes. Our heads were shaved and then we were made to shower – all together. Can you imagine the indignity of it? To them we were no better than simple criminals – *Häftlinge*.' He closed his eyes and paused for so long that Irena thought he'd fallen asleep. As she gently laid a blanket over him he began to speak again.

'It was a hell. Our accommodation was in long rows of barracks arranged around a large central yard. This was where we had to stand for roll call, for hours at a time, three times a day. It was so cold and all we had to wear were thin prison clothes. The only ones who had caps were the "functionary prisoners", he almost spat the words, 'criminals who had the privilege of beating the other prisoners whenever the whim took them. The camp was run by SS men, with the army manning the watchtowers. There were others: young, shady-looking men in long black coats with what looked like pieces of shin bones on their lapels. We heard that they were SS men sent to Schutzstaffel to do penance or for special training. They were referred to as the fallen angels. Fallen Angels! It was a good description of the devils. We were more frightened of them than of anyone else.

'The routine was the same every day: we rose at six, washed, had a drink of some brown stuff they had the nerve to call coffee, before the first roll call – one of many. Often they lasted longer than an hour. They took this opportunity to torture us. If we stopped standing to attention they would beat and kick us. It's almost impossible to stand still when you are freezing. Sometimes they would punish us as a group. Several times we were made to kneel in the mud on one knee and hold our hands in the air. Like so.'

He dropped to his knees and demonstrated. The sight of him like that was impossible to bear. 'Tata, please, don't!' She scrambled to her feet and helped him up and back into his chair. She didn't want to hear any more, but she knew he wouldn't rest until he'd finished his story.

'After Christmas it became even colder and we began to despair of our survival. Influenza and pneumonia began to spread but we had nothing to treat it with. Many died. It was the worst time.

'A week or two later there was a longer roll call, almost three hours. It was the coldest day so far. Many, many people froze to death and we had to leave them where they fell.

The younger men were selected for work in the rock quarry at Mauthausen. At least they got a little more to eat. All the rest of us were given was watery vegetable stew and a small lump of hard bread once a day, and once a week, a little margarine or fruit pulp, perhaps fish paste or a piece of black pudding. It wasn't long before we began to look like walking skeletons. Then, suddenly – we didn't know why – they called the names of a hundred of us, the older ones. We thought we were going to be driven to a forest and shot, but instead they gave us back our clothes and put us on a train. Every moment we expected they would stop the train and pull us off again but they didn't. They just let us go. I came to you soon as I could. But, Renia, they still have the younger professors and there is talk that they won't rest until the intelligentsia of Poland has been wiped out. I'm afraid that could mean the students next – people like you.'

'What can they possibly hope to gain by their actions? What are they scared of? That we will kill them with words?'

'This is a different type of world to the one that existed when you were born. They want to destroy us so that they have nothing to fear from us in the future. That is why you must look out for yourself.'

'It's bad here, too.' She wrapped her arms around her knees and hugged them to her, trying to instil some warmth into her body. 'It doesn't seem to matter who you are or what you do. Only last week they executed hundreds of innocent people, because one German policeman was killed by our underground army. Others just disappear.'

'I've heard the Russians are no better. There are rumours of arrests and executions there too. And the camps there are as bad as here,' he murmured, his voice raspy from talking. Telling his story had clearly taken its toll.

Sweet Mary, the Russians and their camps! He didn't know about Magdalena. How could he bear it?

When she shivered again her father reached out and patted her hand. 'I am not telling you this to frighten you, but to convince you to go.'

'Tata, I have something to tell you. It is more bad news, I'm afraid.'

He leaned back in his chair and folded his hands in his lap. She noticed they were trembling. 'You have had word of Aleksy?' he said finally.

She crouched in front of him and took his cold hands in hers. 'No. It is Magdalena and her mother. I'm sorry to have to tell you, they are both dead. In a camp in the east.'

What little colour he still had in his face drained away. 'Are you sure? There is so much confusion.'

She nodded, rubbing his hands to try to bring some heat into them. 'I'm afraid so, Tata. Magdalena wrote to me and Aleksy. Her mama had already died and Magdalena knew she didn't have long. A nurse posted the letters after Magdalena passed away.'

A tear dribbled down his cheek. 'That poor girl. And her mother. Oh, my poor boy. If he is still alive this news will break his heart.'

They sat in silence, the clock ticking away the minutes. 'You see why you must go,' her father said finally. 'If you won't leave Poland, you must at least leave Warsaw. There is nothing here for you now. No reason for you to stay. I have to go back to Krakow to help with the underground university but I have a friend, a doctor who trained under me, who is working in Rozwadow in the south. It is a just a village, so not important to the Germans, and I think you would be safer there. You can continue to work as a medical student on the wards. Dr Palka – Henryk – is in charge there. He will be a good teacher.'

'If it's safer there you should come with me.'

'They need me in Krakow.'

'*I* need you. What if they arrest you again?' He would never survive if they did.

'It is a chance I must take.'

'I'm begging you, Tata. Don't go back. Please! It's too dangerous.'

He frowned. 'My child, don't you see? It is my way of fighting. It is more important than ever that we train the young people so they are ready when Poland is liberated.'

She had to make him see sense. He had to stay alive, if not for his sake, then for hers. 'And when will that be?' she asked bitterly. 'I see no sign of it.'

'This war won't last forever. It will end one day. Whether it is the Nazis who are the victors or the Allies, one day this nightmare will stop.'

'If you won't stay here, I'll come with you to Krakow.'

He shook his head. 'It is too dangerous. They'll be watching me and if they are watching me they will be watching you, too.' He pressed her fingers. 'I'm old, Irena. I don't mind dying, but you and people like you are the future of Poland. You must do whatever it takes to stay away from the attention of the Nazis.'

'Please, Tata. Don't ask me to do this. If anything's happened to Aleksy and Piotr, you are all I have left.'

'And you, my darling, are all I have. That is why I need you to survive. When the war is over, we will need people to rebuild this country,' her father continued. 'We will need doctors, lawyers, teachers, engineers. The very people the Nazis want to crush. If you stay here you could be caught in one of their round-ups. You could be shot. Then where would I be? Or, if God has spared him, Aleksy? Or Piotr? What would we have to live for if you are not in this world?'

Irena looked at his dear face. Although she couldn't bear to leave him, she knew he was right. Hadn't she promised Piotr she would do everything she could to live? She could just as easily help in a hospital in a village as here in Warsaw, and at least there, she would be closer to Krakow and her father. 'Very well, Tata. If you insist, I will go to Rozwadow when you are better. It is not far from Krakow. You could come to see me – or I can come and see you.'

He sighed with relief. 'I have something for you.' He dipped into his pocket and brought out a necklace. On the end of a thin gold chain was a tear-shaped ruby, surrounded by small diamonds. 'It belonged to your mother. Keep it safe. If you need to sell it, then do so, but make sure you get the best price you can for it. The money I have in the bank is worth a fraction of what it was before the Germans devalued the zloty.'

Irena wrapped her fingers around the necklace. This had belonged to her mother and she would die rather than part with it. 'I'll look after it until we can be together again, Tata.'

Krystiana was waiting for her in the sitting room when she returned from seeing her father to bed.

'Bastards!' Krystiana spat. 'How could they treat a man like your father like that? My God, they deserve everything our men will do to them.'

'Our men have done their best, Krystiana. They can do no more,' Irena said wearily.

'That's where you're wrong.'

Krystiana turned away but Irena grabbed her arm and pulled her around until she was facing her. 'What do you mean?'

'I didn't want to tell you before – I thought it would be too dangerous for you – but our men are fighting back. It's not just a few people shooting soldiers and putting up posters, there are thousands. They didn't capture everyone. Many of our soldiers refused to surrender and escaped into the hills and they're re-forming an army. Here in Warsaw, Krakow, too. Everywhere. There are many such groups but the biggest is the Armia Krajowa – the Home Army. We will be ready when the Allies come to rid Poland of the Nazi bastards.'

'How do you know all this?'

Krystiana smiled. 'My son. He is a commander. Remember near the beginning when I didn't come in for a few days? I was hiding him.'

'Why didn't you tell me? Didn't you trust me?'

Krystiana touched her cheek with a gnarled finger. 'I didn't tell you because you didn't need to know. It was safer for you. I wouldn't have told you now, but I overheard what they did to your father. He's right, little one. You must leave this place. They will be watching you. And if ever they capture my son, God forbid,' she murmured a few words and kissed the cross she wore around her neck, 'they will take me. Then they might come for you, too. It is good you are going away. It will be safer for us all.'

Despite what her father had just told her, Irena felt lighter than she had since the invasion. Piotr could be with this secret army. Poland wasn't defeated yet. She kissed the older woman. 'Thank you for telling me. Thank you for giving me hope. May God protect you and your son.'

Chapter 15

Over the spring and summer, the round-ups and arbitrary executions continued. The underground army became increasingly active and every day another poster would go up on a wall with the names of those who had been shot – either for aiding a Jew or in retaliation for the death of a German. No one knew who'd be next, so everyone kept their heads down and their eyes averted, in a desperate hope not to attract attention. The Jews, however, couldn't avoid being noticed.

In April, the Central Government issued another decree. All Jews had to leave their homes and find new ones in a part of Warsaw especially designated for them; the Poles who lived there having had to find new homes of their own. Not all Poles were unhappy. Some of the Jewish homes they acquired were far superior to those they'd left.

Despite the danger, the underground press continued to publish papers and Irena and her colleagues read them avidly. Radio Swit started broadcasting, bringing news of what was happening inside and outside Poland. It made everyone feel they weren't alone and that, in some small way, they were resisting the Germans too. There had been reports – reliable reports – that several thousand men of the Polish army had escaped and regrouped in France. There was jubilation at first, everyone, Irena amongst them, hoping that their missing loved ones had made it safely to France and were preparing to attack Hitler's armies in Poland. Their optimism was short-lived. In May, France fell and the Allied forces suffered a terrible defeat at Dunkirk. It looked as if Hitler was unstoppable.

Now, as a second winter under occupation approached, Irena had heard that the Jews inside the ghetto were starving and freezing to death, their corpses stripped by the living and left on the street, no one it seemed having the energy or the resources to bury them. Although they had little to spare for themselves, and although they risked arrest by doing so, some Poles tried to smuggle food into the ghetto. But mostly people kept off the streets as much as they could.

It was the search for food that had brought Irena out in the freezing weather. If Tata were to continue to regain his strength, he needed fruit and vegetables – something more nutritious than the bread and thin soup that they ate most days. But all she'd managed to buy on the black market were a few shrivelled plums.

The rain fell in sheets, obscuring people and buildings, splashing up from the pavement, soaking the hem of her coat until it clung heavily to her shins.

Trying to keep the cold rain from sliding down her neck, Irena pulled up the collar of her coat and rearranged her headscarf until it covered the lower part of her face as well as her head. She curled her hands deep into her pockets in an attempt to generate some warmth, careful not to squash her precious booty. An old man almost bumped into her as he hurried past, his shoulders hunched against the wind, his fearful eyes sliding away from hers.

The rain eased then turned to snow, her feet, already frozen in her leaky shoes, leaving smudged footprints behind her.

A woman stepped out of a doorway and into her path. Her

sunken eyes were large in her gaunt face. Tattered, dirty strips of cloth covered her feet and she clutched a bundle of rags to her chest with hands swollen and raw from the cold. She said something in Yiddish that Irena couldn't understand and hesitatingly opened one palm to reveal a torn Star of David.

Irena's heart leaped to her throat and she glanced behind her. The street was empty, but for how long? To be even seen with a Jewess outside the ghetto was dangerous.

'I'm sorry but I can't help you.' She dug around in her pocket for the plums and tried to press them into the woman's hand. 'Take these. It's all I have.'

But the woman shook her head impatiently, and speaking more urgently thrust the bundle at Irena. Irena looked down and sucked in a shocked breath. Nestled within the clumps of dirty rags was a baby and even in the dim light she noticed the sunken cheeks and stretched skin of starvation.

The mother pushed the infant towards Irena more forcefully, her intention clear. She wanted Irena to take her baby.

Appalled, Irena took a step backwards. 'I can't. I'm sorry.' Over the frantic mother's shoulder she saw that three soldiers had turned in to the street and had huddled together to light cigarettes. Fear closed her throat. If the soldiers discovered the Jewess out of the ghetto and without her armband there was no telling what they'd do.

The woman thrust her child at Irena again, talking urgently, pleading with her. If she took the child the soldiers could punish her too. Arrest her – shoot her even.

Irena pushed the child away. 'No!' It came out louder than she'd meant and had attracted attention. One of the soldiers had stopped talking to his companions and was watching them with interest.

'Don't turn around,' Irena told the woman, praying that even if she didn't speak Polish she could understand it. 'There are soldiers at the end of the street. Just walk away.'

Soft wet flakes of snow swirled around them as the woman's desperate eyes bored into hers.

Irena hesitated. She could pretend the child was hers. She could take the baby to the hospital – someone would look after it.

But it was too late. In the seconds it had taken for the thoughts to flash through her head, the soldiers had started walking towards them.

'Go!' Irena hissed. 'In the name of God, go!'

'Hey, you,' a soldier called out. The mother turned a ghastly bleached white. She shoved the armband into her pocket, covered her child quickly in the folds of the rags and started to walk away.

'Halt!'

The woman walked faster. The soldier raised his gun and fired a shot over her head. She stopped, but didn't turn around.

While his two companions went to her, the other stood in front of Irena. 'Papers!'

She pulled them out of her handbag and held them out with trembling fingers.

'Do you know her?' He tipped his head in the direction of the woman.

'No. She is a stranger. I . . .' Even from here Irena could sense the mother's fear as the soldiers demanded to see her papers too. When she shook her head, one of the soldiers reached into the pocket of her threadbare coat and pulled out an armband. '*Juden!*' he spat.

Irena watched helplessly as he opened the bundle the woman was carrying. Exposed to the chilly air, the baby gave a feeble cry. The mother clutched her child closer and although Irena couldn't understand what she was saying she knew she was pleading for the life of her child.

'You can go,' the soldier said to Irena and left her to join his companions.

He snatched the bundle from the mother's arms and laughed while his friend held his gun to her head.

Irena had only just turned out of Zlota Street when she heard the short but unmistakable spurt of machine-gunfire, followed by an anguished cry. A cry so filled with pain and rage and desolation it froze the blood in her veins.

Another staccato burst and the cry was silenced.

On leaden legs Irena continued on her way.

She only just made it home in time before she vomited. She hung over the toilet bowl long after her stomach was empty. She slid down onto the bathroom floor and wrapped her arms around herself. Why didn't she take the baby when she had the chance? She could have saved its life – if not the mother's. But she'd been so frightened, so terribly, terribly frightened.

Unable to move, she stayed there until she heard a key turning in the lock.

'Irena?' her father called. 'Where are you?'

She used the lip of the wash basin to haul herself from the floor.

'Irena! For God's sake, answer me!'

She opened the bathroom door, wiping the vomit from her mouth with the back of her hand.

'My child, what's happened? Are you all right?' Her father hurried towards her and led her into the sitting room. She crumpled into a chair and wrapped her arms across her stomach, squeezing her eyes shut to block out the pain and horror.

'Tata, they shot her. The bastards shot her.'

'Who? Who did they shoot? Krystiana?'

'No. Not Krystiana. A mother. A young, defenceless mother. And her baby. They shot her baby, too.'

'I'll fetch you some vodka.' He returned a few moments later with a tumbler filled to the rim. 'Drink this,' he instructed before tucking a blanket around her.

Her hands were shaking so badly she spilled most of the contents of the glass down her cardigan. She swallowed, gasping as the liquid burned her throat, but as the warmth of the liquor spread through her, the trembling in her hands lessened.

When she was sure she could speak without breaking down she told her father what she'd witnessed. 'I could have saved the baby at least – if I hadn't hesitated. If I'd been braver.'

'Hush, Renia. What happened is not your fault.'

She wished she could believe him. 'It was my reaction that made the soldiers come over.'

'Oh, Renia. They would have caught her eventually. A Jew on the street with a child. What hope did she have?'

'I was her hope, Tata. Her one chance. And I failed her.'

He squeezed her hand. 'No one could have saved her.'

But she couldn't get the mother's desperate eyes and final hopeless scream out of her head. She took another gulp of vodka. 'I know God says we should love our enemies, but he couldn't mean these monsters. They have no souls.'

Her father sighed. 'You mustn't hate, Renia. It will eat away at *your* soul. They might kill us but don't let them take your soul. Then they will have won.'

'I can't help it.' She took a shuddering breath. 'I will never forgive them.' Or herself.

'You mustn't think that way. We are all God's children. Only He can judge.'

'Then you are a better person then I'll ever be,' she replied. 'If there is a God, one day they will pay for what they've done. I will make certain of it.'

She wanted to run out into the street and confront the Nazis, to shout her grief and rage, to batter them with her fists until they were bloodied. But she wouldn't last a minute if she did.

Her father gripped her hands more tightly. 'Listen to me, Renia. One day the world will know what has been done to the Polish nation. One day the Nazis will be brought to justice and made to answer for their barbarity and it is up to us to bear witness for all those who can no longer speak for themselves.'

She didn't want to live in a world where people could be treated as if they were bugs to be crushed underfoot, but her father was right. To give up now would mean those she loved had died for nothing. She owed it to them and their memories to live.

All she had to decide now was how.

Chapter 16
Rozwadow, Poland, 1940

Irena washed her face in cold water, applied a smear of lipstick – it was her last tube so she wanted to make it last – and let herself out of the main gate of the hospital where patients were already queuing for the outpatient clinic. Desperate faces glanced at her as she passed, some calling out a greeting, others just watching her mutely as if they had already given up.

The street was busy with farmers and their carts, although Irena knew the pickings of their produce would be thin. She stopped several and asked if they could sell her something, but they all shook their heads, indicating with a nod the German soldiers who leaned against the walls, smoking cigarettes while keeping an eye on the locals as they went about their business. Irena didn't look at them, not wanting to catch their eye and bring attention to herself. She'd learned that the trick was to seem invisible.

Rozwadow was typically Polish with the centre built around the square and a mix of one- and two-storey houses and surrounded by farmland. Like almost every city and town in Poland, it had an area into which all the Jews had been corralled. No one was allowed to enter or to leave it – not even to get medical treatment – on the pain of being shot on the spot.

Not having family in the village, Irena had a room at the hospital, although with the number of empty houses, she could easily have found lodgings in one of those, but she was happier staying at the hospital. Anything was better than occupying the bedroom of a beloved missing son or the home of a Jewish family now relocated to the ghetto.

The hospital had over a hundred beds, yet there were only two qualified doctors, Stanislaw and Henryk, and half a dozen nurses to care for the sick. The patients were largely fed and bathed by relatives, mostly female, who brought in rolls of blankets and slept by their loved ones' beds. Although a few of the patients in the hospital had wounds – many caused by the butt of a SS rifle - most were being treated for some kind of infectious disease or another, diabetes, heart conditions and, now that winter had truly set in and fuel was almost impossible to obtain, pneumonia. Occupation didn't stop people from getting sick, it just made them harder to treat.

Two of the wards had been allocated to German soldiers, one for the enlisted men and one for the officers, although it was Polish nurses and doctors who cared for them. Most of the soldiers had either dysentery or venereal disease. The German wounded were admitted to their own casualty station or military hospitals. Despite the presence of the Germans, she knew they were lucky. She'd heard rumours about other hospitals being taken over by the Germans, the male doctors either sent to work camps or arrested as the professors in Krakow had been. Since her father's return there, she worried constantly about him.

In a narrow lane behind the baker's she managed to buy a small loaf of day-old bread and a lump of cheese. Pleased with her prize, she returned to the hospital and slipped into her room. She used a penknife to cut a slice of bread and cheese and finished her breakfast with a cup of cold water. Then she washed her face again, put on her pyjamas, pulled the thin blanket around her shoulders, crunched herself into a ball for warmth, and, praying that tonight the nightmares wouldn't come, closed her eyes.

Irena finished wrapping the dressing on the man's arm, pleased with her work. A little rest and some nursing care and he'd be as good as new. Sadly the same couldn't be said for the boy in the bed next to him. He was losing his fight.

She wrote some instructions for the nurses and left the ward, heading for the laboratory. She was due to assist in theatre this afternoon when her work in the lab was finished.

Hearing the clatter of boots on cobbles she stopped by a window and looked out to the square. The Nazis were at it again – going from house to house and taking away men in their trucks. There was one of these raids at least once every week.

She wrapped her arms around herself and watched as the soldiers shouted out names and, giving them only a few minutes to dress and pack a small suitcase, roughly dragged men and the older boys out onto the street. There were some cries of protest, but most of the men did what was asked silently, staring straight ahead, not wishing to draw the soldiers' attention to their children, wives or mothers.

But one woman clung to her father's arm, shouting defiantly at the young German soldier who was using the barrel of his gun to gesture that the man should take his place in the square. It was Nurse Honisz – Wanda. Irena had worked with her on several occasions and hadn't taken to her. Although clinically she was excellent, she had a hardness to her features and a way of dealing with the patients that could be rough at times. She was of German origin, one of the Volksdeutsche, and Irena wondered if she was beginning to see the Poles in her care as less worthy of her attention. However, as long as the nurse did her job, there was little anyone could do about her attitude.

'He is sick! Don't you understand? Sick and old. He can't work. Just look at him, he can barely walk.' Wanda's voice carried across the square.

Her father seemed bewildered, as if he didn't know where he was or what was happening. His daughter tried to pull him back inside but the soldier barked something at her, swinging the barrel of his rifle around from father to daughter while looking uncertain.

Perhaps if Wanda hadn't carried on screaming abuse at the soldier, perhaps if she'd just gone quiet and hustled her father inside, the soldier would have let them go. But her shouts had attracted the attention of the SS officer in charge of rounding up the work detail.

He left the soldiers, who seemed to have found everyone that they had come for, and marched across to the commotion. Then, without saying a word, he drew his pistol and shot the old man through the head. Wanda cried out as her father fell to his knees and almost in slow motion toppled to the side.

Irena's stomach clenched. It was Warsaw all over again. 'Don't say anything,' Irena whispered. 'Bow your head, go back inside, save yourself!'

But the nurse seemed beyond caring. She dropped to her father's side, cradling his bloodied head in her lap. She raised her eyes to the officer and slowly, but very deliberately, spat at him.

Irena wanted to close her eyes, wanted to turn away, terrified to watch what came next, but she couldn't. She'd done that too often and she wouldn't do it again. Even if the soldiers shot her too, one death couldn't be worse than the thousand she died every day. She ran downstairs and hurried into the courtyard. A soldier had pulled the nurse to her feet and the major's pistol was pointing at the terrified woman's chest.

'Wait!' Irena called out in German, thankful it was one of the languages her father had insisted she learn when she was younger. She murmured a prayer under her breath as the major turned around and stared at her, his pistol now pointing in Irena's direction.

'This woman is a nurse. She is needed.' Her legs were trembling so much she was scared they wouldn't support her, but somehow she managed to make them move. She carried on walking towards the nurse, talking calmly all the while. 'She has been working very hard. She is over-tired, that's all. She has forgotten herself. But she is a good nurse. She has cared for your soldiers on her ward as if they were her brothers.'

Behind the major, one of the regular soldiers was hanging his head. He had been a patient, treated for VD, and she worried suddenly that she'd overplayed her hand and made things worse for Wanda. As she drew closer to the officer, she realised she recognised him too. The last time she had seen him, he'd been in pyjamas and she'd treated him for an acute attack of dysentery. He'd only been in the ward for a couple of days but they'd treated him no differently to the locals while he'd been under their care.

Although her muscles were rigid with fear, she forced a smile. 'Oberführer Bilsen, it's good to see you looking so much better.'

He lowered his pistol and clicked his heels together. 'Fräulein Kraszewska, if I remember. I am pleased to meet you again.' He waved his gun in the direction of Wanda who was still being held by the soldier. 'This woman is a nurse, you say?'

'A good one,' Irena repeated, striving to sound nonchalant. 'And you know we need every nurse we can get. Especially if we are to keep disease from spreading.'

It was her trump card. The Germans were terrified of catching infectious diseases, particularly typhus.

The major replaced his pistol in his holster and nodded to the soldier to release Wanda. 'She can go – this time. But I'm warning you, don't interfere again, Fräulein. The people must learn to obey orders without question. It is better for everyone.'

The truck, loaded with the men who had been rounded up, started its engine and the German officer took his place in the side car of the waiting motorcycle.

Quickly Irena moved towards Wanda and took her by the arm. She needed to get her inside before she said or did anything to jeopardise them both. The villagers would see to Wanda's father's body as soon as the soldiers left. As the convoy drove away, Irena dragged the nurse inside and sat her down on a chair. She poured a glass of water from the jug on the table and handed it to her. She placed her hands over Wanda's, whether to steady the nurse's or her own she couldn't be sure.

'Are you going to be all right?' Irena asked.

'My father. Why did they shoot him? He was no danger to anyone. He didn't even understand what they wanted him to do. If they'd waited a few minutes I would have explained.'

Irena thought it was unlikely that, even if Wanda's father had been able to follow orders, he would have been saved. The rumours had it that those who were taken for the work camps and couldn't work were simply shot. At least then Wanda would have been spared the sight of him being killed in front of her. Now it was over she felt the familiar anger against the Germans return. Did they not have fathers and mothers? Grandmothers and grandfathers, too?

'You did your best for him.'

'Thank you for what you did,' Wanda whispered after she'd gulped some water. 'If you hadn't helped me, they would have shot me too. I owe you my life.'

'We need good nurses,' Irena said lightly. She felt a little ashamed of the assumptions she'd made about the nurse. Not all the Volksdeutsche had gone over to the side of the Nazis, even if their lives would have been easier.

'They could have shot you too. Weren't you scared?'

Irena forced a smile and held out her hands. 'Look at me! I'm still shaking. Of course, I was terrified. But we can't let them do whatever they want to us. One way or another we have to keep some dignity.'

After she'd left Wanda in the care of a neighbour, the father's body having been removed to the church, Irena collapsed on a chair and, suddenly faint, lowered her head. Yes, she had been terrified.

But she had stood up to the Germans and it felt good.

Chapter 17
London, 1989

Matthew was waiting for Sarah in the arrivals hall at Heathrow. He was leaning against a wall, leafing through some papers, and she paused to study him for a moment. He looked every inch the successful banker in his dark grey tailored suit, a red and white pinstriped shirt and polished hand-made shoes.

She tucked her T-shirt into the top of her jeans to hide the small hole she'd picked with nervous fingers on the flight down, wondering if there would be time to go shopping while she was here.

Although the flight was only fifteen minutes behind schedule she knew Matthew would have been checking his watch constantly, keen to get back to work. Where had the man she'd met at university disappeared to? Matthew cared little about politics now – unless events in other countries affected the rates of exchange or other fiscal policies. Immediately she was ashamed of her thoughts. Matthew was still a good man underneath the swagger.

'Good trip?' he asked as she reached him, turning her face up for his kiss. 'How's your mother?'

'About the same.'

'And Gilly?'

'She sends her love.' That wasn't true. Although she'd never said so, Sarah suspected her friend disliked Matthew.

The muggy heat of London hit her the minute she stepped

out of the air-conditioned terminal, frizzing the fringe of her recently blow-dried hair.

She waited until her bag was in the boot and they were on their way to Matthew's flat in the Docklands.

'I have something to tell you.' When she'd called him to let him know she was coming to London, he'd been about to go into a meeting and there had been no time to bring him up to date with what had been happening.

He glanced at her. 'Something good, I hope.'

'I'm not really sure. Earlier this week I went to see a firm of solicitors on behalf of my mother.'

'Go on.'

'It's very strange, but it appears my mother has been appointed executor of a Lord Glendale's estate.'

'Who the hell is he?'

'That's the thing, I don't know. At least, I don't know why he made my mother executor. I don't think she knows either. What I do know now is that his name was Lord Richard Maxwell before he inherited the title of Earl and that he was in the RAF during the Second World War. Apparently, his estate – a house in Charlotte Square and one in Skye – goes to a woman called Magdalena Drobnik, supposing she's still alive or can be found. If not, it goes to my mother.' She filled him in on everything she'd discovered, including that her mother was adopted, and had only just come to the end of her account when they stopped outside his flat.

Matthew whistled. 'Are you certain the child in the photo is your mother?'

'There's no doubt. Mum confirmed it too.'

He looked surprised. 'She's talking again?'

'No, not really. There are signs that her speech is improving but the few words she does manage are slurred. Mostly she still uses her walking stick to communicate.' Her throat tightened and she swallowed.

Matthew reached for her hand. 'Are you okay?'

She blinked rapidly. 'Not really.'

She rummaged around in her handbag until she located the envelope with the black and white photograph of her mother as a child. She passed it to him.

He took a moment to study it. 'It does look like her. So what now?'

'The solicitors are looking for Magdalena. If they find her she might be able to explain Lord Glendale's connection to Mum.' She shrugged. 'I was so sure she was Mum's natural mother, but Mum says no. I have no idea how my mother knows her, but I'm determined to find out.' She tried to smile but couldn't quite manage it. 'I know so little about Mum's life. I didn't even know she was adopted. If she lost her parents as a child, if something happened to them, if they gave her up, Matthew, no wonder she finds it difficult to show her feelings.'

Matthew eyed her thoughtfully. 'And not just her. I'd like to know what goes on inside *your* head. Why you won't agree to get engaged.'

Sarah sighed. 'Can we not talk about this now, Matthew? I can't think about marriage when Mum isn't well.' But if she were honest she hadn't been able to make herself say yes to his proposal before her mother had become ill. What was stopping her? Matthew was everything she wanted. Decent. Kind. Safe. *Staid?* a little voice whispered, but she batted it away. Matthew wasn't the boring one, she was.

Matthew waited until they were inside his flat before he pulled her into his arms.

'God, I've missed you,' he murmured against her lips. 'What do you say we skip dinner and go straight to bed?'

Held in the safety of his arms, Sarah felt the doubts slip away. They were only there because they'd spent so much time apart.

She smiled up at him. 'Dinner can wait.'

Later they lay in bed wrapped in each other's arms. 'Hungry?' Sarah asked.

'Sure.'

'You stay where you are and I'll bring us some supper.'

She threw aside the covers, bringing the sheet with her and wrapping it over her nakedness. Her clothes were neatly folded on the chair – her torn T-shirt tossed in the bin – Matthew's already consigned to the laundry basket.

She took one of his shirts from his wardrobe, slid into it and went to the kitchen, which took her all of five paces. Matthew's flat was on the sixth floor with a fantastic view of the docks from its floor-to-ceiling windows. Furnished simply with plain but expensive furniture and the latest hi-fi equipment, it was a little clinical for Sarah's taste, but Matthew loved it.

She set a tray with cold chicken and salad from a pre-packed carton from Marks & Spencer. In anticipation of her arrival, Matthew had chilled a bottle of Sauvignon Blanc for her and opened a Merlot for him before he'd left for the airport. Trust him to be organised.

They'd met at a party in their first year. She hadn't wanted to go, but Gilly, typically, wouldn't take no for an answer. Sarah had known it was a mistake to come the moment they'd arrived. The flat was heaving. The Specials had been blaring, causing the whole flat to vibrate. Several people, arms held rigidly by their sides, jumped up and down as if on pogo sticks.

Gilly had hurried away to find them drinks before Sarah had the chance to protest, leaving her on her own and feeling horribly exposed.

She'd noticed him straight away; at six foot five he wasn't the kind of man you could miss. He'd been standing against the wall, a pint in his hand, and a glazed expression on his face, as a woman stood on tiptoe to shout in his ear. He'd looked over and caught her staring. She'd blushed and lowered her lids.

When she looked up again, he was in front of her. The Specials' 'Too Much Too Young' had come to the end and there was a merciful silence while someone put on another record. 'I don't think we've met. I'm Matthew Morgan.' His voice was deep, with just a touch of an English accent.

'Sarah Davidson.'

'First year?'

She nodded. 'Is it so obvious?'

'A little. All the first years have one of two looks. Either the *first-time-away-from-home-so-I'm-going-to-get-as-drunk-as-I-possibly-can* or the *oh-shit,-why-is-everyone-staring-at-me?* look.'

Sarah didn't have to ask which one he thought she had. A flush was creeping up from her chest and working its way up to her scalp.

'What are you studying?' he asked.

She glanced over his shoulder hoping to see Gilly re-emerge from the crowds.

'English Literature. You?'

'Economics and Maths.' He paused. He was staring at her if she were the only person in the room. 'You're not interested in joining the Political Society, are you?'

She should have guessed. He hadn't come over because he was interested in her but because he was trying to recruit for his society. Ever since she'd arrived at the halls of residence, she'd been inundated with leaflets suggesting she join this club or that. Gilly had made her sign up for too many as it was. Besides, politics bored her.

'I'm not interested in joining more societies,' she said. 'I'm here to study.'

He laughed. 'I'll give you a week,' he said. Then his face grew serious. 'We're protesting against the presence of British soldiers in Ireland. Don't you think it's time the British Government gets out of that mess?'

She didn't have a clue what she thought about Northern Ireland. Like most people she hated what was happening there, but she didn't have any pat answers; she just wished the killing would stop. She was about to tell him so, when he tipped his head to the side and grinned. 'If you come, I'll buy you a beer afterwards.'

'How does bribery fit with a social conscience? Doesn't one preclude the other?'

He laughed again. 'Smart as well as pretty, but I see you have a lot to learn.'

Gilly had drifted back and thrust a glass of cheap, warm white wine in Sarah's hand. 'Hello, I'm Gillian.'

'Oh, hi.' Unusually, Matthew's eyes didn't light up when he saw Gilly the way most men's did. Neither did he invite her to join the political society. Instead, his attention was fixed on Sarah. Behind him, she noticed the girl he'd been standing with waving. The music started up again. Frankie Goes to Hollywood's 'Relax'. The girl lifted her arms in the air and gyrated her hips in their direction.

'I think your friend wants you.'

Matthew flicked a glance over his shoulder. 'Yeah, you're right. Duty calls. I'll phone you. Which halls are you in?'

Before Sarah could answer Gilly did it for her. 'She's in Pollock Halls, Harrington Court, number 401. And I'm next door in 403.'

Later Sarah came to realise he'd mistaken her shyness for cool self-assurance. By the time he discovered the truth, he was in love with her and she with him.

Matthew had left university two years before Sarah and had taken a job in London with one of the banks. They'd commuted between London and Edinburgh – mainly her doing the travelling on Fridays after lectures and returning on the last train on Sunday night. As he'd begun to earn more he'd flown up sometimes to see her. When she'd finished her degree, earning a first, she'd taken a job with a small publishing house in London for a couple of years, renting a flat near his. At first she'd only been a general dogsbody but soon she'd been allowed to work on the copy-edits for a couple of mid-list authors and she found she liked the attention to detail the job required. But opportunities for promotion within the publishing house were limited and Sarah didn't have the heart or the confidence to push herself forward so when an opportunity had arisen to join a smaller press in Edinburgh, she'd applied. It had caused their first major row. Two months ago he'd given her an ultimatum: marry him and move back to London or their relationship was over. Soon after that her mother had had her stroke and the ultimatum had gone on the back burner, where she knew it wouldn't be allowed to stay for long.

She returned with a tray and Matthew lifted the duvet so she could clamber in beside him.

They settled back on the pillows with the tray on their laps.

'So what are you going to do?' Matthew asked.

She wasn't sure whether he was alluding to their engagement or the inheritance. She chose to answer the latter.

'I'm going to find out why Lord Glendale had a photo of Mum. I'm going to find out everything I can about Magdalena and what her connection is to my mother.'

Matthew sighed. 'And after that? Will you marry me?'

'You know I can't even think of marriage while my mother is ill.'

He took the wine glass from her hand and placed it on the bedside table. 'Why do I feel that you are never going to say yes? You promised to give me an answer one way or another and I think I deserve one.'

She snuggled down against him, avoiding his eyes. 'I've got so much on my plate right now, Matthew. As soon as I know what's happening with Mum, I'll be able to think about the future. Just give me a little more time.'

Chapter 18

Rozwadow, 1941

Irena was worried. Her patient, a boy of six, should be doing better than he was. His temperature was down, his cough had improved, but still he was refusing to eat or drink. He was already too thin, his arms and legs like grasshopper limbs jutting out from his body, his eyes over-large in his gaunt face.

The nurses had tried to make him take some fluids but the boy pursed his lips and turned his head away. No one knew where his parents were; they had simply, according to the neighbours, disappeared the day after the boy was admitted to hospital. It was possible they had been taken away by the Germans, or even that they had seen an opportunity to escape and seized it while they could, but whatever had happened to them it seemed they weren't coming back.

'Try a little soup, Dominik,' Irena coaxed. 'Just for me.' They couldn't call him 'boy' so they had chosen a name to give to him.

But Dominik continued to stare at the ceiling, refusing to acknowledge her with so much as a glance. He had lost the will to live – she'd seen it before, mostly among the elderly patients who'd lost husbands or wives, even their whole families. They literally turned their faces to the wall until one day they slipped away. And this child was going the same way. All the medical care in the world wouldn't keep him alive if he wouldn't eat or drink.

She brushed a lock of hair from his face. How much longer could she do this? She should be in her fourth year of medical school. She should be looking after patients in a clean hospital with modern, up-to-date equipment. Instead, she was here, fumbling around with almost no equipment and only basic medicines. And she was so tired.

She gave herself a mental shake. There was no point thinking about what should be. She was here and she had to do the best she could with what she had.

In the meantime the patient in the bed next to Dominik needed a new bottle of saline.

'I'll be back in a moment,' she told the boy. As always there was no response.

But when she went to the store where the medical supplies were kept, she discovered they were almost out of saline. Yet only yesterday they had had plenty left. Concerned, she checked all the supplies. The bandages were low, the supply of sulphonamide definitely far less than it should be. She knew all the regimes the patients were on and there weren't that many on the antibacterial agent at the moment. Someone was stealing from the store. Either for themselves or to sell on the black market. God damn the way this war made people behave.

She made up her mind. She'd see to her patient then go in search of Stanislaw or Henryk – the two doctors needed to know what was happening as soon as possible so they could put a stop to it. She returned to the ward and attached the fresh bottle of saline to the patient's drip. Dominik had fallen asleep so she pulled the blanket up over his thin shoulders.

'I'm going to find Dr Palka,' she told the nurse. 'I want to ask his advice about a patient.'

After stopping by her room to pick up her coat, Irena slipped outside. No one was supposed to be out after the curfew. The punishment for being caught could be a beating or worse.

The moonlight cast a ribbon of light on the darkened street but Henryk's house was only a short distance from the hospital and, as long as she kept to the shadows, there was little likelihood of being spotted. Most of the soldiers would have already congregated in the village square to enjoy glasses of the best Polish vodka along with their expensive cigarettes. There were patrols on the streets, of course, but the sound of their boots would carry for miles on the still night air, giving her enough warning to duck into a doorway. Nevertheless, she could hear her heartbeat pounding in her ears as she stole along the street.

Like all the houses, Henryk's was in darkness. He and his family were probably asleep.

She crept up to the door and knocked softly before slipping inside. The embers of a fire cast a reddish glow over the small sitting room. The house was perfectly quiet.

She hesitated. Like all of them Henryk worked an eighteen hour day and sometimes more. But she had to alert him to the theft of the medical supplies. Who knew how much more would be missing by morning if she didn't?

She tapped on the door she guessed was his bedroom. 'Dr Palka! It is me, Irena. I'm sorry to wake you but I need to talk to you.'

A sound came from inside the room – the dull thud of feet landing on the floor – and a few moments later Henryk's wife, Elena, opened the door. The flickering light from the candle she carried made her face look ghostly.

'For goodness' sake, lower your voice,' she hissed.

'I'm sorry. There is a patient at the hospital . . . ' she tailed off. Elena looked frightened.

'I'll not wake him,' Elena said, closing the door behind her. 'He needs his sleep. You must manage as best you can.'

'I wouldn't have come if it wasn't urgent. I have to speak to him.' She made to step past Henryk's wife, but Elena stretched her hands wide, barring her way.

'Please, Elena. I promise you, it will only take a minute.'

Why was Henryk's wife being so obstructive? It wasn't as if Irena had ever come here in the night before. She must know it had to be urgent for Irena to risk being out after curfew.

But no one behaved the way you expected them to any more. Everyone was so frightened all the time.

A muffled crunch of boots came from outside and Elena and Irena froze.

They stared at each other in horrified silence as the sound came closer. Had a villager seen Irena and reported her to the soldiers?

Unable to move, she watched as the door opened, sagging with relief when she saw it was Henryk. He hurried into the room, closing the door behind him. He looked surprised and not at all pleased to see Irena. Elena stepped forward to take his coat. Henryk was carrying his medical bag, which he placed carefully on a chair before turning to his wife and raising his eyebrow.

'Irena came to see you,' Elena said. 'I . . . I told her you were sleeping. I must not have noticed you going out.' Her laugh sounded forced and unnatural to Irena's ears and she had the distinct impression Elena was lying. When she woke up she would have noticed that her husband wasn't in the bed beside her and in a house of this size, it was inconceivable that she wouldn't have known her husband was out.

'I came to tell you that someone has been taking supplies from the pharmacy store. All sorts of things – bottles of saline, bandages, sulphonamide – are missing.'

Elena darted an anxious glance at her husband.

Henryk grabbed Irena's elbow. 'You fool. You shouldn't have come here. Were you followed?'

'I don't think so.' She tried to pull her arm away but his grip was too strong.

Henryk glared at her. 'Don't think so? That's not good enough.'

'I'm sure I wasn't.' She tugged her arm away. 'Tell me what this is about. Did you know about the missing supplies?' He hadn't seemed surprised when she'd told him. Her stomach churned. Was he taking them for his own purposes?

He raked a hand through his hair and turned back to his wife. 'It's all right, Elena. I know Irena's father. He's a man of unquestionable honour. His daughter would never put our lives in jeopardy.' He faced Irena. 'Would you? Because you must know I could never allow it.'

She shivered. This was a side of the normally affable Henryk she hadn't seen before.

She lifted her chin and met his eyes. 'If you're selling medical supplies on the black market – it's despicable. Worse still, you're putting us all in danger.' The German authorities insisted on a careful inventory of all drugs and medical supplies and if they found out someone was stealing them, reprisals would be swift – and brutal.

'You think I'm stealing from the hospital?' He glared at her in disbelief. Then his face softened. 'I can see why you might.'

'And are you?'

He rubbed a hand across the back of his neck.

'I will tell you what's going on, but before I do I have to know you can keep your mouth shut. I have to know I can trust you.'

'For God's sake, Henryk, my brother and fiancé have probably given their lives for Poland. And you know my father – you know what he endured at the hands of the Nazis. How could you think I would betray my people or my country?'

Henryk studied her for a long moment, making up his mind. 'Very well then, but you mustn't breathe a word of what I'm about to tell you. Not to anyone – except Stanislaw. Do you understand? If you do, so help me, I'll break your neck.'

Irena kept silent. She had said all she was going to say. Now it was up to him to decide how much he was prepared to trust her.

Elena moved the coffee pot onto the stove and placed two mugs on the table. Then she disappeared back inside the bedroom, leaving them alone.

Henryk poured some of the thin brown liquid into the mugs and sat down at the table, indicating with a nod of his head that she should do the same. 'You are correct about the supplies. But it is I – and Stanislaw – who have been "fiddling the books", so to speak.'

When she started to speak he held up his hand. 'Let me finish. Before you came, Dr Zumbach, an excellent doctor and a fine man, was in charge of the hospital. He was one of the first to be taken by the Germans and corralled with the rest of the Jews. The fence of that damn ghetto borders my back yard. It makes it a little difficult to ignore, don't you think?'

Irena nodded. Some of the villagers even envied the Jews – said that they didn't have to go to work camps like them.

'Someone came through the fence a couple of months ago,' Henryk continued. 'He told me that Dr Zumbach was ill and that they didn't know how to save him. He was the only doctor for all those people and without him they knew they didn't have a chance. I went to see him. There is a place in the fence where a person can slip through and as long as he is careful and goes in the night . . . ' He shrugged. 'Dr Zumbach had pneumonia. I did my best. It is cold there, Irena. They are without fuel to keep themselves warm and they have very little food. Conditions are not exactly conducive to recovery and Dr Zumbach died. Since then Stanislaw and I have been taking medical supplies – as much as we dare – and smuggling them inside the ghetto. We try to give them to only the most seriously ill, but to tell the truth that is most of them. Almost all of the younger, stronger men and women have been taken away. It is really only the elderly and the children and their mothers who are left.'

Irena felt light-headed with relief. She didn't know what she would have done had Henryk been stealing for his own ends. To turn him in to the Nazis would have been unthinkable.

'You must know you are risking your life.'

'That is what Elena says. I didn't want her to know. In these times it is more true than ever that what a person doesn't know can't hurt them.' A wistful expression crossed his face. 'But it is difficult to slip out of the marriage bed for hours at a time without a wife wanting to know where you are.'

'The Nazis would kill her and your daughter too if they discover what you are doing.'

He spread his hands wide and shrugged. 'What else can I do? I am a doctor. There are sick people who need me. With Dr Zumbach dead, there is no one else. We can't stand by and do nothing.'

With his words an image of the slaughtered Jewish mother flashed into her head. 'I could go,' Irena said, before she was even aware she was going to say it. The time for standing back and doing nothing was over. And maybe, just maybe, she'd feel better for failing to help the woman and her child.

Her lips felt frozen and not just from the cold. 'I have no family, apart from my father. I have no children. There's no one to get hurt if they catch me.' And it would reduce the time

Henryk spent inside the ghetto and therefore the risk to him and his family.

She almost wanted him to say no. But she knew he wouldn't refuse. She wasn't qualified but she could be of some use. Joining the resistance and being involved in killing Nazis, however much she hated them, was impossible. But this she could do.

'They will kill you if they find out. You mustn't be in any doubt of that.'

She closed her eyes. God knew she didn't want to die, but she'd made her decision.

'I'm not. They might take me to one of their work camps one day anyway. I would rather die knowing I had done my part to help Poland.'

For the first time that night, he smiled. 'Very well. The next time they need me, you can come too.'

Chapter 19

Aware that soon she would have to go behind the fence, Irena slept badly. Sometimes, in the darkest hours of the night, when she lay staring up at the ceiling, she wished she'd taken her father's advice and left Poland.

It was almost a relief when Henryk came to see her in the laboratory one evening. 'Our Jewish friends have sent a signal.' He'd explained that the signal was either a piece of white cloth tied to the fence or, if there was an emergency during the night, a couple of flashes from a lit candle in a window. 'I was going to go but our German friends have brought in a soldier with a suspected ruptured appendix. I have to open him up. You'll have to go tonight.'

Her insides flipped. 'With Stanislaw?'

Henryk shook his head. 'The Nazi bastards are insisting he assists me. They're probably worried I'll let their comrade die if I'm on my own. They're even insisting one of their officers is in theatre too. They're also demanding we both stay with the patient through the night, so there's no chance of either of us getting away later – at least not for long. I'm afraid that means you'll have to go on your own.'

Irena's mouth dried up. When she'd imagined going behind the fence she'd thought it would be with Stanislaw or Henryk. Not on her own. But no matter how terrified she was she couldn't refuse.

Unable to speak, she nodded.

'Good. Come to my house tonight, at one o'clock. One of us will try to slip away for a bit – say we have another emergency. If there are any soldiers patrolling, wait until it's clear. Either me or Stanislaw will meet you there and show you the way in.'

Irena found her voice. 'What should I bring?'

'I'll have a medical bag packed and ready for you with everything you'll need – at least everything that can be found. If you're not sure how to treat a patient, then do nothing. We will discuss his or her symptoms together in the morning and decide what is to be done.'

He leaned across and squeezed her shoulder. 'You don't have to go, you know. Neither Stanislaw nor I will think any less of you if you decide it is too dangerous.'

Perhaps not. But she would think less of herself. And in the end, that was what mattered.

'I'll be there,' she said.

That night, alternating between fear and excitement, Irena let herself out of the heavy front door, wincing as it creaked. The cold sharp air made her catch her breath. The street was deserted, except for an emaciated alley cat rooting around for scraps.

She hurried towards Henryk's house keeping to the shadows, and a few tense minutes later she was inside where she found Stanislaw waiting for her.

He was younger than Henryk, quieter, and as far as she knew, had never married.

'You're here!' he said simply. 'Come on, there's no time to waste. I need to get you inside then I have to get back to the hospital before they notice I'm gone.'

The door to the bedroom was closed. Henryk's wife and

child must be asleep inside, or, more likely, keeping out of the way.

He studied her thoughtfully, nodding approval at her dark trousers and black belted coat, before tugging a black knitted hat from his pocket. 'Put this on. Your hair is so blond it will stand out.'

Irena did as he asked and then followed him out of the back door and across Henryk's back yard. Bending low, Stanislaw felt along the line of the fence until he found the spot he was looking for. Wasting no time, he removed some of the wooden slats and placed them on the ground. Behind the wooden fence was a steel one.

'We have a hole cut here. When you come back through, one of the men will come with you and put the fence together again. But it is your responsibility to replace the slats of the fence from this side and make sure that it looks perfect. Do you understand?'

Irena nodded. Unlike the rest of the village, the ghetto was closely guarded, although Stanislaw had explained that most of the guards hung about the barricaded entrance at the front and made only a couple of tours of the perimeter throughout the course of the night.

A few moments later Stanislaw had unwound the steel loops that were keeping the fence together, exposing a gap large enough for a person to squeeze through. As they emerged on the other side three men detached themselves from the shadows behind one of the houses and moved silently towards them.

'This is Dr Kraszewska.' Stanislaw introduced her in a whisper.

She wasn't a doctor. Not yet. Perhaps not ever, but the people in the ghetto weren't likely to worry about the finer points of her qualifications.

'I have to leave you now,' Stanislaw whispered to her. 'Don't worry, you'll be looked after from here on in. They'll return you to the fence when you've finished and see you safely through.' And with that he turned and disappeared back into the darkness.

Someone took her by the arm and hurried her along the short piece of open ground.

She strained to see through the darkness, her heart pounding so fiercely it was difficult to breathe. A dog barked and she froze as the sound of a man's voice carried on the cold night air.

'Come on,' her companion urged, dragging her forward.

She stumbled along beside him, expecting at any moment to hear a voice ring out demanding they stop – or to feel the punch of a bullet. The Nazis were notorious for shooting without feeling the need to ask questions.

After what seemed like hours but could have been only a few minutes, they reached their destination. The door was flung open and she was ushered inside.

The room was lit only by two single candles and she had to squint to see. When her eyes adjusted she sucked in a breath. Normally the house would shelter no more than a family of six or so, but there had to be several times that number in it now: infants wrapped in their mother's arms; young children staring listlessly; older men and women, with dull eyes and sunken, gaunt faces. Those who couldn't find enough space to lie down, slept upright huddled into blankets.

Despite the number of people, the house was freezing, her breath visible as she exhaled.

This wasn't good. Disease loved nothing better than conditions of overcrowding and poor ventilation.

The man who'd taken her by the arm pulled off his cap, revealing dark, curly hair and even white teeth.

'I am Bernard,' he said. 'This is Feliks and Eugene.' His companions were much older than him although they seemed to defer to him. Feliks had most of his front teeth missing, while the loose skin on Eugene's ruddy jowls suggested that before the war he'd overindulged in vodka and good Polish country food. But there was something about their solidity, their calmness, that reassured her.

'There shouldn't be so many people in here,' she murmured.

'We have no choice,' Bernard said. 'There aren't enough houses for everyone. They keep taking people away, but they bring others to take their place.' He rubbed a hand across his face. 'To them we are animals and can live like animals.'

'When Dr Zumbach was still alive we had one house that we kept for the sick,' Feliks said, his voice hoarse. 'But when the bastards discovered it they took all the sick away. Now we hide the ill amongst the healthy. You say it's not good. Don't you think we know that?'

She clicked her tongue and rolled up her sleeves. 'Who has my medical bag?'

Eugene lit another candle so she could see better before clearing a space on the single small table. Irena noticed a pile of small notebooks in one corner.

'We try to keep the children up with their lessons,' Bernard said, catching her look.

Her shock at the living conditions was replaced with admiration. They were doing the best they could in this hell-hole. If life outside the ghetto was hard, it must be near impossible here. All she could do was offer what medical assistance she could.

'Who's my first patient?' she said.

Chapter 20

Over the next two months, Irena went behind the fence at least once a week. Going through the wire still frightened her, but less so every time. A person could only stay terrified for so long. Each time there were several missing faces and some new ones.

Bernard was always there. He'd explained that he, Feliks and Eugene, the leaders of the ghetto, hid under the floorboards whenever the soldiers came. The three men had been trapped in the ghetto right in the beginning before the Germans could complete a full record of who was who and had decided to stay. 'They must think,' he told Irena, 'that we all escaped right at the beginning of the war. Some of the men did take their chances in the mountains, while the others—' He pulled his lips against his teeth and shrugged.

Today she was testing some urine in the hospital's small laboratory when Stanislaw threw open the door. 'Where is Henryk?' he asked. His normally pale face was flushed, his eyes so bright they looked almost feverish.

'Over here,' Henryk replied drily, glancing up from his microscope. 'What the hell is up with you?'

'My good friend Grzegorz has been admitted. They let him go from the work camp to come here. They have given him three days before he must return. But the stories he tells!'

Stanislaw shook his head. 'People are dying every day in these camps. They work them into the ground without feeding them. When they can no longer work they just shoot them. He says it is slaughter.'

Irena and Henryk shared a look. The round–ups had become more frequent lately. Already at least half the population of their village and the ones nearby had been taken but they'd allowed themselves to hope that the Germans would look after them well enough so they could get the maximum work out of them. The largest number of Poles were labourers and used to tough conditions, but no one could work eighteen hours a day in sub–zero temperatures with almost no food and stay healthy. The occupiers' behaviour didn't make any sense.

'Yet they let him return here for medical treatment?' Henryk said. 'Are you sure you can trust him?'

'I've known him all my life. He wouldn't lie to me. He says they let him come back because he was an engineer before all this happened and the Nazis need him fit enough to supervise the bridges they're building. He thinks the bastards don't have enough engineers in Poland for all the bridges and building work they are doing.'

'Then he is lucky.' Henryk's smile was tight.

'We have to stop them taking more people to these places,' Stanislaw said, pacing the small laboratory. 'It is a death sentence for everyone who ends up there.'

Henryk lifted his shoulders. 'But what can we do? You know what happens when anyone refuses to go – the Germans just shoot them and others. Resisting is futile. At least at the work camps they have a chance. If they are shot by the Nazis, they have no chance at all.'

'That's just it! That's what I have come to tell you! I have an idea. I'm not sure if it will work and if it does I am going to need your help and Irena's. My friend has already agreed to act as a guinea pig.'

Henryk straightened, looking interested. 'Go on.'

'What are the Germans most scared of?' Stanislaw asked.

'They seem scared of very little.'

'Disease,' Irena said instantly. 'That's why they don't bother with the hospital very much. They're scared of catching whatever illnesses our patients have.'

Stanislaw grinned at her as if she were a pupil who had given the teacher the answer no one else knew. 'And what disease in particular?'

'Typhus,' Henryk and Irena said together. It was true. The Germans hadn't had an outbreak of typhus for years. Although they occasionally came to the hospital with sore throats or for treatment of venereal diseases, Irena hadn't seen a single case of typhus among them.

'Exactly! Typhus. Before the war one of my German colleagues wrote a paper in a medical journal about it. He claimed that it was evidence of German superiority. A load of rubbish, of course. The wealthier citizens and the officers get vaccinated against it, a fact they keep from their underlings. But their fear of the disease is something we can use to our advantage. And I have a plan how we can do that. A way to save hundreds, perhaps thousands, of lives.'

'And how precisely?' Henryk asked, scepticism lacing his voice. He was the expert surgeon while the younger doctor was the diagnostician. Stanislaw had been heading for a professorship at Warsaw University before the invasion. He'd had madcap ideas before and none of them had come to anything.

'I took a dead virus and injected it into my friend. I waited twenty-four hours, then drew a blood sample. I checked it last night and it works! It definitely showed evidence of precipitation.'

Henryk raised his eyebrows.

'I can see that you don't believe me,' Stanislaw said, 'So I'll prove it to you. I have another blood sample here to test. Let me show you.' He held out the small tube of blood and crossed over to one of the benches. He took a pipette and dropped some anti-serum onto a slide. Irena and Henryk went to stand next to him. They waited the few minutes necessary for the blood to react with the anti-serum.

'Now look. What do you observe?'

Stanislaw peered down the microscope than stood aside to let Irena take a look. The cells had clumped together, giving the sample a cloudy appearance – evidence of typhus.

'But what makes you so sure you haven't infected your friend, Stanislaw?' Henryk said. 'You could kill him.'

'I told him there was a small risk that would happen. He wanted to take the chance, but just in case, I've kept him isolated. I saw him this morning. He is perfectly well. No fever. No joint pain. Nothing.'

'I still don't understand. How will this help?' Irena asked.

Stanislaw turned to her, grinning widely. 'You said it yourself. The Germans are terrified of typhus and they'll do anything to avoid the risk of infection. So we use their fear against them. The beauty of this is that they will be giving us the diagnosis themselves when they test the blood samples we send them. We will tell them that we have to quarantine the streets in the villages where there is evidence of epidemic typhus. They won't go near them.'

'And what about the men and women you are intending to inject?' Henryk said calmly, although Irena could see the rising excitement in his eyes. She felt the first stirring of optimism. If Stanislaw was right . . .

'I will tell them I'm vaccinating them against disease and that they must keep to their homes until I say. Even if they wonder, they will be glad to be spared from the work camps.'

'And we can do it for the people in the ghetto too!' Irena said.

Stanislaw's smile disappeared. 'I thought about giving it to our friends in the ghetto. But I've heard rumours. If there is infectious disease amongst the Jews and the Germans hear about it, they take everyone out, shoot them and set fire to every building. We can't risk it.'

'But how can you be sure they won't burn our homes and shoot us?'

'The Germans need us for their work camps. I'm confident they'll wait until the village is free from disease before they start taking people again.'

'Won't they get suspicious?'

'Perhaps. But at the moment it's all we can do. We have to try. Who knows, before they get too suspicious, we might be liberated.'

Irena doubted that. But he was right. They had to try. 'You know I'll help in any way I can,' she said.

'I know you will,' Stanislaw said, his eyes soft. 'We couldn't manage without you, Irena. Now I'd better get on and vaccinate as many people as I can.'

He grinned and Henryk slapped him on the back. 'You know, old friend, I think you might have something.'

Chapter 21

As they'd hoped, the Germans accepted the so-called typhus epidemic and allowed Stanislaw and Henryk to quarantine roughly half the homes in the village and those in the surrounding areas too, after which the SS all but abandoned Rozwadow, leaving only enough men to guard the ghetto and keep an eye on the villagers. Subsequently there were fewer raids. It seemed as if Stanislaw's plan was working.

One afternoon, during her break, Irena left the hospital and went to sit on a bench in the square. It was cold but the wind had dropped and the sun was shining.

She wasn't alone. Most of the benches were occupied, either by older women taking a rest on their way home with the shopping or by young mothers watching over their children as they played.

Almost everyone was underweight now. At least, unlike the Jews in the ghetto, they weren't starving. With the smaller Nazi presence, farmers had returned to the village bringing the odd chicken or bunch of carrots to sell or trade in the square. Most of their produce was appropriated to feed the German army but what they didn't take, the farmers sold.

She turned her face to the sun and closed her eyes, enjoying the feeling of drowsiness that swept over her. Perhaps they could find a way to survive this war after all?

When she heard the crunch of boots she didn't pay any attention.

'Good day, Fräulein.' She opened her eyes to find the German SS major who had almost shot Nurse Honisz standing in front of her. Since that day she'd only seen glimpses of him as he'd led the round-ups or inspected his men guarding the ghetto.

She suppressed her fear and revulsion and forced a smile.

'Good day, er, Oberführer Bilsen, isn't it?' she replied in German.

'You remembered. I am flattered.'

Don't be, she thought. I plan to remember every soldier's name that has ever committed an atrocity. I plan to remember every action, every death, every cruel act, so that one day you will all be held to account for your actions.

'You have fully recovered?' she asked, getting to her feet.

'Yes. Thanks to you and the other nurses.'

Irena didn't want his thanks. She just wanted him to keep away from her. 'Please, Fräulein,' he added, 'sit down. Don't let me stop your enjoyment of the sun.'

'I should go, really. I have work to do.'

'I said sit down, Fräulein.' He smiled but his eyes had lost their boyish glint. 'Please.'

She had no choice but to do as he asked.

He wiped the space next to her with a handkerchief before taking a seat. She was aware of the eyes of the other women on her. One by one, careful not to attract too much notice, they gathered their shopping bags and their children and melted away.

Irena waited for him to speak.

'You were brave that day, when you intervened for the nurse,' he said finally.

Irena's mind raced as she thought about what to say. 'I remembered you from the ward. I knew from meeting you that German officers are civilised men. I was certain you didn't want to shoot that sick man or his daughter. Not if you could help it.' It was a lie, of course. Nothing over the last few months had led her to believe that the Nazis were anything but men who had lost their humanity. Nevertheless, he seemed pleased by her answer.

'We do what is necessary to impose order,' he said. 'That is all. The sooner your people realise this, the better.'

She wanted to claw at his face. They could impose order without killing innocent people. She twisted her hands together as she struggled to keep her temper under control. He was a dangerous man.

'This place is sick,' he said after a long pause. At first she thought he was talking about the way the villagers were being treated, that somewhere hidden deep inside, he regretted his country's actions.

'So much illness,' he continued. 'Typhus. Strange that it should be so much here, don't you think?'

Her heart banged against her ribs. Did he suspect? Suddenly she wished Henryk and Stanislaw hadn't taken her into their confidence. She was sure guilt was written all over her face.

'Typhus is like that.' She was pleased that even to her own ears her words sounded casual, bored even. 'When it takes a hold it can be difficult to eradicate as it spreads so rapidly from one person to the next. Isolation and simple nursing is all that can be done. It will disappear when it has run its course.'

'Perhaps it is better to burn it out.'

Dear God, the man was a monster!

'As I said, it will go soon enough. The men and women will recover and be fit for work again.' She looked him in the eyes and forced herself to smile coquettishly at him. 'Like dysentery, typhus is a disease of war.'

His cheeks reddened. 'Let us not speak of war. Not today. Not when the sun is shining. No, today I prefer to enjoy the company of a beautiful woman and talk of other things. More pleasant things.'

More pleasant things!

'Then let us talk about you. You are married?'

'Ah, yes. My wife is back in Berlin with our children.' He slipped a hand inside his jacket and brought out several photographs and Irena was forced to exclaim over each of them. He had three children all with blond hair and blue eyes and his blond-haired blue-eyed wife was clearly their mother. Did she know what kind of monster she'd married? Did she even care? And did the man sitting next to her, regarding the photographs of his family with unmistakable pride, see no irony that only a few yards away, behind the barbed wire of the ghetto, children the same age as his were dying horribly and slowly from starvation?

'And you? Are you married?'

'No,' she said softly. She didn't tell him she was engaged – she didn't want to share any part of her life with this man.

'You are too young, perhaps?'

'It isn't the time to think of marriage.'

'You know with your blond hair and pale skin you could almost pass for a German. Are you sure you don't have German blood in your antecedents?'

Irena made herself hold his gaze, hoping he couldn't read the revulsion in her eyes. 'I am Polish.'

She made a show of looking at her watch before rising to her feet again. 'You really must excuse me. I need to get back to the hospital. They're expecting me on duty.' She held out her hand although the thought of touching this man turned her stomach. 'Goodbye, Oberführer Bilsen.'

He had risen too. He bowed over her hand and clicked his heels together. 'Goodbye, Fräulein. I look forward to talking to you again.'

Chapter 22

As winter turned to spring and the days grew warmer, they no longer had to forage for firewood just to keep themselves and their patients from freezing. Aside from taking her share of the trips into the ghetto, doing what she could for its occupants, her days followed a familiar routine: work, then something to eat, and perhaps a short walk if the weather was fine. The German presence was less than it had ever been and so far she had managed to avoid bumping in to the major. One afternoon, Irena, Henryk and the nurses were discussing patients when Stanislaw burst into the room, looking agitated. He waited until the nurses had left before he spoke.

'The Germans have become suspicious. I suppose it was bound to happen. They want to know why we have so many cases of typhus. They're sending a team in to visit the hospital.'

Icy spiders of fear crept up Irena's spine. 'What are we going to do?' she asked.

'We are going to keep our cool,' Henryk said calmly. 'Remember the results have come from their laboratory.'

'Then it's all right?'

'Not entirely.'

'Do we know when they are coming?'

'Tomorrow.'

Irena wasn't sure how, but Stanislaw and Henryk seemed to

have advance warning of what the Germans were going to do. She suspected that one or both of them were part of the underground army – or in contact with them – but she knew better than to ask. The knowledge could only endanger them all.

'With doctors?' Irena asked.

'Experienced doctors,' Stanislaw replied.

This was bad. A doctor would know as soon as he examined the patients who were reported to have typhus that there was nothing wrong with them – or at least that they didn't have typhus. It wouldn't take them long to realise that Henryk and Stanislaw had been deceiving them.

'I don't know who is to be part of the team,' Stanislaw continued, 'but we must stay calm. We must pretend that everything is as it should be.'

It was mid-afternoon the next day when the German doctors came, two with the rank of major and three more junior officers. Irena's heart had been in her throat all morning, although she'd been told by Stanislaw and Henryk to keep out of the way.

'If they discover what we've been up to they will arrest us and you will be needed here more than ever. It is better that they believe you to be a nurse or a ward assistant. You will have a chance that way.'

Given that the Germans often shot people who were completely innocent, Irena didn't care for the chances of anyone who worked at the hospital.

'If they arrest us, we will say nothing,' Stanislaw said. He held out a little pill on the palm of his hand. 'We will die first.'

Irena felt sick. She had grown fond of the two men and the possibility she might have to run the hospital without them didn't bear thinking about.

Despite her anxiety, she couldn't help but find an excuse to be near the front door when the Germans arrived. Henryk was there to greet them and introduced Stanislaw who managed an ingratiating smile.

'It is good of you to come and visit us here,' Stanislaw said. If the doctors were aware of the irony in his voice they made no sign of it. 'Although I'm afraid you will find our hospital a little provincial.'

'It is either a disgrace or there is something wrong here,' the major said. 'You have the largest number of patients with typhus in the country.'

Henryk smiled ruefully. 'It is simple people who live here. They are peasants mainly and their hygiene is not the best. We try to tell them to keep themselves clean.' He shrugged. 'But what can we do? When they come to the hospital they are covered in fleas. Of course we disinfect them, but then a family member comes in,' he spread his hands, 'and before you know it the fleas are back.'

'Perhaps you have a solution for us?' Stanislaw said. 'Your medicine is ahead of us. We are only simple country doctors.'

Don't overplay it, Irena thought. They're not stupid.

But it seemed as if Stanislaw and Henryk had judged it just right. The major's mouth turned down in distaste. 'You Poles will never be civilised. You should be grateful that the Reich is willing to show you how you should live.'

Stanislaw's eyes flashed and Irena sucked in a breath.

'Now, let us get on with it,' the major went on, ushering them ahead of him with an impatient wave of his hand. 'The sooner we have sorted out this problem, the better.'

'Of course, of course. But you have come a long way. Let us have some refreshments first. Then we will take you to the patients. We have some on the wards – the sickest – the ones who we think will die regardless of what we do. The others, as you know, have been quarantined in their homes as there isn't space in the hospital for all the sick. After you've visited the wards I can take you there so you can see them for yourself.'

'We will want to take some blood from the infected patients, but perhaps we should have some tea first,' the captain said, looking at the major. He clearly was in no hurry to examine the patients.

'Or a little vodka? And something to eat?' Henryk turned around and indicated to one of the ward assistants who had the misfortune to be passing by to come forward. The woman glanced at Irena, her face slack with fear. Although she wasn't aware of what they'd been doing, no one wanted to be noticed.

Irena stepped forward, ignoring Henryk's tight shake of the head. They couldn't let the Germans think that they had anything to be frightened of.

'What would you like, Doctor?' She kept her head bowed submissively and coarsened her accent.

'Bring some food and a bottle of vodka to my office.' Henryk clapped his hands. 'And hurry. We don't want to keep our visitors waiting.'

If Irena had her way she would put rat poison in the Germans' drinks. She grabbed the ward assistant by the hand and led her out of hearing. 'You'll find what you need on the table in the kitchen. Take it to Dr Palka's office. Keep your head down and say nothing. Don't even look at them.'

The woman nodded and scurried away, clearly relieved to be out of sight of the German officers.

Irena waited as Henryk ushered the visitors into his office. Two of the soldiers with them took up positions outside the door while the others remained at the hospital entrance.

None of the soldiers could be long out of their teens, yet many of them had surely used their weapons on women and children. Did any of them have nightmares – or even doubts –

about what they were doing? Would they be the ones to shoot her and her colleagues? The German doctors weren't stupid. As soon as they examined the patients, they would know they had been fooled and retribution was bound to follow. She wished she could pray, but she hadn't been able to turn to God since the death of the Jewish mother and her child. Whatever happened now, it was out of their hands. All she could do in the meantime was carry on as if everything were normal.

Avoiding the soldiers' stares she headed back to her patients.

Two hours later, the German doctors arrived on the isolation ward. Surprisingly it was just the three juniors, who couldn't have been long out of medical school.

Irena continued to help her patient, a young woman with dysentery, eat her soup, but all the while she watched the doctors from under her lashes. All the patients in the ward with a diagnosis of typhus did have the disease, so it wasn't them she was worried about. If the junior doctors were here that meant the more experienced medical officers had gone out to the villages with Stanislaw and Henryk to the patients who didn't really have typhus.

She wondered if she would ever see either of the doctors again.

A nurse hurried over to the German doctors. 'I understand you are here to see our typhus patients,' she said.

'Some syringes and specimen bottles please,' the captain replied, covering his nose with a handkerchief. Clearly the smell in the ward was getting to him. The nurses had left a pile of soiled sheets in the corner, behind a screen, something they never did. Irena hid a smile. It was a small act of defiance but one that hopefully meant it was unlikely that the doctors would stay a moment longer than they had to.

And it seemed she was right. They took bloods from the three patients without even examining them and wrapped the vials in plastic bags to take away. Nodding curtly to the nurse, they snapped their heels together and left the ward.

It was late afternoon before Stanislaw and Henryk came to find Irena in the laboratory. The two men looked pale and tired but they hadn't been arrested – at least not yet. A small flame of hope flickered in her chest. Was it possible they had got away with it?

'Thank God!' she said. 'I wasn't sure I'd see either of you again.'

Henryk perched on a laboratory stool and dragged a hand through his dark hair. As vodka fumes filled the room, she noticed Henryk was decidedly unsteady on the stool while Stanislaw's eyes were bloodshot.

'How much have you two had to drink?'

'I lost count.' Stanislaw grinned.

'They might not care for our country and its people but these Germans like our vodka,' Henryk added. 'I hope you're up to taking care of the hospital tonight, Irena. At least until Stanislaw and I have slept it off.'

'Yes, yes,' Irena said, 'but what happened?'

'It seemed that the major and his lieutenant weren't too keen to actually examine patients with typhus – especially dirty Poles.' His lip curled on the last phrase. 'Particularly not after some decent food and several vodkas. In the end they decided to send the junior officers with Stanislaw while they stayed behind with me to finish the vodka and to discuss the best methods of blood transfusion.'

'They came up to the ward but they hardly looked at the patients,' Irena told them. 'They just took blood and left. I think the fact that the nurses had left a load of faeces-stained linen out of sight and hadn't opened a window all day might have had something to do with it.'

Henryk's grin was wide. 'They did look a little pale around the gills when they came back down.'

Stanislaw slapped his friend on the back. 'It was the same at each home I took them to. I made sure they were the dirtiest, most overcrowded and the poorest. The Germans could hardly bear to step inside. They didn't even want to touch the patients – so I took the bloods while they watched and then we left.'

Unsteadied by relief, Irena felt her legs give way. She reached behind her for the bench. 'So it's going to be all right?'

'I don't see why not,' Stanislaw said. 'The bloods will come back positive.'

'It's over then?'

Stanislaw yawned. 'My dear, it's a long, long way from being over. Let's just say it's over for the time being.'

Chapter 23

Irena couldn't avoid the SS major for ever. Not unless she never put a foot outdoors. It was a week after the doctors' visit when she almost bumped into him on the pavement.

'Fräulein,' he said, clicking his heels together and bowing. 'I was hoping to see you again.'

As a shard of fear pierced her, she forced a smile.

'Oberführer Bilsen! I thought you must have been posted elsewhere.'

'I spend most of my time in Krakow these days, but I thought I should check up on what's happening in the other areas under my jurisdiction.' He smiled. 'I must admit, if we hadn't met today I would have come to seek you out.'

'I'm not sure it's safe for you to be here,' she said. 'As you know we have had so much illness in the district.'

He gave her a sharp look. 'So I'm told,' he said.

Her heart jerked again. 'I should get back to the hospital,' she murmured. She made to pass by him but he blocked her way.

'Why always in such a hurry? It is lunchtime. I'd be honoured if you will join me for something to eat.'

'I really do have work to do. Perhaps another time?' She would rather eat from a rubbish bin than dine with him.

'I'm afraid I'm going to have to insist, Fräulein. I don't care to dine on my own.'

The steel in his eyes chilled her. She wouldn't put it past him to arrest her – he wouldn't even have to give a reason. She moistened her lips. 'Very well. If you like.'

He hooked her arm into his and led her off in the direction of the German part of the village and into one of the cafes reserved for the soldiers of the Reich.

Almost every table was occupied with German army personnel, some with female companions – not every Polish woman stayed away from the Nazis – and the sound of their voices merged with their cigarette smoke. Apart from the language and the military uniforms, it could have been any cafe in Poland before the war.

He pulled out a chair for her. A waiter scuttled over to them with a menu, but the major didn't even glance at it. 'Bring me your best bottle of wine and the best meat dish on the menu.' He smiled at Irena and her skin crawled. 'I hope you're hungry?'

Was he serious? He had to know that their rations were barely above starvation levels. She'd almost forgotten what fresh meat tasted like. Saliva flooded her mouth and her stomach clenched. However, she didn't think she could swallow even a mouthful of food in the company of this man.

'Not really,' she lied. 'I had some soup and bread a short while ago.'

He leaned back in his chair. 'You must have something, if only to keep a lonely man from eating alone.'

'You haven't been back to Berlin to visit your wife?' she said pointedly.

'As a matter of fact, I was there two weeks ago.'

'And she is well?'

'Of course.'

'And your children?'

'They are well too. However, I didn't invite you to lunch to talk about me. I would much sooner talk about you.'

His words sent waves of panic through her. Was it possible the German doctors hadn't been deceived? Or that they'd found out that they were helping the Jews? At that moment the waiter appeared and set down a plate of stew and vegetables along with a carafe of wine in front of them.

'Would you excuse me while I freshen up?' Irena said. She needed time to collect herself. He mustn't suspect she had anything to hide. He'd expect a little nervousness – he'd be stupid otherwise, and she knew he wasn't – but she mustn't show how terrified she felt.

'Of course,' he said, getting to his feet. 'Don't be too long. We don't want our food to get cold.'

She rinsed her face and hands with cold water and, leaning against the rim of the basin, drew in a shuddering breath. She had to stay calm and answer his questions as best she could without giving anything, or anyone, away.

When she returned he leaped to his feet again and once more held out her chair for her.

'What did you do before the war?' she asked. If only she could keep him talking about himself.

'I was a teacher,' he replied. 'Of physics.'

'Really?' She couldn't help but show her surprise.

He studied her. 'And you? Were you always a nurse?'

'I've always wanted to care for people,' she replied evasively.

'Please, eat.' He gestured to her plate. Reluctantly she picked up her fork.

'Are you not frightened that you'll get the disease, this typhus, from the people you look after?'

She couldn't tell whether he was genuinely interested or sounding her out. 'It is a chance I have to take. I'm safe as long as I follow the rules of good hygiene. Wash my hands after seeing to each patient, that sort of thing.'

'You know you don't have to stay here. You could come with me to Krakow. As my guest. You must miss your old home.'

She paused, her fork halfway to her mouth. She wasn't sure which bit of what he'd said frightened her most. Why did he imagine she'd want to go anywhere with him? And if he knew she came from Krakow then he knew more about her than he'd let on. In which case he was toying with her. She forced herself to chew the lump of stew.

'I am happy here.'

'I should tell you that soon the Reich will be requiring more people to help the German effort – people in your age group. You are what? Twenty-one? Twenty-two?'

She nodded. 'About that.'

'Conditions aren't always easy in the factories. If you came to Krakow you wouldn't have to work. I could find you an apart-ment and come and visit you. We could go to concerts. You would like that, I am certain.'

And be his mistress? She would rather die.

'If I went to Krakow I would stay with my father.'

He swirled the wine around his glass. 'Ah, yes, your father. Professor Kraszewski. I believe he was a guest of the Reich for a while.'

It was as if someone had tipped ice water down her neck. So he did know who she was. 'He was released.'

'Which is not to say he couldn't be a guest again.'

Despite her nausea, she forced a smile. 'Could I have some time to think about it?' she said.

He took a gulp of wine and dabbed his lips with his napkin. 'Don't keep me waiting too long. I'm not a patient man.' There was no mistaking the threat in his words. 'I'll be back in a month and I'll look forward to hearing your answer then.'

He insisted on accompanying her back to the hospital. As they walked Irena was uncomfortably aware of the glances of disapproval from her fellow countrymen and women.

'Thank you for lunch,' she said, when they reached the hospital gates.

He looked down at her, a small smile tugging at his lips. 'I promise you, Fräulein, that you will be much happier – and healthier – if you come to Krakow.' He studied her for a moment longer. 'In fact, I am not certain that I shouldn't take you away right now. Put you somewhere where you'll be safe from disease. I don't want to take any chances that you will bring it with you.'

Somehow she managed not to react to his words. 'I promise you I'm perfectly healthy. At least as far as I'm aware, although as you know, given the right conditions, illness can strike suddenly.' She decided to take a chance. 'But if you're concerned perhaps you could get me some typhus vaccine? That would make sure I don't get it.' She could give it to the residents of the ghetto.

'I'm afraid that won't be possible.' He clicked his heels. 'Until next month, Fräulein.'

Irena was in her room, attempting to scrub the taint of the encounter with the major from her skin, when Stanislaw and Henryk marched in without knocking. She whirled around, pulling her robe closed to hide her nakedness.

Neither man was smiling.

'I imagine you've heard about my meal with the major,' she said. 'I was planning to come and tell you.'

'What are you up to, Irena?' Stanislaw demanded. 'Have you told him what's going on here?'

Outraged, she lifted her chin. 'How can you even think that? After everything I've done? Don't you know by now how much I hate the Germans?'

'Come now, Stanislaw, give her a chance to explain,' Henryk interjected, laying a placating hand on his arm. 'We've trusted her this far and she's not let us down.'

'Her neck hasn't been truly on the line before.' Stanislaw shook Henryk's arm away and glared at Irena. 'Are you planning to save it by dropping us in the shit?'

'No,' she said sadly, 'of course not.' How could these two men, who'd she'd come to think of as friends, think, even for a moment, that she would betray them? 'He asked me to go to Krakow. As his mistress.'

Henryk and Stanislaw exchanged a look. 'And what did you say?'

'What do you think? *Oh yes, Herr Oberführer, I would love to sleep with you? I would love to be held in the arms of a man responsible for murdering innocent men, women and children.*' She shook her head. 'I told him I would think about it, but only to give me enough time to work out what to do. I'd rather be arrested and imprisoned for the rest of the war than share a bed with that beast.' She shuddered and dropped her voice. 'Do you think if I wanted to save my skin I would have become involved in helping the people in the ghetto? Don't you think that as soon as I knew you were helping them I would have gone to the Gestapo? And what about the typhus scam? I risk my life every day too.' For the first time Stanislaw looked uncertain. 'You must believe me.'

Stanislaw sighed. Either her words or whatever he'd seen in her face appeared to have convinced him. He turned to Henryk. 'There's a chance we can turn this to our advantage.'

'What do you mean?' Irena said. Her skin crawled as she realised there was only one thing he could mean.

'If you became his mistress, you could find out all kinds of information and pass it on to us. We could know their movements in advance – find out who is on their lists and when they are planning to do a round-up. Whatever he shares with you – whatever you overhear – could save lives.' He took her hand. 'You would be doing it for Poland, Irena.'

Appalled, she snatched her hand away. 'Please don't ask me to do this,' she whispered. 'I could never sleep with him. I couldn't pretend for a second that his touch didn't revolt me. Please don't ask it of me.'

'It's too dangerous,' Henryk said to Stanislaw. 'Irena's not a member of the resistance. She hasn't the training to do what you want.'

'We need more people to tell us what the Germans are planning, Henryk,' Stanislaw said softly before turning back to Irena. 'At least think about it. When does the major want his answer?'

'He's coming back to Rozwadow in a month. He expects my decision then.'

'Then we have time.' He took her by the shoulders. 'You could help save thousands of lives. Maybe more. Think it over.'

Chapter 24

A few days later, Irena was in her room doing her laundry when one of the nurses knocked on her door.

'You have a visitor,' she said. 'He's in the courtyard.'

She dropped the blouse she had been washing in the basin of soapy water and dried her hands. She hoped it wasn't the major. Since his visit she'd spent nights tossing and turning, thinking about what Stanislaw had suggested. She wished she could bring herself to sleep with the Oberführer. She *could* find out valuable information and it might go some way to atone for not saving the Jewish woman and her child. But after turning herself inside out, she'd come to a decision. She couldn't do it. The thought of his hands on her body revolted her and she'd never, in a million years, be able to pretend otherwise.

But Oberführer Bilsen had made it clear he was suspicious of her and when she refused to become his mistress, it would be only a matter of time before he brought her in for questioning. Behind that benign urbane manner was a man who would shoot her in the head without blinking. And if they did arrest her, if they beat her, would she be able to keep her secrets? She couldn't be sure. How could anyone know what they would say under torture?

If she broke and told them about the work Stanislaw and Henryk had been doing here, they would be executed and the scam uncovered. Thousands who might otherwise be saved, would die.

Of course she could be mistaken about the major's suspicions, but even if she was, she might still end up in a work camp. As the major had said, the Nazis were starting to take women between the ages of fifteen and twenty-four for their work camps – or for other reasons the older women in the village only whispered about. What good would she be to her country then?

Neither Stanislaw nor Henryk had said anything more about the matter, and she hadn't been able to bring herself to tell them about her decision.

'Who?' she asked now through frozen lips.

I don't know. He didn't say. An older man.'

'A German?'

The nurse looked at Irena, surprised. 'No. He is Polish. I must go. I have work.'

Wondering who it could be, Irena hurried outside.

It took her a moment to recognise the frail, elderly figure on the bench.

'Tata! I didn't expect you.'

A smile of delight spread across his face. 'My child!'

She ran across to him and, as he enveloped her in his arms, she felt all the fear and tension of the previous months melt away. He smelled of tobacco smoke and wet wool – familiar, comfortable, safe smells.

He ran a hand through her hair, murmuring words of endearment that warmed her soul. Finally he held her away from him. As he studied her, his eyes clouded. 'You are thin, Renia.'

'We are all thinner than we were, Tata. But why are you here? Is it safe?'

His mouth twisted. 'The Germans do not seem to care any longer what I do.'

'And the other professors and doctors?'

A spasm of grief crossed her father's face. 'Some they leave alone. Some they take away to prisons – others to work camps.' He shook his head. 'It is all so arbitrary.'

There was no answer to that. 'Sit, Tata. Rest a while. You are still not strong.'

'There are only a few of us doctors left in Krakow and only the older ones. It means we do not get much rest. At least there are some of us left to care for the sick and to teach.'

'So why *are* you here, Tata? Not that I'm not happy to see you but it must have taken you the best part of the day to get here – unless you have come to stay?'

'No, I must get back. I had to see you. I have some news.' The sun was beginning to disappear and her father pulled up the collar of his coat.

'Let's go inside,' she said, tucking her arm through his. 'We can speak there.'

'No, what I have to say must be said where there is no danger of anyone overhearing us.'

'Is it good news, Tata?'

Her father's face broke into a wide smile. 'Yes. It is about your brother. I have word. He made it to England and has joined the British RAF. He is safe. He will continue to fight against the German invader from there.'

Happiness bloomed inside her chest. 'Aleksy is alive! But that is wonderful! Are you sure?'

'Absolutely. He managed to get a letter to me. It was in code and not signed but I knew what it meant.'

Her heart soared. Her brother, her darling Aleksander, was safe. Now, if only she could get news of Piotr, she could live through anything.

'Have you heard any news of Piotr?'

Her father's expression changed and in that moment Irena knew that she did not want to hear what he had to tell her.

'No, Tata!'

'I am sorry, my child. There have been reports. Terrible reports.'

'Go on,' she whispered.

'It is only rumour. We can't be certain.' He touched her cheek. 'There is talk that the Germans executed many of our officers that they kept as prisoners-of-war. Word has it that Piotr's regiment was amongst them.'

The ground seemed to shift beneath her feet. 'You said you can't be sure!'

'No. It's possible his regiment escaped execution and was taken to a Russian gulag in Siberia. But even if that is true,' he laid his hand on top of hers, 'it doesn't mean he is still alive.'

'He's not dead! Not Piotr. Krystiana told me thousands of our soldiers are in the Home Army. Thousands, Tata! And even if he was captured – he's strong. He'll come back to me. You'll see!'

She could tell he didn't believe it but he didn't know Piotr the way she did. 'At least we know for certain Aleksy is alive. We must be grateful for that.'

'Which brings me to the other reason I've come. I've asked you before, but now I'm telling you. You must leave Poland. You're not safe – even here. I have seen terrible things and I have heard worse. They are killing more and more of us. They won't be satisfied until there isn't a Jew or a Pole left on this earth.'

'I know, Tata.'

He gripped her hand tightly. 'It is more dangerous than ever. The Germans have been asking about you. They want to know where you are. I told them that I lost touch with you when Warsaw was bombed, that I think you are dead, but I don't think they believe me.'

She didn't want to tell him they already knew who, and where, she was. He'd be even more worried.

'If you stay here you will die,' he continued, 'I am certain of it. More than ever.'

Her heart shuddered as his eyes brimmed with tears. 'Tata!'

'I couldn't go on if anything happened to you, Renia. You must leave.'

Leave Poland? To abandon her country when it needed her most? Yet, although everything inside her rebelled against it, she knew she had no choice. Her father was right. It was too risky to stay here.

'If I agree to go, will you come too?' she asked, even though she already knew what his answer would be.

'You know I can't. I am too old to start a new life in another country. I must stay. But it will give me a reason to live if I know my children are safe.'

Irena chewed her lip. How could she leave her father when she might never see him again? And Piotr? Perhaps he'd escaped and was with the underground army, and might come to find her. Although so far, he hadn't even found a way of sending her a message.

She shook the doubts away. He was alive somewhere – even if it was in one of Stalin's camps – and she'd promised him she'd try to survive so that one day they could be together again. And to be free, to see Aleksy again, to live without fear. To be able to tell the world what was happening here . . .

'If I disappear, will they not come looking for me?'

'I'll persuade Henryk to say that you died of typhus. He can write the death certificate. It won't be difficult to find an undertaker who will swear he buried you.'

'How will I get out?'

'There are ways. You must know that Stanislaw and Henryk

have their contacts – people who will help you. Do you remember the name and address of the Englishman I gave you when we were still in Warsaw? I am sure he will help you too.'

'I don't know if I can bear to say goodbye to you.' Her voice thickened as tears clogged her throat.

Her father lifted her hand and kissed her fingers. 'You must be brave. I will rest easier knowing you are safe. If you won't do it for me, do it for Piotr and your dead mother's memory.'

Chapter 25

London, 1989

Sarah lingered outside number 95 Grosvenor Street, summoning up her courage. Like the house in Charlotte Square, it was Georgian with an imposing front and tall windows. Even the door was similar, although this one was painted a cheerful fire-engine red. However, the Glendales' London home was three or four times the size of the one in Edinburgh and took up the best part of the street. Houses in this part of London must be worth a small fortune. The Glendales had to be minted and she was glad she'd swapped her jeans and T-shirt for a suit she usually wore to work. Taking a deep breath, she rang the doorbell.

'Yes? Can I help you?' A harassed-looking woman in her late twenties or early thirties with a fair-haired toddler clinging to her skirt answered just as Sarah was beginning to give up hope of finding anyone at home. Sarah took an involuntary step backwards. Somehow she'd been half expecting a butler to open the door.

'Please forgive me for intruding on you like this, but I was wondering whether you knew a Lord Glendale?'

'I'm Lady Glendale. Lord Glendale is my husband.'

It took a moment for Sarah to work it out. Of course with Richard's death his title would have passed to the next male heir. At least she'd found his family.

'I mean the former Lord Glendale. Richard Maxwell.'

'Richard? Yes, he was my husband's second cousin – his grandmother's nephew.'

'Do you mind if I come in for a moment? I'd really like to speak to someone about the late Lord Glendale. I know I should have telephoned first, but your number isn't in the book ... ' Sarah tailed off. 'Anyway, I was in the area.'

The woman eyed Sarah doubtfully. 'What did you say your name was?'

'Sarah Davidson. I'm not sure if you're aware, but Lord Glendale – the former Lord Glendale, I mean – made my mother, Lily Davidson, executor of his estate. I'm not at all sure why and I thought someone in the family might be able to tell me.'

The woman stood aside. 'You'd better come in.'

Sarah followed Lady Glendale through to a large sitting room scattered with toys. She removed a toy monkey from a wing-back chair and indicated to Sarah that she should sit, before lifting the child onto her lap. 'This is my daughter Chloe. Chloe, this is Miss Davidson.'

'Hello,' her child said shyly, before giggling and turning her face into her mother's chest.

'So your mother is one of the mysterious benefactors of Richard's will,' Lady Glendale said, patting Chloe's back. 'I have to admit, we did wonder.'

'It was as much of a surprise to me as it must have been to you, Lady Glendale.'

'Oh, please, call me Elizabeth.' She smiled suddenly and it changed her face from plain to pretty. 'I still haven't got used to the title yet. Only a few weeks ago, I was plain old Elizabeth Maxwell. To be honest, the British aristocracy scares the living daylights out of me.' She tightened her hold on the squirming child on her lap. 'Now what exactly would you like to know? I'm not sure I can be of much help.'

'As I said, I'm at a loss as to why Richard – Lord Glendale – made my mother executor and a possible beneficiary. Unfortunately, she's not very well at the moment, so I thought I would find out on her behalf. Apparently she's to inherit his properties in Edinburgh and Skye should the solicitors fail to track down a Magdalena Drobnik. I don't suppose you happen to know who she is?' In her haste to explain, her words were falling over one another. She couldn't shake the conviction that a stern-faced butler would appear at any moment to turf her out.

Elizabeth shook her head. 'I'm afraid not. My husband received a copy of Richard's will from the solicitors and I have to admit he was a little surprised at its contents – we all were. He'd never heard of either your mother or Miss Drobnik.'

Damn. She'd really hoped she'd find some answers here. 'Then he doesn't know why Lord Glendale would have done what he did?'

Chloe wriggled again in her mother's arms and Elizabeth placed her on the floor.

'If you're worried that my husband might contest the will – if that's why you're here – I'm afraid he hasn't made up his mind. I rather think he won't.' She gestured to the room. 'He has this place and when his father died, he inherited another house in Kent. He had to sell that one to pay inheritance tax, but we could have never afforded the upkeep anyway.' She pressed her lips together. 'I'm being more forthright than I expect my husband would wish, but I do hope you're not going to make trouble for the family.'

Sarah was aghast. 'Make trouble? Why should I do that?'

Elizabeth pursed her lips. 'People can behave strangely when money is involved.'

'I promise you I have no intention of upsetting your family

in any way.' Sarah took the envelope out of her handbag. 'What I would really like to know is why Lord Glendale would have had this particular photograph of my mother in his possession.' She handed it to Elizabeth who took a pair of reading glasses from the table by her side and studied it.

'I'm afraid I can't tell you. I don't recognise her. I certainly haven't seen her in any of the family photographs.'

A bell tinkled from somewhere deep in the house and Elizabeth sighed. 'Grandmother must have heard the doorbell. She'll be wanting to know who's visiting.'

'Your grandmother?'

'Grandmother-in-law, to be precise – Lady Dorothea.'

'Lady Dorothea is still alive? But she must be—' In the nick of time Sarah stopped herself from saying 'ancient'.

'Almost a hundred. Ninety-nine and eleven months, to be exact. She wouldn't thank either of us for adding any more years onto her than she has already.'

'Is it possible I could speak to her? Lady Dorothea might be able to tell me something about Magdalena Drobnik.'

'As you'll appreciate, Grandmother is very frail.' Elizabeth's lips twitched. 'At least physically.'

'I promise I won't take up too much of her time. Please, I wouldn't ask if it wasn't important. I really need to know—'

Before she could finish, the door was flung open revealing an elderly lady with a shock of white hair and a face with so many lines they looked like cobwebs. She was wearing a bright pink waistcoat trimmed with feathers and leaning heavily on two ebony sticks. However, there was nothing elderly about her piercing blue-green eyes. 'I heard the door. Why didn't you come when I rang, Elizabeth?' She peered at Sarah. 'I see we have a visitor. Well, aren't you going to introduce us?'

Elizabeth jumped to her feet and hurried to help the old lady.

'I thought you were resting, Grandmother. I was just coming to see what you needed.'

So this was Lady Dorothea.

The old lady batted Elizabeth away with one of her sticks. 'There's plenty of time to rest when I'm dead. I keep telling you I'm old, not senile.'

Elizabeth rolled her eyes behind Lady Dorothea's back. 'Grandmother, may I introduce Sarah Davidson? It's her mother who is to inherit Richard's estate should Miss Drobnik no longer be alive. Sarah, this is my husband's grandmother, Lady Dorothea.' She turned back to the old lady. 'You know the doctor said you were to take it easy.'

'Fiddlesticks! He's only a child. What could he possibly know?'

Chloe ran to Lady Dorothea, wrapped her arms around her legs and looked up at her adoringly.

Lady Dorothea patted her head and smiled. 'You know I'm not past it, don't you, darling?'

When Elizabeth moved towards them, Lady Dorothea waved her stick again. 'Don't you even attempt to take my elbow!'

Sarah suppressed an impulse to giggle. If she did, she wouldn't put it past Lady Dorothea to whack her too. As Elizabeth backed off, the old lady lowered herself carefully onto the seat of an upright sofa. After she was settled she looked at Sarah. 'So tell me, why are you here?'

From what she'd seen of Lord Glendale's aunt so far Sarah decided it was better to come straight to the point. 'As Elizabeth said, your nephew left his properties in Edinburgh and Skye to a Magdalena Drobnik, or, should she have passed away, to my mother. Do you have any idea why he should do such an extraordinary thing?'

'None whatsoever. He didn't choose to tell me what was in

his will. That's as it should be. His business was his own.' Her eyes softened. 'He did love that house in Skye. He spent so much time there it's where we buried him.'

'At the house?'

'Don't be ridiculous, child! In the cemetery, of course. Glendales don't get buried in their back gardens!'

Elizabeth gave Sarah a sympathetic look and took her daughter by the hand. 'Could you help me make some tea for Grandmother and our guest, darling?'

When they'd left, Sarah leaned forward in her chair. 'What I'd really like to know is whether you could tell me anything about Magdalena Drobnik. The woman Richard left his estate to.'

'I know who Magdalena Drobnik is.'

'You do? How? When did you meet her?'

'I didn't say I had ever met her — just that I knew Richard had left his estate to her. The only Polish woman I knew was an Irena.'

'Irena?' A frisson of excitement ran up Sarah's spine. Perhaps Irena and Magdalena were friends?

'A girl who came to stay during the war.'

'Are you sure her name was Irena and not Magdalena?'

'My dear, I might forget what I had for breakfast this morning, but my memory of the past is perfectly intact. The young woman's name was certainly Irena, although I forget her last name. It certainly wasn't Drobnik. Polish surnames are so complicated, aren't they? All I can remember is that it was something that sounded like crash.'

'You're quite certain you didn't know a Magdalena?'

A flash of irritation crossed the old lady's face. 'Very certain.' She fiddled with her stick. 'I imagine you're wondering why Richard didn't leave this house in his will, too?'

'Oh no. Absolutely not. To be honest, I'm just surprised he's left his other properties to my mother – if Magdalena doesn't claim them of course – especially when he has family alive.'

Lady Dorothea pinned her with a look. 'This house was never his. Richard's father passed it to me after my husband died.'

'He didn't leave it to his son? Wasn't that unusual back then?'

'You mean the whole inheritance malarkey being entailed down the male line? Yes, you're correct. But Richard's mother – my sister-in-law – bolted after the war. To America. My brother never got over it. Caused no end of upset. Not that I could blame her really.'

Although this didn't have anything to do with her Sarah couldn't help but be intrigued.

'Why couldn't you blame her?' she asked. 'Your brother couldn't have held Richard responsible for his mother's actions, surely?'

Lady Dorothea lifted her chin. 'That's family business, Miss Davidson. It really isn't any of your concern.'

Sarah winced inwardly. Lady Dorothea was right. She was here to find out about Magdalena. 'I'm sorry. Forgive me.'

A flash of annoyance crossed the old lady's face. 'Don't tell me you're one of those young women who are always apologising. Can't bear it. We had more backbone in my days. If you want to know something, ask. If I don't want to tell you, I shan't.'

Although Lady Dorothea made her feel like a naughty schoolgirl, Sarah told herself not to be a wuss. She might never get another chance to ask her questions.

'What else can you tell me about Irena, then?'

'Not very much, I'm afraid. I only met her once or twice. She arrived on my brother's doorstep one day – around the end of the Blitz. I gathered she'd escaped from Poland.'

Sarah's pulse was bounding. Two Polish women and both

with a connection to the Glendales. Surely they had known each other? She sat on the edge of her chair.

'Do you know if Irena's still alive? Did she have family? Brothers or sisters?'

'I really couldn't say. As I said, I didn't know much about her. She was studying medicine, I do remember that. She helped out at one of the first-aid posts during the Blitz. Then the Hun stopped bombing us.' Lady Dorothea clicked her fingers. 'Just like that. Irena left London shortly afterwards. The Bolter arranged for her to live at Charlotte Square and I never saw her again. So many people came into one's lives back then and just vanished.'

The old lady closed her eyes, seemingly lost in her memories. Thoughts tumbled through Sarah's head. If Magdalena wasn't Mum's mother, perhaps Irena was? If she were a friend of Magdalena's – or her sister – that would explain the connection between Magdalena and Mum. If Irena was here during the war, and if she was still alive, then she might still be in the country. She might even be in Edinburgh. If Sarah could track her down she might be able to tell her about Magdalena. At least it was a lead of sorts. And Richard could still be Mum's biological father.

'Do you know why Richard had a photograph of my mother as a child?' Sarah asked.

Lady Dorothea's eyes flickered open. 'Absolutely no idea.'

'Is it possible that Richard could have ...?' She hesitated then remembered what Lady Dorothea had said about coming right out with her questions. 'Do you think Richard could have had a child you didn't know about?'

'Richard? Most unlikely.' Lady Dorothea shuffled forward in her chair and leaned on her stick, clearly ready to rise. Sarah resisted the impulse to help her to her feet. 'If he had made some woman pregnant he would have had the decency to marry her.'

'Perhaps he couldn't? Perhaps they were separated by the war? Or he simply didn't know he'd fathered a child?'

All of a sudden Lady Dorothea looked every day of her advanced years. 'I've told you everything I can – or at least everything I know that might help you.' She looked towards the door. 'Where on earth is that girl with my tea?' It was clear that the conversation was at an end.

Realising that her time with Lady Dorothea was over, Sarah handed her one of her business cards. 'If you think of anything else – anything at all – could you call me?'

Lady Dorothea placed the card on the coffee table. 'Yes. Now you are going to have to excuse me, Miss Davidson, I'm feeling a little tired.'

Later that evening, Matthew took Sarah out to dinner at their favourite Italian restaurant.

She waited until they'd ordered, before she told him what she'd learned.

However, he didn't seem to share her excitement. On the contrary, he was unusually subdued.

'I've been offered a posting in Geneva,' he said suddenly. 'My boss called me in this morning and told me that the job was mine.'

Sarah frowned. 'You never told me you were applying for a job abroad.'

He smiled wryly. 'It's not as if we speak very often these days.'

'I know.' She placed her hand over his. 'I'm sorry.' The last time she'd seen him was shortly after her mother's stroke. They'd spoken on the phone once or twice since then but it wasn't the same. One or both of them was always on their way somewhere and their conversations were always brief.

He lifted her hand and wrapped it in his. 'I'm afraid this job makes the question of marriage rather more urgent. I want you to come with me to Geneva – as my wife. You know if your mother does end up inheriting those houses, you could sell them and use the funds to find a decent nursing home for her.'

Sarah snatched her hand away. 'I can't just put Mum in a nursing home and then abandon her!'

Matthew fiddled with the stem of his wine glass. 'But it's not just that, is it? You could have stayed in London. You know I would have supported you until you found a job with another publisher. If you come with me to Geneva you could give up your job. I can easily afford to support us both. You could even start writing that novel you're always talking about.'

Sarah cringed. She wished she'd never told him. It was only ever a pipe-dream then and even less likely to be written now. She couldn't focus on anything except Mum at the moment and if Matthew couldn't see that . . . 'Let me be clear. Are you asking me to leave my mother and come with you to Geneva?'

'I'm asking you to marry me, Sarah.' He took a sip of wine and swirled it around his mouth before placing his glass on the table. 'Geneva's not far. You could fly back whenever you wanted to see Lily.'

'Don't you realise, Mum could die!' Her voice rose on a wail. 'She could have another stroke and die, Matthew. How can you even think I would leave her now?'

'I'm not asking you to leave her right now, Sarah. I'm just asking you to set a date for our wedding.'

They stopped talking as the waiter placed their plates in front of them, but neither made a move to start eating.

'You haven't answered my question. Will you marry me and come to Geneva?'

She plucked at the silk of her blouse. 'I can't think about anything until I know what's happening with Mum.'

He sighed. 'I'm going to take the job, Sarah. I think I've waited long enough for you to decide whether or not you want to marry me. It shouldn't be a difficult question to answer.'

Her hands were shaking as she lifted her glass. He was right. She wasn't being fair. If she loved him the way she was supposed to love the man she was to spend the rest of her life with, shouldn't she have married him as soon as she could?

But if he loved her, shouldn't he wait?

Chapter 26
London, 1941

Two weeks after Irena left Poland she was standing on the steps of a grand building in the centre of London. All she had was one small suitcase, the clothes she was wearing, a few zloty and her mother's necklace, which thankfully she hadn't had to sell or barter on the long journey.

Henryk and Stanislaw had accepted her decision without trying to argue her out of it. But they'd insisted, if she were going to go, it had to be immediately, before Oberführer Bilsen returned. Events had moved quickly. They'd organised false papers for her and injected her with the 'virus'. She'd spent a couple of days in Henryk's house being cared for by Elena before Stanislaw had announced her death. As Tata had hoped, the doctors had found a sympathetic undertaker to bury a body – an elderly woman without a family – and so Irena Kraszewska had been laid to rest.

A man she'd never met before had come for her during the night. As a large part of their journey was to be on foot, her small bag was packed with very little: a dress, a skirt and blouse, a change of underwear and a few toiletries. She hadn't been able to take the photograph of Piotr with her – if German soldiers stopped and searched her and found a photograph of a Polish cavalry officer on her, it might be enough to make them take her in for questioning. So she'd left it with Elena who'd promised to take care of it until she was able to reclaim it. She had, however, taken her mother's necklace, sewing it in to the lining of her coat.

The fraught journey to Zakopane by train, never knowing if her new papers would pass muster, had been followed by a trek across the Tatra mountains, taking sheep-trodden paths, sleeping in safe houses at night and scavenging for food wherever they could find it. They'd slipped across the border into Hungary where new papers were waiting for her before continuing south through Yugoslavia. From there she'd taken a boat, landing in England ten days after she'd left Rozwadow.

The journey had been miserable and had taken its toll, but abandoning Poland – because that was how it felt – had been the hardest part. For what seemed like the hundredth time, she wondered if she had done the right thing. She could have taken the new papers Henryk had organised for her and found somewhere else to live in Poland where she still might have been of use to her country. But, as Henryk had pointed out, if Oberführer Bilsen returned to find her simply gone, he might have her father re-arrested. And there was always the possibility she'd be picked up in a round-up in one of the other towns or villages and that the major would have found her that way. Then she would have been questioned and might still have led the Gestapo to Henryk and Stanislaw. It was, she'd had to agree, an unacceptable risk.

She felt disorientated by London: the street signs in English, the red London buses, the large balloon-type objects hanging over the city.

Yet, in other ways, the British capital wasn't so very different to Warsaw in the days before the occupation: many roads were cordoned off and impassable because of craters in the road or unexploded bombs; almost every building showed signs of damage, some reduced to rubble, others still smouldering, those still in use protected by sandbags, their windows criss-crossed with black tape. Families picked through the ruins of what had once been their homes, while others sat dazed, boiling kettles on small stoves under makeshift shelters. And still most people went about their business, stepping around craters in the road as if they were part of the normal landscape. Despite the devastation, Irena felt safe.

Ignoring the dull ache behind her ribs she knocked on the door.

After a few moments the door was opened by a man in a dark suit.

Irena held out her hand. 'I'm Irena Kraszewska. I have come to see Lord Glendale.'

The man ignored her outstretched hand and looked her up and down before peering behind her. He didn't seem too pleased to find her on his doorstep.

'This *is* ninety-five Gros-venor Street?'

'If you mean ninety-five Grosvenor Street,' he said haughtily, pronouncing the street name without an 's', 'then yes, this is it. Is Lord Glendale expecting you, miss?'

Irena was relieved that whoever this disapproving man was, he wasn't the man she needed help from.

'Who is it, Smith?' A woman's voice came from within the hall.

'Since when have I needed help answering the door?' Smith grumbled, but he stood aside. 'It is some young lady requesting to see his lordship.' He sniffed. 'His lordship never mentioned he was expecting a visitor.'

A stout woman with grey hair shoved him out of the way. She was wearing an apron over a dress sprigged with flowers.

'Don't leave her standing. Can't you see she's almost at the end of her tether?' She took Irena by the arm. 'Come into the warmth, dear. My goodness, you look half starved.'

Even in her state of exhaustion Irena was aware of the splendour of the house with its high ceilings, marble floor and grand staircase.

'You look worn out, dear. Have you come far? This war is terrible, just terrible, the way it flings us all about, isn't it? But don't you worry, we'll get you sorted. I'm Mrs Smith, by the way – his lordship's housekeeper – and cook come to that.'

Irena was relieved when Mrs Smith didn't appear to expect a response to her chatter. The housekeeper led her through the hall, down a flight of steps and into a large kitchen. 'You take a seat there, pet, while I get the kettle on.'

Mrs Smith's accent was different to her husband's; softer with a lilt to it almost as if she were singing. She placed a kettle on the cooker. 'Irena, did you say your name was? And where have you washed up from?'

'Washed up?'

'Come from, pet, come from.'

Irena wondered how to reply. Months of being secretive had become a habit.

Happily, once again, Mrs Smith didn't wait for an answer. 'I don't know what my husband – that's Smith who opened the door to you – was thinking leaving you on the step like that. Now, is his lordship expecting you? The thing is, dear, I don't think he could be else he would have told Smith.'

'No, he's not expecting me. But I need to speak to him. I was given this address by a friend of his.' She stumbled over the unfamiliar words. Although her father had insisted she learn English as well as German it was a long time since she'd spoken it. 'He told my father Lord Glendale might be able to help me.'

'Oh, I'm sure he'll help you if he can, pet. He's awfully kind that way. Was it work you were looking for because I can always use a hand? The girls have all left to do war work.' She sniffed.

'Not that I can blame them but they've left me in a pickle. This house is too big for me and Smith to manage on our own even if his lordship does spend most of his time down the club and with her ladyship up in Scotland doing her doctoring thing. Lord Richard, their son, isn't here very often either, although he's here on leave at the moment. He's with the RAF, you know.'

For the first time since she'd left Poland, Irena felt her spirits lift. The son might know where she could find Aleksy. She wouldn't feel so alone then.

Her stomach clenched at the aroma of baking: she couldn't remember when she'd last eaten. Steam rose from the kettle and Mrs Smith heaped tea leaves into a pot.

'Are you all right, pet?' Mrs Smith said, peering at her. 'You don't look too well to me.'

'I'll be fine after a cup of tea. And perhaps a slice of bread if you have some to spare?'

'A slice of bread? Of course. I have a couple of loaves in the oven as we speak and a couple that are just done. Now if you'd asked me for an egg or a chop that would be a little more difficult – what with the rationing, and all, but we can certainly manage some bread and soup.'

As the warmth of the kitchen seeped into Irena, the tension of the last weeks left her and she began to feel sleepy. What she would do if Lord Glendale wouldn't help her, she wasn't entirely sure, but if necessary she would take the offer of work here in the house – at least until she'd recovered her strength and could start searching for Aleksy.

Mrs Smith put a bowl of soup in front of her and Irena made herself take small sips. A few minutes later, a warm slice of bread was placed next to her bowl and she ate that too, breaking off tiny bits at a time to prevent herself from stuffing the whole thing into her mouth in one go.

When she'd finished the soup and the tea – which was milky, not at all how she was used to taking it, but welcome nevertheless – Irena suppressed a yawn behind her hand. If only she could curl up in the armchair next to the stove and go to sleep.

'You look as if you need your bed,' the older woman said. 'I don't know when his lordship will be back but what about you take Doris's bed? She was a maid here before she left to work in the munitions – more money, you see? More freedom too, I suspect. She always was a flighty thing. This war has turned everything upside down. Anyway, what was I saying? Yes, why don't you take her bed and have a bit of a sleep?' She paused suddenly and covered her mouth with her hand. 'You're not a German spy by any chance, lass? You don't look like one but you can never tell.'

Irena almost laughed. It clearly hadn't occurred to Mrs Smith that if she were a German spy she'd be unlikely to admit it. She shook her head. 'I promise you, I'm as far away from a German spy as you can imagine.'

'You do sound foreign though, lass.'

'I'm Polish.'

'Polish! Well I never. I've heard there's a few of you about since the war started, but I would have never taken you for one.'

Irena was pretty sure Mrs Smith had never met a Pole before and was therefore hardly in a position to judge, but she kept her thoughts to herself. The woman was being kind.

'Now then, dear, why don't you leave your bag down here and I'll take you to Doris's old room? It's on the top floor so there are a few steps, I'm afraid. Smith will bring your suitcase up to you later.'

Irena was so tired she could barely speak but she wasn't about to be separated from the few belongings she had left in the world, least of all her coat with her mother's necklace sewn into its lining.

She picked it up, along with her small bag, ignoring the look of disapproval on Mrs Smith's face. 'I'd rather ... ' Her voice cracked.

Mrs Smith's expression softened. 'Of course you would. Now come with me. You'll see. Everything will seem a lot better once you've had a good rest.'

Irena woke to a gentle tap on the door. At first she didn't know where she was but then she remembered. She was in England in Lord Glendale's house and in the absent Doris's bed.

She threw the blankets aside and opened the door to find Mrs Smith holding a large jug. 'His lordship is home and asking to see you. I brought you some water to wash with. The bathroom is down the hall but the water in the tap is cold at the moment so you'll be better with a basin.' She placed the jug on a small washstand and handed Irena a towel. 'I don't want to rush you, pet, but let's not keep his lordship waiting longer than necessary.'

'He didn't mind my taking a sleep, did he?'

'Of course not. He's a good man, is his lordship. You'll see for yourself. Now when you're ready, come downstairs to the hall. Can you find your way back there all right?'

Irena nodded. 'Down the back stairs, two flights and turn left.'

'Right. Smith will be waiting for you there anyway. He'll take you in to his lordship.'

When Mrs Smith left, Irena hurriedly washed her face and hands and brushed her hair, before twisting it into a chignon. She slipped on her only spare dress, which, although more threadbare than she would have liked, was at least clean. She pinched her cheeks to add some colour, wishing she had some powder left to disguise the shadows under her eyes.

When she had made herself as presentable as possible she went downstairs. Smith looked her up and down, no less disapproving than he'd been before. She returned his gaze steadily. She might be a refugee but she was still a Kraszewska.

'Lord Glendale is waiting for you in the library, miss.'

She followed him up the main staircase and into a wood-panelled room lined with books. Unlike the chilly hall and bedroom, this room was warm and cosy, a fire burning brightly in the grate, despite the sun streaming in the window. There were two men present, an older man with greying reddish-blond hair, his left sleeve pinned up at the elbow, and a younger man wearing a red silk scarf that seemed out of place against his blue serge uniform.

Both men stood. 'Now then,' the older one said sternly, 'suppose you enlighten me as to why I have a woman whom I have never met sleeping in my house.' He looked over at the man by the fireplace. 'Lord Maxwell – my son – assures me he doesn't know you either.'

Irena twisted her hands together so they couldn't see they were shaking. 'My name is Irena Kraszewska and I have come from Poland. My father, Professor Julien Kraszewski, was given your name by an old friend and colleague – Dr Hoffman – who said that you might be able to help me.'

'Now why would Maximilian give you my name?' Lord Glendale didn't ask her to sit down so she remained standing. His son, however, glanced at his father with a frown. 'Please, Miss Kraszewska, take a seat. I'm sure we can get to the bottom of this.'

Irena shot him a grateful smile before sinking into the armchair opposite Lord Glendale. 'My father has known Dr Hoffman for as long as I can remember,' she said. 'Dr Hoffman is my godfather.' She smiled. 'We weren't always at war with the

Germans, you know. After Czechoslovakia was invaded Dr Hoffman tried to persuade my father to leave Poland with my brother and me. He told my father if we ever found ourselves in London and needed help, we should come to this address.'

'He did, did he?' Father and son exchanged glances. Irena knew how it must sound. Why would a German try to help a Polish family when they seemed bent on destroying the Polish nation?

'Where's your father now?'

'Still in Poland. I tried to persuade him to leave but he wouldn't.'

'And how did you get here?'

'I was given false papers—' Just in time she bit back the words she was going to say about being helped by the underground army. 'I came through Hungary.'

Lord Glendale studied her through narrowed eyes. 'I'm sorry, my dear, but I will have to ask you to be more specific. I'm sure you will understand why we have to be careful. At a time like this, there are those who come to this country in order to help the German cause.'

'I'm a medical student!' Irena cried. 'You can't think I'm a spy! No one could hate the Germans more than I do. They've murdered so many people in my country and those they haven't murdered they have taken to their factories where they're working them to death.'

The son poured a glass of water from a jug on the tray and passed it to her. 'We just need to be sure you are who you say you are.'

Irena stumbled to her feet. 'I'm sorry. I shouldn't have come here. I'll go.'

'Sit down, Miss Kraszewska. Please,' Lord Glendale said. 'I will need to check your story thoroughly but if you are telling the truth, of course we will help you.' He rose to his feet as a gong sounded from somewhere in the house. 'That is Smith letting us know dinner is ready. I'm afraid you'll have to excuse me as I've a previous arrangement to dine at my club, but Richard will keep you company.' He glanced at his watch. 'I should be back later. Perhaps you would stay up until then and we will talk some more?'

Lord Maxwell – or Richard, as he insisted she call him – ushered her into the dining room. She was still burning with indignation at the way Lord Glendale had questioned her, but she waited until they had soup in front of them before speaking.

'You're in the RAF. Perhaps you can tell me why the British didn't come to help Poland when they promised.'

Richard started. He raised an eyebrow. 'You wish me to defend my country's policies? And over dinner?'

'Poland could have been saved if Britain and France had attacked Germany right in the beginning.'

'Possibly. We'll never know now.' His eyes glittered. 'Our boys have taken quite a beating in defence of your country.'

'In defence of my country or yours? You must be worried Hitler will invade you.'

'You make it sound very simple, Miss Kraszewska.'

'Please don't patronise me.'

He placed his spoon down and leaned back in his chair. 'Very well. This is how I see it. If we'd thrown everything at Hitler right from the start, perhaps we could have stopped him. Unfortunately we didn't have the resources, or the men. Not then – hence the shambles at Dunkirk.'

'But—'

'You ask why we didn't come to Poland's aid right at the beginning. The RAF boys were keen as mustard to go into action, but our planes didn't – still don't for that matter – have the fuel capacity to fly to Poland to engage the enemy. It was that simple. I can assure you, Miss Kraszewska, pilots want nothing more than to take a shot at the Boche.'

The fight went out of her. 'Irena,' she muttered. 'My name is Irena.'

Smith cleared their plates and replaced them with others. Irena didn't even glance at hers.

Richard smiled tightly. 'Have I answered some of your questions?'

She sighed and pushed away her plate. 'At least the British are still fighting. As long as they hold out, there is still hope for us.'

'Oh, we shall hold out, Irena. Have no doubt about that.'

'My brother is a pilot too,' she said. 'I heard he made it to France and, when it fell, to Britain.'

'He's a Polish pilot?' He lowered his knife and fork, his gaze sharpening. 'In that case he could well be nearby. We have a number of Polish pilots within our squadrons as well as one or two squadrons made up entirely of Poles. They have quite a reputation.'

She threw down her napkin. 'Can we find out?'

Richard's eyes darkened. 'It's been a rough few weeks. You may not know but the RAF has been involved in some heavy fighting over the last months and your countrymen played a major part.' He shook his head. 'A lot of pilots bought it.'

'Bought it? I don't understand.'

'Died.'

She sank back into her chair. She couldn't bear it if she'd come all this way only to find her darling brother was dead.

'Look, Irena, it's possible that your brother – if indeed he is here – wasn't involved in the fighting. I know it's difficult, but try not to worry.'

Try not to worry! All she'd been doing since the war started was worry. As Richard turned his attention to Smith to indicate he could remove their plates, she studied Lord Glendale's son more closely. He was older than her, in his late twenties, she guessed, and good-looking in the way that she thought of as quintessentially British, with his blue eyes, high cheekbones and haughty expression. But behind his eyes she thought she saw shadows – and the same aching sadness that was inside her.

'Were you involved in these battles?' she asked, once their plates had been cleared.

'Yes,' he said shortly. 'Now I'm afraid you will have to excuse me. I have to get back to base. Mrs Smith will look after you. If the air-raid sirens sound, don't panic. One of them will take you to the cellar. If you happen to be outside, the underground shelters are all signposted. Or just follow the others. Make certain you take a gas mask with you – I believe there's a spare that Mrs Smith can let you have.'

He clearly had no idea what she'd been through. Nevertheless, it felt good to have someone look after her for a change.

But she had no intention of going anywhere. Even her bones were heavy with fatigue. 'I must wait up for your father, but after that – unless he has decided I am a spy,' she managed a smile, 'I shall go to bed.'

'When I get back to my base I'll make enquiries about your brother.'

'Would you? I'd be very grateful.'

'Don't worry, if he's in the country I'll track him down. I promise.'

Chapter 27

When Lord Glendale returned, it seemed that whatever he'd managed to find out about Irena, from whatever sources he had, had satisfied him.

'I've spoken to my wife and told her about you. She tells me that there is a medical school in Edinburgh that is run by Poles for Poles. She thinks you might wish to finish your studies there.'

'They would take me?'

'It seems so. Richard is going to visit his mother in a couple of weeks and, if you chose to go, he could accompany you. I'm afraid it will take a week or two to make the necessary arrangements. Our railways are rather in demand at the moment. Now should I tell Lady Glendale to expect you? It would be better than staying here. London's not safe.'

She couldn't leave London without finding Aleksy first. However, she had a week or two to track him down. 'Thank you, I'd very much like to resume my studies.' At least then, when she returned to Poland, she'd be able to start work straight away as a qualified doctor.

'Good show! I'll sort out the necessary documents, identity book, ration cards, gas mask and so forth. In the meantime, you're to treat this house as your home.'

His unexpected kindness brought a lump to her throat.

'I've asked Mrs Smith to move your possessions into one of

the guest bedrooms,' he continued, 'and Lady Glendale has suggested that Mrs Smith gives you some of the clothes my wife has in her wardrobe. There are additional questions that the authorities would like to ask you, but apart from that, you must pass the days as best you can. I don't spend much time at home so you'll have to make do with your own company, I'm afraid.'

In the morning, as promised, there was a dress lying on the end of her bed along with some underwear, still in its wrapping paper. The simple tea dress with a lace collar would have been too tight had she not lost so much weight, but it was a good length, coming to just below her knees. She and Lady Glendale must be a similar height.

She made her way back down to the dining room to find Lord Glendale finishing his breakfast.

'Good morning,' he said, glancing up from his paper. 'Did you manage to get some rest, my dear?'

'I did, thank you.'

She laid her napkin on her lap while the still-disapproving Smith served her bacon and toast. The bacon, the first she'd had in months, smelled and tasted so good she ate it one small piece at a time, savouring every delicious mouthful.

'I'd like you to come to my office this afternoon to tell my colleagues more about what is happening in Poland,' Lord Glendale said. 'I shall send a car around three if that suits?'

As if she could refuse. 'I'll be ready.'

The car came to collect her promptly at three, and delivered her to a large, imposing building. After a long wait in the foyer, she was shown into a room with several men in officer's uniform, including Lord Glendale. She was given a cup of tea and asked about her journey. Then the questions became more searching.

What was happening in Poland? Was she aware of any resistance groups where she'd lived?

She answered as best she could, omitting the part about the typhus scam, and although she told them that the underground army was active, she wasn't specific. She wasn't altogether sure she could trust them not to leak information that would get her Polish friends in trouble, even shot.

When they had finished with her, she was driven back to the house on Grosvenor Street. As a wave of exhaustion washed over her, she decided to leave exploring London until another day and, finding a well-stocked library, curled up in a chair with a book instead.

The next morning she went down to breakfast to find a middle-aged yet still beautiful red-haired woman wearing a khaki uniform, her hair neatly rolled above her collar, sitting opposite Lord Glendale. She had a piece of toast in one hand, and was talking rapidly, her free hand gesticulating as she spoke.

When Lord Glendale noticed Irena he got to his feet. 'My dear, may I introduce you to my sister, Lady Dorothea? Dorothea, this is Irena Kraszewska, the young lady I was telling you about.'

Irena crossed over to the woman and held out her hand. 'Pleased to meet you.'

Lady Dorothea shook it and smiled. 'How do you do?'

Irena sat and helped herself to a slice of toast. Smith placed a boiled egg on her plate and returned to his place at the sideboard.

'I gather you're a medical student,' Lady Dorothea said, dabbing her lips with a napkin.

'Yes.'

'You must have had experience of dealing with casualties in Poland then.'

'I was working in a hospital until I left.'

Lady Dorothea slid a triumphant glance at her brother. 'I told you she'd be perfect.'

'Leave the poor girl be, Dorothea. She's been through hell in the last months.'

'Perfect for what?' Irena asked. She wouldn't be talked about as if she weren't there.

'My sister is with the FANYs,' Lord Glendale told Irena. 'Now we're at war, she sees it as her duty to keep London running – single-handed if necessary.'

'FANYs?'

'First Aid Nursing Yeomanry.' Lady Dorothea sent a scornful glance in her brother's direction. 'We do loads to help the war effort – not just nursing.'

'My sister is a Staff Commander. She was in the last war and I dare say if they'd allow her she'd be in the thick of things overseas.'

'I am in the thick of things, Simon, right here. It can't get much thicker, can it? Not when that dreadful man is determined to pulverise us into submission. I've had to send my only child to the country to keep him safe – God knows when I'll see him again – and my husband is overseas doing his bit, so naturally I have to do mine.' Lady Dorothea flicked her fingers at her brother. 'But never mind all that now, I have to go in a minute.' She turned to Irena. 'We need more people to man our first-aid posts. We're terribly short of recruits. All the decent nurses have joined the forces or are employed in the hospitals. If you were working in a hospital in Poland, you must have bags of experience.'

'Yes, I do.' Irena closed her eyes briefly. *Bags of experience* – that was one way of putting it. Images of mutilated and dead bodies spooled through her mind, and she shook her head to push them away. 'Of course, I'd be happy to help,' she said. 'Just tell me where and when.'

'Not so fast,' Simon protested. 'There are procedures to follow. An application process . . . '

Lady Dorothea smiled sweetly at him. 'Fiddlesticks! What is the point in having a brother in the War Office, Simon, if not to bypass procedures and rules?' She stood. 'Shall we go, Miss Kraszewska?'

Lord Glendale tossed his napkin to the table and got to his feet too. 'At least let the poor girl finish her breakfast.'

Irena placed her half-eaten toast on the plate. 'I'm ready now.'

Lady Dorothea drove her to the Red Cross headquarters and introduced her to one of the women in charge. After telling her that Irena was top dollar, able to drive and happy to work the nightshift, she'd hurried away to 'check up on her girls'.

Following a verbal check of her credentials, Irena was given a tin hat with FAP stencilled on the front, a short-sleeved blue dress and an apron with a red cross emblazoned on it, and told to report to a station that evening where 'someone would show her the ropes'.

That evening, after a solitary supper, Irena took the bus to her first-aid post. Contrary to what she'd been led to believe, there were only two of them – herself and Gladys, a thin woman somewhere around thirty although it was difficult to say for certain. Gladys had almost no nursing experience, had only been working there for a week or so and was, she freely admitted, terrified.

A number of people stopped by with cuts and scratches as well as a few complaining of sore heads and abdomens. Irena dealt with them quickly, showing Gladys how to clean wounds and re-bandage them properly. She gave out aspirin to the people with headaches and stomach aches, advising them to go to their doctor in the morning if it didn't get better. She suspected that the cause of the vague aches and pains was fear and stress but she sympathised. What she did find remarkable was the attitude of the Londoners as they waited patiently to be seen. Many of them had lost loved ones and everything they owned, yet they smiled and joked with each other as if they were at a tea party.

By eleven there were no more patients to see. Gladys had just poured them a cup of tea, when the siren wailed.

'We need to get to Marble Arch underground. That's the nearest shelter to us. Come on.' Gladys yanked her by the arm and away from their post.

Like rabbits emerging from rabbit holes, figures appeared, joining those already on the street: men and women, coats thrown hurriedly over nightclothes, hurried to the bomb shelter, holding babies in their arms or tugging children along by the hand. Suddenly the night sky was illuminated by searchlights criss-crossing the sky.

Down in the bowels of the underground station, people unrolled mattresses and blankets and calmly set about getting their children back to sleep. Some men gathered around a pack of cards and started a game. Others unscrewed the tops of flasks and poured cups of tea for themselves and their neighbours. At the far end of the tunnel a man had taken out a squeeze box and, as he played, many began to sing along.

The unreal, almost festive, atmosphere changed when the first bombs fell, making the ground shake. Children woke up and began to cry and mothers tried to shush them.

Over the next hour more and more loud explosions echoed through the tunnels.

'We have to get out of here,' a woman cried after a particularly close explosion, one that showered plaster and dirt from the ceiling. 'I'm not going to let them bury me alive.' She'd been pacing up and down all evening, a child clutched to her chest.

A nearby man grabbed her by her shoulders. 'Sit down, Mother. No one is to leave before the all-clear.'

The woman looked around frantically as if searching for an escape route.

Irena crossed over to her. 'Is that your baby?' she said. 'Let me see.'

The woman paused. Her child was wrapped in a blanket but one chubby leg had worked its way through the folds and was waving up and down. At once an image of the baby she hadn't tried to save leaped to Irena's mind. As her chest tightened, she pushed the memory away.

'What a lovely, strong baby,' Irena said. 'A boy or a girl?'

'A girl. Daisy, I call her.'

'And what's your name?'

'Sandra.'

There was a loud crump that made the ground beneath them shake. Sandra shrieked and glanced around in panic.

'How old is Daisy, Sandra?' Irena asked to distract her.

'Nine months.'

Daisy looked up at Irena and grinned, exposing two tiny lower front teeth in her otherwise toothless mouth.

'She's beautiful. Can I hold her?'

Sandra held out the infant and Irena took her. Holding the baby was a small balm to her soul.

'Why don't we sit down?' she suggested. 'Perhaps we could have a cup of tea while we are waiting for the raid to finish?'

A couple of women in uniform had set up a trolley with large urns from which they were dispensing hot drinks.

'A cup of char would be good,' Sandra agreed and, to Irena's relief, settled down on one of the benches lining the platform.

Irena handed Daisy back to her. 'I'll get it for us, then perhaps you can tell me all about little Daisy?'

When the all-clear sounded, people began to fold their blankets and make their way outside. Irena and Gladys had to wait in line until eventually they emerged from the stairs and onto the street.

As she took in the scene, Irena's heart kicked against her ribs. It was Warsaw all over again. On the far side of the street buildings were alight, the flames reaching to the sky, turning it red. There were gaps where shops and homes had once stood, the remaining houses almost cut in two, ragged shards of wallpaper the only evidence that a short while ago people had lived there. The contents of shop windows – coats, dresses, silk shirts – were strewn across the debris. Cinders swirled around them like a hellish snow storm. A foot, still in its tiny shoe, lay close to a pile of rubble. Huge craters, with flames leaping from them, punctuated the road. A woman, missing most of her clothes, staggered along the street, keening. Firemen trained their hoses on the burning buildings while the clanging of ambulances couldn't quite drown out the screams of distress. Men and women immediately started tearing at the piles of rubble that had once been homes and offices, looking for survivors.

Irena felt a hand on her arm.

'Poor devils,' Gladys muttered, 'but if the Boche think we're going to give up just because they drop a few bombs on us, they have another think coming.'

A short distance away, a man had unearthed the body of an old lady. He felt for a pulse before shouting for an ambulance, but the ambulances were overwhelmed. It might be hours before some of the casualties received medical attention.

'Come on, Gladys,' Irena said, taking her companion by the arm. 'We must help.'

'We can't abandon the first-aid post,' Gladys replied. 'Sister will have my guts for garters.'

'We're needed here.' When Gladys didn't respond, Irena sighed. 'You go back – fetch me if you need me. But I'm staying here.'

She worked until she could hardly think. She applied tourniquets and pressure bandages made from anything she could get her hands on, soothed the injured and the dying and announced deaths so that the rescue workers wouldn't waste time and energy trying to revive those who were beyond hope.

It was a long, dreadful night, but when the casualties had all been taken to hospital and the dead to the morgues, Irena sat on a broken piece of masonry and stared up at the clear blue sky above the smoke. She was tired and dirty and some of what she'd seen would stay with her forever, but, despite all that, she felt a strange sense of peace.

She'd been manning the first-aid station for less than a week when the bombing stopped. There was still no word about Aleksy and she was terrified the lack of news meant he wasn't in Britain as she'd hoped or, worse still, that he was dead.

But just as she'd decided to visit every RAF base on her own, Richard brought news.

She was ringing the doorbell so that Smith could let her in when there was a loud roar behind her. She turned to find Richard, in flying cap and goggles, astride a motorcycle. A girl in the uniform of a WAAF was perched on the seat behind him.

'I've found him!' he said, taking off his goggles. 'Your brother. Flight Officer Kraszewski is with the famous squadron 303. They're based at RAF Northolt. At least they were until a few days ago.'

'Isn't it marvellous?' said the girl who was with him. 'You must have been so worried.'

'This is Susan,' Richard said. 'Or Captain Mortram, should I say.'

Irena was too stunned to do anything except shake the hand Susan was holding out to her.

'Aleksy is all right?' Irena hardly dared believe it.

'He was yesterday.'

Happiness soared through her with such ferocity, she was almost dizzy. 'I need to see him. Can you take me to him?'

'Thing is, 303 squadron has been sent to Dumfries in Scotland for a few weeks' respite. They took a bit of a beating over the last couple of weeks. They'll be back, but no one knows when.'

'Then I'll go there.'

'I thought you might say that. I've wangled us a couple of tickets on the sleeper to Edinburgh for Friday,' Richard said. 'You can get to Dumfries from there easily enough.'

'But I'd like to go now,' Irena protested.

'Sorry, old thing. Train tickets are like gold dust – at least for civilians. I was lucky to get the ones I did. You'll have to wait. I've let Mother know to expect us.'

A warm glow spread through Irena. Her prayers had been answered. Aleksy was still alive. She'd be resuming her medical training shortly. It was a beautiful summer's day. If only Tata and Piotr were here, her happiness would be complete. And Magdalena, of course. Just as suddenly as it had arrived, the joy went out of her day. Aleksy had to be told that his beloved fiancée was dead.

'In the meantime,' Richard continued, 'I have his address for you. I am sure that you will wish to write to him. To let him know that you are here and being looked after.'

She wouldn't write to Aleksy. She'd be seeing him soon and what she had to say to him had to be said in person.

Richard revved the motorcycle. 'Now, I'm afraid you'll have

to excuse us. I managed to escape for an hour so I could give you the good news. We're on alert back at the base, so I need to get back and I have to drop Susan here off on the way.'

He seemed very cheerful at the thought of going into battle. But that was men for you. They seemed to think that their very existence depended on proving their courage. But if it meant that he would be shooting down German planes, who was she to disapprove?

The next evening, her night off, she was on her way to the library to return a book when she met Richard at the foot of the stairs.

'I have come to take you to a club,' he said.

'To be honest, I'm happier staying in and reading.'

'Rubbish. You can't spend every evening inside on your own when you're not working.'

'I enjoy my own company.' It wasn't altogether true. Since she'd left Poland the nightmares had become more frequent. They were vividly real and almost always of sightless babies, their arms reaching out for her. At other times she'd be running but going nowhere. She would wake covered in perspiration, her heart hammering against her ribs. Even worse, she'd been getting flashbacks during the day. Reading kept the memories at bay for a little while, as did work, but now, with less to do, her heart would often start racing for no apparent reason and then at other times she'd feel a terrible, all-consuming lethargy creep over her.

'Too much time on your own isn't good for anyone.' A shadow flitted across his face. 'Trust me, I know.' Almost immediately the smile was back in place. 'I need an evening out and I'd like you to join me. I won't take no for an answer. Go on, put your glad rags on.'

Irena hesitated. Why not? He was right. It would be a

distraction and she had yet to celebrate finding Aleksy. Then she remembered: apart from the few clothes she'd brought with her, all she had were the dresses of Lady Glendale's Mrs Smith had given her, which were now well worn and hardly suitable for a club.

'I don't have anything to wear.'

Richard looked her up and down. 'You look pretty good to me, but if you're worried, why don't you raid Mother's cupboard for a cocktail frock? She has more than enough. Not sure about the shoes, though. I think your feet might be a little bigger than hers.'

Irena was amused. It seemed improbable that this man could know anything about women's clothes, although she'd already formed the impression that Richard knew a lot more about women than most men. He reminded her of Polish officers with their easy charm and expectation, too often confirmed, that girls would fall at their feet.

'I'll be twenty minutes.'

He grinned. 'In my experience when a woman says twenty minutes she means at least twice that.' He picked up a newspaper from the stand in the hall. 'Take your time – things don't start happening at the club until later anyway.' He looked over her shoulder. 'Would you mind bringing a whisky to the library, Smith. In fact, bring me the bottle.'

Irena started. She hadn't noticed Smith standing in the shadows, waiting to attend to his employer's son. 'Very good, My Lord. And for the miss?'

She smiled. 'Miss will have some champagne.'

By the time Irena came back down, Richard appeared to have had more than a glass or two of the whisky. However, his eyes were focused and alert.

Looking up from his paper, he whistled. 'That dress suits you.'

She'd selected a dress in pale shimmery green that she knew set off her eyes and went well with her mother's necklace, and she'd taken time with her hair, fashioning it into a style she'd admired on the young female Londoners. Pleased that for the first time she looked like the Irena Kraszewska before the war, she'd applied some deep red lipstick she found on Lady Glendale's dressing table. As a final act of vanity, she'd squeezed her feet into some heels belonging to her absent hostess that, as Richard had guessed, were really a size too small.

'Are you certain Lady Glendale won't mind me helping myself to her wardrobe?' she asked.

'My mother has more clothes than she knows what to do with. She'd be delighted to know someone was making use of her dresses.'

To Irena's surprise, it appeared Richard intended they use his motorcycle to get to the club. 'Isn't petrol rationed?' she asked.

Richard grinned. 'It is for some. And you can't walk very far in those heels.'

Irena pressed her lips together. It seemed the aristocracy were having a different war to everyone else.

The club was filled with cigarette smoke, and the sound of laughter and raised voices almost drowned out the five-piece band. Most of the men were in uniform, the women wearing either evening dresses or smart frocks. The band was playing 'Only Forever' by Bing Crosby, one of Irena's favourites.

Richard spotted some friends, and he led Irena across the room by the elbow.

Like Richard, the men were RAF, and like him, wore red socks, their dress jackets lined in silk in the same colour. The women with them were exquisitely dressed and heavily made up but one in particular stood out from everyone else in the room.

She was tall and slim and had black wavy hair that contrasted with her alabaster skin.

'Irena, may I introduce Lady Eleanor Fellows and Lucy Marksman? Ladies, this is Irena Kraszewska. She arrived from Poland a few days ago.'

The beauty, Lady Fellows, raised her face to receive Richard's kiss. 'How do you do, Miss Kraszewska?' She held out a slim hand. 'How very clever of you to have escaped.'

'And these reprobates are Julian, Bill and Scotty.'

The RAF officers raised their beer glasses in Irena's direction.

'How do you do?' Bill said. 'I'm Flight Officer William Pickard.'

Richard laughed. 'Close your mouth, Bill, there's a good chap. You're positively drooling over our guest.' Irena felt her cheeks redden. The sandy-haired officer hadn't taken his eyes off her. 'Besides,' Richard continued, his eyes lingering on Irena, 'she's already taken.' The way he looked at her made her uncomfortable.

They squeezed into the booth and ordered drinks – Gin Fizzes for the women, beers with whisky chasers for the men.

The music throbbed through Irena and she found herself tapping her foot to its beat.

'Have you known Richard long?' she asked Eleanor as the number drew to a close.

'A few years.'

The band had struck up a tune, the words of which oddly sounded like 'let's hang up our washing on the Siegfried Line'. Almost everyone except Eleanor, Richard and Irena lined up and formed a circle, their hands on the waist of the person in front of them.

'What do the words mean?' Irena asked.

Eleanor laughed. 'The Siegfried Line is the Germans' line

defending their borders. It means that we don't believe that they'll be able to prevent us from invading them.'

The room was hot and Richard's companions had unbuttoned their jackets. As they danced the red lining of their jackets flashed.

'Why do they wear red? I can't help but notice they wear red socks too.'

Eleanor smiled at Richard. 'Shall I tell her, darling?'

Richard downed the last of his pint. 'Be my guest. More drinks, everyone?'

When Irena and Eleanor shook their heads, Richard headed through the throng towards the bar.

'The red is a sort of a tradition for the boys of the Millionaires' Club.'

'Millionaires' Club?'

'It's how people refer to the squadron. All the members are disgustingly well-to-do. It was formed in nineteen twenty-four or 'twenty-five, no one is quite sure which. Gossip has it that the son of the Duke of Westminster had the idea at a dinner at White's – that's a men's club in St James's. He wanted the officers to be men who could hold their drink and who were of the same sort as him and therefore wouldn't be overawed by him. He also wanted them to have sufficient funds to be able to enjoy the good things in life.' She smiled softly. 'They make it their mission to do exactly that – while they can. To them red is a symbol of defiance as well as cocking a snook at the RAF. Richard and my husband,' she paused and swirled the drink in her glass, looking unbearably sad, 'joined while they were at Cambridge. One of them is the son of Lord Beaverbrook, who owns many of the newspapers in London. The others are all of that ilk. When petrol was rationed, Julian simply went out and bought a filling station.' She took a sip of her drink and when she raised her eyes again they glistened with unshed tears. 'It's not all fun and games. They're brave men. The best. Nine of them died during the Battle of Britain, my husband included.'

'I am so sorry,' Irena said. Her heart went out to her. Everyone had lost someone.

'We hadn't been married long.' Lady Fellows smiled wanly. 'But heigh-ho, chin up and all that.'

The dance had come to end and Richard returned, accompanied by a woman in WAAF uniform with dyed blond hair and slightly glazed eyes.

'This is Martha,' Richard introduced her. 'One of the WAAFs from the base. She's a plotter.'

'That means she works in the ops room at the airbase,' Eleanor said, seeing Irena's bewilderment. 'They use markers on these enormous maps to show the controllers where the enemy planes are as well as to keep track of our boys.'

'The name is Marion actually, not Martha.' The woman clinging to Richard's arm pouted. 'Do keep up, darling.'

Richard looked at her and laughed. She tried to pull him away but Richard ignored her. They shuffled up as the rest of Richard's friends joined them at the table, Richard squeezing in beside Irena, the others on the other side of Eleanor. Irena could feel his thigh pressing against hers and smell the faint citrus scent of his cologne.

'I'm going to freshen up,' Marion said to Richard, with a glare at Irena that couldn't have said more clearly 'Hands off' had she worn a sign around her neck.

'What do you do?' Bill asked Irena.

'I was training to be a doctor when war broke out.'

Bill grinned. 'You could be my doctor any time, miss.'

'Please, call me Irena.'

'Down boy,' Richard said from her other side. Although the

words were said lightly, his eyes flashed. 'Irena is a guest of my father's.'

'Knowing Richard, he just wants to keep you to himself,' Bill whispered. 'As if he doesn't have more than his fair share of girls. But life is too short to hang about, don't you think?'

'Yes,' Irena answered distractedly. From the corner of her eye she noticed Richard staring at her, an almost hungry expression in his eyes. Quickly, she looked away.

'I think you'd rather talk to Richard,' Bill sighed. 'Most girls do.'

Irena felt the heat rise to her cheeks. 'Not at all,' she protested. 'Actually, I'm engaged to be married.'

Bill studied her through half-closed eyes. 'Where is he, then?'

'I don't know. I'm not even certain he's still alive.' To her chagrin her voice wobbled.

Bill was immediately contrite. 'Gosh, I'm sorry. I can be such a big mouth at times.'

Eleanor leaned over. 'Leave the poor girl alone, Bill. There're plenty of others who will give you the time of day – and anything else you ask if you give them a chance.'

Marion had returned with another woman Irena hadn't met. After a while, when Richard continued to ignore Marion, they drifted on to the dance floor where they wrapped their arms around one another, holding each other up as they swayed in time to the music. No one seemed to give their extraordinary behaviour a second glance. Indeed, as the night wore on couples were openly kissing on the dance floor and a woman was dancing on the table, her eyes closed, a lit cigarette hanging from her brightly painted lips.

Irena felt distant, apart. She wished she could be like the other women – forget – even for a moment – what she'd lost.

She took a long sip of her drink and gathered herself together.

She was meant to be celebrating finding Aleksy. 'Do you dance?' she asked Bill.

He grinned. 'Like a giraffe on gin, but I'll give it a go.'

But Richard was on his feet before him. 'May I?' he said.

Irena let him lead her onto the dance floor. The band struck up a waltz and she tried to relax into his arms, but she was too acutely aware of the pressure of his hand on the small of her back and the way she fitted under his chin. How safe it felt to be held like this.

A couple swirled past, the woman, breath-stoppingly like Magdalena with her petite frame and dark hair.

Madzia and Aleksy should be married by now. Magdalena should be dancing somewhere having fun, dressed up and smiling. The waltz finished and all of a sudden Irena couldn't bear to stay a moment longer. It didn't feel right to be enjoying herself when thousands were dying every day. It didn't feel right to be enjoying herself when Magdalena was dead. She grabbed her bag and mumbled something about leaving, before squeezing through the crowded dance floor and outside.

She leaned against the door for a moment sucking in lungfuls of air, trying to stop herself shaking.

'For God's sake, Irena, what is it?' Richard said, gently pulling her around to face him. She hadn't thought he'd come after her.

'I need to go home.' Her teeth were chattering.

'I'll take you, then.'

She shook her head. 'You go back inside. I can get a taxi.'

'You'll be lucky. No, my girl, you're coming with me.'

'I'd prefer to be on my own.'

But he took her elbow and steered her along the street, towards his motorcycle. 'Something has upset you. Did someone say something?'

'No, I was thinking of my friend – and my fiancé.'

'You're engaged?' He removed his cap and ran a hand through his hair. 'My bad luck. I should have guessed someone as beautiful as you would be taken. So where is he?'

'I'd rather not talk about it.'

He touched his fingers to his cap. 'I promise I won't tell anyone else. Scout's honour.'

How could this man understand? He strode about going to nightclubs, laughing with his friends as if hell itself wasn't banging on the door. He had his family, his friends, his home. How could he know what it felt like to have lost everything? That even the memory of the man she'd promised to love for ever was slipping away, and that it felt wrong to be laughing and dancing.

'Irena?'

Suddenly, without knowing how, she was in his arms and sobbing against his chest.

Two days later, she was in the library immersed in a book when Richard threw open the door.

'Smith said I'd find you in here. The squadron has been stood down for the day and a gang of us are going for a picnic and we – I – would like you to come too.'

'I don't wish to intrude,' she said stiffly, embarrassed that he'd witnessed her falling apart the other night. When she'd stopped crying, she'd told him about Piotr and Magdalena. He'd listened without saying anything, then taken her home, calling for Mrs Smith to make her a hot-water bottle and help her up to bed.

'Eleanor and Lucy are coming too. They've packed a picnic.'

Undecided, Irena chewed her lip. She'd liked Lucy and Eleanor, but it didn't feel right to spend time with Richard, particularly as he'd made it clear he was attracted to her. Then again, judging by the number of women vying for his attention, it appeared that he flirted with every woman he came across.

'Come on – you owe me after dragging me away from the club. Martha had already agreed I could see her home.'

'Marion,' she corrected. 'And I didn't ask you to come after me . . .' She tailed off when she saw he was grinning. It couldn't hurt. They'd be going their separate ways soon enough. 'Very well,' she said. 'I'd love to.'

They set off in two cars, Irena with Richard and Eleanor in one, while Lucy was in the other with Julian and Scotty. Despite the low cloud, it was warm with only a slight, pleasant breeze.

After a while, they pulled up beside a field. 'This is it,' Richard said. 'There's a river about a mile from here. It's sheltered enough to swim in.'

'I haven't a bathing costume,' Irena protested.

Richard raised an eyebrow. 'We don't tend to bother with costumes, at least the lads don't. The girls swim in their underwear.'

'Don't tease, Richard,' Eleanor said, tucking her arm through Irena's elbow. 'You can have mine, darling girl. I don't mind swimming in my underwear. I've known these boys for ever.'

That afternoon was one of the happiest Irena had had since the war started. They swam, the women squealing as they submerged themselves in the cold water, while the men pretended an immunity to the freezing water that fooled no one. Richard's body was more muscled than his lean frame in uniform had led her to expect. To her mortification, he caught her staring at him and grinned. She looked away, furious with herself for even noticing.

When they'd finished swimming, they dried themselves in the sun and sipped champagne. There was no talk of war. Instead, the conversation ranged from films they'd seen, to books they'd read and concerts they'd attended. More than once she looked up to find Richard's eyes on her and was dismayed by the jolt of pleasure it gave her. She tried to bring Piotr's face into focus but his image slipped from her mind like a fish.

She lay on her back and closed her eyes and, instead, let herself imagine that she was back in Poland, in the park behind the university, with her friends as their lazy chatter, not dissimilar to this, ebbed and flowed around her.

She sensed someone sit down next to her and opened her eyes. Water dripped from Richard's wet hair and followed the curve of his cheekbones, down to his mouth. He really was a remarkably beautiful man.

'Penny for them?' he said, throwing himself back on the blanket.

She knew she was blushing. 'I was just thinking that it wasn't too long ago that I was doing something similar in Poland. It feels as if it happened to a different person.'

He propped himself up on his elbow. 'The war changes us all. I doubt if any of us will be the same when this is over. We're all going to have to find a way to live with our demons.'

So he had demons too.

'Why didn't Bill come with us today?' she asked, remembering the sandy-haired pilot at the club.

'Poor bugger bought it yesterday. Somewhere over France. He wasn't the only one. We lost three planes.'

She sucked in a breath. 'Oh no! I'm so sorry. I liked him.'

Anger flashed behind his eyes. 'There were fifteen of us in the club to begin with. There are only five of us left.' Suddenly he smiled. 'That's why we have to make the most of the time we have.' He pulled her to her feet. 'Come on, I'll race you in.'

Later, after everyone had been dropped off, Richard suggested that they go to see a film. Irena couldn't think of a reason to refuse and besides, there was something reassuring, almost comfortable, about being with him. She was beginning to suspect that behind the languid, couldn't-care-less attitude, was a man who cared deeply.

The cinema was packed and, as it had been in the club, it was difficult to see clearly through the thick cigarette smoke. She and Richard found two seats together near the front.

The Pathé newsreel started up. Planes filled the screen and everyone hushed as the cheerful voice of the narrator filled the cinema. 'A day that will go down in British history. Here are our boys showing the Hun what we can do.' The camera focused on a Spitfire attacking a yellow-nosed Messerschmitt and moments later the enemy aircraft went down in a plume of smoke. 'Time and time again our boys went back to the fray, returning to base only to refuel and rearm before heading back into battle. The Hun didn't know what he was letting himself in for.'

Irena felt Richard stiffen next to her. When she glanced at him he was staring straight ahead. The newsreel flickered on, showing dog fights as the narrator continued to boast about what they were calling the Battle of Britain. When the film finished, a couple behind them stood and, looking at Richard, started clapping slowly. Soon the rest of the audience were on their feet and clapping too. One by one several men in RAF uniform stood and the woman behind them tapped Richard on his shoulder. 'Stand up, lad. People want to see you.'

Reluctantly, Richard got to his feet. The applause intensified and several men whistled and cheered. Richard responded with a mock salute. As the feature film started, and everyone sat down again, Richard grabbed Irena's hand. 'Let's get out of here.'

She didn't try to argue. Instead, she followed him out of the auditorium and into the dark street. She said nothing as she walked alongside him, struggling to keep up with his long strides.

Eventually he stopped at a bridge crossing the River Thames.

He stared out over the water, seemingly preoccupied with his thoughts. She waited for him to speak.

'It's all hokum,' Richard said finally. 'The whole lot of it.'

'You should be proud.'

'Proud? Yes, we're proud, but that's not the whole story.' He reached into his pocket, brought out a pack of cigarettes and offered her one. When she shook her head he took one out and tapped it on the back of his hand. 'What they don't tell the public is that the RAF lost over a thousand planes over that period. They say "planes" not "pilots" because they don't want Joe Public to remember it's men that are in the burnt-out wrecks. Over five hundred and forty of them bought it, if you're interested. It's not to say they don't care about the pilots, they do – but only because there aren't enough of us. The death of one experienced pilot is worth the loss of ten planes to them. They have to be replaced and quickly.' He lit his cigarette and drew smoke deep into his lungs. 'Some of the chaps they send to us only have a few hours' flying time and no battle experience whatsoever. There was one lad who joined the squadron two weeks ago. He was eighteen. You'd think to see him in his uniform that he'd been given a present. All shining and gleaming. He went out with us like that and he came back a shaking mess. Nobody said anything – that wouldn't do. The second time the lad went up I could tell he didn't want to go, but of course he had no choice. I kept him near me, but there was a dog fight and we got separated and he was shot down. We're supposed to fly in a V formation, that's what they teach us, but we know that's not the right way. Bloody Group thirteen were late to the party because their commander insisted that they couldn't take off unless they were in the right formation. Damn rules. Those chaps haven't a clue. We should do it the way the Poles do. Break away and go in close and fast.' He paused and looked out over the river. 'There are only three things a pilot has to know: keep the sun behind you, go in and get out fast and never fly in a straight line for more than thirty seconds.' He sucked in a breath and attempted a smile. 'Sorry, don't know what's got into me. I keep forgetting your brother is a pilot. It can't help my telling you this shit.'

She touched his shoulder. 'I know what it is like to be scared, so scared you think you will die from the fear. I also know that a person can't feel like that all the time. Eventually feeling scared to death becomes normal.' She placed her hands on the rail and followed his gaze out over the river. 'It's only the absence of fear that makes you truly realise that you've been frightened all the time. But there are worse things than feeling scared.' She bit her lip. 'Much worse things.'

He reached for her hand. 'Tell me what it was like. You can, you know.'

She returned the pressure of his fingers. 'One day, perhaps. But not yet. Come on, I'm working tonight. Let's go home.'

Chapter 28

Edinburgh, 1989

Back in Edinburgh, Sarah took a taxi straight to the hospital. Her parting from Matthew had been cool. She'd decided on the flight not to say anything to her mother about what she'd learned in London. There was no point in getting her all agitated and upset – at least not until she knew more. If Irena was still alive she was determined to find her – although she wasn't sure how. Then she'd tell Mum.

After leaving the Astley Ainslie, Sarah dropped her bag at her flat and set out towards the Old Town and the university. Although she should drop in at the office she wanted to chase up the Irena lead.

But how to find someone who could tell her something about the graduates, particularly the Polish ones? She headed down George IV Street, towards the Central Library. Her job as a copy editor often involved checking up on facts, so she was a well-known figure there.

After a few false starts she found a member of staff who was able to help.

'We hold a medical directory – it lists all the qualified doctors, their specialities and where they are working currently. I'm not sure how up to date it is but it could be a start?'

The book, it couldn't really be called a formal directory, contained the names of the doctors currently working in hospitals across Edinburgh. There were three with Polish-sounding surnames, one of whom worked at the City Hospital, the other two at the RIE. Next to their names was the date they had been entered onto the medical register. To Sarah's disappointment, most of the dates were after 1950.

She considered phoning the RIE's switchboard and asking to be put through to the doctors, but as the hospital was only a short distance from the library, and thinking she might learn more if she talked to them in person, she jotted down the names and, after thanking the librarian who had helped her, left the library and headed back towards Lauriston Place and the Royal Infirmary.

Seeing the hospital brought back sickening memories.

It had been four in the morning when she'd been called by the A & E nurses and told that her mother had been brought in by ambulance and was seriously ill. She'd thrown on her clothes, terrified that she wouldn't make it in time. When she'd got to the hospital, her mother had still been unconscious and the sight of her, in that hospital bed, her mouth pulled down at the side, had made her want to howl. She'd only been allowed a few minutes with Mum before they'd taken her up to the ward and she'd whispered to her that she loved her – words she'd never been able to say before or since and didn't even know if her mother had heard.

She took a deep breath and went inside.

The large Victorian hospital was as grand inside as it was out. In the wide, high-ceilinged entrance hall was a desk with a middle-aged woman in a blue overall standing behind it. Judging by her anxious smile and the pristine state of her uniform, she had to be new.

'Hello,' Sarah said. 'I wonder if you can help me.'

The woman, whose name badge identified her as Jane Kennedy, pointed to a sign on the counter, and grinned. *The WRVS welcomes you to the Royal Infirmary of Edinburgh. We are here to help you.* 'That's what we're here for. What can I do for you?'

'I believe you have a Dr Wilinski and a Dr Sobíeski on your staff?'

Jane pulled a buff-coloured A5 book towards her. 'If they are they'll be in the hospital directory. I haven't been here long so I don't know all the doctors' names yet. There're so many of them and they keep changing – at least the junior doctors do.' She flicked through the book, running her finger down a list of names. 'Oh, you're in luck. Found them. Which one do you want?'

'You couldn't put me through to Dr Sobíeski, by any chance?' Sarah replied, aware she couldn't say she didn't know.

'I don't think he'll be in his office. The doctors here are really busy. But I could put you through to his secretary, if you like. She'll be able to get hold of him for you.'

At that moment an older woman arrived at the desk. 'You can go for your tea-break now, Jane.'

'I was just going to put this lady through to Dr Sobíeski's office, Mrs Gray. I'll do it before I go, shall I?'

Mrs Gray snatched the receiver from Jane's hand. 'You can't just call the doctors – or their secretaries! We'd have people bothering them all the time if we did.' She turned to Sarah. 'I suggest you write to Dr Sobíeski, care of his secretary, and make an appointment.'

Jane gave Sarah a regretful smile and shrugged her shoulders. The two women turned away and started talking in low voices.

Shit. So near and yet so far. But she was damned if she was going to write any letters. And even more damned if she were going to wait weeks for a reply.

She noticed Jane had left the directory on the table. Sarah glanced around, slipped it under her arm and walked away. As soon as she was out of sight she rifled through the pages until she found Dr Sobíeski's name. It listed him under 'ward eighteen, surgical'. Dr Wilinski was listed under 'ward three, medical'.

When she returned to the desk the older woman was talking to a porter and, as casually as she could, Sarah replaced the booklet on the reception desk.

She took the lift to the third floor. To the left and almost immediately outside ward eighteen was a door with a nameplate: DR SOBÍESKI.

To her frustration there was no reply when she knocked. She tried the door but it was locked. Taking the stairs she went back down to the second floor and after getting lost several times, managed to find her way to the medical block and Dr Wilinski's office.

She knocked on the door and, without waiting for a reply, opened it. Two women were sitting at a table that ran the length of the room, bent over a pile of case notes. One was wearing a blouse and skirt, the other a white coat. They looked up in surprise.

'I'm sorry to interrupt,' Sarah said, 'but I'm looking for a Dr Wilinski.'

'I'm Jozefa Wilinski,' the woman in the white coat said, raising an enquiring eyebrow.

'Do you have a moment?'

'What is this about? Are you a relative?'

'No. I'm trying to find someone who could tell me about the Polish School of Medicine. I was hoping you might know or point me in the right direction.'

Dr Wilinski stretched her arms above her head and smiled. 'Good God! I thought my father and I were the only people left who gave a rat's arse about it.'

Sarah's breath came out in a whoosh. 'No. Let me assure you, I give a lot more than a rat's arse about it. Do you have a few minutes?'

Chapter 29

'This is my father, Dr Marian Wilinski.' Jozefa introduced Sarah to an elderly man, who immediately pushed himself out of his armchair by the fire. 'Father, this is the young woman I was telling you about – the one who is interested in the Polish Hospital.'

After talking to Sarah, Jozefa had arranged for her to meet her father, but not until today. In between visiting her mother, and hoping to appease her boss, Sarah had spent the last three days catching up on work.

'Forgive me, my dear, but these days it takes me longer than I care to admit to get to my feet. Old age with a hefty dash of arthritis, I'm afraid.'

His voice was still heavily accented. Although he stooped slightly he must have been tall as a young man as he still topped Sarah by several inches. He held out a gnarled hand with over-long fingernails. 'I'm pleased to meet you, Miss Davidson. My daughter has told me you're interested in the Paderewski Hospital.'

'Yes. Please, don't let me keep you standing.'

However, he waited until she was seated opposite him before he sank back in his chair. The room was filled with books and Sarah cocked her head to one side to read the spine of the one on the table next to her. The title was in Polish.

'Tea? Coffee?' Jozefa asked.

'Tea would be lovely.'

Dr Wilinski waited until his daughter had left the room. 'Jozefa tells me you're trying to find someone who may have been at the medical school in the Second World War. Is that correct?'

'Yes. Two women, actually. A Magdalena Drobnik and an Irena. I'm afraid I don't have Irena's last name. Apparently it sounded like crash.'

He smiled, his cheeks sinking a little in his already gaunt face. 'Kraszewska?'

'I don't know. Could be.'

'Irena Kraszewska.' He rolled the words around his mouth. 'The name sounds familiar. Yes, I believe she was one of the students.'

A tingle ran up Sarah's spine. 'Can you tell me anything about her?'

'What do you know about the Paderewski Hospital?'

'Very little. I gather there were medical students – refugees – from Poland who studied there.'

'Then you know more than most.' He looked pleased. 'After Poland was invaded many hundreds of Polish doctors and medical students ended up in Britain, particularly Scotland. I was one of them. I was in the Polish army – I escaped . . . ' He was silent for a few moments. 'Professor Jurasz was the driving force behind the hospital. He thought it was important that we continued our studies so he persuaded some influential Scottish professors to lend their support to a Polish medical school. We were given part of the Western General – a block that used to house the children's wards – to use as a Polish hospital. It was well equipped, thanks to financial aid from the Paderewski fund in New York. We were also given access to the teaching at the Royal Infirmary.'

'Was it only Polish troops that studied there? What about women?'

'You're quite right. It wasn't just troops. Although most of the doctors and medical students were in the army, Polish civilians who'd been medical students were welcome too. It opened in March nineteen forty-one and there were two women in the first year and, if I'm remembering correctly, Irena was one of them.'

'Do you remember the other woman's name?'

He shook his head. 'No, but I don't think it was Magdalena.'

Jozefa came in with a tray and set it down on the coffee table. 'You should keep the rug on your knees, Father,' she scolded, reaching down for the blanket that had fallen to the floor and replacing it across her father's lap.

'Never think we'd survived a war,' Dr Wilinski muttered, but behind his daughter's back, he winked. 'Do you know there were thousands of us – Poles, I mean – fighting in Britain during the war?' he continued.

'Now, Papa, don't start—' Jozefa began but her father cut her off.

'If Sarah wants to find out about two Polish women I'm sure she'll be interested in our history.' He looked to Sarah and when she nodded encouragingly, he continued. 'Our boys flew with the RAF during the Battle of Britain. They had more kills than any squadron. They were fearless. Their fellow pilots knew that, of course . . . ' He took a noisy gulp of tea. 'They were also paratroopers, commandos, in the Royal Navy – everywhere. They even took Monte Cassino for the British.' He paused. 'No, not for the British, for Poland. Because that's what we all wanted – an end to the Nazi regime and to return to our country. We couldn't fight in Poland, although many of us did with the resistance, so we fought alongside the British in order that Poland could be free. Of course, we didn't know that the British would betray us again by signing over Poland to the Russians.' He leaned forward. 'Do you know not a single Pole was invited to take part in the victory parade in London in 'forty-six? Czechs marched, Chinese, Indians – every nationality that fought alongside Britain except us. All because the British government didn't want to offend Stalin. After all we'd done.'

'It wasn't as simple as that, Papa,' his daughter remonstrated gently. 'The British government has apologised, and there is that lovely memorial to the Polish Air Force near Northolt.'

'Too little, too late.' He shook his head as if to chase the images away. 'But you're right, my dear, there is no point in raking up old grievances, especially as Poland is free again. Took fifty years, but she's free.'

'I'm not sure that's what Sarah has come to learn,' his daughter said. 'Why don't I leave you two to talk?'

He waited until they were alone again, before he continued. 'I'm sorry. Your being here does rather bring it all back. Let's return to what you want to know. I'm pretty certain about Irena Kraszewska, although the name Magdalena doesn't ring a bell. Doesn't mean to say she wasn't there – my memory for names isn't as good as it once was.' He pushed the blanket aside and heaved himself out of the chair again. 'But I do have something that might help. I've been collecting as much as I can from those days. One of my colleagues is writing an account of the Polish Hospital and he's asked for my help in compiling memorabilia from that time. I think I have a book in my study upstairs that lists all the graduates. If you'd excuse me for a few minutes?'

While she waited for him to return, Sarah studied the books on the shelf. Apart from the medical books and several in Polish, they were mostly non-fiction – history and autobiographies. She also discovered a couple of contemporary romances she was pretty sure didn't belong to the older Dr Wilinski. She liked the thought that the erudite woman who'd invited her here might be a secret reader of romances.

She'd finished her tea by the time he returned. 'It was under a pile of papers in a corner,' he said. 'Took me a bit of time to find it. Knew it was there, though.' He laid an ordinary hardback notebook on the table, changed his glasses and started flicking through it. 'Ah, yes,' he said. 'Here she is. Irena Kraszewska – graduated in nineteen forty-three.' Sarah held her breath as he continued flicking. 'No, no mention of a Magdalena.' He turned to Sarah. 'I remember Irena quite well. She was a good student, excellent actually. Kept herself to herself. All she really wanted to do was work.'

'Do you know where she went – what she did when she graduated?'

He shook his head. 'She left pretty soon after she qualified. Many of our students stayed and worked as doctors here or in other parts of Britain, but Irena,' he shrugged again, 'she simply disappeared.'

Sarah chewed the inside of her lip unable to think of anything else she could ask that might help. She'd been so sure that he'd be able to tell her more about Magdalena or Irena, but it seemed she was no closer to finding either.

Chapter 30

Scotland, 1941

Irena had slept fitfully on the train, wakening every time it pulled into a station with a screech of metal on metal. Then there would be the bangs and crashes as porters loaded supplies on board as well as the muted chatter of passengers as they boarded the train.

When she joined Richard in the dining car for breakfast the next morning, they were, he said, still in England.

'We're not far out of Carlisle,' he told her as a waitress poured their coffee.

'Where is Carlisle?' she asked.

'Just about on the border between Scotland and England.'

'Isn't that close to where Aleksy is?'

'Fairly. Dumfries is about an hour away. By car, that is.'

'There might be a bus.'

'Possibly. I couldn't say for sure.'

'I would like to get off at Carlisle,' Irena said. She couldn't bear to be so close to her brother and not see him.

Richard looked at Irena, raised an eyebrow, then smiled broadly. 'Go and get your stuff together. Lord knows how we'll get to Edinburgh but we'll worry about that later.'

Irena could have kissed him for not trying to argue with her.

He beckoned to the train conductor. 'When will we reach Carlisle?'

'Who can say, sir. Perhaps in fifteen minutes, perhaps an hour.'

It was, in fact, half an hour before the train pulled into the station. It had only taken Irena a few minutes to pack her case and she was waiting for Richard outside her compartment when he came for her.

'The conductor tells me we will probably have to take another train to Dumfries and then find a taxi to take us to the airfield. You do know your brother might be on a sortie when we get there?'

'Then I will wait. You mustn't feel you have to wait with me. I am sure you would rather go on to Edinburgh and see your mother. I don't want you to waste your leave on me.'

'I couldn't possibly abandon you to your own devices. Anyway, Mother will probably be at work,' Richard said. 'That's where she spends most of her time.'

'But she will want to see you, her only son?'

'Of course. But my mother has always spent most of her time at the hospital. She loves what she does. I think you and she will get along famously.' The admiration in his eyes made her heart catch.

She wished he wouldn't keep looking at her like that.

They discovered that the next train bound for Dumfries wasn't scheduled for several hours and even then the station guard couldn't promise them that it would arrive or depart then. 'Priority is given to the troop trains, miss.' He turned to Richard. 'You'll understand that, sir, being in the RAF yourself. And could I just say, sir, that we are all so grateful to you chaps. If it wasn't for your lot we could all be speaking German by now.'

When Richard slid her a look and raised an eyebrow, she knew he was thinking of the conversation they'd had that night on the bridge. 'Is there a car that can take us? Or that I can hire?'

The train guard tipped his hat back on his head and rubbed his chin. 'The station master has one. He might be persuaded to let you have it for a couple of hours. We like to do what we can for our RAF boys.'

In the end, the station master agreed that they could take his car on condition they brought it back before he was due to go off duty at five. There was a train departing for Edinburgh mid afternoon and after a brief discussion Irena and Richard decided that they would return in time to get that train – if it was running.

'Your brother is unlikely to have much time off. If he's not in the air, he'll be on standby. You do appreciate that?' Richard said.

'If I can get five minutes with him, it will make me happy. Even just to see him. It's been more than a year ...'

'If he's out on a shout, then we'll wait for him,' Richard said. 'One way or another you are going to see him.'

Irena watched as there was an exchange of notes between Richard and the station master. It seemed that the station master wasn't so patriotic that he would let them have the car for nothing.

'I will pay you back,' Irena promised as they set off down the narrow road in what she assumed was the right direction. All the road signs had been removed.

'Certainly not,' Richard replied. 'I'm not exactly short of a bob or two.'

'Nevertheless, I will. As soon as I can.'

Richard smiled and shook his head but said nothing.

'You are sure we are going the right way?'

He raised an eyebrow. 'Don't you think a pilot has to know where he is going? I'm just following the sun.'

They passed through Dumfries and out back into the country. Soon she'd be seeing Aleksy again, and although she'd longed for this moment, she dreaded having to tell him about Magdalena. As if Richard sensed what she was thinking, he reached for her hand and squeezed it.

'I can see the control tower of the airbase,' he said, pointing to a grey stone building in the distance. 'We're not far now.'

They were stopped at the perimeter fence while Richard showed his papers to the soldier on duty at the barrier.

The soldier looked her up and down. 'Visitors are not allowed on the base, sir.'

Irena's heart sank.

'This lady is with me. Her brother, Pilot Officer Kraszewski, is one of the pilots here.'

'In that case, sir, and as long as you will sign her in, you may proceed.'

There were dome-shaped huts spread across the camp. Outside them, men in flying suits sat in armchairs, smoking pipes and reading newspapers. To their left a number of planes, around thirty, Irena guessed, sat on the tarmac. Men in khaki boiler suits scurried around and over them like ants.

'The engineers. Checking the planes,' Richard explained.

He stopped the car in front of a group of men and asked for the Polish unit. A sergeant pointed towards the rear of the camp. 'That's their Nissan hut over there, sir. They should be hanging around dispersal.'

Richard started the car and they bumped their way along the last few yards until they came to a halt in front of a Nissan hut flying the Polish flag.

The sight made Irena want to cry. Here, at last, was proof that Poland was not completely beaten.

And then she saw him. He was walking towards them wearing a sheepskin-trimmed leather jacket over his uniform and carrying an oxygen mask in one hand.

'Aleksy!' She leaped out of the car before Richard had a chance to bring it to a complete stop.

'Aleksy!' she called again.

Her brother turned around and for a long moment they just stared at one another. Then she was running towards him, stumbling in her haste to reach him.

He dropped the mask and stepped towards her. 'Irena!'

She was in his arms and he was whirling her around. She hadn't known it was possible to laugh and cry at the same time.

'Dearest sister!' he said in Polish. 'I was so worried. I didn't know what had happened to you. The stories we hear . . . '

'I am here! And I have found you.'

Aleksy placed her on the ground and gripped her shoulders. 'Let me look at you.' He studied her for a moment. 'I can't believe it! My darling Renia. Here. How did you get out? How is Tata? And Magdalena? Are they with you?' He looked over her shoulder as if expecting them to materialise.

Then he noticed Richard, who had kept his distance, turning his back slightly to give them some privacy. 'Hello,' he said, reverting to English and holding out his hand. 'A fellow pilot, I see.'

'Oh, Aleksy, this is Flight Commander Richard Maxwell. His family have been so good to me. He's taking me to stay with his mother. She's arranged a place for me at the University of Edinburgh to continue my medical studies.'

The two men shook hands.

'You chaps are doing a terrific job,' Richard said. 'I'm glad I finally have a chance to say so.'

'We try,' Aleksy responded with a smile of his own. 'Thank you for taking care of my sister.'

There was an awkward silence for a moment. 'I'll just go and see the boys,' Richard said. 'There's bound to be someone I know here.' He glanced at his watch. 'We only have an hour or so if we're to make our train.'

'I'll be here,' Irena replied. Only an hour to spend with her brother. In that case she had to make the most of it. She shrank inside knowing she had to tell him about Magdalena.

Aleksy took her by the arm and led her away from the group of men who had studiously returned to whatever they were doing. 'How is Magdalena?' Aleksy asked. 'Have you seen her? Did she come with you? Is she all right? I've been so worried about her. I wrote her many times but she never replied.'

'Aleksy ... can we find somewhere private ...'

He stared at her, the light leaving his eyes. 'Just tell me.'

'I have bad news, I'm afraid.' She hesitated but there was no way to soften the blow. 'Aleksy, Magdalena is dead.'

The colour drained from his face. 'She can't be.'

'Oh, Aleksy, I'm so sorry. I know how much you loved her. The Germans took their house from them and gave it to a family. I think Magdalena and her mother were trying to go to Colonel Łaski. They were taken by the Russians and put in a camp.'

When Aleksy continued to stare at her without saying anything, she continued. 'She wrote to me. Her mother had died and I think she knew she didn't have long either.' She took the note from her bag and held it out. 'This was enclosed with my letter. It's for you.'

Aleksy made no move to take it from her. 'I trusted you to look after her,' he said dully.

Although he was only echoing what she'd thought so often, she recoiled from the censure in his voice. 'I tried. But none of us even guessed what would happen. You can't have any idea what it was like, what it is like, in Poland now.'

'I shouldn't have left. I should have joined the resistance. I would have saved her.'

'You did what you had to do, Aleksy.' She was crying now. 'We all did what we had to do.'

'I need some time,' he muttered and before she could reply, he walked away from her.

'Give him a few moments.' She hadn't been aware that Richard had returned. He passed her his handkerchief and she blew her nose.

'I should be with him. Make him understand.'

'Make him understand what? That while he's been here knocking the hell out of the Jerries the woman he loves was starving to death? How can anyone make sense of that?'

She drew a shuddering breath and tried to steady her voice. 'Aleksy's right. I should have made them leave.'

Richard took her by the shoulders and turned her to face him. 'You can't blame yourself. If this war is anyone's fault it's the Germans.' He lifted his hand from her shoulder and rubbed his thumb across her cheek. 'Come on, dry your tears. What's happened to the brave, resolute young lady I knew in London?'

She blew her nose and handed him back his handkerchief. 'I'm not brave.' She sniffed. If he knew what she'd done, or more correctly, hadn't done, he wouldn't say that.

Aleksy was coming back. 'If you need me I'll be in the officers' mess,' Richard said and with a final squeeze of her shoulder, walked away.

'I'm sorry, Renia,' Aleksy said, his expression remote, his brown eyes empty. 'I shouldn't have said those things. It was the shock.'

He folded the note and placed it in his top pocket. 'You haven't told me about our father.' His lips twisted. 'Is he dead too?'

'No, Aleksy. Tata is still alive. Or at least he was the last time I saw him, but the war has taken its toll on him too.'

She told him about their father's arrest and her move to Rozwadow, about going into the ghetto and the typhoid scam, but she left out the bit about the Oberführer Bilsen's interest in her. There were some things that her brother didn't need to know.

'I wish you hadn't risked your life like that,' Aleksy said when she'd finished. An image of the woman trying to hand her the child flashed into her head and she shivered. For a second, she was tempted to tell him about the Jewish woman and her child. She longed to lay down her burden – to admit what she'd done. But would Aleksy understand? Would anyone who hadn't been in Poland then understand? She didn't know if she understood herself.

'You risk your life every time you go up in a plane. Everyone in Poland risks their life every day. But I ran away.' Her voice cracked. 'There are so many people left behind and we don't know what will happen to them.'

He pulled her to him and hugged her fiercely. 'What could you have done if you'd stayed? I might have lost you too.' Aleksy held her for a moment longer before releasing her. 'Couldn't you have persuaded Tata to come with you? From what you have told me it is only a matter of time before he is arrested again.'

Maybe she should have tried harder to make Tata leave, but she couldn't bear it if Aleksy thought she'd run away without caring what happened to their father. 'I begged him to come with me. But you know how stubborn Tata can be.'

Aleksy slung an arm around her shoulder and hugged her. 'At least you are out of danger.'

'Yes,' Irena said heavily. *She* was out of danger.

Too soon it was time to leave for their station. Aleksy walked with them to their borrowed vehicle.

'Will you come and see me in Edinburgh?' she asked. 'When you get leave?'

'Of course.'

Richard scribbled something on a piece of paper he'd torn from a small notebook. 'This is my parents' address in Edinburgh and the phone number. You'd be most welcome to stay.'

'Thank you.' Aleksy shoved it in his pocket.

The sound of a phone ringing came from the hut close to where the other pilots were gathered.

'That's a scramble,' Richard said.

'Scramble?'

'It means Aleksy's squadron has to get airborne.'

'No! Tell them you can't fly today, Aleksy.'

A tired smile crossed her brother's face. 'If ever I needed to fly, it's today.' He held Irena for a few moments before kissing her on the cheek. 'Stay safe, Renia.' He turned to Richard. 'Look after her.' And then he was running again, stopping only to pick his Mae West from a chair before clambering into the back of a jeep. As it sped away, Irena wondered if she'd ever see him again.

Richard saluted the retreating jeep. 'As if she were china, son,' he murmured, looking at Irena. 'As if she were china.'

Chapter 31

A chauffeur-driven car was waiting for them outside the station when they reached Edinburgh. The rain was falling steadily, combining with the smoke from the chimneys to create a heavy smog.

'Good evening, sir,' the driver said to Richard.

'Evening, Crawford. This is Miss Kraszewska.'

Irena held out her hand. There was an awkward moment where Crawford looked at Richard before stretching out his hand and giving her fingers the briefest of squeezes – almost as if he couldn't bear to touch her.

'You've confused Crawford,' Richard whispered as the man put their luggage in the boot.

'Why?'

'He doesn't expect to shake hands with my guests. He's old school.'

None of it made sense to Irena.

'What old school?'

Richard threw back his head and laughed. 'It's an expression. I'll fill you in later.' He slid her a glance. 'That means I'll explain.'

Although she was almost fluent in English, the expressions and idioms people used still bewildered her sometimes. Of course, they had nonsensical ones in Poland, too, but those she could follow. It was at times like this, she felt most dislocated.

Despite the kindness the British people had shown to her, she doubted she would ever feel at home in this country.

They drove through cobbled streets before turning into a large square surrounded by elegant houses. They'd barely stepped out of the car before a woman in a dark suit ran down the steps to meet them.

'Darling! It's so lovely to have you home again.' She lifted her face to receive Richard's kiss before turning to Irena. 'You must be Irena! Are you exhausted? Come inside out of the rain.'

Another woman, pin thin and with a worried, time-wrinkled face, met them at the top of the steps. When she saw Richard her face broke into a smile.

Richard picked her off her feet and hugged her. 'Hannah! You're even more beautiful than the last time I saw you.'

The older woman blushed. When Richard put her back on her feet she swiped him on the arm. 'Away with you and your nonsense. Oh but, your lordship, it's good to have you home.' She stood back and surveyed Irena with a frown. 'I don't know what my sister has been feeding you in London, lass, but it looks to me as if you're in need of fattening up. I'll get back to the kitchen and get something sorted for you. Dinner won't be until seven.'

As soon as Hannah scurried off and Crawford had relieved them of their coats, Lady Glendale led them into a large, high-ceilinged room where a fire was blazing in an elegant marble fireplace.

'Take a seat by the fire, Irena,' Richard's mother said quietly. In the light of the room Irena was able to see her better. She was older than she had appeared out on the street, but she was beautiful in a way Irena suspected would never fade. Her honey-blond hair was swept up in an elegant chignon, but where Richard's eyes were blue, hers were a deep chocolate brown.

'As soon as you have warmed up, I'll show you to your room so you can freshen up. Hannah will bring you a tray,' Lady Glendale said to Irena.

'Freshen up?'

'Mother means a wash or a bath and change,' Richard explained.

'Thank you. And thank you for being so kind, Lady Glendale.'

'I think it is more appropriate if you call me Dr Maxwell if we are going to be work colleagues.'

'How have you managed to get it all arranged so quickly?' Irena had imagined it would take weeks.

'Mother never wastes time when she has something that needs doing,' Richard said, dropping a kiss on the top of his mother's head.

'It wasn't very difficult,' she replied. 'There are several Polish medical students here already. All of us at the university think we should do what we can for those of you who managed to get away. We have decided that you must have your lectures with the Scottish students at the university, but you are to have your clinical training at the Polish Hospital. It's part of the Western General, which is being used as a military hospital.' She slid a mischievous smile at Irena. 'Don't worry, we'll find you plenty to do.' Dr Maxwell stood. 'Now I'm afraid you are going to have to indulge me for a few minutes while I find out what my son has been up to.'

'Perhaps I could go to my room now and have a wash before dinner?' Irena said. She felt awkward intruding on the family's reunion.

'Of course. Richard, would you take Irena up to the green room? I'm afraid all the maids have gone off to do war work of one kind or another. It's only Crawford and Hannah left.' She gave Irena another smile. 'Although with Richard and his father away, there's only me rattling around. Speaking of which, how is your father, Richard?'

Richard stood and held the door open. 'He's well. I'll take Irena to her room and then I'm all yours, Mother.'

Irena luxuriated in a long hot bath, until she'd washed away every last speck of grime and dust. When she returned to her bedroom, there was a tray of tea and scones on her bedside table. Nibbling a scone, she brushed her hair before tying it into a knot. She peered at her face in the mirror, grimacing at the reflection staring back at her. There were still dark circles under her eyes and lines around her mouth she was sure hadn't been there a few months ago. Although she'd put on a little weight while she was in London, she was still thinner than she could remember ever being. But then wasn't that fashionable these days?

Why was she worrying about her appearance anyway? What could it possibly matter? Nevertheless, rightly or wrongly, she longed for a tube of lipstick to replace the one she'd finished, or some foundation – anything to put some colour into her too-pale complexion.

As she made her way back downstairs, just before seven, a gong sounded and Richard and his mother, their arms linked, walked into the hall. Richard had shaved and changed out of his uniform into a dark suit and white shirt and bowtie. His mother was wearing a short evening dress. They looked up at her, but if they noticed she was wearing the same dress as earlier, they didn't comment.

'Come along, my dear,' Dr Maxwell said. 'I'm afraid you missed the glass of sherry we always have before dinner, but I'm sure Crawford will have unearthed some wine to have with dinner.'

They sat at a long, polished mahogany table set with fine

china and crystal. Crawford came around to her left and poured her a glass of wine, so red it seemed to glow. Irena took a sip and as the alcohol hit her stomach, she felt herself relax. Dr Maxwell waited until they had been served with a thick vegetable soup before she spoke.

'I understand you were working in a hospital in Poland during the first months of occupation. That must have been a terrible experience.'

Richard raised his glass to his mother. 'Mother has some idea what it must have been like for you. She served near the front line in the last war, you know.'

For a moment Irena glimpsed a profound sadness behind Dr Maxwell's brown eyes, then Richard's mother blinked and it was gone.

'I believe it is so much worse what we do to one another now,' Dr Maxwell continued. 'At least in the last war – who would ever have thought we'd see two? – we didn't have the weapons we do now. I see some of the aftermath in the Western General. I do a round there once a week, Irena, as well as work at the Royal Infirmary.'

'Mother ran a small private hospital for years. She was one of the first women in Scotland to qualify as a surgeon after the war so they are pleased to have someone with her experience at the military hospital.'

'I still have the hospital, Richard, although I tend to leave it in the hands of my very capable colleagues now that there's a war on. Unfortunately, we need surgeons more than ever. In which field do you hope to specialise in, Irena?'

'Paediatrics.' Then before she could help herself she was telling them about the children in the ghetto and how so many had died from lack of food or safe water. Richard and Dr Maxwell listened in silence.

'Oh, my dear, how awful. Did you tell any of this to my husband? He works for the War Office. I think he'd like to know.'

Richard was watching Irena closely, admiration and sympathy in his blue eyes. She swallowed the lump in her throat. She didn't want – or deserve – either.

'Most of it. Not everything. You get so used to keeping quiet about everything. It had to be secret.'

And she should have remembered that. What had she done? If word ever got back to the Nazis about the help Henryk and Stanislaw were giving in the ghetto they'd be arrested and then their typhus scam would also have to stop. How could she have been so stupid? She reached out a hand. 'Please don't tell him. I mean, of course he should know what the Nazis are doing to us and particularly to the Jews. Someone needs to do something to help. But ... ' She tailed off. Of course she couldn't expect them not to disclose where they had got their information. And of course they would never do anything to put people in danger. At least not knowingly.

Richard had come to stand behind her. He rested a hand on her shoulder for a moment. 'You can trust us not to give your chums away.' He sat back down, his mouth set in a grim line. 'None of us in the RAF like it that we're not bombing that lunatic Hitler to smithereens. But the men in the war cabinet are so bloody cautious. Sometimes I wonder if they are ever going to let us fight this war they way we should.'

'Richard!' Dr Maxwell interrupted. 'We have to trust that Churchill and people like your father know what they are doing.'

'In the same way the British government knew what they were doing when they refused to accept your lot in the last war? They've changed their minds since then. It only took them twenty years to do so.'

'What do you mean?' Irena asked.

Richard waited until Crawford had cleared their soup plates and placed some fish in front of them before he answered.

'Mother was with a unit of women who called themselves the Scottish Women's Hospital. They were led by a Scottish doctor called Elsie Inglis – she's dead now.' He glanced at his mother, all traces of his earlier anger appearing to have disappeared. 'But it's your story, Mother. I think you should tell it.'

'It all seems a little tame now compared to what you have been through, Irena,' Dr Maxwell said quietly. 'When the last war broke out, Dr Inglis gathered several women together: doctors, nurses, orderlies, chauffeurs – everybody and everything that was needed to set up a field hospital. However, when she offered their services to the British government they were less than impressed. In fact, they rejected her offer outright.' She took a sip of her wine. 'But Dr Inglis was the sort of woman who wouldn't take no for an answer. She went to the Serbian and French governments and offered to help them instead. Naturally, they were only too delighted to accept.'

'Mother went out with one of the first units. To Serbia, if I remember correctly?'

'Yes. Richard's Aunt Dorothea – my husband's sister – was there too. In the beginning she was an orderly in a unit in France. Later she came to Serbia as a chauffeur.' The colour drained from her face and she raised her hand to her forehead.

'What is it, Mother? One of your headaches?'

Dr Maxwell nodded.

Richard was instantly at his mother's elbow with a glass of water. 'I shouldn't have brought up the last war,' he said to Irena as Dr Maxwell took a sip. 'Mother doesn't like to talk about it.'

Irena could understand only too well. There were many things she could never speak about.

'When are you leaving tomorrow, Richard?' Dr Maxwell asked.

'I'm on the sleeper, so I'll be here when you get home from the hospital.'

'You have to go back so soon?' Irena said. 'I thought you were on leave?'

'I am. Forty-eight hours.'

'Yet you took the time to come with me to Dumfries?'

'It was my pleasure.'

Once more she was forced to revise her opinion of him. Under his flippant exterior he was a decent man. When Richard's mouth twitched and he raised an eyebrow, she realised she'd been staring at him.

'Could I fetch you something for your headache? A cold compress – an aspirin perhaps?' she said to Dr Maxwell, flustered.

'Would you mind dear? There are pain killers on my dressing table. My room is the first one on the left at the top of the stairs. I'd ask Crawford or Hannah, but they're kept so busy and neither manage the stairs as well as they used to.'

'Of course.'

Irena found Dr Maxwell's bedroom easily enough and as she'd said there was a bottle of aspirin on her dressing table. As she reached over to pick them up she noticed a photograph lying face down and instinctively picked it up to set it upright.

It was of Richard's mother when she was younger, standing next to a dark-haired man Irena didn't recognise but who was clearly not Lord Glendale. There were mountains in the background so it could be Scotland, but she didn't think so. Isabel's skirt was long, falling to just above her ankles, and she was wearing a white blouse, buttoned up to the neck. There was something familiar about the man next to her. He wasn't in uniform, although what he was wearing could have been military issue: a plain shirt without an insignia and a leather jacket. But it was the way they were standing that made Irena wonder. Although they weren't touching and both were staring into the camera and smiling, they were leaning into each other in a way that strangers wouldn't.

Was the man a lover from a time before Isabel had married Lord Glendale? If so, it was odd that she kept the photograph in her bedroom.

It was none of her business and she was keeping Dr Maxwell waiting. She placed the picture back the way she'd found it, hurried back downstairs, and handed the bottle of pills to Richard's mother.

'Thank you.' Dr Maxwell tipped a tablet into her hand and swallowed the aspirin with a sip of water.

'Could I come with you – to the hospital, I mean?' Irena asked. Now she was here she was keen to get back to seeing patients.

'Not tomorrow. Perhaps the next day. You should rest a little. Once we have you on the wards, you'll be worked hard, I promise.' She rubbed her temples. 'Would you excuse me? I'd think I should lie down for a while.'

After Dr Maxwell had left, Richard seemed to change again. He tapped his foot on the floor as if desperate to be away from her company. No doubt he had plans for that evening.

'I should go to bed too,' Irena said.

'I'm going to see if I can find some chums of mine down at the club. Won't you join me?'

'No, thank you. But you go.'

Richard seemed disappointed. 'If you're sure? It doesn't seem polite to leave you on your own on your first night in Edinburgh.'

'I am perfectly sure.'

The darkness in his eyes cleared. 'I'm hoping to meet a friend for tea tomorrow if she's free. Why don't you come along?'

He was only being polite. If this friend was another girlfriend she was unlikely to want Irena there.

'I can't imagine your friend will want to share you with a stranger. Especially if she only gets to see you for a short while every so often.'

'Oh, Kat won't mind. She's not my girlfriend, if that's what you're thinking. We've known each other all our lives and could never be anything but chums. She's training to be a nurse at the Royal. I'm certain the two of you will hit it off. You know, with both of you having medical backgrounds.'

Irena hid a smile. Men were simple creatures if they thought a shared interest meant two women would get along.

It seemed Scottish men weren't different to Polish men at all.

Chapter 32

'Katherine, may I introduce you to Irena Kraszewska, a medical student from Poland?' Richard said to the attractive, freckled-faced woman with thick, curly hair and a cheerful, open expression. They'd met in a crowded tea room in the Old Town, close to the Royal Infirmary.

'Irena, this is Katherine, the old friend I told you about.'

'Not so much of the old, Richard.'

She held out her hand. 'Pleased to meet you. Now, shall I order us some tea?'

Irena smiled. Did the British ever drink anything else? 'I'd prefer coffee.'

Richard summoned the waitress and gave the order.

'Irena is going to be working at the Polish medical school at the Western,' Richard explained. 'She's staying at Charlotte Square with Mother for the time being.'

'I'm a student nurse – otherwise known as a slave – at the Royal Infirmary,' Katherine said. 'It's the best hospital in Scotland. As least we think so, although the girls in Glasgow would beg to differ. They say we're too old-fashioned, but they're just jealous.' She chewed her lip. 'We *might* be a little traditional, but we like that. Most of the time.'

'We'll be having our lectures at the Royal,' Irena said when

Katherine paused for breath. 'We might come across one another there.'

While they drank their tea, Katherine made them laugh with her stories of life on the ward. After a while, Richard got to his feet.

'If you ladies would excuse me? I have somewhere I need to go.'

'A woman?' Katherine asked with a teasing glance. 'Anyone I know?'

He shook his head and tweaked her nose. 'A gentleman never says.'

Katherine turned back to Irena. 'He's incorrigible. It's bound to be a woman. He always has one in tow.'

Irena wasn't quite sure what to say to that. Richard's love life was no concern of hers.

'How do you know Richard's family?' Irena asked when they were alone.

'You mean, how can I, a lowly student nurse, move in aristocratic circles?' Katherine smiled, apparently not in the least bit offended by the question. The truth was it was exactly what Irena had been thinking. In Poland it was the same; they had their counts and countesses and they rarely mixed with the lower and middle classes.

'I suspect I wouldn't have been taken on by the Royal if Dr Maxwell hadn't put in a word for me. She and my mother have known each other since they were children, and I've known Richard since I was a baby. Mum – she's a midwife – used to meet Dr Maxwell in the park and Richard and I played while they talked. Well, not played exactly, more me following him around like a puppy, if I'm honest. I thought he was wonderful. Then we sort of lost touch for years until one day we bumped into each other at a club. He was with some of his chums from the RAF. We had quite a night.'

'Aleksy, my brother, is in the RAF too,' Irena said. A woman carrying a crying toddler pushed the door open with her shoulder and sank into a chair with a sigh of relief. 'He also managed to escape from Poland.'

'Did he really? Tell me more. It's all so thrilling. I can't wait until I can join the QAs so I can get in amongst it all.'

'The QAs?'

'The Queen Alexandra's Imperial Military Nursing Service – it's a bit of a mouthful so everyone calls them QAs for short. They're out with our forces right now. I hope to goodness the war doesn't end before I finish my training.'

When Irena kept quiet, Katherine covered her mouth with her hand.

'Oh, I'm sorry. That was stupid and thoughtless. You must be desperate for it to end. Me and my big mouth. I open it and all this stuff just seems to pour out. Mum says I'm like a leaky bucket.'

'You shouldn't wish to go to war. It's horrible and bloody and heartbreaking. The wounded and the dying are so young, and you don't have enough medicine, or supplies. Conditions are rarely like you're used to in hospital.'

'That's what Mum says.'

'And she's right.'

Katherine slid her a glance. 'Did you hate it all the time?'

Irena thought for a while. She hated what the war had done – was still doing – to those she loved. She'd been terrified of going behind the fence of the ghetto and she'd hated not being able to save more of the people, particularly the children inside it, but she'd been thrilled when those she'd treated had got better. And, at the beginning of the war, when Warsaw was under attack, being in the thick of life-and-death decisions at the hospital had exhilarated her. It didn't seem right, but looking back, that was how she'd felt.

She realised Katherine was waiting for an answer. She chose her words carefully. 'I hated it when there was nothing I could do for a patient and very often I was scared that I wouldn't know what to do, but mostly, if I'm honest, it was the most exciting time of my life. It's what we nurses and doctors train to do, isn't it?'

'I knew you'd understand! Perhaps you can help me persuade Mum that I should join the QAs then,' Katherine said. 'I'll be twenty-three by the time I finish my training and no longer a minor, but I've always done what Mum wants.'

In many ways Katherine seemed younger than her years. On the other hand, it could be because Irena felt so much older than her own twenty-three years.

'Tell me more about your brother,' Katherine said. 'If he's in the RAF does that mean he knows Richard?'

'They've never flown together, but they have met. It was Richard who found him for me. We lost touch when Germany invaded Poland.'

Katherine placed her cup back on its saucer. 'Richard might like the fast life but he's a good man at heart.'

Irena wondered if Katherine felt more than friendship for Richard. She hoped not, for the nurse's sake. Although she didn't know much about him, she strongly suspected Richard was unlikely to settle with one woman.

'Have you seen your brother?' Katherine continued. 'You must have been so delighted to discover he was safe.'

'It was a big relief. And yes, I've seen him. He's stationed in Dumfries. Richard came with me on the train and was kind enough to agree to get off at a place called Carlisle so we could go and see him. Aleksy and I only had a short while together, but I hope to visit him there again when I can, or perhaps he'll visit me in Edinburgh when he has leave.'

'When you go and see him, I could come with you. If it coincides with my day off, that is,' Katherine offered. 'It will be a day out.'

'I would like that.'

'Now that that's settled, shall we go shopping when we finish our tea? I'm in desperate need of some new nylons.'

Irena was in urgent need of more than nylons, but she still didn't have money. Until she did, darning and mending what she had would have to do. In the meantime, Katherine's cheerful, uncomplicated company was a balm to her bruised soul.

Chapter 33

Instead of waiting until the new term started, Irena resumed her studies by working as a dresser at the Polish Hospital. Work kept her from dwelling on what was happening in Poland and the weeks passed quickly. Scotland's summer was far colder, wetter and windier than Poland, but there were no air raids – in fact, there was very little evidence, apart from the rationing and blackouts, that a war was going on. Every day she perused the papers avidly and she listened to the BBC news whenever she could. Unbelievably Hitler had invaded Russia and his former ally was now on Britain's side.

Irena wasn't sure what to make of it; she remembered too well what the Russians had done to Poland and didn't trust them an inch. But, she consoled herself, with Russia on the side of the Allies, Hitler was bound to be defeated.

Sometimes when she was in bed, she'd trace the outline of Piotr's features in her mind, filling in the details of his eyes and the shape of his mouth like a painter colouring in a sketch. Yet even though she'd concentrate as hard as she could, she couldn't quite capture the essence of him. He was fading from her memory bit by bit and the harder she tried to hold on to his image, the more elusive it became.

In the evenings, when Dr Maxwell returned from work, they would sit by the fire and talk about medicine and, for those short hours, Irena was able to forget her loneliness, and her worry about Piotr.

She was in the drawing room, looking out over Charlotte Square and watching the people making the most of the evening sunshine, when Isabel – the doctor had long since insisted Irena call her by her first name – hurried in brandishing a telegram. Her eyes were shining and she had a broad smile on her face.

'Richard has a week's furlong. He should be here tomorrow evening. Isn't it wonderful?'

Irena felt a rush of unexpected pleasure. 'You must be so looking forward to seeing him.'

Isabel's face clouded. 'Unfortunately I won't be able to spend as much time with him as I'd like. I'm much too busy between my hospital and the infirmary to take more than a day or two's leave.' Then she brightened. 'At least I shall see him at dinner and some of the evenings. You will keep him company sometimes, won't you, my dear?'

'Me?'

'Yes. I know you have your work at the hospital, but you do have the evenings and some days free, don't you?'

It was true. There were so many Polish medical students in Edinburgh now, that there wasn't enough work for them all on the wards – even split between the hospitals. Nevertheless, Irena doubted that Richard would want to spend too much time with her instead of Katherine or one of his girlfriends and she told Dr Maxwell as much.

'Naturally, he'll be delighted to spend time with you. You're our guest. It would be remiss of him not to. You haven't had much fun since you've been here and it's time you relaxed a little. You're a young woman.'

Irena grimaced. 'I don't feel young.'

'I know you are mourning for everything you have lost,' Isabel said. 'And I know what that feels like.'

Irena left the window and sat down next to Isabel. 'You lost someone too?'

'I doubt there is anyone who didn't lose a brother, son, friend or lover in the last war.' The look of pain in her eyes made Irena think of the photograph she'd seen in her bedroom.

'Did you?' she ventured.

Isabel rose from her chair and went to stand next to the fire. She held out her hands to the flames, keeping her back to Irena. 'My brother Andrew was shot down. He was so young. He was a pilot too. As was my husband.'

'Is that how Lord Glendale lost his arm?'

Isabel turned back to Irena. 'Yes. It stopped him from flying – at least for the rest of the war. It didn't stop him flying for pleasure, though. He's always kept a plane of his own. He manages all right, despite having only one arm. I think he would have given anything to have been able to join our RAF boys when this war broke out, but even if it hadn't been for his injury, he was too old.' She tucked a lock of hair behind her ear. 'I think that's where Richard inherited his love of being in the air. Simon – Lord Glendale – took him up almost as soon as Richard could walk. I protested, of course – aeroplanes weren't as safe back then as they are now.' Her eyes clouded again. 'Perhaps I should have tried harder to stop him, but Richard loved it and I've always found it difficult to refuse my son anything.'

'Aleksy always wanted to fly too,' Irena said. 'He and Richard are very alike in many ways.'

The two women shared a long look. Both knew that pilots had the greatest chance of dying.

'I think Simon finds his work at the War Office almost as

exciting as being a pilot,' Isabel continued. 'It's much safer, of course, but no less important,'

Irena had suspected as much when he'd taken her to be interviewed when she'd first arrived.

Crawford brought in a tray of tea and they waited until he'd left before they resumed their conversation. 'Will you go back to Poland when this is over?' Isabel asked as Irena poured their tea.

'Of course! It is my country. I belong there. I long to be back, although I can't imagine what sort of Poland – what sort of life – I'll be returning to.'

'The war – all the horror – will end, Irena. You must have faith. Then everything will return to normal and you will be able to resume your life. It won't be the same as it was before the war, but there will be compensations.' A shadow crossed her face. 'A life still to lead.'

'Was that what it was like for you when you came back from the Great War?'

Isabel fingered the pearls at her throat. 'It wasn't the life I imagined living, no.'

'But you are happy?' The words slipped out before she could stop them. Isabel didn't invite confidences, but there was something about her today that made her seem more approachable. 'You must be. You have everything. Your work. Your husband. Your son.'

Isabel smiled sadly. 'And I am grateful for it all.'

Irena decided to take advantage of Isabel's mood. 'Has Lord Glendale said why the British aren't attacking the Germans in Poland?'

'He tells me very little. The Official Secrets Act, you know. However, sometimes he shares a snippet or two.' She smiled mischievously. 'I can be very persuasive when I want to be. I do know that we are concentrating most of our energies on defeating Hitler in Africa and stopping him taking over the rest of Europe. After that, I'm sure Britain and her colonies will turn their attention to getting Hitler and his Nazis out of Poland.' Dr Maxwell glanced over her shoulder although there was no one else in the room and lowered her voice. 'My dear, I don't want to raise your hopes – indeed, I'm not sure if I should be telling you – but I have heard that the Russians are releasing their prisoners-of-war and that will include the Polish soldiers they captured.'

Irena sat up, almost splashing tea all over her dress. 'Then Piotr could be amongst them!'

Isabel smiled. 'It is possible, isn't it?'

The next day, in order to welcome Richard, Isabel took a rare day off work. She was a bundle of energy, picking flowers from the garden and arranging them herself in tall crystal vases. It had rained continuously for a week and although coal was rationed she had insisted that Hannah light a fire in Richard's bedroom. Irena had enjoyed witnessing the usually imperturbable doctor's excitement.

Shortly before dinner, Richard arrived. He'd changed in some way she couldn't quite put her finger on. The assurance was still there, and the smile she remembered still hovered around his lips, but when he thought no one was looking Irena noticed the darkness was still in his eyes – if anything deeper than before.

He kissed his mother and held out a hand to Irena. 'I'm pleased to see you again, Irena.'

'And I you,' Irena replied, hiding her discomfort. It wasn't just his words that unsettled her, but the way he was looking at her. As if he were drinking her in. 'If you don't mind, I think I shall have supper out,' Irena said, uncomfortably aware of the flush travelling up her neck.

Isabel started to protest then gave her a grateful smile. 'On your own? That wouldn't be much fun.'

'Some of my colleagues are having dinner at a club. They invited me to join them.'

That was true but she had no intention of going. She enjoyed the company of her fellow Poles but, sooner or later, talk always returned to what was happening in Poland and the news was never good. She wasn't really hungry anyway.

She let herself out of the house and turned towards Princes Street Gardens. The earlier rain had stopped and the sky was a glorious shade of blue, feathered with skimpy clouds, the streets still busy with people, mainly women and older children, making the most of the break in the weather. At seven o'clock it was still light and would remain so for a good while yet. Not that she intended to be out late. A couple of hours at the most, then she'd slip inside and up to her bedroom without disturbing Richard and his mother.

At the top of the hill, Edinburgh Castle glowed in the evening sun, reminding her of Wawel Castle and Poland.

She'd dreamed about Piotr last night. He'd been walking towards her. It had been so vivid, so real, she could feel the sun on her arms, hear the song of the birds, see the dark hairs on his arms. But when she'd called out to him, he'd smiled and stretched out his hands, his palms facing towards her – as if to tell her that he was in a place where she couldn't go. When she'd woken to find it was only a dream, it had been unbearable.

She found a bench and sat and watched as the sun dipped behind the city. One day she'd be back in her homeland where she belonged and she and Piotr would get married, her father leading her up the aisle. She could almost hear Aleksy giving the best man speech and although Magdalena wouldn't be with them, she'd be there in their hearts. The image sent a jolt of grief and longing through her. Surely it couldn't be much longer until the war was over?

Until then, she would never give up hope.

The next morning was unusually warm and Isabel insisted that Irena and Richard take advantage of the sunshine.

'I shall ask Hannah to pack a picnic. You can take the car, Richard. Neither Irena nor I use it much and I've been saving the coupons for when you're home.'

'I'm sure Richard would prefer to invite some of his friends,' Irena said, horribly embarrassed that her company was being foisted on Richard again.

'I would like it very much if you would come, Irena. You'll save me from my own company,' Richard said with a smile.

As Isabel left them alone to organise the picnic, Irena turned to Richard. 'I really don't mind staying at home. I'm sure you have friends . . . and I have some studying I should be doing.'

'On a day like this? Absolutely not. You can catch up on your studies any other time. You must have realised by now that in Scotland the sun rarely shines for more than two days at a time – so we must make the most of it.' He lowered his voice. 'Besides, it's you I want to spend time with.'

A short while later, they were heading out of the city, and, sooner than Irena thought possible, into the countryside.

'How do you like Edinburgh?' Richard asked.

'Very much. Your mother has made me feel very welcome.'

'I knew you two would have a great deal in common.'

'It is nice to have someone to talk medicine with. I know it must be an imposition to have me stay. There are lodgings available for us Poles but when I suggested I move out, she wouldn't hear of it. She says she likes having someone in the house.'

'Poor Mother. What with both Father and I in London, she must get lonely sometimes.'

'Yet she doesn't visit you there?' It was something that had been puzzling Irena.

'I'm usually at the airfield and Father's war work keeps him busy. I doubt she'd have much more company there. Anyway, Edinburgh is where her hospital is. I can't see Mother ever abandoning it.' He grinned at Irena. 'I spent a good part of my childhood in her office hoping she'd remember I was there, waiting for her.' If he resented being forgotten by his mother he gave no indication of it.

Being the children of occasionally neglectful medical parents was, it seemed, something they had in common.

'I used to spend time with my father at the hospital. He took me on his ward rounds at the weekends and during the summer holidays. I think that's when I decided to become a doctor.'

'And that was when I knew I'd never be a doctor. But like you Katherine's always wanted to be a nurse. Clearly the cries of agony we could hear through the office walls didn't put her off.'

'She told me you've known each other a long time.'

'For as long as I can remember. Mrs Stuart, Katherine's mother, worked as a nurse at my mother's hospital. When we weren't hanging around there, my nanny looked after us both. I used to resent having this little girl always toddling after me, so I learned to ignore her. Back then I didn't like associating with girls.' He shot Irena a grin. 'That's all changed, of course.'

'Are you sure Katherine isn't one of your girlfriends?'

Richard threw back his head and laughed. 'Katherine?

Absolutely not. I'm afraid she knows me too well to ever want to fill that role.' Irena was relieved. Katherine was too innocent to be romantically involved with a man like Richard. He was the kind of man who made women fall in love with him. Why wouldn't they? Most women adored pilots and he was good-looking, titled and charming. But, she suspected, having watched him at the club, as soon as the woman fell in love with him, he would move on to another one.

'What will you do after the war?'

The light left Richard's face. 'Most of us don't think too much about the future. *Carpe Diem* – seize the day. That's our motto. Plenty of time to be serious after this is all over.'

He turned down a dirt road and the car bounced along a rutted track for a mile or two before they came to a halt.

As far as Irena could tell they were in the middle of nowhere. There was a small farmhouse on their left and in front of them, a hill.

'How do you like walking?' Richard asked. 'Either we follow a path around the side of the hill and have our picnic there or we can go straight up. What would you rather?'

Irena breathed in the damp air, realising for the first time how accustomed she'd become to the smog that always seemed to hang over Edinburgh. 'Let's go up.'

Richard lifted a canvas bag from the back seat of the car and slung it over his shoulder. 'Come on then.'

She was out of breath by the time they reached the top. Richard put down the bag he'd been carrying and opened it. 'Knowing Hannah we'll have everything we need.' He pulled out a small blanket and laid it down next to a mound of stones. The blanket was followed by sandwiches, a flask of coffee, a bottle of champagne and two glasses. He flourished the champagne. 'Good for Hannah. She knows me too well.' He popped the cork and, ignoring Irena's protests, poured them each a glass. The bubbles in the wine tickled her nose and she laughed.

'Do you know, that's the first time I've seen you laugh,' Richard said, lowering his glass. 'You should do it more often.'

Irena felt the heat rise to her cheeks under his frank admiration. 'I wasn't always serious. Before the war I was as carefree as anyone.'

He tipped some more champagne into her glass. 'In that case, why don't we forget about the war – just for today?'

He stretched out on the blanket and rested his head on his hands. 'Tell me more about Poland before the war.' He leaned over and pulled her down beside him. When she resisted he grinned again. 'Don't worry, I've never laid a hand on a girl – not if she didn't want me to.'

Irena relaxed. She lay down next to him and tucked her hands behind her head. 'Life in the cities wasn't so very different to how it is here in Edinburgh or London. Many Varsovians have, or had, houses in the country. Perhaps the biggest difference between our countries is that a greater proportion of the population live in the country than they do here.' A bee buzzed around some yellow flowers and directly above her the sky was clear with only the merest whisper of clouds.

'My earliest memories are of the time I spent with my grandmother at her farmhouse,' she continued.

He propped himself on his elbow and looked down at her. 'What was that like?'

'Wonderful. When I think back to those days I remember sunshine and the smell of cooking. My grandmother loved to cook. In the early summer she'd send me out just as the sun was coming up to pick rosebuds before they opened so we could make jam.'

'Jam? From rose petals?' He widened his eyes in mock disbelief.

'I can't imagine you know much about cooking.'

His lips twitched. 'And you'd be right. Not one of my skills. Never found it necessary to learn, thank God.'

She was so lost in the world of her childhood, she barely heard him. 'We'd cover the petals with sugar and pound them with a mortar. It was delicious.'

'Go on,' he murmured.

Irena closed her eyes. 'There were always herbs hanging from the rafters in her kitchen. We'd go for long walks to search for them. Peppermint to make a syrup to cure stomach ache, stinging nettle for arthritis, as well as others I forget. I think that's where my interest in medicine first started. I was so proud when people used to come to the farmhouse to see my grandmother and get one of her cures. When we weren't searching for plants, she was teaching her recipes.'

'Where was your mother?'

'She died. In a riding accident.' She lifted her necklace from under her blouse and showed him. The ruby and diamonds flashed as they caught the sun. 'This was hers.' To her mortification, her voice cracked. 'It's my talisman — as long as I'm wearing it, it feels as if she's watching over me.'

'Poor darling.'

The sympathy in his voice made her eyes smart. She blinked away the tears. She'd cried in front of him once and wouldn't do so again. She tucked the necklace away. 'I had Grandmother and Tata and Aleksy. I managed fine.'

His eyes creased at the corners. 'I'm sure you did.' He lay down on his back again. 'Go on, tell me more. I like listening to your voice.'

'I was four and Aleksy two when Mama died. Tata always worked long hours, but after Mama's death he spent even more time at the hospital, returning home only to eat and sleep.

Although Maria, our housekeeper, did her best to care for us, she had children of her own so Aleksy and I were sent to live with our grandmother on her farm near Krakow. I loved it there – apart from missing Mama. When I started school I went back to live with my father, under the care of Maria, returning to the farm – and darling Aleksy – during the school holidays. But then Grandmother died and Aleksy was sent away to school. It was a horrible time. I was lost and lonely in the Krakow apartment, so I asked Tata if I could wait for him in his office after school until he finished work, which was often very late, but I never minded. I would sit on his office floor and flick through his medical journals and textbooks, fascinated by the diagrams of body parts and photographs of rare conditions. When my interest still hadn't waned by the time I got to secondary school, Tata started taking me on his hospital rounds at the weekend. I couldn't talk to him about Mama, but I could talk to him about medicine.'

She slid him a look from the corner of her eye. He was watching her intently, as if every word she said mattered.

She went on to tell him about the narrow cobbled streets of the village near her grandmother's farm, the terracotta-roofed houses and the churches filled with the smell of incense. All of a sudden, a pang of longing for Poland so fierce it almost took her breath away surged through her and she tailed off.

Richard was so quiet that for a moment she thought he'd fallen asleep but when she turned her head to check it was to find him watching her through half-closed, sleepy eyes.

'I'm sorry,' she said. 'I didn't mean to bore you.'

'Rest assured, there is nothing boring about you.' It might be the way he talked to all women, but she couldn't help the little pulse of pleasure his words gave her. 'What about you?' she asked quickly. 'What did you do before you became a pilot?'

'I studied law at Oxford. My Aunt Dorothea is a lawyer so you could say I was following in family footsteps.'

'I met her in London. She seems a formidable woman.'

He grinned. 'She is.'

'Will you practise when this is over?'

'I plan to.'

'Yet you still want to fly planes – even when you know what the chances of being shot down and killed are?'

The lines between his eyebrows deepened and he studied her thoughtfully. Then his lips curved into a smile. 'You really are quite something. D'you know, you're the first person to come right out with that question? No one talks to us pilots about dying. Everyone prefers to pretend it's not going to happen – or refuses to acknowledge it when it does. When we come into dinner after a sortie and there's an empty chair at the table, no one says anything. We have to keep up the pretence that we're having the best time of our lives – and in a way we are. When you're up there, you don't have time to feel fear, but when you get back, or when you're on standby, that's when it kicks in. We know death is always a possibility but we choose not to dwell on it. If we did, we would become cautious and if any thing's going to kill you, that will.'

'Aleksy tells me that his squadron always toast the dead and missing before dinner,' she said softly, 'but then we Poles have had longer to live with death. He always wanted to be a pilot, too. But not Piotr. He preferred the cavalry. He said it was safer to keep his feet on the ground.'

Thinking of Piotr brought the familiar ache of longing, but it wasn't as intense as before. She couldn't shake the feeling that it was only her love that would keep Piotr safe, yet she was here with another man, a man she enjoyed looking at and talking to. She shivered as foreboding washed over her.

She sat up and hugged her knees. 'We should go.'

Richard reached out and turned her face towards him with a fingertip. 'Now I've made you sad again.'

'I'm tired of feeling sad all the time.' She tried to smile. 'It doesn't make me a very good person, does it?'

Richard pulled her back down. 'You have nothing to feel guilty about. Your fiancé wouldn't mind, you know. If anything happened to me and I left a girl behind I'd want her to find happiness any way she could.'

Piotr had said the very same thing to her that last night. 'Perhaps he's looking for me now.'

'If you were my girl, I'd search heaven and earth until I found you.'

Her pulse skipped a beat.

'How long will you wait for him?' he asked quietly.

'Until the war is over and all the men have returned.' She scrambled to her feet and started packing up the basket. 'Let's go,' she said.

Richard suggested they attend an open-air recital in Princes Street Gardens. Not ready for the day to end, Irena agreed.

By the time they returned, Isabel had gone to bed.

'What about a night cap?' Richard asked.

'I'm a little tired.' She was increasingly aware of the way he kept looking at her and her own reaction to him.

'Please. Sit with me a while. I don't always find it easy to sleep.'

'Neither do I.'

His admission touched her more than anything else he'd said or done, so she took a seat by the fireplace. He placed a record on the gramophone and as the voice of Glenn Miller filled the room, he crossed over to the drinks tray and poured them both a whisky.

'What keeps you awake?' she asked.

He handed her the tumbler before lounging back in a chair. 'I dream I'm flying. Sometimes it's peaceful, just me and the clouds. Other times I'm being chased or my plane is on fire and I know I have to bale. The worst ones are when I see another plane being chased and I know he's going to go down but I can't do anything to stop it.'

Not so different to her nightmares.

His mouth curved in a smile. 'Other times I dream I'm dancing with a beautiful woman in my arms. I don't know her name but I know she's meant to be there. Come to think of it, she looks like you.' He leaned across, looking directly into her eyes. As he touched her face with his fingertip, a shocking wave of desire pooled low in her abdomen. She drew back and stood, placing her unfinished drink on the table. 'I think I'll go to bed now.'

He dropped his hand. 'I'm sorry. I didn't mean to chase you away. That was clumsy of me. You're like no other woman I've met and I don't know how to be around you.' He rubbed the back of his neck and she could see the genuine regret in his eyes. 'I'm really not so bad once you get to know me.'

Despite herself she smiled. 'And am I? Going to get to know you?'

'Oh yes,' he said, 'I rather think you are.'

Chapter 34

February 1942

The numbers of students at the Polish Hospital continued to increase until they reached almost three hundred. Although Irena had little to do with them outside working hours, she would sometimes meet them in the doctors' mess, where the talk was always of what was happening in Poland and whether their loved ones were safe.

As Isabel had suggested they might, the Russians had released thousands of Polish prisoners and, although many had joined the Russian army, some had trickled in to Britain, a few coming to work at the Polish Hospital. There was, however, no word from Piotr. She asked every new arrival about him, but no one was able to tell her anything. Now at night when she dreamed, Piotr's face and Richard's blurred together. Being with Richard made her happy, made her feel more alive than she'd done in months, but he also made her feel tangled up inside. She knew she was in danger of falling in love with him – whatever she'd tried to tell herself – and everything inside her shrank from the knowledge. So Richard's departure back to his base in London had almost been a relief.

The newly arrived Poles brought terrible stories with them – about the camps they'd been held in and the conditions, but most alarmingly about the way the Germans were exterminating Jews. No one could believe it was true, even if one of the doctors swore his brother had evidence it was happening.

'They take them to camps in Poland or Germany and separate them into groups: those who can work and those who can't. Then they burn those who can't – mainly the women, children and old people.'

'How can your brother be sure?' one of the other doctors asked sceptically. 'Not even the Nazis would do such a thing.'

'My brother knows Jan Karski. Jan told him that he went into one of the camps to get proof and escaped with it. He took it to the British government, the Americans too, but all they say is that they need more evidence.'

'Perhaps he's making it up. To make the British bomb the Germans in Poland?'

'I'm telling you, I've heard only good things about Jan – there is no way he'd make up stuff like this. No one *could* make up stuff like this.'

Irena excused herself. She was expected at afternoon rounds on male surgical. But as she hurried along the corridor to the ward, she wondered. Could the rumours about the extermination camps possibly be true? She thought about the mother and baby – the casual way the soldiers had killed them as if they weren't human – and she was filled with a dreadful foreboding.

Irena stood on the doorstep of Charlotte Square and shook the rain from her umbrella. As soon as she stepped inside it was clear that something was wrong. There was a suitcase in the hall and Hannah was standing next to it wringing her hands. Irena had never seen the usually stalwart housekeeper looking so distressed. Her skin chilled.

'What is it, Hannah?' she asked. 'Is it Richard?'

When she nodded Irena's chest squeezed. 'Is he ...?' She couldn't continue.

'His plane took a hit. He managed to land in England. He's

alive, but hurt. I don't know what her ladyship will do if he doesn't make it. That boy is the very soul of her and of his lordship.'

A knot twisted high in Irena's chest.

'Where is Lady Glendale?'

'She's in her bedroom. She's planning to get the train down to London tonight. Lord Glendale is making the arrangements.'

Irena unpinned her hat and tossed it on the hall table. 'I'll go to her.'

'Yes. Please. I've never seen her in such a state.'

Irena ran up the stairs and knocked on Isabel's door. She went inside without waiting for a reply. Isabel was sitting at her dressing table, a photograph in her hand.

Irena hurried over to her and knelt by her side. The photograph slipped from Isabel's fingers and fell to the floor. Irena picked it up. It was of Richard in his RAF uniform standing in front of a plane. He was grinning directly at the camera, looking relaxed and pleased with himself.

The knot in her chest tightened.

'Any news?' she whispered, handing back the photograph.

'His father phoned a little while ago. Richard's in hospital. No one can – or will – tell me how badly he's hurt. Apparently he was shot up over France but instead of bailing, he went after another plane and shot it down. He managed to make it back and land the plane. That's all I know.'

Irena took Isabel's hand, surprised to find her own was trembling. 'Will he be all right?'

'There's no way of telling at the moment. His father doesn't really understand what the doctors are saying. That's why I must go. I can't bear it that I'm not with him now.'

'Of course you must go to him. Did you manage to get a ticket?'

Isabel smiled wanly. 'It can be useful to have a husband working in the War Office.'

'Would you like me to come with you?'

Isabel took a breath and straightened her back. 'No, thank you all the same. I shall be all right. Besides, you have your work. But I would be grateful if you would go to the Royal tomorrow and explain what's happened. They will need to arrange for someone else to take over my theatre list in the afternoon. Let them know I might be away for a few days. I shall telephone them once I've seen Richard and have a clearer idea how long I'll be away for.'

'I'll let them know. There must be something else I can do?'

'You can pray.' Isabel smiled faintly. 'The train isn't for another hour, but I shall leave for the station quite soon. I've packed an overnight bag. I have everything else I need at the London house.'

Irena squeezed her hand. 'Let me know how he is as soon as you can. Tell him . . . tell him I was asking for him.'

'You care for him?'

More than she wanted to admit. 'Of course. He's been a good friend to me.' She got to her feet. 'I'll ask Crawford to call for a taxi.'

It wasn't until the evening of the following day that Isabel phoned.

Irena had been unable to stop thinking about Richard while on duty and had almost given a patient plasma instead of saline. She'd given herself a mental shake and forced herself to concentrate. Back in Charlotte Square she'd wandered from room to room, picking up a book and putting it down without being able to remember a word she'd read.

According to Isabel the burns to Richard's arms and legs

weren't serious, but he'd also sustained a fractured tibia, which would keep him from flying for a few months. It was a relief to know he wasn't badly hurt but an even bigger relief to know he wouldn't be flying for a while.

The hospitals in London were all needed for the wounded men sent back from the front so it was standard practice to admit injured soldiers to hospitals near their home once they had received immediate attention and his mother had arranged for him to have his convalescence at the Western so that she could supervise his treatment herself.

It was a couple of weeks before Richard was transferred to the Western. The day after he'd been admitted there, Irena slipped away from her ward and went to see him.

He was in the officers' ward, sitting at a table with his injured leg propped up on a chair, and playing cards with the other men who were out of bed. Irena's heart jerked. Apart from his broken leg he had cracked a rib and his chest was strapped. He also had a fading yellow bruise to his cheekbone and a multicoloured eye.

A nurse leaned over him to give him some pills in a plastic cup and he grinned at her and something bloomed inside Irena's chest that felt suspiciously like jealousy.

He looked up and saw her and his eyes lit up.

'I expected you yesterday,' he said petulantly.

'I wanted to give you time to settle in. I knew the doctors would be assessing you.'

He tossed his cards on the table and reached for his crutches. 'Sorry, boys, you're going to have to finish this game without me.'

Irena helped him to his feet and walked beside him as he hobbled over to his bed.

'I've been waiting for you. The only good thing about being cooped up here is that I know you're nearby.'

'Been practising your flirting skills on the nurses?'

'Don't be coy, Irena. You know you're the only one I want to flirt with.'

Her heart gave another little run of beats.

'I should be getting back to the ward.'

'Come on, Krash. An injured pilot and all that. Don't you have an ounce of sympathy in your bones?'

'If it's sympathy you want then I'm not the girl for you.'

Realising what she'd said she blushed and jumped to her feet. 'I need to go.'

She turned away, but not before she heard him say, 'Oh, but I think you are, Irena, and I think you're beginning to realise that too.'

Chapter 35

It was a couple of months before his plaster was removed and Richard was discharged home. Having him at Charlotte Square was wonderful and painful in equal measure. Irena found herself looking forward to seeing him and being with him made her happy, but when she was alone, she was tormented by guilt. She told herself that she'd done nothing to betray Piotr – it wasn't as if she ever encouraged Richard, or even hinted that she welcomed his attention – and Piotr would have wanted her to find happiness, but it didn't change the way she felt. She was as married to Piotr as if she had his ring on her finger.

As usual Richard was waiting for her when she returned from work – in the garden today – a newspaper on his lap and a half-finished crossword on the table next to him. She could tell immediately that something had disturbed him.

'What is it?' she asked. 'Bad news?'

'Good and bad news,' he said slowly. 'I've been given new orders. As soon as the army medic passes me fit to return to duty, I've to go to East Fortune to help train new pilots.' He flung his newspaper on the ground. 'I suspect my damn father is behind this.'

She drew up a chair and sat next to him. It was bound to be safer training pilots than flying fighter planes. However, if she had her way this war would be over before Richard ever had to get behind the controls of an aircraft again.

'But that's good news, isn't it? You've been keen to return to work.'

'I want to go back to my squadron – what's left of it, at least. Training pilots is one thing, but I want to be up there with my men, teaching the Jerries a thing or two.'

'Don't you think you've done enough?' she said.

'It'll never be enough. Not until we've killed every last Nazi. I hate not being with my squadron. These men are like brothers to me. They need me flying alongside them.'

'I feel the same. I think of my people in Poland still dying in their thousands and there's not one day when I don't feel guilty that I'm not there with them.'

He reached for her hand. 'And if you were, you might be dead. How would that help?'

'I know, but it doesn't stop the way I feel.'

'Then you of all people must understand why I have to get back to my squadron? Why I need to be back in the real action.'

'You keep telling me that the new recruits need to be taught by someone who knows how to fly in combat. What better person than someone who has done it?'

'It's not the same.'

'Do you know you sound like a sulky child?' she said, trying to lift his mood. 'You should be glad that you have a chance to survive this war. I know your parents will be relieved. You're their only child.'

But Richard wasn't to be mollified. 'If I find out that my father has pulled strings to get me out of active duty I'll never forgive him.'

Irena was becoming exasperated. 'It might only be for a short time. I suspect they won't keep experienced pilots away from active duty for too long. If your father has pulled strings, then I for one am glad.'

The shadows left his eyes and he grinned. 'Are you, Krash? That almost makes it worthwhile.'

She felt the heat suffuse her face. She hadn't meant to say what she had, but the words had come out before she could stop them.

'Does that mean you have come to care for me, even a little?' he continued.

'It means that I want you to stay alive.'

He leaned forward again and traced the line of her lips with the pad of his thumb. 'It's enough, for now.'

Although there was still no news of Piotr, Irena woke every morning with a lightness of heart she never thought she'd feel again.

Richard still hadn't regained full use of his leg, but it was healing sufficiently well for him to get about with a stick which, needless to say, he hated. At the weekends, when Irena was free, they would take a tram and visit the National Portrait Gallery or one of the museums. She discovered that behind his easy, superficial manner he had a sharp brain and liked many of the same things she did. They talked about authors and artists, their debates often becoming heated – but they never spoke about what they would do after the war.

One afternoon when they'd walked to the foot of Arthur's Seat and back, without Richard needing his stick, he turned to her.

'I've to report for duty tomorrow. Will you miss me?'

'I'm sure you'll come to Edinburgh when you can,' she said evasively.

'Will you come to see me at East Fortune? It's not far.'
'If you like.'
He smiled. 'I like.'

An invitation to attend a concert at RAF East Fortune came two weeks later. Irena arranged to have the day off and took a bus to the airfield. The short Scottish summer was coming to an end and, although it wasn't quite six, it was already getting dark outside.

The driver let her, along with several excited women around her age, off at the bus stop outside the camp and she had to stand in line to show her invitation to the guard at the gate.

But she didn't have to wait long. Richard appeared and taking her elbow steered her to the front of the queue, handing her invitation to the guard.

When they were away from the crowd he stopped to kiss her cheek. 'I wasn't sure if you'd come.'

'Why wouldn't I? I love Gilbert and Sullivan.'

He raised an eyebrow. 'If you're telling me that's the only reason you're here, I'm going to be a broken man.'

'Of course I wanted to see you too,' she said lightly, although her heart tripped. 'We're friends, aren't we?'

His eyes slid to hers, a small smile playing around his mouth. 'I think we're a little more than that, don't you, Krash?'

Not sure how to answer, she kept quiet.

'The concert doesn't start for a while,' he continued. 'Would you like to come to the mess for a drink? Meet some of the other chaps.'

'Why don't you show me around, Richard? Apart from that day in Dumfries, I've never been on an airfield.' She tucked her arm into his. 'Is it always this busy?'

'This is quiet. We're usually doing training flights day and night, but the weather forecast isn't good so there's no flying for anyone tonight.'

He led her over to one of the long huts, shaped like a semicircle and with a tin roof. The planes were parked at the same angles in lines on the runway, apart from the few outside one of the large hangars, with women in blue serge jump suits clambering over them.

'These women are mechanics?' Irena asked.

'Certainly are and pretty good at it too.' Another woman trundled past them driving a large lorry with packages loaded in the back.

'Do they share the same quarters as the men?'

Richard grinned. 'Good God, no. Their COs watch them as closely as if they were nuns in a nunnery – or at least they try to.' He pointed to the far side of the airfield. 'That's their barracks over there, behind a wire fence that's supposed to keep the airmen out. As you can imagine, it doesn't work too well.' His grin grew wider. 'The women are good at finding a way across.'

She felt a stab of unwelcome jealousy. How many of them had found their way to Richard? Or he to them?

'Come on, I'll show you where they check our parachutes. It's where the pilots try to hang out when they're waiting to fly.'

They stopped in front of one of the huts and Richard opened the door, standing aside to let her go in first. It was pleasantly warm inside out of the drizzle. Parachutes billowed from the roof, hung over lines that looked like the pulley Hannah had in her kitchen to dry the washing when it was raining.

'The girls have finished for the day, but since they always have the heaters on so their fingers stay agile, it stays warm for a while.'

'What do they do with the parachutes?'

'Check them for tears. Make repairs. We rely on them completely. One day our lives might depend on our chutes.'

A chill swept over her skin and she shivered. But Richard was a trainer now, no longer engaging the enemy in the skies. He had a good chance of surviving the war as long as he was here.

He switched on a radio that rested on an empty barrel. 'Would you care to dance?'

'Here?'

'Why not?' When she took his hand, he pulled her into his arms. Feeling awkward, she held herself stiff.

But Richard kept the pressure of his hand on her lower back, pressing her into him. He rested his cheek against her hair and she could feel the softness of his breath on her neck as he hummed along to the music. Irena closed her eyes, acutely aware of his warmth and the hardness of his chest against her body. She could see their reflections mirrored in the dark window as he guided her slowly round in time to the waltz. They looked right together. She relaxed into him. It felt so good to be held again.

'That's better,' Richard said softly, tightening his arms around her.

'Of course you'd say that.' She tilted her head back so that he could see she was smiling. 'Because, as always, you've managed to get your way.'

Even in the dim light, she could see his eyes glinting. 'Ah, if only that were true. I haven't always got my own way with you, have I?'

She didn't know if it was the soft music, or the way he was looking at her, or just that she longed to feel safe and loved even for a short while, but when he brought his mouth down to hers she didn't pull away. Instead, she threaded her fingers into his hair and kissed him back. He groaned and cupped his hands round her buttocks, pressing her against him. His lips trailed down her neck, shooting sparks of pleasure along her spine and then he was lifting her up and sitting her on one of the tables. Instinctively she wound her legs around his waist, pulling him closer.

'God,' he murmured against her mouth. 'You have no idea how long I've waited for this moment.'

His fingers brushed her breasts as he unbuttoned her dress, making her nipples tighten. Her dress fell to the floor and his hands skimmed over her skin, pushing the straps of her slip aside, sending shock waves of desire through her. She could hardly think. All she knew was that she ached for him.

He stopped suddenly and reached into his pocket. It was the practised way he did it, so smoothly, as if he'd done it many, many times before, that hauled her back from the brink. She pressed her palms against his chest and pushed him away. 'No, Richard, don't. Please stop.' She wriggled out of his arms and onto the floor, scooping up her dress from where it had fallen.

He stepped away from her, the sound of their ragged breathing almost drowning out the music from the radio.

'For God's sake, Irena, why not? You don't know how long I've imagined this moment – how hard it's been for me to keep my hands off you. I didn't plan for it to be like this but, God, I want you so much.'

Her heart was pounding so hard she could barely breathe. She stepped into her dress and started doing up the buttons.

'I know you want me as much as I want you,' he continued.

'Yes,' she admitted. She'd come within a whisper of letting him make love to her.

He stepped towards her but she held up her palms. 'No, Richard. Don't.'

His hands fell to his sides. 'Is it because of Piotr? Are you still in love with him?'

Was she? She didn't know any more, but even if she hadn't

been engaged to Piotr she couldn't and wouldn't fall in love with another man – especially one who could break her heart. Every time Richard went up in a plane there was a good chance he wouldn't come back. She couldn't risk loving him. 'I'm still promised to Piotr.'

'That's not the same as being in love with him.'

'I don't know, Richard. I don't know. But please, if you care about me, let me be.'

'Care about you?' He dragged a hand through his hair. 'Christ, Irena, I love you. I think I fell in love with you almost the moment I met you. You were so brave, so defiant, so beautiful, so damn sad. How could I help myself?'

'Richard, I'm sorry. I—' His face blurred as tears burned behind her lids. She felt wretched, right to her core. She'd never meant to hurt him.

He moved then. Wrapping his arms around her, he brought her to him and stroked her hair as if she were a child again. 'Hush, darling. Don't cry. It's all right. I can wait. I won't stop loving you. When you're ready, I'll be waiting. However long it takes.'

She stopped his words with her fingertips.

'No,' she said. 'Don't. You'll be wasting your time.' She looked him in the eye. 'I think it's time for the concert to start.'

Chapter 36

Irena was sitting in the doctors' lounge, taking a break before going back on the wards, when several of the doctors entered, talking and gesticulating. When they saw her they became quiet and she noticed none of them would look her in the eye.

She jumped to her feet. 'What is it? Has something happened?'

There was an uneasy silence. One of the doctors she knew well came and took her by the hands. 'There has been an announcement on Berlin radio. We know that everything they say isn't true, of course, but we have reason to think on this occasion it might be.'

'What did they say?'

'Tell me, my dear, was your fiancé with the Uhlan?'

'Yes.' Everyone knew that. She'd asked about him often enough.

He ran his tongue over his lips. 'They say they have discovered a mass grave near Katyn forest. They say it contains the bodies of thousands of Polish officers murdered by the Russians.'

Irena sank into the chair behind her. Katyn forest was to the east – the direction Piotr's unit had been heading on their way out of Warsaw.

'They could be lying. It could be propaganda.' Her mouth was so dry she could barely speak.

'That might be so, but another of the medical students has a brother who's just come from Russia and he tells the same story. He was there when they were captured by the Russians. He had a bad feeling about it so he removed everything from his uniform that identified him as an officer. There was a Captain Kopiewski in his unit. That was your fiancé's name, wasn't it?'

Kopiewski wasn't an uncommon name.

'He suggested to him, to all the officers, that they do the same. But they wouldn't. You know how proud our officers are.'

'But that doesn't mean anything,' she whispered, queasiness catching at her throat.

Dr Bratek sighed. 'This man, the brother, was there when the Russians separated the officers from the non-commissioned men. They were led away into the forest. He heard shots. Then the Russians came back. There were no prisoners with them. I am so sorry, my dear, but I think what the Germans are saying is probably true.'

'Perhaps they escaped? I can't imagine Polish officers going meekly to their deaths. Piotr would have fought with his bare hands rather than do that.'

'The Germans say the grave they uncovered contains the bodies of as many as four thousand Polish officers, still wearing their uniforms. It wouldn't have occurred to the men that the Russians were going to shoot them in cold blood. They would have assumed they were being taken to a camp under guard. By the time they realised what was happening it would have been too late.'

Her whole body was shaking. She knew they wouldn't have told her unless they were absolutely sure. But she still wasn't ready to give up on Piotr. Not until she had evidence. She stumbled to her feet. 'I must go. I'm due in theatre.'

Dr Bratek pressed her back down. 'You're in no state to work. Go home. Take compassionate leave.'

She couldn't bear to be alone with her thoughts. 'I'd rather stay here.'

Dr Bratek shook his head. 'No. I forbid it. I've arranged for someone to take you home.' He looked over his shoulder and one of female medical students stepped forward.

She took Irena gently by the elbow. 'Come. Come with me.'

Irena unlocked the door of Charlotte Square and stumbled inside. She felt strange – detached – as if the world no longer existed.

Dr Maxwell was waiting for her. 'Oh my dear, they telephoned me at the hospital. I'm so sorry.'

She took Irena's hands in hers. 'Come and sit by the fire.' She rang the bell in the hall before taking Irena by the arm and leading her into the smaller sitting room on the ground floor.

Despite the warmth of the fire, Irena's teeth were chattering.

Isabel crossed over to the side table where the drinks tray sat and poured a large measure of whisky into a glass before handing it to Irena. 'I'm sorry we don't have vodka. However, this will serve the same purpose.'

The fiery liquid burned her throat but she didn't care. She didn't think she would care about anything ever again.

Isabel sat silently across from her, her dark eyes filled with concern and pity.

'Maybe Piotr managed to escape somehow,' Irena whispered, hoping Isabel would agree with her.

'My dear, I phoned Lord Glendale. He has a list of names – given to the War Office by the Germans. I'm so very sorry, but your Piotr's name is on it.'

'I want to see it.'

'Of course. But I have to tell you, Irena, there is no hope. No hope at all.'

267

Chapter 37

Lord Glendale rarely came to Edinburgh; he'd only been twice in the last year, so Irena decided to go to see him in London. Before she accepted that Piotr was dead, she needed to see his name on the list, to extinguish the last, lingering hope. She also desperately wanted to see Aleksy whose unit had been transferred back to Northolt a couple of months ago. He, of all people, would understand how she felt.

Reluctantly, Isabel arranged travel warrants for her to go to London. Irena wrote to Aleksy and told him about Piotr, asking if they could meet.

But when she got to the house in Grosvenor Street and saw Lord Glendale he confirmed that Piotr's name was indeed on the list. He even showed it to her.

There it was: in black and white and amongst a list of thousands of other names. Captain Piotr Kopiewski. Isabel had been correct. There was no more hope.

The next morning she met Aleksy in a park near Selfridges department store where they were to have tea.

He looked more relaxed than the last time she'd seen him and if she didn't know better she would have said he was happy.

'It's good to see you, sister,' he said in Polish, eyeing her warily.

'It's all right. I'm not going to cry.'

'I was sorry to hear about Piotr. Every time I'm in the sky and have one of the Huns in my sights I think of him.'

'You're the only one who can understand how I feel – we've both lost our loves.' She stopped to hug him. 'At least I still have you. And Tata.' She prayed she did. She hadn't heard anything from her father, although she didn't really expect to. Not until the war was over.

Aleksy gently disentangled himself from her embrace and stuffed his hands in his pockets. 'Renia, life goes on. It has to. You'll find someone else to love. Just as I have ... '

She looked at him in disbelief. 'Surely you can't have forgotten Magdalena already!'

He shook his head. 'I'll never forget Magdalena, but I can't spend the rest of my life mourning her either.'

The calm, matter-of-fact way he said it shocked and infuriated her.

'Is that it? Pff,' she snapped her fingers, 'Magdalena's dead, time to move on to the next woman? Dear God! What's happened to you, Aleksy?' She backed away from him. 'It's this bloody war, isn't it? It changes everybody and everything and nothing, nothing is as it should be!'

'Irena, calm down.'

'You were going to marry her. She was the love of your life.' All the fury, despair and anguish that had been churning inside since she'd heard about Piotr came spewing out and she hit his chest with her bunched-up fists, again and again. 'How can you forget her?'

Aleksy grabbed her hands. 'Irena, for God's sake. Not here. Not in front of everyone.' People were steering a path around them, eyeing them surreptitiously, before looking away quickly. 'I loved her. You know I did. But she's dead. So is Piotr. But we are still alive.'

They glared at each other, much the same way they had done as children. He took her arm. 'Come on, let's go and get that cup of tea.'

He led her into the tea room and she studied him while they waited for the waitress to bring their order. Now she looked at him, really looked at him, she saw the terrible sadness in his eyes. All the anger leaked away from her like a tide on the ebb.

'I'm sorry,' she said when they had their tea in front of them.

'It's all right. You must know I would give anything for Magdalena not to have died, but I'm no longer the man she fell in love with, just as you are no longer the woman Piotr knew. We can't mourn them for ever. We're alive and they are dead. I know I might not see the end of the war, and I want to make the most of the life I have left. I want to love and be loved. I want to make love, as often as I can, eat good food, drink good vodka, I want to feel the sun on my face, and you should too. We should live the lives Piotr and Magdalena and all the others who are dead would have lived if they could. Anything else is a disservice to them. We will always remember them but the best way to honour their memory is to live the life they couldn't.'

It was the longest speech she'd ever heard him make. But it made sense, even if didn't altogether sound like Aleksy.

'So tell me about this woman you've met,' she said

Aleksy stirred sugar into his mug. The waitress must have kept some aside for him.

'She's a QA and very pretty. Do you know that they get sent to Peebles to train in what used to be the Hydro?'

Irena nodded, remembering what Katherine had told her about her plans to join the QAs.

'That's where I met her. I had the day off from flying and she was in the town with a friend doing some shopping. Meeting her was the best thing that happened while I was in Scotland.'

'What's her name?'

'Fiona. She's from Aberdeen.' He grinned again.

'Where's she now? Still in Peebles?'

A shadow crossed his face. 'She's gone with her unit to Africa. I'm not supposed to know but she wrote to me and gave me enough clues for me to work it out. There couldn't be that many places where the hospital is under canvas and there's sand everywhere.'

Irena reached across and pressed his fingers. 'It's all right. I'm happy for you.'

'I did love Magdalena, you know.'

She sighed. 'I know. I think she'd be glad you're happy.'

'What about you? Will you be all right?'

'I'll have to be. It helps that I love my work in the Paderewski Hospital – Dr Maxwell is very kind to me, she treats me almost like a daughter ...'

Aleksy narrowed his eyes and studied her speculatively. 'Her son is the pilot who brought you to see me, isn't he?'

'Richard? Yes, we've spent a lot of time together. He's a good friend.'

Aleksy raised his eyebrow. 'A good friend? Are you sure that's all?'

'What do you mean?' Blood rushed to her cheeks.

'Oh come on, dear sister, you can't be that blind! I saw the way he looked at you when you came to the airfield, and you've gone bright red.'

She shifted in her seat and decided it was best to change the subject. Just talking about Richard was making her uncomfortable. It hadn't been fair to accuse Aleksy of forgetting Magdalena when she'd kissed Richard. Perhaps it was guilt that had made her attack her brother?

'You know we had a Polish paratrooper admitted to the ward

the other day – that's the third in just over a week. He was a bit cagey when I asked him where he was based. I mean, I know there are Polish forces all over Scotland, I just didn't know about a parachute regiment nearby.'

'You don't know?'

'Know what?'

'They're dropping men – women too, I've heard – into Poland – to work with the AK – the Home Army. They have a training centre in Fife.' He leaned forward. 'They're going around the Polish forces asking if anyone wants to take on special operations.'

Her heart started racing.

'What did you say?'

'I thought about it. If I wasn't flying I would go back too.'

Instantly she knew. It was what she had to do.

That evening, unusually, Lord Glendale dined at home. Irena was relieved. Now she had made up her mind she needed his help.

'Is there any news of what is happening in my country?' she asked.

Lord Glendale rustled his paper and peered over the top at her. 'I expect you miss it.'

'I'd like to go back.'

'You will, my dear – as soon as we've thrown the Germans out of there.'

She ran her tongue over lips, suddenly dry. 'Perhaps I could have a moment of your time? I have something I would like to speak to you about.'

She waited until the servants had left the room before continuing. 'You know I speak German? Russian, too, for that matter?'

'I do.' He looked puzzled.

'I've heard that the British are training Poles to go back into Poland.'

Something flickered behind his eyes she couldn't define. He set the paper down carefully, and looked at her keenly. 'Where did you hear that?'

She thought it better not to tell him Aleksy had told her. 'It appears to be well known amongst my countrymen. We've had a few men admitted with injuries, broken legs, the odd bullet wound. It doesn't take too long to put it all together – not when you think about it.'

He leaned back in his chair and filled his pipe. 'You don't mind, my dear?' he asked. She shook her head and waited until the pipe was lit to his satisfaction. 'I think I see where this is going.'

'I want to go back to Poland. I don't want to wait until it's free. I need to go now.'

He puffed on his pipe for a while longer. 'We do use Poles for a certain type of work, but it's extremely dangerous, my dear.'

Her skin prickled. 'It's what I want to do.'

'Even if it means risking your life?'

Her heart banged against her ribs. Although she knew she'd be going back to live with constant fear, there was only one answer to that. Piotr was dead. She'd finished her training. All these months she'd been waiting, longing to return to Poland, the guilt at not being there gnawing away at her. It was time for her to help her countrymen and women.

'Yes.'

When he smiled it changed his face completely. 'I want you to take time to think about it. It is a risky business – a very risky business. Life-threatening, to be clear. The Nazis are utterly ruthless.'

'I know.'

'Very well. I shall talk to my colleagues. It may come to nothing. There will be a selection process – interviews, aptitude tests, and so on. Then there will be intensive training. Not everyone makes it through. Someone will contact you soon. Until then, say nothing. Not to my wife. Not to Richard. Not to your best friend. Do I make myself clear?'

'Perfectly,' Irena replied.

He lifted his paper. 'Oh and Lord Glendale . . . '

He lowered his paper and peered at her over the top.

'I'd like to go as soon as possible.'

Chapter 38

'So, Dr Kraszewska, I understand from Lord Glendale you wish to return to Poland.'

'That's correct.'

It was only two days after her conversation with Lord Glendale. He'd asked her once more if she were sure and when she'd assured him she was he'd given her an address and told her that it would be up to the person who interviewed her to decide whether she was a suitable candidate for further training.

The woman shuffled some papers before looking up at her. 'Why?'

'Because I am Polish. And because I know what is happening there.'

'And how do you know that?'

'I was there. You don't round up people, work them into the ground without feeding them properly and expect them to live. And I've heard worse – rumours that the Jews are being exterminated in so-called relocation camps. I work with Poles. They get news from their families sometimes. It only seems to be the British and Americans who won't believe what is happening. I lived under occupation for more than a year and I know what the Germans are capable of.'

'We feel that these rumours have been exaggerated.'

'Then you must need better intelligence. That's why you

need me. I am Polish, I know the country and I wouldn't exaggerate. I'm fit and healthy. I speak fluent German and Russian and with my medical training I could have the perfect cover as a nurse.'

'Do you not think it would be better if you stayed in Britain and continued to work as a doctor?'

'I promised myself I would return to Poland when I was qualified. I see no reason to wait now.'

And so the questions went on. For over an hour. She was asked about her parents, her brother, her life in Poland before the war and her life since she'd come to Britain, including whether she was romantically involved.

'I was engaged. I found out recently that my fiancé was killed near the beginning of the war. By the Germans or the Russians, no one is quite certain which.'

'The Russians are our allies now. If we do send you out, we can't have you waging your own private war. Is that understood?'

'Perfectly. I only want to help my country. If the Russians are Britain's allies then they are ours too.' She pushed away the thought of what the Russians had done. Many of the Polish doctors, medical students and patients had been prisoners of the Red Army and had suffered almost as badly as those taken by the Germans.

Eventually the interview came to an end. 'You will need to go through a four-day assessment before we can decide whether to accept you. Will you be in London for long?'

'I'd planned to return to Edinburgh tomorrow, but I've been given compassionate leave from my hospital and I'm not due back for another week.'

'Could you delay your return? I might be able to arrange for you to attend the course this week if you could.'

'Then I'll stay.'

She had her hand on the door and was about to leave, when the woman cleared her throat. 'One last thing, Miss Kraszewska. You're a doctor or about to become one. What if you have to kill a Nazi? What if you have to shoot him, or slip a knife between his ribs?'

Irena turned around. 'If you'd asked me this even a week ago I would have said no. But I promise you, if it meant saving my life or one of my fellow Poles, I would do it. God forgive me, I would do it.'

Chapter 39

The day of her graduation was warm. She'd sent a ticket to Aleksy but he'd been unable to get leave. Isabel was unable to come either.

She'd not seen Richard since the evening at East Fortune. He'd sent several invitations to concerts and dances at the airfield, but she always wrote back with an excuse. In the last weeks she'd thought a lot about what Aleksy had said. Why shouldn't she and Richard grasp happiness where they could? Yet a part of her resisted. She was going back to Poland and there was a chance she would be killed. She had nothing to give him, especially not now. Nevertheless, knowing he was in the world and not far away was a sweet kind of torture.

When she was handed her diploma her pride was tempered with sadness. If only Tata could have seen this day. His daughter was finally a doctor. It was what they'd both wanted. Along with her fellow graduates she repeated the Hippocratic Oath, closing her eyes when it came to the part of Doing No Harm. Despite what she'd told the people on the assessment course, she wasn't sure she could kill anyone.

She walked out into the sunshine to find Richard amongst the crowd waiting in the square outside McEwan Hall. Seeing him, silhouetted against the sun, his blond hair like a halo, sent a shock of desire and longing through her. She knew it then.

Whatever she'd tried to tell herself, she loved him. She'd loved Piotr, but this was different, no less intense but stronger, surer.

Catching sight of her he walked towards her. 'Well done, darling,' he said, kissing her cheek.

'I didn't know you were coming.'

'If Muhammad won't come to the mountain, and all that . . . '

'Richard, I—'

'Mother told me about Piotr. I'm so sorry.'

'Would you like me to take your photograph?' Natasza, one of Irena's fellow graduands, interrupted. 'I can see you don't have a camera.'

'Thank you,' Richard said quickly. 'Where would you like us?'

'What about on the steps? It's where most people are having theirs taken.'

Irena stood beside him, feeling awkward, certain everyone could see the way her body reacted to being so near him – as if every part of her was reaching out to him.

'Where shall I send it when it's developed?' Natasza asked.

'Nineteen Charlotte Square, please. Care of Dr Maxwell.' Richard turned the full force of his smile on Natasza. 'I don't suppose you could make two copies?'

She blushed and smiled back. 'I could.'

When Natasza had left to join her friends, Richard took Irena by the elbow. 'I'm taking you for lunch. No arguments.'

'Why are you here?'

'Because I couldn't stay away.' He said it matter-of-factly, but the look in his eyes told her all she needed to know.

They crossed the road to The Doctors, a pub that Irena had been to before with Katherine. He raised a glass. 'To Dr Kraszewska. What will you do now? Will the Polish Hospital keep you on?' Although it would be the first time she'd lied to

Richard, it was time to use her cover story. She'd received a letter asking her to report to an address in Scotland in two weeks' time. She had been warned that there would be several stages to her training and it could be discontinued at any point. But she knew she wouldn't fail. She would do whatever it took to return to Poland.

'I've been asked if I would fill in for doctors on leave in the military hospitals.'

'In Scotland?'

'It could be anywhere.'

'England?'

'Perhaps.'

'It would be good if you were sent to England. I've to report back for active service in ten days' time. They need experienced pilots more than ever.'

It felt as if she there was a band of steel squeezing her heart. 'No!'

He frowned. 'No, because you don't want to be near me?'

'No, because I don't want you to go back into active service.'

'So you do care for me, just a little?'

'You know I do,' she whispered.

'Before I leave, I need to go to Skye to check on my father's lands and houses. I also want to see how the tenants are coping with the war. I want you to come with me.' The look in his eyes sent a tingle from her toes to her fingertips. 'What do you say? Will you come?'

She had two weeks before she was due to report for her preliminary training and to spend some of that time with Richard was suddenly irresistible. How could she bear to say no? God help her, she wasn't strong enough to deny herself just this little time with him.

'Yes,' she said. 'I'll come.'

Chapter 40

Skye, 1943

Although it was late by the time the train chugged its way into the station at Kyle, it was still light. Richard took their bags and hefted them onto his shoulder. 'We need to take a boat across to Skye,' he said, 'but we'll have to wait until morning to do that. In the meantime, I booked us a couple of rooms in a hotel close by.' He looked at her hopefully.

Irena just nodded. She would sleep with him, but not tonight. When she did she wanted it to be perfect and that excluded furtive visits along a hotel corridor.

The next morning they took the small ferry across to Skye. Richard, a secretive smile playing on his lips, disappeared into a small, single storey-building next to the post office and emerged with two heavy bicycles.

'Our mode of transport for the next few days,' he said, grinning broadly.

Irena was dismayed. 'I can't ride that,' she said. 'I don't know how.'

His eyebrows shot up. 'You can't be serious. Everyone knows how to ride a bike.'

Irena shook her head. 'Not me. Not many Poles can.'

'Then I'm afraid you are going to have to learn. There's no spare petrol to be had. It's either this or we walk.'

She eyed the bicycle, and walked around it.

'Come on, give it a bash,' Richard coaxed.

Tentatively, with him holding onto the edge of the saddle, Irena straddled the bicycle.

'The road is flat. It'll be a piece of cake. Don't worry, I won't let you go until you're ready."

A woman emerged from the post office and stared. Within moments she was joined by an assortment of villagers: two women with shopping, an old man with a pipe who watched with frank curiosity and several children who nudged each other and, giggling, pointed at Irena. The post master brought out a chair for an old woman dressed in black who'd been carrying a basket of fish on her back. They talked amongst themselves in a language Irena hadn't heard before.

'In front of these people?'

A man in a flat cap grinned at something the old woman said. He was missing a tooth at the front.

'Don't mind them,' Richard said. 'They're just here to cheer you on.'

Irena smiled vaguely in the direction of her audience and gritted her teeth. 'It's just a matter of confidence,' Richard continued. 'A kind of self-belief. If you think you can do it, then you will. Are you ready?'

She nodded. Then she was being pushed along by him. 'Peddle like mad,' he said, 'and keep both hands on the handle-bars.'

She did as he asked. The bike wobbled a little as she set off, but steadied as she gathered speed. Soon she was going along at a decent pace and she risked a glance behind her to check Richard was still holding onto her. When she saw that he'd let her go and was watching her from several feet away, she panicked and before she knew it she'd toppled into a ditch, her hands and knees tangled up with the bicycle.

She looked up to find Richard standing over her, his blue eyes creased with concern. Directly behind him was their audience. No one was laughing any more.

'Are you all right?' He crouched by her side. 'Can you stand?'

She moaned. 'My leg. I think it's broken. Perhaps my arm, too.'

'Bloody hell, Irena. I'm sorry. Here, let me help you up.'

He seemed so crestfallen, she couldn't help herself. She laughed and scrambled to her feet. 'I'm perfectly fine. This verge is as soft as a feather mattress. I just thought you deserved a scare for letting go of me.' She dusted herself down. 'I'll give it another shot.'

Richard couldn't hide his relief. He leaned across and removed something from her hair and showed it to her. It was a stalk of hay. 'Not quite what the best-dressed women in London are wearing, darling, although I have to say you'd look stunning in a sack.'

She spent another hour or so practising until she was sure she'd mastered her new transport. She tried going up a hill, around a few corners and, trickiest of all, down a slope. She took another spill, but managed to stop herself from landing on the ground by putting her feet down just in time. She noticed that her audience had swollen in numbers and although embarrassed by the attention, she smiled and waved to them. They nodded their approval when she signalled to Richard that she was ready to start their journey.

'I think that's enough cycling for one day,' he said, to her relief. It had been a long time since she'd done much vigorous exercise and her legs and bottom were already aching. 'Ian here says he'll give us a lift to Glendale House.'

It appeared that the man in the flat cap was the post office van driver. He tossed their luggage and their cycles into the back of his van, while Richard and Irena squeezed into the front.

It was a perfect afternoon, only a smear of white in an otherwise cloudless sky.

'And how are Lord and Lady Glendale?' Ian asked. 'It's been a long time since we've seen either of them.'

'They are both well,' Richard said. 'I know they'd like to have been able to come to Skye themselves, but they're always so busy.'

'I met your mother and grandfather when I was just a young lad,' Ian said. 'A ram butted me and broke my leg. Lady Glendale was just a slip of a girl back then, but I've never forgotten the way she rolled up her sleeves and helped her father fix it without batting an eyelid.'

'My mother is a remarkable woman,' Richard agreed.

'She and Lord Glendale must be very proud of you,' Ian continued. 'The newspapers have been full of what you lads did to keep the Jerries out of Britain.' He took one hand off the steering wheel to light his pipe. 'Some people thought you'd turn out more like your Uncle Charles, but me and the wife always knew you wouldn't let the earl down.' He turned to Irena. 'We like to keep up with what the family is doing, miss.'

Irena shot Richard a look and raised an eyebrow in question. *Tell you later*, he mouthed.

'And how is your wife? And the children? Not children now, are they?'

Ian's smile dimmed. 'My son David is in France with the Lovat Scouts. The wife worries about him but I tell her he'll be all right – as long as he keeps his head down. At least we've got that Hitler fellow on the run. And now the Americans are in it too, we can't fail to win, can we?'

He brought the van to a halt while they waited for a shepherd driving a flock of sheep to pass. 'My daughters are both doing army work,' Ian continued. 'One is with the ATS and the other is a VAD in London. Their mam is hoping they'll get some leave soon enough. She doesn't like having an empty house. Mind you, we're kept busy growing crops to send to the mainland. You just let me know if you need anything and I'll send it over.' He gave a conspiratorial smile. 'If you fancy some venison that could be arranged, too.'

While Ian and Richard chatted about the people they knew, Irena stared out the window. Skye was a beautiful place, with mountains on one side and lochs on the other. In the fields women in trousers, their hair hidden under scarves, wielded scythes to cut the hay. As the van passed them, they stopped to wave. The rich scent of freshly mown hay transported Irena back in time to her grandmother's farm and a sense of peace flooded through her. Here, except for the noticeable absence of young men, the war might not be happening.

Irena must have nodded off, because the next thing she knew, they had turned off the main road and were bumping down a narrow track.

'Good, you're awake,' Richard said. 'You looked so peaceful I didn't want to disturb you.'

'What time is it?'

'After three,' Richard replied. 'Are you hungry?'

'Starving.'

'Mrs Nicholson should have something prepared for us. I telephoned to let her know we were coming. I told her we could see to ourselves today, but she wouldn't have it.'

'Let your lordship look after yourself? And you with a guest?' Ian snorted, slamming the door of his van. 'Of course she wouldn't. She's been like a woman possessed since she heard you were coming.' He doffed his cap. 'I'm away then before Mairi sees me. She's always bending my ear about the mail. I think she holds me personally responsible for it not getting through.'

Richard and Irena were greeted by a woman wearing a scarf

that couldn't quite contain her wild grey hair. Her dress had been darned many times and her cardigan was missing a button.

'Lord Richard,' she said in her musical voice, 'I wondered if I'd see you again before God saw fit to take me.'

He took her hands in his. 'It's been too long, Mairi. How are you?'

'I'm fine, just fine.' Her eyes clouded. 'You heard about my Kenneth?'

'I did. I'm so sorry. He was a brave lad. A credit to you and Hector.'

Mairi pulled a handkerchief from the pocket of her apron and blew her nose. 'God only takes the good. Now who is this you have with you?' She turned her light blue eyes to Irena.

'This is Dr Kraszewska, a friend of the family. She'll be staying here too.'

'*Fáilte* – welcome,' the woman said simply. 'I've made some scones and soup. I imagine you'll be hungry?'

'Ravenous,' Richard answered. 'Scones and soup will be just the ticket.'

After another long look at Irena, Mairi sniffed and retreated back inside.

'I'm not sure she cares much for me,' Irena said.

Richard looked surprised. 'Does it matter?'

Inside, the house was comfortable without being overly grand. It was a large two-storey building with two sitting rooms, a library, a dining room and several bedrooms. Hers overlooked the garden and despite the heat of the sun outside, Irena shivered. Had she done the right thing coming here with Richard? Was it fair to him when she knew this could be the last time he saw her?

A short while later there was a knock on the door and she opened it to find Mairi holding a large jug.

'There's no running hot water in the house, so I thought you might need some to wash up.' She nodded towards a basin on the dressing table. 'If you leave it outside your room door, I'll get rid of it later.'

'Thank you.' Irena took the jug from her. 'Have you been with the family for long?'

'Since Lord Richard was a lad. My mother was here with the previous Lord and Lady Glendale. I took over from her when she got too old to work. The family don't come here much any more, but these big houses soon get damp if they're left to their own devices.' She wound her fingers together and gave Irena a hard look. 'The last time Lord Richard was here, there was a sadness in his eyes I didn't like to see. He looked like a man who'd seen too much death. He might have been able to fool the others with his big smile but he couldn't fool me.'

'I expect we're all sadder than we were before the war,' Irena said gently.

'I didn't say he was sad *this* time. Strikes me that he's happier than he's been for a long time. I suspect it has something to do with you.'

'What do you mean?'

'That lad is in love with you. If you do anything to take away the light in his eyes, you'll have me to answer to.'

Irena's heart splintered. 'I care for him too, Mairi.'

The housekeeper shuffled her feet. 'Aye, well, now I've got that off my chest, how are Lord and Lady Glendale?'

'They're both well.'

'It's a shame they don't come here any more – not that she ever came much but Lord Glendale used to pay us a visit once or twice a year. As for the house in Borreraig, no one has stayed there for years now – not since before the war and Lord Richard brought his friends up for the Skye Ball. I suspect he wanted to keep out of the way so no one would know when they got up to their usual high jinx.' Her mouth turned up at the corners. 'He always was a mischievous scamp.'

'Is it far away? The other house?'

'Not by car. It would take you a good while to get to it by bicycle. Why? Will you be going there?'

'I'm not sure of our plans, but we might. I imagine Richard will want to check on it.'

'I imagine he will. Right then, best not spend all day chatting – not when I've work to do.'

Later, when Irena had freshened up, she went downstairs. She found Richard in the library looking through some of the books on the shelves. He'd changed out of his uniform and into a pair of trousers and an open-necked shirt. He looked so different she almost felt a little shy of him.

'Did you find everything you needed?' he asked.

'Yes, thank you. Mairi brought me up some water to wash.' She slid him a look. 'And gave me a bit of a talking-to.' She knew it amused Richard when she used British idioms.

He grinned at her. 'What did she say?'

'Something along the lines that she'd have my guts for garters – is that the right expression? – if I hurt you.'

'Good old Mairi. She's always been on my side.'

'What did Ian mean about your uncle?' she said, more to change the subject than because she really wanted to know.

'Uncle Charles? I gather he came to a nasty end. He disappeared before I was born. A couple of years later his body was found. It had been buried. Clearly he fell foul of someone on the island.'

'He was murdered! That's terrible.'

He lifted his eyebrows. 'I suspect every family has their share of skeletons in the closet. Why should we be any different? It was a long time ago. My parents don't talk about it much but the islanders have always had their views.'

Irena was intrigued. Nothing she knew of the Maxwell family had hinted that they had their secrets. But how well did she know them? Certainly not well enough to be privy to things that had happened in the past. However, it was reassuring to know they weren't perfect.

She took a seat by the fire. Although it was summer, Mairi had lit it and Irena was glad of its heat. This old house with its thick walls was cold.

'And what views do the islanders hold?' she asked.

'They believe that one of the crofters did away with him.'

'Why?'

'That's the part no one seems sure about. My uncle was a bit of a drinker apparently and a womaniser too.'

Irena hid a smile. Uncle and nephew had something in common then. Or at least they'd had once.

'There's a rumour of an illegitimate child.' He shrugged. 'Perhaps that had something to do with it? An angry father, a scorned lover – although ... ' He stopped and for a moment she thought he was going elaborate but then he shook his head. 'It's all speculation and happened a long time ago. Let's talk of something else. Have you warmed up yet?'

'Perfectly. So you have two houses on Skye. Is that not a little greedy?'

He looked surprised. 'This one is part of the estate. We let the tenants do what they like with the land. They can even buy their crofts if they choose, although most prefer to remain tenants. The estate brings income to the island. We pay for repairs to the crofters' homes, employ as many as we can and, before the war, employed several more to keep the house running.'

He clearly didn't care for the implied criticism. Most of the time she forgot he was an aristocrat and used to the privileges of his class, no doubt without thinking too much about them. It was the same in Poland, but she couldn't see that it could continue in whatever new world was going to emerge after the war.

'And the one in Borreraig?'

'It belongs to my mother. Although she doesn't go there, she won't part with it. My father would like her to sell it. Unlike this house it doesn't have an estate to go with it. And, despite what you think, my father doesn't like holding on to property for the sake of it. But neither will he sell it without my mother's agreement.'

Mairi popped her head around the door. 'Your dinner is ready. It's not what you're used to but I've done the best I can.'

Irena and Richard shared a smile. 'I'm sure it will be wonderful.' He held out his arm for Irena to take. 'Shall we eat?'

The dining room was glacial. Mairi had set a place at one end of the long table for her and another at the other for Richard so that they were separated by an expanse of polished wood.

Mairi served them their soup. It was some sort of broth with lumps of meat in it. Although it didn't look very appetising, it smelled delicious. 'There's roast mutton and potatoes in the oven,' Mairi said, 'and I made some seaweed pudding for after.'

'Thank you, Mairi,' Richard said. 'Why don't you get off home? We can see to ourselves.'

'If you're certain? It's just that my Hector is waiting for his dinner at home. He's useless when it comes to seeing to himself. He seems to think that his arms and legs stop working as soon as he steps inside my kitchen.'

'Off you go, Mairi. Give him my regards.'

Mairi paused by the door. 'He wants to know whether you'll be needing the boat while you're here. He pulled it onto the shore down at our house but he says he can fetch it for you no bother if you'll be wanting it?'

'Tell him thank you from me, but I might collect it myself tomorrow if the weather's fine.'

When Mairi left, Irena took a mouthful of soup. It was good, but already chilling in the cold dining room. She picked up her plate. 'Let's eat in the kitchen,' she said.

'In the kitchen?' He grinned. 'Why not?'

It was much warmer there than in the dining room, the stove giving off a good heat. Clearly Mairi's domain, there was a scrubbed wooden table in the centre of the room with a bench on one side and chairs on the other, linoleum on the floor and two wooden sideboards stuffed with pots and pans as well as a dresser filled with plates.

'I wonder what Mairi will say if she finds out we've been making ourselves at home in her kitchen?' Richard said.

'I like it,' Irena said. 'It's cosy.' For the first time she could remember their conversation was stilted.

They ate in silence for a while. When they'd finished, Irena took the food out of the oven and served them both.

'I never had you pegged as being domestic,' Richard said. 'I rather like this different side to you.' His eyes glittered as he held her gaze. 'Although you must know by now, there isn't much I don't like about you.'

Her heart hammered. 'I can cook, you know,' Irena said. 'One day I'll make you some Polish food to prove it.'

'Just as I thought. Perfect.'

'If you mean me, you're wrong. I'm not perfect. I want you to love me despite my faults – not some mythical version of me.'

When she realised what she'd said, she bit her lip and rushed on. 'I hate being cold and when food isn't rationed, I eat too much.'

He was still looking at her. 'I think you're the bravest, most adorable woman I've ever met.'

Her face grew warm under his frank admiration. 'Please, Richard, don't.' She sucked in a breath. Before she knew it the words were spilling out and she was telling him about the mother and baby she didn't try to save – telling him of her fear, and her guilt – her awful, awful guilt. 'I could have taken the baby. There was a moment … before the soldiers came around the corner … but I didn't. So you see – I'm not brave.'

'My darling girl, how long have you being keeping this inside? You could have been killed. They might have shot you too.' He scooped her into his arms and onto his lap, soothing her with words of love.

'I could have saved their lives,' she whispered.

'I still think you're the bravest, most adorable woman I've ever met. But you don't have to be brave any more, my darling. I'll never let anything happen to you.'

She buried her face in him and cried. For the child she hadn't been able to save, for Piotr, for Magdalena and all the dead, for Poland.

She must have fallen asleep because she woke up on the sofa with her shoes off covered by a blanket. There was no sign of Richard.

The curtains were open and the moonlight flooded through an open window. After the smog of Edinburgh, the air, delicately scented with the smoke from the fires, smelled better than any perfume. The gentle swishing of the branches of trees as they swayed in the breeze filtered in from outside.

She heard a crunch of gravel and the rasp of a match striking. Moments later the smell of tobacco drifted into the room. She pushed the blanket aside and padded over to the window.

Richard was standing looking out over the garden. There was a full moon and she could see him clearly. Her heart banged against her ribs. He was a golden man. A good man. Possibly a man without a future. He'd be going back to active service when they left here and might never return.

And she loved him. God help her, she loved him. He hadn't been repulsed by what she'd told him. He still loved her.

They had nine days left and for that time she was going to forget about Poland, forget about young men dying, forget about everything. She was going to pretend that she was safe and everything was all right with the world. She wouldn't think about the past or the future. For the next nine days she'd be the Irena Kraszewska she was before the war – she would be a woman who could love without fear.

She opened the door and ran out into the night. He didn't turn around at the sound of her footsteps. 'Go back to bed, Irena,' he said quietly.

Her heart still beating a tattoo she stepped towards him and wrapped her arms around him, resting her face on his back. 'Only if you come too,' she whispered.

The next morning she lay for a while staring down at him. She felt lighter, freer, than she had in years. Leaving Richard sleeping, she threw her robe over her shoulders and crept down to the kitchen. Mairi was already there, stirring something on the stove.

'Good morning. I was just making the porridge before I brought you up some hot water. If you're wanting a bath you'll have to wait until the pans on the stove are boiling.'

'A wash will be fine. I might have a bath later. I don't want to put you to any trouble.'

Mairi's eyebrows shot up. 'It's no trouble. It's what I'm paid for.' She lifted a kettle from the stove, poured some water into a teapot and placed it back on the hot plate. 'I was about to bring you up a tray.' She seemed a little put out to find Irena in her kitchen. 'Did you eat in here last night?'

'It was warmer.'

'Lord Maxwell eating in the kitchen! Dearie me.'

'Does it matter?' Irena asked.

'It does to the earl. I can't imagine Lord Glendale eating in a kitchen.'

'Times are changing.'

'Aye, well. Perhaps where you come from. But not here.' She finished setting the tray and placed the teapot on it along with a cup and saucer. 'I'll just take this up to his lordship.'

'I'll take it,' Irena said quickly, reaching out.

When Mairi eyed her, Irena blushed. 'So that's the way it is,' the older woman said. 'Can't say I approve, but who am I to say what's right and what's wrong? At least the boy's happy. I'll bring up some water – to *your* room – in a minute. Did you find the towels I left at the end of your bed?'

Irena took the tray back upstairs. Richard was still sleeping, his arms flung wide and a smile on his mouth, so she left the tray by his bed and returned to her room.

As she washed, she thought about the night before. Making love to Richard had been everything she'd imagined and more. She could still feel the touch of his hands on her skin, his mouth kissing places she'd never imagined could be kissed – the feel of his hard, strong body against hers – the feel of him inside her – the look on his face when she'd cried out with pleasure.

Her heart was singing as she dressed in slacks, a blouse and a cardigan. Downstairs she found Richard waiting for her in the dining room. As soon as he saw her, he stood and held out a chair for her to sit.

'How did you sleep?' he asked, smiling. 'I was disappointed to find you gone when I woke.'

She blushed. 'After we, er, I remember putting my head on the pillow and then nothing.' No nightmares, no dreams. No more eyeless women and dead babies reaching out to her. Just deep, peaceful sleep. 'What would you like to do today?'

A slow smile spread across his face. 'I know what I'd like to do, but I doubt if Mairi would approve. She's already ticked me off.'

'Can't we persuade her she's not needed?' Irena whispered.

'I have an idea. Why don't we stay at my mother's house? We'd be alone. We could spend all day in bed if we wanted. We could cycle there or take the boat and Mairi could arrange to have our bags sent over.'

'I would like that. Perhaps we could go out in the boat later?'

He hooked his arms behind his head and grinned. 'I told you, you are my perfect woman.'

Later that morning they cycled to the house in Borreraig. As soon as she saw it, Irena knew why Isabel loved it. It was set at the end of a dirt road and hidden by trees but at the bottom of the track the vista opened up directly onto a loch. On the other side, lush green mountains echoed with the sound of sheep. Birds swirled overhead as waves shushed on the shore.

'What a lovely place to have a house,' she said.

Richard looked pleased. 'I thought you'd like it. I have to admit I've only stayed here once – with friends.'

She took him by the hand. 'Let's explore.'

Inside it was as if the house was waiting for them; Irena went from window to window, opening the curtains and shutters to let in the light and pulling the dust sheets from the furniture.

'When was the last time someone lived here?' she asked.

'My father's factor stayed here before the war for a month or so while the gate house in Glendale was being prepared for him and his family and I came here with friends a few years ago, but otherwise it's been empty.'

'A house like this needs to be lived in,' Irena said. 'It should have a family and children.'

Richard grinned, pulling her towards him. 'Is that a hint?'

She wriggled out of his arms. 'I'm not talking about us . . .' She bit her lip. No matter how much she wished for it, whoever lived here, it wouldn't be her. 'But you will marry one day.'

'The only woman I want to marry is you.'

The world seemed to stop turning. Irena sucked in a breath. She turned to him and traced the line of his jaw with her fingertip. 'You mustn't wish for something that can never be.'

'I love you, you must know that.'

'You're only saying that because you think it's the only way you can have me,' she said lightly.

The smile left his face. 'Don't pretend, Irena. It doesn't suit you. I've never told a woman I loved her before, and I wouldn't say it now if I didn't mean it. And I certainly wouldn't propose if I wasn't sure you were the only woman I'll ever love.'

He looked so much like a petulant little boy whose toy has been taken away from him, that for a moment she wanted to laugh.

'I won't give up, you know,' she said. 'I'll wait for as long as it takes.'

His hand was on her shoulder and she could feel its heat through the thin material of her blouse. Hadn't she promised herself last night that she wouldn't think of the past or of the future? Piotr was dead and this man made her feel more alive than she could remember. But it wasn't fair to let him believe that they had a future when she knew she was going to leave him. And despite everything, she was still going to leave him.

'Are you worried I won't make it?' he said softly, as if reading her mind.

She couldn't tell him that it wasn't him she was afraid wouldn't make it, but her. 'You'll make it,' she murmured. 'Of course you will.'

'Is it because of Piotr? Do you still love him?'

'I did love him, very much. I won't pretend that I didn't. But he's dead and nothing can bring him back. You'll have realised I'm no virgin, Richard. I slept with him. Once. And I'll never regret it. But I'm tired of feeling sad. I'm tired of feeling lonely.' She stepped forward until she could feel the heat of his body and raised her face. 'Let's just pretend,' she whispered. 'For the next few days, let's pretend we are married, that there is no war and that we have day after day to be together.'

He bent his head and kissed her. 'Let's go upstairs.'

Time passed too quickly. At night, after they'd made love, they lay in each other's arms listening to the sound of the sea. During the day they fished or swam, sometimes cooking their catch over a fire outside the boathouse close to the shore. It had become their favourite spot. Down there, hidden from view, looking out over the changing waters of the loch, the war receded from their thoughts and they let themselves believe it wasn't happening. Irena found rubber boots in the porch and they tramped across the moors for miles, keeping away from the road. Richard pointed out sea eagles and the dolphins who visited the shore nearby. Sometimes they startled a deer or a rabbit, but Richard never took a gun with them on their walks. He'd had, he said, his fill of death.

Most days they would call on a family living on the estate. Richard would ask about husbands, sons, brothers, and sisters who were with units far away, impressing Irena with the way he seemed to recall names and regiments with ease.

In the evenings she would cook pierogi for him from cabbage and rabbit meat and he'd stand behind her, snaking his arms around her waist and nuzzling her neck, until laughing she'd give up and let him take her to bed.

She began to dread the coming of the night, knowing that it

signalled one less day they had to spend together. When they returned to Edinburgh she would be leaving him for good and she couldn't even tell him. It seemed so cruel and sometimes, for the briefest moment, she wondered if she was doing the right thing. She also knew she had no choice. Often, in the heart of the night, she would slip out of bed and curl up in the armchair and watch him sleep in the shaft of moonlight from the window, trying to imprint every line of his face and body onto her mind. Then she'd ease back into bed and wrap her arms around him, letting the strong beat of his heart lull her back to sleep.

Every morning they'd open the back door to find a different gift on their doorstep: a salmon wrapped in newspaper, a few eggs, potatoes, carrots, some flat baked bread, a brace of rabbits, a haunch of venison or an urn of creamy milk, still warm from the cow.

One day, the warmest of the summer so far, they changed into bathing costumes and swam in the loch. Laughing, Irena clung to him, wrapping her legs around his waist. When he touched her it was as if every cell in her body came alive and she could never resist him. They made love in the loch, a golden eagle their only witness.

Out of the water it was cool. Richard gave her his shirt to put on and she sat on a rock drying her hair.

'Stay exactly like that.' He bent down and picked up a camera. 'Do you know I've never seen you so happy.'

She smiled into the camera as he took her photograph. It was true; her happiness was dimmed only by the knowledge that she'd be leaving him soon.

On their last night, as the sun was sinking in the sky, they retreated to their favourite rock, outside the boathouse. Richard sat behind her, Irena between his legs, his chin resting on the top of her head.

'I wish I could keep you with me,' he murmured. 'Always.'

She wriggled in his arms until she was facing him. She placed her hands on either side of his face. '*Kocham Cię*. I love you,' she said. 'I love you more than I thought it was possible to love anyone. You are the other half of my soul.'

'Then if you love me, why won't you marry me?'

'Love isn't everything, Richard. I can't marry you – not yet – not until I feel right with myself.'

'How can you not? What is it? What are you keeping from me?' His face hardened. 'If you won't marry me, why are you with me?'

She searched for the words that would make him understand, that would make him realise there was no hope. 'Being with you makes me happy. I could die a hundred times and I'd still love you. But this, being here, is not the real us. You have to go back to your world and, sooner or later, I'll return to mine.'

'Your world is here with me.'

'I wish it could be.' She shushed his protests with the tip of her finger. 'Please, Richard, don't spoil the little time we have left.'

Time both elongated and contracted. She wanted to stop the clock, spin out every second. Sometimes she allowed herself to dream that one day, when it was all over, they would come back here. Richard would look after the estate while she worked as the island doctor. They would live in the house in Borreraig and fill the empty rooms with children.

Of course she knew it was just a dream. Richard was going back to his squadron and she was going to Poland. This time might be all they ever had.

Chapter 41

Edinburgh and Skye, 1989

'So you're going to Skye,' Gilly said. They had met at the Portrait Gallery for lunch. Sarah had made one of her increasingly infrequent trips into the office and was expected back. Her boss hadn't been too pleased when she'd asked for more time off, and had warned her that unless she came back to work full time, he'd have to replace her. They were a small firm, he'd said, and as much as he sympathised with her situation, they had to have employees they could rely on.

She was crazy to be risking her job. If she lost it, she wouldn't be able to make her mortgage payments, never mind employ someone to look after Mum when she came home. Yet, she couldn't bring herself to care. The need to find out what happened to her mother as a child consumed her to the point she could think of little else.

Sarah broke off a piece of bread and spread it with butter. 'It seems the next logical step. I don't know why I didn't think of doing it before. There's nothing else to learn here. I want to know what happened to Mum before I tell her what I've been up to. Sometimes the doubts creep in. What if Mum doesn't want to remember and my dragging up her past means she has to confront things she'd rather stay forgotten?'

'But she wants you to find Magdalena. And Magdalena is the

key to her past. Besides, whatever happened to your mother, it's your story too,' Gilly said gently.

'I know. I need to find Magdalena,' Sarah swallowed, trying to relieve the pressure in her throat, 'before it's too late.'

'I thought your mum was showing signs of improvement?'

'Yes, but—' Sarah's voice hitched. 'That doesn't mean she won't have another stroke. I can't get over this feeling that knowing I'm trying to find Magdalena has given her hope. I know that sounds crazy, but,' she lifted her shoulders, 'it's how I feel.'

Gilly covered Sarah's hand with hers. 'I don't think it's crazy at all. I know how much you love her.' She waited until Sarah blew her nose and wiped her eyes. 'Are you going to stay in the Glendale's house in Skye?'

'I don't see why I shouldn't. The solicitors gave me a set of keys and it's not as if there is anyone who can object.'

'What does Matthew say?'

'Does it matter? He's my boyfriend, not my keeper.'

Gilly leaned back in her chair, tapping her soup spoon against her lips. 'So the worm is turning.'

'What do you mean?'

'Oh, for heaven's sake, Sarah, don't you realise he's not for you?'

'He's perfectly right for me. He's good to me, he has a great job and most importantly he loves me.'

'If he loved you it would never have crossed his mind to ask you to go to Geneva when your mum is ill. He would have turned down the job and kept shtum about it. God, you don't even have the same interests. You like reading but I doubt he's ever picked up a book in his life. You like country music, he's an opera buff.' She narrowed her eyes. 'You've never even admitted to him that opera bores you to tears, have you?'

Sarah squirmed in her seat. 'No but—'

'I suspect he only goes because he wants to be seen at the right places with the right sort of people.'

'You're being unfair,' Sarah retorted, stung.

Gilly sighed. 'Am I? Think about it, Sarah. Mr Perfect-for-you might not be so perfect after all. He has his future all mapped out. A future that suits him. But what about you? Are you sure it's what you want?'

No, she wasn't. And that was the problem.

It was a long drive to Skye but Sarah didn't mind. She always thought best when driving. She felt she was getting closer to finding out about her mother and, with a bit of luck, this trip would give her another piece of the puzzle.

It was raining heavily by the time she reached the island and found the road that would take her to Dunvegan and, ultimately, to Borreraig House. The lower slopes of the Cuillins were only just visible, their summits completely hidden by clouds, and it took all her concentration to see where she was going on the single-track roads.

Coming to a dead end she realised she must have missed her destination and had to turn the car around, rolling down the window as she snaked along, trying to find it. Finally, there it was. An open gate hung half off its hinges, the name of the house on a small rusty plate on the fence post, almost overgrown by a creeping hedge of wild roses. No wonder she'd passed it.

She drove down the rutted driveway bordered on both sides by trees that blocked out the sunlight. As she clambered out of the car, easing the stiffness in the small of her back, the rain stopped and the sun came out. She gasped with delight.

The house was close to the edge of Loch Dunvegan and if it hadn't been so isolated, hidden as it was from any other house, it would have been perfect. Sarah sniffed the air – there was a pungent smell she didn't recognise – like coal but sweeter. Shouldering her bag, she unlocked the door and let herself in.

She found the kitchen and, dropping her bag to the floor, looked around curiously. There was an ancient black-leaded stove on one side, lino on the floor and a pine table with an armchair in the corner. A door led through to a pantry where she found several tins of Frey Bentos corned beef that looked as if they'd been there for years.

The other rooms seemed frozen in time too. The sitting room was furnished with what must have been the original furniture: high-backed, upholstered armchairs and a faded rug covering a wooden floor. There was even an antiquated gramophone with a pile of long-playing records next to it. She rifled through them. Bing Crosby – she'd always thought of him as an actor – some classical records and some jazz.

Upstairs there were several bedrooms and she chose the smallest, on the basis it would warm up quicker. It had a single cast-iron bed, a bookcase, dressing table and, to her delight, a view over the loch. She found blankets and linen in one of the cupboards and quickly made the bed. When she finally crept between the sheets, having warmed them with a hot water bottle, she fell asleep as soon as her head hit the pillow.

The next morning, realising she hadn't asked exactly where Lord Glendale was buried, she studied the map of Skye she'd brought with her. About five miles away was the village of Glendale. It seemed an obvious place to start looking.

The village was little more than a scattering of houses, a small shop with a post office sign, a community hall and two churches. Imagine having a village named after you – or was it the other way round?

A bell tinkled as she let herself into the General Dealers.

There was a counter with a till, a large fridge and an old-fashioned freezer, and some shelves with an eclectic assortment of tins and packets. Sarah selected a couple of packets of pasta, and a few tomatoes and potatoes from the tired-looking array on a bottom shelf as well as a bottle of white wine. Just as she was beginning to wonder whether the shop was completely unmanned, a stout middle-aged woman appeared from somewhere in the back.

'Oh hello, dear. Have you managed to find what you're looking for?'

'I don't suppose you have any sweet potatoes?'

'Just what you see on the shelves. Now if you'd come a couple of days ago, you might have been in luck. We get a delivery from the mainland on Mondays and Thursdays. That's when most locals do their shopping. But you wouldn't know that, would you, dear? You're not from these parts.'

'I'm from Edinburgh.' She waited while the woman rang up her purchases.

'Five pounds and thirteen pence. Edinburgh. Well, then. It's a lovely city. Are you staying long?'

'A couple of days.' Sarah tipped her purse onto the counter and counted out the money. 'I'm staying at Borreraig House. Do you know it?'

'Oh, the doctor's house – that's what the locals call it. Katherine didn't mention it had been let.'

Sarah's heart skipped a beat. 'Katherine? She knows the Glendales, then?'

'Oh, aye. Well, she did. You do know Lord Glendale died recently, don't you? He's buried in the cemetery just across the road.'

Sarah's fingers tingled. Her instinct had been right. She would go and find Richard's grave as soon as she was finished here.

'You don't have a number for Katherine, by any chance? Or an address?'

The shop assistant folded her arms, curiosity shining from her bright blue eyes. 'An address is easy enough. She lives in the house on the hill opposite one you're staying in. Can't miss it. You can see it from the road.'

Sarah picked up her shopping. 'Thank you so much.' She paused at the door. 'The cemetery's across the road, you say?'

'Aye. If you're looking for Lord Glendale's grave, it's the big one on the right.'

A few minutes later, Sarah was standing in front of it. On top of the recently filled mound of earth was a bouquet of wild flowers. Along with his dates of birth and death and his RAF rank, his simple granite headstone was engraved with a few lines. She traced the words with the tip of her finger and whispered them out loud. *'At the going down of the sun and in the morning, we will remember.'*

As eager as she was to talk to Katherine, Sarah forced herself to wait until mid-morning.

There was only one house on the opposite side of the road to where she was staying, an old-fashioned crofthouse, the likes of which she'd seen dotting the landscape as she'd driven through Skye. She knocked tentatively on the door but, receiving no reply, wandered around to the back of the house where she found a woman, somewhere in her late sixties, pinning washing to a line.

'Excuse me, are you Katherine?'

The woman swung around and smiled around the peg she was holding in the corner of her mouth. She removed the peg and held out her hand. 'That would be me. You must be the lass staying in the doctor's house. What can I do for you?'

Sarah had expected someone much frailer, not this energetic, slightly plump woman with bright blue eyes and, albeit grey in places, curling hair. 'I'm looking for someone who can tell me about the late Lord Glendale. I was told you knew the family.'

'Yes, I did.' A sad smile flitted across Katherine's face. 'Let's go inside and have some tea.' She picked up the empty washing basket in one hand and a bucket of what looked like clods of earth in the other.

'Shall I take that for you?' Sarah offered, but when Katherine passed it to her it almost fell from her hands. It was far heavier than it looked.

Katherine led her into a kitchen similar to the one in Borreraig House. It had a Rayburn and a scrubbed table with several chairs around the edge. It was warm and bright and smelled of baking.

'Now then, let me get you a cup of tea and then we'll talk properly.' Katherine shifted a heavy black kettle onto the stove and bent to stoke the fire. 'Is the house warm enough? It's been empty for quite a time.' Her voice was soft, almost musical.

'It is a bit chilly. I didn't have much luck lighting the stove.'

'It's easy enough when you get the knack. I could send my grandson down if you like, to give you a hand? He won't be in until later, though.'

'Thanks, but I'm sure I'll work it out.'

Katherine placed scones on a plate and took some pancakes from her larder and set about buttering them.

'How many children do you have?' Sarah asked. Desperate as she was to quiz Katherine, she couldn't launch in straight away with her questions.

'Three – two daughters and a son. Five grandchildren as well.' She tipped her head towards a shelf filled with photographs.

Responding to the unspoken invitation, Sarah picked up a

photograph of a woman in a graduation gown. There was one of another woman and a man, both holding degrees and looking self-consciously into the camera. The rest were of children at various ages as they grew into adulthood. 'Do they live here?'

'Heavens, no. They come home on holiday but they prefer the city. 'My daughter, Emily, is a thoracic surgeon in Glasgow; Susan is a lawyer in London and Donald is in Italy.' She smiled. 'Now come to the table and have your tea.'

She set a plate piled high with scones and pancakes in front of Sarah. Surely all this wasn't for her alone? It seemed, however, that indeed it was. Katherine poured Sarah a cup of tea so strong a teaspoon could have stood up in it, before taking a seat on the other side of the table.

'Aren't you having anything?' Sarah asked.

'Oh, no. When you get to my age you have to watch your weight.' She patted her slightly rounded stomach. 'Emily is always telling me off for baking every day even when I'm on my own.' She grinned. ' My grandson does his best when he's here, but even he can't keep up. The deep freezer is full to the brim and I hate to throw anything away.'

Sarah bit into a buttered scone thick with cheese and washed it down with a sip of tea. Emily's loss was her gain, although how she was going to get through all of it, she had no idea.

'Now, my dear,' Katherine said, topping up Sarah's teacup, 'what is it you want to know about the Glendales?'

'Lord Glendale left the house I'm staying in to my mother as well as one in Charlotte Square – in the event a certain Magdalena Drobnik isn't alive to claim them. Does the name ring a bell?'

Katherine's brow knotted. 'I did wonder how you came to be staying in Richard's house, but I assumed his family had decided to rent it out before putting it on the market. I'm afraid the name Magdalena Drobnik means nothing to me. Doesn't your mother know who she is?'

'Mum had a stroke a couple of months ago. She can hardly speak now, but she did seem to recognise Magdalena from an old photograph Lord Glendale left to her. I would have brought it to show you, but Mum insisted on keeping it. I think Mum must have known Magdalena when she was younger – and she wants me to find her.' Sarah's throat tightened. 'I only recently found out that Mum was adopted when she was a little girl.'

'I'm not surprised you didn't know your mother was adopted,' Katherine said. 'In those days most people kept it quiet. They believed it was better for the child that way.'

'If you don't know who Magdalena Drobnik was, I don't suppose you know anyone who might?'

Katherine shook her head. 'I really wish I could help you.'

Sarah sagged back in her chair, realising she'd been pinning her hopes on Katherine knowing something.

'What about an Irena Kraszewska, then?'

Katherine sat up straighter. 'Irena? Yes, I knew her.'

'You did?' Excitement jolted through Sarah and she leaned forward. 'I was wondering if Magdalena and Irena knew each other. Were sisters even.'

'I don't believe Irena had a sister. If I remember correctly she had a brother – Aleksy, I think his name was – who was with the RAF.'

'Do you know what happened to him?'

Katherine shook her head. 'I'm sorry, I don't.'

'What can you tell me about Irena? I'm convinced there's a connection between her and Magdalena. And between them and Richard.'

Katherine pulled out a chair and sat down. 'I can fill in *some* of the blanks. At least about Irena. I met her during the war.' Some of the light died in Katherine's eyes. 'I haven't thought about the war in a long time, but perhaps it will be easier for you to understand what I do know if I start there.

'I met Irena through Richard, Lord Glendale.' She smiled. 'I thought she was the most beautiful yet the saddest woman I had ever seen. She had this hair I envied – it was like a cloud of gold – and blue eyes paler than a summer sky. It was Richard who introduced us. She'd turned up on his father's doorstep one day – it must have been 'forty-one. No, was it 'forty-two? I can't remember. Wait, it was 'forty-one because I was in my second year as a student nurse in the Infirmary, although that wasn't where I met her first.' She shook her head. 'Oh dear, I'm not telling this very well, am I?'

Although Sarah had several questions she was burning to ask – such as how Katherine knew Richard in the first place – she decided it was better to let the older woman tell her story in her own way and in her own time.

'Anyway, whenever it was, I soon found out why she was so sad. She'd been in Poland – she was Polish, you see, did you know that?'

When Sarah nodded, Katherine continued. 'She was there when war broke out and had seen some awful things, I imagine – I couldn't then, of course, not really. At that time I hadn't seen much of the war first hand – we were spared the worst of it in Edinburgh. That changed when I joined the QAs.' She paused and sat in silence for a while.

'The QAs?' Sarah prodded gently.

'The Queen Alexandra's Imperial Military Nursing Service. We called it the QAs for short. I joined them as soon as I could, but I couldn't go out with them until I had finished my training and that wasn't until 'forty-three. So that's right, it must have been 'forty-one when I first met Irena.'

'Lady Dorothea told me the same thing – I mean the part about Irena coming to London after escaping from Poland.'

'Richard's aunt is still alive? Goodness. She must be a very old lady.'

'Almost a hundred. But pretty sharp with it.'

'I never met Lady Dorothea,' Katherine said, 'although my mother spoke of her. But that has nothing to do with Irena – or maybe it has. Anyway, let me carry on before I get even more muddled.

'Irena was a medical student. There were Poles all over Scotland at that time, my dear, in our air force, in our army. Just everywhere. We loved them. They were so polite and so fierce. They hated what the Nazis were doing to their country and were determined to do what they could to make it free again.'

'Do you know why Irena sought out Lord Glendale's family?' Sarah asked.

'That I can't tell you. Some sort of connection in the past, perhaps? Or in Poland? Does it matter?'

'I don't know. I'm sorry I interrupted. Please go on.'

'Irena stayed with Richard's mother, Lady Glendale, or Dr Maxwell as she was better known at the hospital. Dr Maxwell was one of the first women surgeons at the Royal Infirmary. Were you aware of that?'

Sarah shook her head.

'Well, I suppose there is no reason for you to know. From what Irena told me they got on well and she stayed with them until she'd graduated. By that time I had joined the QAs and been posted to North Africa.' She smiled again. 'That's where I met my Johnny.'

She bent and took some peat from the bucket, opened the door of the Rayburn and threw it in. Sarah had the impression that Katherine wasn't a woman who liked to sit still for very long and right enough as soon as she sat down at the table again she picked up some knitting, a man's sweater from the look of it, and her needles started clacking. Sarah was impressed that she didn't seem to need to look at what she was doing. The most she'd ever knitted was a teddy bear in primary school and that had turned out badly.

'Johnny was with the SAS.'

'I didn't know the SAS were around then.'

'They were formed during the Second World War. By someone called David Stirling. He was an aristocrat from Bridge of Allan way.'

'Was Johnny an aristocrat? Is that how you knew Richard?'

Katherine laughed. 'Johnny? No, he was an engineer. And and a rugby player – played for Scotland, as a matter of fact. I think that's why the SAS took him. They liked people who could think on their feet and were physically tough.' She laid her knitting on her lap and stared into space. 'He never played rugby after the war – he took a bullet to the knee. Although he returned to engineering, I'm not sure he ever really settled down to civilian life.' Katherine picked up her knitting. 'And *your* boyfriend?' she asked. 'I'm assuming a pretty girl like you has one. Where is he?'

'London. He works for a large bank.'

'I see.'

'He wants us to get married. At least he says he does,' Sarah blurted.

Katherine raised an eyebrow. 'A man doesn't usually propose marriage unless that's what he wants, but I get the feeling you're not too sure?'

Sarah placed her cup on its saucer. 'How do you know? I mean, how can you be certain that someone is the person you should be spending the rest of your life with?'

Katherine frowned. 'Oh my dear, if you have to ask me that, then I'm very much afraid he's not the man for you.'

'But he's kind, safe, reliable. We could have a good life.'

'You don't marry someone because they are kind, safe and reliable. You marry someone because it's the only thing you can do. Because the thought of a life without them is unbearable.'

Sarah grimaced. 'That's a very romantic view.'

'It's the only view worth holding.'

Kind and interested though Katherine was, Sarah wasn't here to talk about her relationship with Matthew.

'What happened to Irena after she graduated?' she asked. 'Do you know where she went?'

'She went back to Poland, my dear.'

Chapter 42

Scotland, 1943

They day after they returned from Skye, Richard left to rejoin his squadron. Although they'd said their goodbyes in Skye, his actual leaving was harder than she'd imagined even in her worst moments. But he couldn't suspect that she knew this might be the last time she would ever hold him so she stayed strong – kissing him goodbye and turning away even though she never wanted to let him go.

As promised, there was a letter waiting for her with travel warrants and instructions. Before she'd left for Skye she'd told Isabel the same story she'd given to Richard – that she was going to be covering leave at the military hospitals around Britain starting at one in Fort William. Her handler had agreed to post the postcards and letters Irena would send her from various places across Britain.

She took the train north from Glasgow, passing through several stations along the way. As instructed, she pretended to be immersed in a book so as not to be drawn into conversations with her fellow passengers.

The station signs had been taken down so she couldn't be sure where she was. However, she recognised Fort William from her trip with Richard as soon as the train pulled into the station.

From there she had to take another train heading west. A few miles outside Fort William it came to a halt and her papers, as well as those of the other passengers, were scrutinised. When the train stopped again, it was, as far as she could see, in the middle of nowhere.

The conductor announced that this was the end of the line and all remaining passengers were to disembark. A soldier with sergeant stripes stood on the platform holding a clipboard.

'Where are we?' a short woman with an impish smile asked in a Polish accent as they gathered their bags.

'I don't know,' Irena replied. It looked a little like Skye, with the same wide-open glens and towering mountains, but they hadn't crossed any water so it couldn't be. 'I'm Anna, by the way,' the woman said, holding out her hand. 'I suspect we're heading to the same place.'

She was right. The sergeant beckoned them over and checked their names and papers from a list. There were six of them – three men and three women – all Poles. They were hustled into the back of an army truck.

A short while later the truck came to a stop and the sergeant came around to the back and lifted the tarpaulin cover. 'Right, you lot. This is your home for the next few weeks. Out you come.'

Their home was a substantial house surrounded by trees. Irena could smell damp foliage and, from somewhere in the distance, hear the sound of trickling water. Inside it was exquisitely furnished with antiques and oil paintings. They each had a bedroom on the first floor. Irena's had double-aspect windows overlooking the garden, a bed so high she could have hidden a small family underneath, a wardrobe and a chest of drawers. The uniform of a FANY captain and some fatigues were neatly folded at the end of her bed.

They were given a few minutes to unpack and change into their uniforms after which they were to meet downstairs.

They gathered in front of the roaring fire in the enormous drawing room and gratefully accepted drinks from Sergeant Fowler, who'd finally introduced himself and everyone to each other. They were a mixed bunch, ranging in age from around nineteen to forty, Irena guessed. The three women exchanged curious looks. In almost a direct contrast to Anna, Martyna was tall, thin and serious-looking.

'Now, sirs, ma'ams, welcome to the first stage in your training. Let me tell you what you'll be in for over the next few weeks. To get you into peak physical condition, there will be a great deal of outdoor training, which will include learning how to survive off the land. You will also be instructed in the use of weapons and how to evade capture. At the end, supposing you get through, you will be taught how to jump from a plane – with a parachute, of course.' There was a rumble of laughter at this, which helped clear the tension from the room.

The sergeant went on to explain the routine of their days.

Their meals would be taken together in the large dining room and in the evenings they had the use of the drawing room with its fire, well-stocked bookshelves and piano. Under no circumstances were they to go into Arisaig, the nearby town – or anywhere else, for that matter – without permission.

They were given supper, a surprisingly lavish meal of lobster and venison. After they'd eaten, they gathered again in the sitting room, where they were introduced to their instructors and told the syllabus for the next four to six weeks.

Every morning they were roused from their beds by Sergeant Fowler who, whatever the weather, had them running and doing press-ups on the lawn. Basic weapons training followed breakfast and Irena discovered she had an aptitude for shooting a rifle, one she prayed she would never have to use. Unarmed conflict was next, something she was less good at, although she did her best. After lunch, they were taken into a smaller room that served as their classroom and shown how to assemble and dissemble a wireless and how to code and decode messages. They also had to learn to read maps until it became second nature and they could pinpoint where they were and where they had to go – if at any time they needed an escape route – in a moment. All the time Irena was aware of being watched, but she didn't let it bother her. She suspected not all of them would make it through this stage of the training, but she was determined to be one of those who did.

Towards the middle of the course they were taught how to use explosives. The house was so remote they were able to practise blowing up make-believe targets without attracting any unwanted attention from the locals.

The physical training became more intense. Twice they were woken in the middle of the night, blindfolded, led to a truck and driven into the countryside before being told to find their own way back to the house. Irena, Anna and Martyna stuck together, helping each other out, not wanting to rely on the men. The first time, it took them several hours to make it back as they kept going around in circles, but the second attempt took them even longer as the low-lying cloud obscured the stars making it impossible to navigate. Knowing it was pointless to stumble around in the dark, they made makeshift shelters for themselves from pine branches and shivered their way to the morning. In the misty light of the dawn, they crept back to base using their new-found skills to avoid the locals and cover their tracks. But if they thought they were going to be applauded by their sergeant, they were badly mistaken.

'Travelling by daylight is dangerous. Are the lot of you mad? I wouldn't give a farthing for your chances with the Nazis. As far as I'm concerned, you might as well stick your hands up and say, "Shoot me now." Next time you stay hidden until nightfall, then you travel. Do I make myself clear?'

Given that he was shouting at the top of his lungs, it was difficult for anyone to pretend otherwise.

Martyna disappeared suddenly one day and when they asked where she was they were told to 'keep their noses out of it', didn't they know 'careless talk costs lives'?

Sometimes they were taken to a deep-water loch where they'd be immersed in the frozen water and made to swim to a bridge, still fully clothed and holding their packs, loaded with explosives, above their heads. Instead of being allowed to dry off, they were made to make their way home on foot, forced to take the most direct route, even if that involved, which it usually did, climbing over fences, or wading through streams and bogs. At night, their muscles aching, they'd trudge up to bed, almost too tired to climb the stairs. It was only her hatred for the Nazis and her longing to return to Poland that gave Irena the strength to get up each morning and head back out into the cold, wet, miserable Scottish weather. Yet, there were good times, too. In the evening after their supper, they would sometimes play cards or charades, Anna keeping them amused as she mimicked Sergeant Fowler. But underneath the light-heartedness and banter, they all knew that they would need every ounce of ingenuity and every skill they were being taught here.

The training that she found most difficult was when they were taught how to kill a man by cutting his throat with a knife or using a garrotte to strangle him. Everything in Irena shrank from it. The Hippocratic Oath had committed her to saving lives, not to taking them, and the thought that one day she might be called upon to do so nauseated her. She even found it difficult to practise on a rabbit, Anna sometimes stepping in when the instructors weren't looking, to do it for her. She got through it by telling herself that it wasn't real, that having to kill another human being would always be a choice.

Missing Richard was a constant dull ache behind her ribs. She scoured the newspapers and listened to the news on the wireless every chance she got. Every time she heard about RAF losses she felt sick. No mail was allowed in or out, all letters and postcards to family and friends being passed on to their handlers and posted from wherever they'd told their loved ones they were. She consoled herself that if something had happened to Richard or Aleksy, Isabel would write and eventually the letter would find her.

When the day finally came for them to leave their home in the Scottish highlands she had mixed feelings. The last part of their training was to take place in England where they'd be taught the specialist skills they would need. Although she was to act as a courier, she was warned that apart from taking part in sabotage, she might also have to act as a wireless operator in emergencies. Before she knew whether she had passed, she had to learn how to parachute from a plane and all her life she'd been sacred of heights.

But she was determined. Nothing would stop her from going back to Poland.

She was given three days off before she was to report to the Polish 'finishing school', as it was euphemistically called, in England.

Although she knew it would have been wiser to book into a bed and breakfast, she was drawn back to the house in Charlotte Square.

She asked the sergeant to send a telegram for her from Fort William, telling Isabel that she had some leave and would be returning to Charlotte Square for a few days.

Isabel was delighted to see her and Hannah fussed over her as if she were one of the family. It was lovely to have nothing to do for whole days at a time, although Richard's presence was everywhere. At night she'd tiptoe into his room and lie on his bed, breathing in the faint scent of him that still lingered on the bedclothes.

On her last night in Edinburgh, she told Isabel that it was possible she might be going overseas to one of the casualty stations after another spell in a military hospital in England.

'Have you told Richard?'

Irena started.

'Oh, my dear, did you really think I hadn't noticed the way you two feel about one another?'

'I thought we were ... discreet.'

'A woman can't hide it when she loves a man and you do love him, don't you?'

Unable to trust her voice, Irena nodded.

'And he's proposed?'

She nodded again.

'I'm assuming you've said yes.'

'No. I can't. Not until this war is finished – it wouldn't be fair.'

Isabel reached over and grasped Irena's hands. 'I know why you think that, but you have to grab happiness while you can. My darling boy might not see the end of this war ... are you prepared to take that chance?'

'It's because we – he – might not survive that I can't marry him.'

Isabel sighed, the firelight playing across her face. 'Before I married Lord Glendale I was in love with someone else.'

'The man in the photo?'

'You've seen it?'

'Yes. Ages ago when I went to fetch you aspirin from your room. I promise I wasn't snooping. The picture was lying face down on your dressing table and I automatically went to pick it up. I didn't mean to look at it.'

'That was Archie.' Isabel's eyes took on a faraway look. 'My love.'

'But you didn't marry?'

'We would have, but the war got in the way. Don't let the same happen to you.' Isabel hesitated. 'Remember I have been Simon's wife for a long time and know a little about his work. I'm not a fool either.'

Irena's skin prickled.

'These stories you're telling me – about working at different military hospitals – they're not true, are they?'

'Why would you say that?'

'You and I aren't so very different, you know. I won't ask you to confirm or deny anything. That wouldn't be fair – I know you'd have no choice but to lie to me. But if you are thinking of doing anything dangerous, have you thought what that might mean? For you and my son?'

Still Irena said nothing.

Isabel sighed. 'At least give him the chance to say goodbye.'

Chapter 43

Audley House, the so-called Polish finishing school, was situated in a large stately home hidden in the depths of the English countryside. If Irena hadn't known it was a training school for the SOE she would never have guessed. Large, manicured lawns sloped down to croquet lawns and to the left there was a tennis court. It was here that the last part of her training – her briefing course – would take place. She was one of only two women – the other, to her delight, being Anna.

The course was taught by one of the captains and involved learning about current conditions in Poland. Most of the students, like Irena, had been in Poland during the early months of the war, but life, they were told, had changed in the time they'd been away. The training officer recounted a story about an agent, working with the French resistance, who'd ordered a 'black coffee', not realising that since milk had become impossible to get, everyone simply ordered a 'coffee'. Mistakes like these, they were warned, could mean their death. In particular, they had to learn the new names of streets. Hitler had renamed many of them and not to know this could prove fatal.

At the end of the course, Irena and Anna were told they had passed. In two days, they would be taken to another house where they would wait until the weather conditions were right for them to be dropped into Poland. Irena was given poor quality Polish clothes and stout shoes, similar to the ones she'd worn when she'd left Poland, but more befitting a nurse.

'You will need to choose a name to be known by,' her handler said. 'Preferably one that means something to you.'

Irena knew straight away which one she wanted: Magdalena. It seemed right to take the name of the woman she'd let down. But not her last name. Both together would link her too closely to Magdalena and consequently her father, the colonel. Drobnik, then. Magdalena Drobnik sounded just right.

'As we discussed,' her handler continued, 'your cover will be that you're a nurse. It will allow you to travel without raising suspicion. You will be based in one of the hospitals but you should be able to travel freely on the pretext of visiting patients in their homes. It is vital you never show your extended knowledge as a doctor. Are we clear?'

Irena nodded.

'I have to reiterate that if you are caught it is unlikely we will be able to do anything to help you. If you aren't shot straight away, it is probable that you will be imprisoned – and tortured.'

They'd gone over this before. Irena knew what to expect. Her handler had given her a small blue pill to take should she be captured. Taking her own life was a mortal sin but she would choose death over betraying anything or anyone.

That night, one of the British soldiers who guarded the gates to Audley House slipped her a note. It was from Richard. He asked her to meet him in a lane not far from the house. He would wait for her all night if necessary. And, if she didn't come, he would have no choice but to report her missing to the police, or go to the War Office via his father.

How had he found her?

But it didn't matter. She had the chance to see him one last time, and God help her, she couldn't resist.

He was waiting for her in an open-topped jeep parked by the side of the road, his head resting against the back seat, his hat pushed down over his forehead. Wild, pulsating joy flooded through her. She hadn't thought she'd ever see him again.

Checking that no one was around to see her, she hurried over to the car and coughed to let him know she was there – she'd learned never to surprise a soldier unless she meant to; it could result in her having her head blown off.

He started and pushed back his hat. 'Christ, I didn't hear a thing.'

She smiled. 'Good. That means I've learned something.' She opened the passenger door and climbed in next to him. The smell of his aftershave sent little spirals of desire through her belly.

'We can't stay here,' he said, starting the car.

'I know a place. Go down the road for a couple of miles and turn right. There's a barn we can park the car in.'

They were silent as Richard drove. He seemed angry with her, as he well might be. She wondered how he'd found her and how much he knew about what she was doing. She pointed to the field she meant and leaped out to open the gate, closing it again once the jeep was through.

She ran past the vehicle and opened the barn doors so that Richard could drive in.

While he parked she leaned against the barn doors, trying to calm her racing heart.

He left the dimmed lights on and leaped over the driver's door.

'Come here,' he said.

She shook her head. 'We need to talk.'

'Yes we do. Damn it, Irena, do you have any idea how long I've been looking for you?'

Slowly she walked towards him. 'I can't stay long. I wouldn't have come if you hadn't threatened ...' She swallowed. Her mouth was so dry.

He stepped forward to meet her and took her face between his hands. 'My darling, my love,' he murmured. Then his mouth was on hers and she was drowning.

After a few moments she pulled away. She reached into the car and switched off the lights.

Now there was complete darkness. She felt him come to stand behind her. He wrapped his arms around her waist. 'I don't remember you being shy,' he murmured in her ear.

'Someone might see the lights through a crack.'

She heard his sharp intake of breath and her skin cooled as he let her go. 'Of course. I'd forgotten for a moment. An agent needs to know all that stuff.'

As her eyes adjusted to the darkness she could just make out the shape of him. 'How did you find me?' she asked.

'Did you really think I wouldn't?' His voice was bitter. 'Did you think those damn letters and postcards would fool me for long? Didn't you think I would find it strange that every time I had leave and wanted to come and see you, you'd moved on to a different hospital? In the end, all it took was a couple of phone calls. None of the hospitals had ever heard of you.'

'That still doesn't explain how you found me.'

'Once the penny dropped it wasn't difficult. There aren't that many training schools just for Poles in the country. Christ, Irena, how could you keep this from me?'

She moved towards him and placed her hands on his chest. 'Don't be angry with me.'

'Why the hell not? You know I love you. I thought you loved

me. Yet you're going back to Poland. For God's sake, darling, you could be killed. You don't need to do this. If you don't care about me, can't you care about yourself? What do you think you're going to achieve? We've got the Boche on the run. My unit is being sent to Italy. That can only mean one thing. It's almost over.'

How many times had she heard that? It wouldn't be over until the last German had been evicted from her country.

'And if I asked you not to go, not to fly missions any more, what would you say?'

'That's different.'

'Why is it different?'

'Because it's my duty. Because I'm an officer in the air force. I can't refuse even if I wanted to. But no one is ordering you back to Poland.'

'And do you want to? Stop flying? Even though you know,' her voice caught, 'that every time you climb in your plane it might be your last?' She hardened her voice. 'You're a rarity, Richard. How many men who started flying with you are still alive?'

'Damn it, Irena, we're not talking about me. You know I have to do what I do.'

'As I do. I love my country as much as you love yours.'

'You're a woman, Irena. A doctor. Let the men go. I'll go to my father if I have to and tell him you have to be stopped.'

She had no doubt he would. It was unlikely Lord Glendale would be able to stop her going, but she couldn't take the risk. She forced a smile to her lips.

'There's no need.'

'What do you mean?' The hope in his voice made her heart tighten.

'I failed the course,' she lied. 'They don't believe I'll use my weapon if I had to. They can't take the chance. They're not sending me back to Poland. I'll be working in Britain as a decoder for the agents in the field. I can't tell you where.'

He eyed her suspiciously. 'Why didn't you tell me this straight away?'

'I would have – if you'd given me the chance.'

He buried his face in her neck. 'Thank God, I've been going crazy thinking about it. If anything happened to you . . . '

'My love, nothing is going to happen to me. We might not be able to see each other for a while, that's all.' She unfastened the necklace and held it out to him. 'If you're going to Italy, you'll be flying missions again. Please take this. It will protect you the way it's protected me.'

He took it from her hand. 'No, darling, it's kept you safe this long – you keep it. As long as you're wearing it, I'll know you're all right.'

She knew him well enough to know there was no point in arguing, so she lifted her hair so he could clasp it around her neck.

When he'd finished, she threaded her hands through his hair. 'Now, *najdroższa*, let's not waste any more time talking.'

Two days later she was parachuted into Poland.

Chapter 44
Skye, 1989

'*She went back?* You mean *after* the war?'

'During.' Katherine placed her knitting on the table and studied Sarah for a while. 'All I know is that she did some sort of training with Special Operations or some such and they dropped her back in Poland. Poor Richard was devastated when he discovered she'd gone.'

'Richard was in love with *Irena*?' She would have sworn he was in love with Magdalena.

'Absolutely besotted.'

'Was she in love with him?'

'Not at first. She was engaged to an officer in the Polish cavalry. I know she hoped for a long time that he survived. Sadly he didn't. But, even before she learned of her fiancé's death, I could tell she was attracted to Richard. It would have been difficult for her not to have been. If you'd met Richard back in those days, you would have known that any woman would have fallen for him. He was RAF and our pilots were heroes. Everyone adored them, particularly after the Battle of Britain. They were the glamour boys of the time. A bit like Rock Hudson was in his heyday.'

Sarah had only vaguely heard of Rock Hudson but she got Katherine's drift. She wondered if Katherine had been in love with Richard too, even a little. It seemed as if Katherine had guessed what she was thinking.

'I never saw Richard that way. I couldn't. Even if I hadn't known him when we were both children, he was my cousin. Not that he knew ... oh, never mind that now. I mustn't let my mouth run away with me. It's just so long since I talked about any of this.'

Although Sarah was curious to know what Katherine had been about to say, she decided to leave it for the time being. She'd learned it didn't take much to distract Katherine and there was so much she was desperate to know. Particularly the bit about Richard being in love with Irena and not Magdalena.

'Maybe Richard met Magdalena later?'

'If he did, he never mentioned her. But then again, our generation is not a kiss-and-tell one and Richard, especially in his later years, was an intensely private person.'

'What happened to Irena's fiancé?'

'He was shot by the Russians. Quite early on in the war, she found out later. I think his death was part of the reason she went back to Poland.' Katherine stood and added some peat to the stove. 'I never actually spoke to Irena about her decision to return to Poland. She was – not secretive exactly – but not prone to confidences. Anyway, I imagine she wasn't allowed to tell anyone about her work with the SOE – Official Secrets Act, you know. And as far as I'm aware she didn't tell anyone, not even Richard – especially not Richard. I suspect, apart from the need for secrecy, she knew he would have moved heaven and earth to stop her.' Katherine glanced at the clock on the wall. 'Is that the time? Neil will be coming in soon for his lunch and I've not got it ready for him.'

'Neil?'

'My grandson. He's been staying with me this last week.'

Sarah reluctantly got to her feet. There was so much more she wanted to know. 'I should let you get on,' she said. 'Perhaps I could come back later?'

'You're very welcome to stay for lunch. It won't be much. Some soup and a little stew and potatoes.'

It was impossible to imagine eating another meal so soon after the feast she'd so recently polished off.

'It's very kind of you to ask me, but I don't want to intrude.'

'You wouldn't be. I'm sure Neil would be glad of some younger company. I worry he gets bored here. Young people do seem to need to be doing things all the time.'

'No, really. Perhaps you could come to me for dinner? What about tonight? Or tomorrow if that suits you better? I'm only here for two more nights. I don't want to leave Mum too long.'

'Could I send Neil down to the house later to let you know? He can help you light the stove at the same time.'

Back at Borreraig House, instead of going inside, Sarah went down to the bay and sat, her knees pulled up to her chest, staring out at the loch. Could Richard have been in love with two women? It was entirely possible – even likely – that Irena had been killed in Poland. Richard might have sought comfort with Magdalena. But that still didn't explain the connection between Mum, Richard and the elusive Magdalena.

However, if the solicitors ever found her, Magdalena might be able to tell her who Mum's parents were. It seemed every time she thought she was getting close to uncovering the truth about her mother's past it was only to find herself in another blind alley.

When the sun disappeared behind some clouds and it became chilly she roused herself and went back inside. No longer warmed by the sun streaming in the windows, the house was getting cool. She tried again to light the Rayburn, but failed miserably. She was ready to kick the thing when she heard a masculine voice call out and a man appeared at her kitchen door.

She pushed a lock of hair from her face. 'I'm sorry, I didn't hear you knock.'

He was tall and wearing jeans and a pair of high wellingtons rolled down to his knees. He looked as if he needed a shave and his jumper had seen better days. His thick dark hair was wind-tossed, his cheeks ruddy from the wind and his eyes a startling shade of blue.

'No one knocks around here.' He held out his hand. 'I'm Neil, by the way.'

This was Neil? Flustered, Sarah rubbed her sooty fingers on her jeans before shaking his out-stretched hand. She'd imagined Katherine's grandson to be younger, just out of school perhaps, and certainly not around her age.

'My grandmother asked me to bring you these.' He placed a plastic Co-op bag on the table. She opened it – stared at the salmon and crab inside – and quickly closed it again.

'Please thank her for me. But what do I do with the crab? It's still alive.'

'Er, boil some water in a pan and drop it in.'

'Alive! I couldn't possibly.'

A slow smile crossed his face. 'My last girlfriend didn't like cooking them alive either. Pass me a knife – or anything else you can find with a sharp point.'

She reached into the cupboard and finding a cake tester, passed it to him. She winced when he stuck it into the shell, but at least the crab no longer waved its claws at her.

'Once it's dead, you have to cook it straight away. Now would be good.'

'For how long?'

Amusement gleamed in his blue eyes. 'Look, why don't you boil the kettle and I'll do it for you? Oh and stick the salmon in the fridge. You should cook it soon as.'

'At least that sorts dinner for the next couple of days.' Sarah set the kettle on the two-ring stove. 'Did your grandmother say which evening suits her best?'

'Tomorrow, she says, if that's all right with you? I have plans to eat out myself so she won't have to make me anything.'

'You won't be joining us then?' She felt vaguely disappointed.

'No, but thank you.' He squatted on his haunches in front of the stove. 'Right then, let's get this fire lit.' He started crumpling some newspapers he'd brought with him and tossed them into the stove. He left the kitchen, returning a few minutes later with an enamel bucket of peat, which he added to the fire. He worked silently, not appearing to feel the need to make small talk.

'Thank you,' she said when the fire was burning to his satisfaction and he'd closed the stove door.

'It's no bother.' He folded his arms and leaned against the worktop.

'Cup of tea?'

'No thanks. I'll need to be on my way once that crab's cooked.' They waited in silence until the kettle boiled. She found a pot and passed it to him. He filled it with water, threw in the crab, jammed a lid on top and put the pot back on the stove.

'I hope I haven't upset your grandmother by asking her about the past,' Sarah said when he was finished.

He laughed. 'Upset Gran! She's as tough as old boots, as you'll soon discover.'

'She told me she was a nurse during the war.'

'More than a match for my grandfather and he was quite a character too.'

'I heard he was a war hero. What about your parents?' For some reason this man piqued her curiosity.

'Dad met my mother when he was nineteen, got her pregnant, married her – as they did in those days – but buggered off soon after. He lives in Italy now. He's an artist, or at least that's what he tells everyone. I doubt he's sold a painting in his life.'

Odd that they should both have parents who were artists.

He peered into the pot. 'This big boy is ready.' He took the pot over to the sink and emptied it, a cloud of sea-smelling vapour rising into the kitchen. 'Wait until it's cool, then break the claws open with a hammer.'

Sarah looked at the crab doubtfully.

'Right then,' Neil said, 'I'll leave you to it.' He shoved his hands in his pockets. 'See you around.'

And with that he was gone.

The following morning the sun had come out. She'd brought a manuscript to copy-edit with her but, unable to concentrate, she decided work could wait. She tugged on her wellington boots and headed up the rutted track that constituted the driveway. Although she'd thought she wouldn't, she had slept soundly last night. Possibly due to the number of glasses of wine she'd glugged with her solitary supper.

She was almost at the end of the driveway when she met Neil. Her heart did a weird flippy thing.

'Hello there. Were you coming to see Gran? She's out, I'm afraid.'

Damn. She was desperate to hear what else Katherine had to tell her. 'Might as well go for a walk then. Can you suggest one?'

'How about Galtrigill? It was where the boatman who rowed Bonny Prince Charlie used to live.'

'Sounds good. Which way?'

'We could follow the road, but let's walk by the cliffs. It's better.'

'We?'

He grinned. 'We.'

She trudged beside him over a stile and onto a narrow track. 'What do you do?' she asked.

'I'm a freelance photographer.'

She was surprised. She'd assumed he was a fisherman. She waited for him to elaborate but it seemed that was all he intended to say on the subject. This was going to be a fun outing if he used words as if they were riches too precious to squander.

'How about you?' he asked.

'I work for a publishing house.'

'A writer?'

'A copy editor.'

'But you'd like to write?' How did he know that? Then again, most people assumed that people who worked within the industry were closet writers.

'I've thought about it,' she admitted reluctantly, 'but I don't have the talent.'

'How do you know? Have you tried?'

On second thoughts, she preferred it when he wasn't talking.

'Perhaps one day when I'm not relying on a job to make a crust . . .'

He slid her a sideways look and raised an eyebrow.

'My mother is an artist – like your dad,' she said, changing the subject.

'I hope she's sold more of her paintings than he did.'

'She's pretty well known.' Sarah narrowly avoided a pile of sheep droppings. 'But she had a stroke a few weeks ago. I doubt she'll paint again.'

'Bummer.'

She was glad that he didn't offer her empty platitudes. However, the look he gave her from his shockingly blue eyes was filled with sympathy.

'So what kinds of photos do you take?'

'I'm a photo-journalist. I take photographs wherever there's a story.'

'Will I have seen your work?'

'Possibly. I was with *The Times* until they were taken over by Murdoch. I went freelance after that. I've had my work published in *Life* magazine, *National Geographic*, Sunday supplements – places like that.'

'Where have you been?'

'Most places. Most recently the Congo.'

'Isn't it dangerous there?'

'Not if you know what you're doing.'

Immediately in front of them was a spread of bracken.

'Make sure your jeans are tucked into your socks,' Neil told her. 'Ticks.'

'Your grandmother said you're visiting. You don't live in Skye, then? I mean, when you're not working?'

His gaze wandered over the hills and to the islands, partly hidden by mist, across the sea.

'I live in London mostly. More practical work-wise when I travel so much. Friends put me up when I need a place to doss – one or two let me use their cupboards as dark rooms when I need to develop my photos – but I come back here whenever I can.'

'And your girlfriend who doesn't like to boil crabs alive? She doesn't worry about you when you're working in politically sensitive areas?'

He laughed. '*Politically sensitive areas?* Fuck-ups would be more accurate. But Jasmine-who-doesn't-like-to-boil-crabs-alive is not my girlfriend any more. Hasn't been for the last six months. Got pretty fed up with the amount of travelling I do. And when I wasn't travelling, the best I could manage was a couple of months at a stretch in London. She came here with me once. It wasn't a success. She was bored in less than a day. Said there was nothing to do.'

For some reason the knowledge he didn't have a girlfriend sent a little shiver of unexpected delight up her spine. If Katherine was Richard's cousin then in some way she couldn't quite work out, Neil was too. Although he wasn't as spectacularly good-looking as Richard, he had the same aquiline nose and high cheekbones. And a certain masculine roughness she found surprisingly sexy. Matthew was fastidious when it came to his personal grooming – he even ironed his jeans or rather, paid a laundry service to do it for him.

She realised she'd been staring and he was waiting for her to say something. 'Well, there isn't much to do here. Not really.'

'That's a matter of opinion.'

They had reached the part of the path that ran along the cliff side. It was a sheer drop to the rocks below and Sarah kept her eyes averted.

'Did you find out what you needed to know from my grand-mother?'

'A bit of it. But not everything. What has she told you?'

'Very little. She's an islander. We tend to keep confidences.'

So she found herself telling him the whole story. He listened without interrupting.

'And the solicitors haven't managed to contact this Magdalena?'

'They hadn't by the time I left Edinburgh, although it's pos-sible they have by now. I need to find a phone box and ring them. The phone in the house must have been disconnected when Richard died.'

'There's one at this end of Borreraig. We'll pass it if we take the road back instead of the track, but I'm not sure if it's work-ing either. You could use the one in our house.'

They stopped to watch a yacht disappear behind a cliff.

'You didn't know your mother was adopted then?' Neil asked.

'She never told me.'

'How old was she?'

'About five, I think.'

'If she was that old, won't she remember something about her natural parents?'

'You would think, huh? But since it wasn't a topic she ever brought up and it's difficult for her to communicate now, I know absolutely nothing.' She bent down and picked a sprig of bog myrtle, inhaling its sweet scent as she rubbed the leaves between her fingers. 'I keep thinking of Irena. What made her go back to Poland? She must have known what was going on there. I would have been petrified.'

'We don't always know what we'd do until we're put to the test.'

'I've a pretty good idea what I would have done. Kept my head down and if I managed to escape nothing would have induced me to go back, especially not as an agent. I'm no risk taker.'

'Maybe her motive was patriotism? Or revenge? Love even?'

'One of those, I'm sure. I guess I'll never know.'

They walked through a small copse before Neil turned away from the sea and headed inland. He stopped in front of a large expanse of land dotted with the overgrown remains of what once had been walls. 'This is Galtrigill, or what's left of it,' he said. He turned back towards the sea. 'If I were to build a house on Skye, it would be right here.'

She followed his gaze to the dazzlingly blue sea, surrounded by green hills covered with pink and purple heather. It was perfectly still except for the occasional cry of a seagull, the air scented by wood smoke or peat, bog myrtle and clover. He was right – it was stunning. She could easily imagine him here, living off the land, fishing for his supper – except, of course, he wasn't a fisherman.

He flicked her a glance. 'Not that I'm planning to settle down any time soon.' He hooked his hands behind his neck and stretched. 'Still got too much to do.'

She studied him from the corner of her eye. He was everything Matthew wasn't. Neil had no house – no permanent job and he travelled to dangerous countries. Yet he was the most intriguing man she'd ever met.

Sarah had to keep putting coins into the phone box while the secretary transferred her call to Alan Bailey. Neil sat on a rock nearby waiting for her. She was almost out of change when Bailey came on the line.

'Ah, Miss Davidson, I was about to write to you.'

'Does that mean you have news?'

'We have located a lady who we believe to be Miss Drobnik. We still have to carry out a few checks, but if she is indeed the person we are looking for, I'm afraid she will inherit the houses in Edinburgh and Skye after all.'

The money from the houses would have helped, but far, far better that Magdalena had been found. It would make Mum so happy. Sarah only wished it had been her that had found Magdalena.

'I'm delighted she's alive,' she said truthfully. 'Could you give me her address?'

'I'm afraid I can't do that. However, if you are happy for me to do so, I shall write to her with your details and let her know you would like to contact her.'

Sarah seethed with frustration, knowing nothing she could say or do would make the obnoxious Alan Bailey change his mind.

The pips were going and she was out of change. 'Please do that. Today, if possible. I really need to speak to her.'

'I can't promise I'll do it today. I have—' and with that, the line went dead.

Sarah opened the heavy door of the booth and called across to Neil. 'Do you have a couple of twenty pences or a fifty?'

He dug around in the pocket of his jeans and handed her two coins. 'I could go back home and get some more, if you like?'

'This should do. I don't expect it will be a long call.'

She dialled Matthew's number and was once again put on hold. As she waited to be connected to him, she drummed her fingertips on the top of the phone. Even if the solicitors wrote to Magdalena today, which was unlikely, it would be another week at the earliest before Sarah heard anything.

'Sarah?' Matthew said from the other end of the line.

'Yes. I'm calling from a phone box just in case we get cut off.'

'You're still in Skye?' She could hear the rustling of paper in the background as if he were reading something while talking to her. She suppressed a flash of irritation. Matthew liked to 'multi-task', as he called it. 'Any news?' he asked.

'I've a lot to tell you. We need to talk.'

There was more rustling of paper. 'Hold on a moment.' He must have placed his hand over the receiver as everything went muffled for a while. The pips went again and she stuck another twenty into the box. 'Sorry about that. Jane's just reminding me I'm due at a meeting. So what have you found out?'

'I'm just off the phone to the solicitors. They've located Magdalena. At least they think they have—'

'So she's alive. Pity.'

'Pity?'

'It means you won't inherit the house in Edinburgh – or in Skye, although that doesn't matter as much – it won't be worth a fraction of the Edinburgh one. You could have used the money to find a home for your mother. That way you'd be free to come with me to Geneva.'

Hadn't he been listening when she told him that this search was so much more than that?

'Sarah, I'm going to have to put you on hold again—' Before she could protest, she heard the piped music his company used.

Her gaze drifted to where Neil was sitting. He was staring out to sea, looking as if he had all the time in the world to wait for a woman he barely knew to finish her phone call. She followed the line of his sight, towards the sea. The wind had risen and crested waves rippled the earlier smooth surface of the water. The sky had darkened, making the landscape wilder. The scene reminded her of her mother's paintings. Sad and angry but utterly beautiful.

A memory of the holiday in Dorset came flooding back.

It had been a success. Her mother, freed from the tyranny of her daily painting schedule, had walked with Sarah along the cliffs most mornings. They would stop for lunch in one of the tea rooms and then, in the afternoons, browse the shops or, if the weather had turned, read their books, Sarah sprawled on the sofa, her mother, more neatly, in one of the arm chairs. There had been no more wine, however, no heart-to-heart of the kind Sarah had hoped for.

She'd waited until their last evening before she summoned the courage to speak about Matthew.

'Once I've graduated, he wants us to live together in London, Mum,' she'd said eventually. Her mother had met him once and behaved with perfect politeness but Sarah had sensed she hadn't trusted Matthew's easy charm. Certainly there had been no suggestion of them sharing a room. Not that that had stopped Matthew from creeping into her bedroom in the middle of the night.

'London! So far away.'

'It's not really. A few hours by train. I could come home at weekends, or you could come and stay with us.'

Her mother's mouth had turned down at the corners. 'If he loves you he'd want to marry you. Not ask you to live in sin.'

Sarah hadn't known whether to laugh or cry. 'Everyone's living together first these days, Mum.'

'But not my daughter.' She'd sat forward. 'Once he gets what he wants, he'll never marry you.'

'He does love me, Mum.'

'In that case he would want to marry you.' Her mother took her hand, surprising Sarah. 'You have one life, Sarah, only one; and we never know when that will be taken from us. You must make the most of it. Don't just settle. I know I've not always encouraged you to spread your wings, but I was wrong. I've not been a very good mother, I'm afraid.'

'Don't be silly.' Although she'd longed to talk like this to her mother, this new openness, this vulnerability, made her uncomfortable.

'You know, when you were born I was so happy. At last I had someone I could love – really love. Oh, I loved your father, at least I thought I did, but he wasn't mine. Not the way you were.'

Sarah stayed absolutely still, not wanting her mother to stop.

'When I held you, I thought my heart would burst right out of my chest. But then I thought, what if I lost you? What if something happened to you? From then on, all I could see were the dangers. You could get croup, I could drop you, your father could crash the car with you in it.' She sat back in her chair. 'So many things could hurt you. The fear of losing you took over me. I started doing little things, not stepping on cracks, all sorts of ridiculous rituals. I made a bargain with God: if he kept you safe, he could do what he liked with me.'

Sarah held her breath. Her mother had never confided in her

before. She'd waited so long for this moment, now it was actually happening she felt strangely uncomfortable.

'Your father tried his best to make me see that I was passing my fears onto you but, even though I knew it was wrong to keep you wrapped in cotton wool, I couldn't stop myself. It was almost a relief when he left. I would never have to wonder again whether I could trust him to protect you – he was so *casual* with you. Flinging you into the air, refusing to get up in the night to see if you were all right.' She smiled sadly. 'He said having you in our room was enough, but I knew, if I didn't watch over you, someone or something could snatch you away from me.'

'But nothing ever happened to me.' Nothing could ever have happened.

'When you said you wanted to go to university, I would have stopped you if I could,' her mother continued, as if now she'd started talking she'd made up her mind to go on. She gave Sarah a wry smile. 'I would have moved into the halls to be with you if they'd let me. At the very least I wanted you to stay at home and commute, but then I thought of you travelling every day and I knew I couldn't risk that either. All I really wanted was for you to stay at home with me where I could watch over you.'

'But that's why I needed to go into halls. I was so shy, Mum. It was horrible without you at first.' She didn't tell her mother that going to university had been almost as much about getting away from her over-protectiveness as it had been about getting a degree.

'You must believe me when I tell you, Sarah, you were loved. Loved so much.' She came and knelt beside her. 'You still are. I haven't always told you. I want you to live the life you dream of, reach for the sky – never, ever settle for second best. Will you promise me, that?'

'I promise.'

Her mother laughed shakily. 'Then, my child, if you do that I may not have been a good mother but perhaps I have been a good enough mother.'

It had been the only conversation of its sort they'd ever had and until now she'd forgotten her mother's words. Or had she put them to the back of her mind, scared to think too deeply about them?

Back then, if he'd asked her, she would have married Matthew like a shot. Had Mum been right all along? Was she staying with Matthew because it was easier than being on her own? If so, didn't she owe it to him to break it off?

'Sarah? Are you there?' Matthew was back on the line. 'Look, can we talk about this another time? I've got to get to a meeting,' he spoke quickly. 'You know how I loathe it when other people aren't punctual. Phone me at home. No damn, not tonight, I'm out.' More rustling of paper as he flicked through his diary. 'Thursday evening. After eight. Call me then. Look, I really have to go.'

'I'm not coming with you to Geneva, Matthew.'

'What?'

'I'm not coming to Geneva and I'm not marrying you. I'm sorry, I have should have told you sooner.' She gripped the phone tighter. 'I'm so sorry, Matthew. I just don't love you the way I should.' Very gently she placed the phone back down in the receiver.

Breathing rapidly, she rested her forehead on the cool metal of the call box. How had it taken so long for her to realise that Matthew wasn't for her? Or she for him.

The door of the booth swung open.

'Hey, what's up?'

Feeling a little dazed, Sarah looked at him. 'I think I've just broken up with my boyfriend. I should probably have done it years ago.'

Neil studied her through half-closed eyes.

'Looks to me as if you need a drink – and I don't mean tea.' He jerked his head in the direction of his grandmother's house. 'Come on, I've a bottle of whisky that's just waiting to be cracked.'

Katherine's kitchen was warm. Every so often the rain would spatter against the window, and there was a slight fug of condensation obscuring the view to the road.

'Where is your gran?'

'She does a couple of hours' voluntary work at the old folks' home most afternoons. She won't be long.'

Voluntary work at an old folks' home as if she were a spring chicken herself! Katherine was exactly the kind of old woman she'd like to be.

Neil placed a bottle of whisky on the table along with a tumbler. 'Help yourself.'

'Aren't you having any?'

'I've work to do.' He nodded behind him. 'I have to finish the copy that goes with the photos I developed this morning. I need a clear head.'

'Can I see them?' Although she was genuinely inerested, she also wanted to think about something other than what she'd just said to Matthew.

'I'm not sure you'd want to.'

'No, really, I'd like to.'

'They're not pleasant.'

'For heaven's sake, let me see.'

He studied her thoughtfully for a long moment. 'Wait here,' he said.

He returned a few minutes later with a sheaf of photos in his hand. Silently he passed them to her. She turned over the first photograph. It was A4 size, a black-and-white glossy. There were four men kneeling in a row with their hands tied behind their back. The next one showed the same four men, but this time there were two other men in the photograph, both in paramilitary uniform. One held a gun against the temple of the first of the kneeling men. She felt sick. Although she knew what was coming next she couldn't stop herself from looking. Sure enough the next photograph was of the man lying on the ground, a dark stain beginning to form around his head. Disgusted she threw the pictures on the table.

'I did warn you,' Neil said, gathering them together.

She was shaking. 'How could you have stood there and done nothing? It was obvious what those men were going to do. Didn't you care?'

'What do you think I should have done? We're there to report not intervene. If we did, we'd probably be shot too. The important thing is to tell the story and make people sit up and take notice. If we try to stop the stuff we see do you think it would stop the wars? Or the deaths? It won't. But what might stop them are photos like these plastered across major papers and on the television.'

'But is it enough?'

They glared at each other.

The sound of crunching gravel as a car pulled up outside broke the silence.

Neil sucked in a breath. 'I bear witness, Sarah. That's what I do.' He gave her one last look and taking his photos, turned and left the room.

She was still trembling. *Listen to me. Scared of my own bloody shadow. Yet I've practically accused a man who probably has more courage in his little pinkie than I have in my whole body of being a coward. Way to go, Sarah. Way to go.*

Chapter 45
Poland, 1944

The instant Irena felt her feet touch the ground, she bent her knees and rolled onto the wet grass, her parachute collapsing around her. She had only enough time to fold it before silent shapes were upon her, tearing it from her hands. They hustled her across the field and through some bushes towards a truck with its motor running and its headlights dimmed, and she and 'Rafal', the other man who'd been dropped with her, were unceremoniously shoved into the back of the vehicle. Irena leaned back against the canvas canopy and breathed deeply, trying to slow her rapid heartbeat. Finally, she was here. Back where she belonged. She'd been warned that on no account was she to try to get in touch with her father, or anyone she might have known before the war. However, as soon as it was all over, nothing would stop her from going to Tata.

Only when the truck rolled away into the darkness did the man sitting next to her speak. 'We're taking you to a safe house for tonight. From now on use only your cover name and story. No matter who you speak to. Is that understood?'

She nodded.

'Tomorrow you will be given the details of your contact. He will be the one to tell you where to go to deliver and collect messages. It will be in different places each time. You can reach me through the Brożeks – the people you'll be staying with – but only if you think that your contact, or the person you are delivering messages to, has been compromised. Are we clear?'

Once again she nodded. He turned away from her and spoke to Rafal, no doubt giving him a similar set of instructions. When the man had finished he sat back and closed his eyes and the rest of the journey passed in silence.

After forty minutes or so, the truck pulled off the road and Irena was instructed to climb out.

'You must go the rest of the way on foot,' the man who'd done all the talking so far said. 'Antoni will take you to the safe house.' He gripped her shoulder. 'Good luck.'

As the truck pulled away, for a moment, in the sudden silence, she felt terribly alone.

Antoni was wearing a woollen hat pulled low on his forehead, and, in the moonlight, she had the briefest impression of a man of average height with a prominent chin before he turned away, beckoning her to follow him.

She kept close to his back as they crossed more fields and climbed over fences until they came to a suburb on the outskirts of the city. He motioned to her to keep behind him as he hurried along the streets, stopping every so often to listen for the sound of approaching vehicles or footsteps. Once, he yanked her into the shadows until a motorcycle with two German soldiers had passed by.

Eventually they arrived at a three-storey apartment block. Her guide let them in through a door that had clearly been left unlocked for them.

A tousle-haired woman wearing a silk dressing-gown met them in the hallway. 'This is your guest,' Antoni said. 'Her name is Magdalena. She starts work tomorrow.' And with that he slipped back into the night.

'I'm Mrs Brożek,' the woman introduced herself. 'You are my niece from the country. Is that understood?'

'Perfectly.' Irena answered. 'I've memorised the details of my identity. You don't have to worry.'

'All we do is worry,' the woman said. Then she smiled briefly. 'Welcome back to Poland.'

The next day Irena strapped her nurse's bag to the carrier of her bicycle. It was filled with bandages, anaesthetic and a few medicines – everything a nurse would be expected to have when visiting patients in a time when medical supplies were in short supply.

The bicycle was more rickety than the one she had ridden in Skye, but after a wobbly start, she found her balance and could take her attention off the road.

As she cycled along the street she forced herself not to pay attention to the German soldiers who seemed to be everywhere. The Varsovians didn't give them a second glance – no doubt after more than four years of being occupied they'd become used to them.

She tried to picture where she was going but some of the landmarks she'd known before were missing – either statues torn down by the occupiers or buildings destroyed during the first month of the German invasion. She smiled when she saw the number of anchors – the symbol of the Polish resistance – painted onto walls and statues. They made her feel less alone.

She found the right place without difficulty: the hours spent memorising the maps had been useful. She leaned her bicycle against the wall, lifted her bag from the carrier, and knocked on the door. It was answered by an elderly lady with glasses.

'Ah yes, the nurse,' she said. 'Come in. My sister is expecting you.'

Unsurprisingly it wasn't another old woman who was waiting for Irena but a man in his forties with muddy brown hair and dark, inscrutable eyes.

'Nurse Drobnik,' he said, 'I am Bronisław. Unless there is an emergency, this is the last time we shall meet. Dr Jawarski will supply you with the names and addresses of the patients to see. Sometimes he will provide you with a message and the address of the person to whom you are to deliver it.' Having genuine patients to visit would help her cover. 'You must burn it or flush it away as soon as you have memorised it. Is that understood?'

'Yes.'

'The Nazis are having more and more sweeps,' Bronisław continued. 'It is possible you will be caught up in one, in which case there is nothing – *nothing* – we can do for you. You will have to take your chances.'

'I understand,' Irena said.

'Good. Now go to our doctor friend and he will tell you where to go next. Sometimes, instead of taking a message to an address, you will be asked to leave it in a safe place to be collected or to pass it to a courier. If it appears that either the drop off or the courier has been compromised, go away, see another patient perhaps and come back later and try to make the drop. Our doctor friend will know how to contact me in case of emergency.'

For the next few weeks Irena carried messages across Warsaw. She was stopped once, but the soldier barely looked at her papers before waving her on. Fear was a constant presence, waking her during the night and causing her to shake when she least expected it. But her work brought her a measure of peace too, easing some of the guilt she'd lived with over the last years. At night, she indulged herself, thinking about Richard and imagining the life they would share once the war was over. If they survived. And if he forgave her. He would know by now that she'd lied to him. Would he understand why she had? And why she'd had to leave him?

One day, having just deposited her latest messages, she was waved down by a middle-aged woman in the street.

'You are a nurse?' she asked.

'Yes. What's the matter?'

The woman chewed on her lip, her eyes darting past Irena.

'You can trust me,' Irena said. 'I promise.'

'I have no choice but to trust you! Will you come with me to my house? Someone needs your help.'

Irena didn't ask why she hadn't taken whoever it was to the regular doctor or to the hospital. She had her suspicions.

Pushing her bicycle, she followed the woman down a narrow street.

'Leave that here,' the woman hissed, coming to an abrupt stop in front of a small lane. 'Put it out of sight. But bring your bag. Hurry!'

She was clearly frightened out of her wits. Irena felt a stirring of unease. Was this a trap? It was difficult to know who to trust and so much easier not to trust anyone. At least she was no longer carrying anything that might incriminate her or her fellow resistors. To all intents and purposes she was simply the local nurse.

She followed the woman up a flight of stairs and into her home. Inside the woman took off her headscarf and gestured to Sarah to sit. In a chair beside the lace-curtained window was a man in a grubby vest and trousers whom Sarah could only assume was her husband. He didn't murmur a word of welcome. Just stared at her fixedly.

'Let me look in your bag,' the woman said to Irena.

Irena opened it for her.

She rummaged around before nodding to her husband who eased himself out of his chair. He beckoned for Irena to follow him into the bedroom. It was small with only room for a double bed, a dressing table and a wardrobe. He dragged the bed away from the wall, exposing a cupboard door. He opened it, revealing a woman and two small children inside in a space no bigger than a large wardrobe. Three pairs of frightened eyes stared out at her.

'We have been hiding them here for the last four years,' Irena hadn't heard the woman join them, 'but the boy is sick. We're frightened he will die.'

They'd been hiding there for four years! It was almost impossible to believe.

'Come on out,' Irena said, crouching down. 'I won't hurt you. I can't examine the boy if you stay in there.'

The mother eased herself out of her hiding space and, taking the children by the hand, pulled them out behind her. 'Don't be frightened, little ones,' she said.

Her daughter was around three or four with wide brown eyes and thick dark brown hair. She gave Irena a shy smile before popping her thumb in her mouth. She was painfully thin, but otherwise appeared healthy enough. The boy, who was a little older, perhaps as much as seven, was a different matter. Bright spots of fever coloured his too thin cheeks. The sour smell of suppurating flesh made her want to gag.

'Jacob went out a few days ago,' his mother explained, 'even though he knows he must never ever do it. He wanted to help get us some food. The Nawarskis had to go away for a couple of days, so, for once, they didn't seal us up. I was sleeping, I didn't know he'd gone. He was foraging in some ruins when rubble fell on him.'

The boy looked at Irena through thick, dark lashes. 'I knew I couldn't ask anyone to help me so I waited until dark. Then I crawled back here.'

'I cleaned and splinted his leg as best I could but I can see it's infected. He needs medicine,' his mother continued, looking at Irena with imploring eyes.

'I'll do what I can. Will you tell me your name?'

'Hinda.'

'Hinda, I need Jacob on the bed so I can look at his leg. Can you help him or shall I?'

'I can do it myself,' Jacob answered, gritting his teeth as he hobbled to the bed and hauled himself onto it. Gently Irena felt along the bones of his legs. It wasn't broken as far as she could tell, but judging by the smell and the dark brown fluid seeping through the bandage, he had a nasty wound that had, as Hinda suspected, become infected. The boy should be in hospital. But that was impossible. Had he been fairer they might have tried to pass him off as the child of an Aryan Pole but with his colouring there was no chance.

'I'll clean the wound,' Irena said. 'I'll try to come back tomorrow with something to stop the infection spreading. For now could I have some boiled water please?'

As she waited for the water to cool, Irena eased off the dressing, stopping when she couldn't remove more without hurting the boy. He stayed still, his pale lips pressed tightly together, the only indication she was hurting him. The girl watched from the corner of the room with sombre brown eyes, sucking contentedly on her thumb.

'How old is your daughter?' Irena asked.

'Leah is almost four. She was born here. Poor thing has never been out of this house. If I hadn't been heavily pregnant with her we might have taken our chance to flee while we could. But we left it too late. Once war broke out, I couldn't leave.' She lowered her voice. 'Their father was killed early on in the war. He was with the Polish cavalry.'

'So was my fiancé,' Irena said. 'I lost him too.'

'Dear Mrs Nawarski was our housekeeper,' Hinda said, smiling up at the older woman. 'She had her chance to go but wouldn't take it. I don't know what would have happened to us if she and Tanek hadn't taken us in.'

'As if I would abandon you,' Mrs Nawarski mumbled softly, 'when you and the children are as precious as my own.' Her voice hardened. 'It does my heart good to know that we're getting one over on those heartless bastards.'

'You have no other family?' Irena asked Hinda.

'No. My mother and father, brothers and sisters were put in the ghetto. We weren't at home when they were taken. I wanted to join them but I was persuaded not to by Mrs Nawarski. She said I must think of the children and should stay with her. I don't know where the rest of my family are now. They were taken away before the ghetto was destroyed, and I've had no news of them.' She glanced at her children before turning back to Irena. 'I told the children that they have gone to the countryside for a holiday.'

It was clear that the woman had a good idea of what had probably happened to her family. Irena straightened and tested the water temperature with her finger. 'I will soak the rest of bandages off,' she told Jacob. 'I'll be as gentle as I can but it will still hurt a little. You are going to have to be very brave and try not to cry out. Do you understand?'

When Jacob nodded, his mother bent to kiss him.

'They know. They are used to keeping very quiet. Sometimes we wonder if little Leah here knows how to speak.'

'She does!' her brother protested. 'She just doesn't like to.'

The boy's mother slid behind her son so that she could hold his upper body in his arms. 'If you need to, my treasure,' she said, 'turn your face into me.'

Gently, Irena removed the remaining bandages, soaking each layer with water before peeling it away. The boy whimpered when she came to the last bit. Even with the water, it remained stuck to his skin. Finally, the old bandage was off. She sucked in a breath when she saw the damage to his lower leg. The wound was red and inflamed around the edges with a line of infection snaking up his leg. He had to be in a great deal of pain. She would do the best she could with what she had, but he really needed to have it treated in hospital.

'I don't have any sulphonamide with me,' she said, when she'd cleaned the wound. 'But I will come back tomorrow and bring some.' She wrapped a clean dressing around his leg. 'In the meantime, keep him cool.' She nodded to the little girl. 'I'll try to find some food too.'

'I don't know how to thank you,' Hinda said.

'We must help one another. The Allied forces are closer now. If we can hold out for another few months, perhaps we will all make it.'

Chapter 46

'Why don't they do something?' Antoni asked, picking lice from the seams of his coat and squashing them between his fingers. 'What more proof do they need?'

Irena had come to the safe house to collect that day's messages. 'You know the British, Irena. What the fuck are they waiting for? All we're asking them to do is bomb the railway lines leading into those Godforsaken camps.'

Occasionally, in the night, she accompanied Antoni and his fellow insurgents to the RAF drops. When the planes flew over, releasing their cargo of rigid metal containers shaped like large green bombs, she found herself wondering if she could be staring up at the underbelly of a plane piloted by Richard or Aleksy.

As soon as the planes left they'd run to retrieve the containers. Apart from weapons they often held cigarettes and tobacco, jars of butter, tins of jam, bicycle tyres and, most importantly as far as Irena was concerned, some basic medicines.

But more often than not, the containers ripped apart when they hit the ground and a large proportion of the weapons were smashed and unusable. She sent messages of her own back to Britain telling them to be more careful, but it didn't seem to make a difference.

Nevertheless, with what they salvaged, the Home Army

managed to blow up the odd railway line and factory. It wasn't enough and much too late to save the Jewish resistance in the ghetto that had been flattened by the Germans months earlier, the survivors – what there was of them – either executed or taken away to camps. There was no doubt now that the remaining Jews were being exterminated in ever increasing numbers. Still the British didn't bomb the camps or the railway lines leading to them.

'Perhaps they're scared they'll kill civilians,' Irena responded.

'Fuck them and their caution. These people are going to die anyway,' said a young woman who was greasing her weapon, squinting up the barrel to see that it was clean.

Irena wasn't so sure. It was one thing to kill Nazi soldiers, quite another to bomb trains carrying innocent civilians. There was only one way to save the Jews. The Allies had to liberate the German-occupied countries.

Having memorised her latest message – another one asking the British government for help – Irena left the safe house and cycled towards the hidden family. She continued to visit them every second day, bringing them what food she could and redressing Jacob's wound, but despite her best efforts, the boy's condition had deteriorated, the infection continuing to spread up his leg and Irena knew there was a good chance he would lose it. The little sulphonamide she managed to acquire for him wasn't enough. He really needed to have the wound cleaned and debrided under anaesthetic.

Away from the city centre and without the trams to impede her progress, Irena picked up speed. Two soldiers, their guns slung over their shoulders, were on the pavement a little further up on the right and they turned to stare at a girl cycling towards them, her bare legs flashing as she pedalled.

One of the soldiers dug his companion in the side and said

something that made him laugh. Irena hoped they wouldn't stop the girl.

She was a only a short distance away when the girl reached into her pocket and pulled something from it. Suddenly there were two bangs and one of the soldiers doubled over and crumpled to the ground. The other one reached for his weapon, but before he could lift it to fire, there was another loud retort. His rifle fell to the ground, as he dropped to one knee, clutching his arm. The girl on the cycle stopped in front of him, kicked his weapon away with her foot and raised her pistol.

'No!' Irena shouted. At the sound of her voice, the girl looked in her direction. Irena recognised her: she was one of the resistance fighters she'd met in a safe house.

Irena brought her bicycle to a halt, leaped off and stood between the girl and the soldier. He was staring up at the girl, his eyes wide with shock and fear. He was really just a boy – not much more than eighteen.

The street had emptied. Irena and the girl stared at each other for one, long moment.

'Go!' Irena urged. It wouldn't be long before other soldiers arrived on the scene. They would kill them both if they found them. Or perhaps worse, arrest and interrogate them.

The girl shook her head tightly and with a quick glance behind her, cycled off. The soldier, his teeth clenched, his forehead and upper lip glistening with sweat, looked at Irena with imploring eyes. She crouched by his side.

'You've been hit in the arm,' she said in German. 'I know it hurts but it's not going to kill you.'

Then she heard it, the sound of a truck coming in their direction. It couldn't be far away.

'I have to go,' she said.

The soldier grabbed her skirt. 'Hans. How is he?' Irena

glanced to her left. The other soldier was lying on his side, his legs pulled up towards his chest. He was facing her and she could see his pupils were fixed and dilated.

Irena shook her head. 'There's nothing I can do for him.' The truck was coming closer. If she were going to get away she had to leave now.

And the injured soldier knew it too. They stared at each other. 'Go,' he said. 'Hurry.'

As the nose of the truck appeared at the end of the street, Irena picked up her bike and pushed it into an alleyway. The ringing of boots on the cobbles as soldiers spilled from the truck filled her with terror. They would be on her in moments.

'Over here,' a voice hissed from an open doorway. A middle-aged woman, her hair tied up in a scarf, gestured to her. 'Quick. Bring your bicycle.'

Irena pushed it into the narrow hall and the woman locked the door behind her. She took the bike from Irena. 'Leave it here, but bring your bag. Come inside.'

'But if they find it!' The blood was hammering in her ears.

'You're a nurse, aren't you? So you're here to see me. Be quick. We don't have much time.'

Irena had no choice but to trust her. She left her precious bicycle in the hall and followed her inside. The woman kicked off her shoes and pulled her dress over her head. Wearing only her slip, she took Irena by the arm. 'I've been sick for days. It is women's trouble. This is the second time you have been to see me. You don't know what's wrong, but I won't go into hospital.'

When Irena nodded, the woman lay on the bed and pulled the thin blanket up to her chin. 'Open your bag. Take something out – I don't care what – and put it on the table. Now for both our sakes, try to look normal – you look frightened to death.'

A moment later, there was a loud banging, followed by the sound of splintering wood.

'*Raus, Raus!*' the soldiers shouted. Irena sucked in a breath and went to the door. Before she could open it, a German soldier flung it open and shoved her aside.

'What is the meaning of this?' she demanded in German. 'I have a sick woman in here. She mustn't be disturbed.'

'Is that your bicycle in the hall?'

'Yes. I am a nurse. I always use it when I need to visit patients who can't come to the hospital. Now would you mind telling me what's going on?'

'Let me see your papers,' the soldier demanded.

Hoping he wouldn't notice that her hands were shaking, she reached into her pocket and passed them to him. As she did, she saw with horror she had a dark stain on her sleeve.

He noticed it too. His eyes narrowed. 'How is it you have blood on you, Fräulein?'

'Nurse!' a querulous voice came from the bedroom. 'When are you going to give me something to stop the bleeding?'

The soldier grabbed Irena by the elbow and dragged her into the bedroom. She wondered how many minutes she had left to live.

'Where are you bleeding? Let me see.'

'Oh, sir. It's down below – women's troubles. I haven't stopped bleeding this last three weeks. The nurse doesn't know what's wrong either, but she was about to give me something that might help.'

She made to push the blankets away but the soldier stepped back, repelled. 'Wait here,' he said.

As soon as he left the room, the woman held out her hand. 'Do you have a scalpel? Anything sharp?'

All Irena had was a pair of scissors. Guessing what the woman intended, she took them from her bag. 'It's better I do it,' Irena said. The woman lifted her nightdress and searching for a vein near her groin, Irena used the tip of the scissors to puncture a hole.

'Bigger,' the woman said through gritted teeth. 'There has to be more blood.'

Taking another deep breath, Irena widened the hole until blood spilled onto the sheets. Judging by the noise of running boots, the soldier was coming back with reinforcements. Irena wrapped the scissors with a piece of lint and replaced them in her bag.

And not a second too soon. The soldier had brought his captain back with him. He threw back the sheets, but when he saw the blood on the woman's thighs, he covered her up again. 'Search this place,' he told his men. 'The nurse's bag, too.' He turned and gestured to a soldier to come forward. Irena felt sick when she recognised him. He was holding his arm across his chest, stemming the blood with a handkerchief. The captain pointed at Irena.

'Is this the woman?'

The world seemed to stop turning. Images of Tata, Aleksy and Richard flashed into her head. She would never see any of them again.

But the soldier shook his head. 'No. It wasn't her.'

'Are you sure?'

'Yes. I have never seen either of these women before.'

Chapter 47

By July the German army was in retreat all over Europe and the Russians almost at Poland's doorstep. The Red Army dropped leaflets and broadcast on the radio that they were coming, exhorting the Poles to be ready to help them. Knowing they were close, the Home Army came out into the open to fight.

To her joy, Irena had met Anna again. She'd appeared at one of the safe houses, wearing an olive skirt and jacket with the Polish Home Army armband on her upper arm.

The two women hugged.

'Why are you here?' Irena asked.

'The time for sending messages is over. Poland is about to be liberated and I want to be standing shoulder to shoulder with my countrymen and women when it is.' Anna glanced over to Antoni, before smiling slyly at Irena. 'With him.'

So that's the way it was.

'We're not waiting for the Russians to liberate us,' Antoni said from across the room. 'We will liberate ourselves – even if it means dying in the attempt. If we don't they will just be another occupying force. Poland must be free again.'

On the first of August the first shots were fired, killing hundreds of Germans. They were quick to retaliate, pulling people from their homes or from the street and summarily executing them. They set fire to houses and buildings, systematically moving from street to street.

Within weeks the city of Warsaw was reduced to rubble. Although they must have known they were defeated, the Germans seemed intent on destroying every building and killing every man, woman and child. The resistance fought wherever and with whatever they could. Even children joined in.

With all pretence of acceptance of German rule gone, and with the Home Army fighting openly on the streets, Irena persuaded Hinda to take her children to the hospital. They would be as safe there, if not safer, than they would be in hiding.

The doctors at the hospital cleaned Jacob's wound under anaesthetic and almost immediately the little boy began to improve. His mother and sister stayed close beside him, sleeping on the floor. Whenever Irena found a few moments to spare, she visited them there and as soon as Irena sat down Leah would climb into her lap and sit there, sucking her thumb, her small body pressed into Irena and her head tucked under Irena's chin. She said the odd word, but on the whole was happy to watch what was going on around her.

In return, Irena couldn't help but love the little girl back. There was something about Leah that reminded her of herself at that age. Despite the trauma of years spent in hiding, or perhaps because of it, Leah rarely cried. Equally, she seldom smiled. Irena hoped that when the war was over, when normal life resumed once more, and with the love of her mother and brother, Leah would learn to behave like a child should.

Irena was at the hospital, caring for the injured and dying as best she could, as best as any of them could without medicine or anaesthetic for those screaming in pain or burning up with fever, when German soldiers stormed in, brandishing their weapons.

'Everyone outside,' they shouted, 'Now!'

One of the doctors raised his head from the patient he was examining. 'We can't leave our patients. They will die if we do,' he said calmly.

'They must go too. Everyone. Out.'

The doctor looked incredulous. 'It is impossible,' he said, turning back to his patient.

An officer walked over to him, pulled the pistol from his belt and calmly shot him in the back of the head.

'Anyone else?' the officer sneered. 'Anyone else who feels they would like to stay?' The remainder of the staff shared terrified glances before turning to the injured and sick and helping them out of their beds. What new horror did the Nazis have in store for them? Irena heard tramping feet in the corridor and glanced over her shoulder to see doctors and nurses, even a nun, carrying stretchers.

'Leave the sickest,' the German officer said, 'they will be seen to. But no doctors or nurses are to stay. You must go with your patients. They will need you to take care of them.'

A worm of fear crawled along Irena's spine. She wanted to believe them. The Russians were almost here, so what use was it for the Germans to waste precious resources, precious ammunition on them?

She picked up a child she had been treating who had crush injuries to both his feet and carried him outside, joining the snaking line of patients and staff. Behind her she heard shots and cries, and she held the child closer, covering his ears with her hands.

'It is all right,' she murmured. 'It's going to be all right. We are moving to another hospital, that's all.'

The procession tore at Irena's heart. Most of the doctors were in front, the assistants next, carrying on stretchers those too weak or injured to walk, and then Irena and the nurses with the remainder of the patients, some still in their underwear, some on crutches, supported by relatives or fellow patients. They shuffled forward, their eyes downcast, each step requiring superhuman effort.

Someone grabbed hold of Irena's elbow. It was the mother of the boy Irena was carrying. 'Let me take him,' his mother said, although she could barely walk herself. Irena passed the boy to her, suspecting that this could be the last time the woman held her son.

They were poked and prodded along Gorczewska Street, where the line turned off into a tunnel and halted. A few moments later the line moved forward again until finally they were herded together in a shed.

After examining their documents, they were divided into groups and the first group of twelve was led out of the back entrance and into what Irena assumed would be a courtyard. A few minutes later the sound of machine-gunfire ripped through the room followed by two or three single shots. There were a few cries from the people waiting, but mostly they just gripped each other tightly, whispering their goodbyes.

So this day, a bright August afternoon, was to be her last. Images spooled through her mind, pictures of herself as a little girl holding her mother's hand, of her and Grandmother in the kitchen, at the piano as Alexsy sat next to her, memories of her father taking her by the hand on his visits to hospital, the first time and the last that she'd seen Piotr and then finally the most painful of all, her curled up in the armchair in the room in Skye watching Richard as he slept. *My love, my love.*

Another group was led away and once again the sound of gunfire rang out. They should do something. Run, attack the guards, anything. They were going to die anyway and she refused to go to her death without a fight. And not here, in this dark place that smelled of blood and terror.

She dragged in a breath. Most of the guards were herding the next group forward at the other end of the shed and only three remained at the entrance. There would be others outside, even if she made it past the ones at the entrance, but at least she would die in the sunshine.

She edged silently towards the guards. All she had was a hat-pin – less than useless against a machine gun. Nevertheless, she removed it from her cap and curled her fist around it.

As she approached, one of the soldiers looked at her and a flash of recognition crossed his face. It was the young German soldier who'd been shot on the street and who in return had saved her life.

'Fräulein?' he said.

She nodded. He glanced to his left where his companion had turned away to subdue a woman who was screaming as her child was wrenched from her arms.

'You are Volksdeutsch?'

She shook her head. She wouldn't claim German ethnicity, not even to save her life.

The soldier stared at her then grabbed her by the arm. 'You are Volksdeutsch,' he insisted. 'You should not be here. Go.'

Just then a small hand slipped into hers. She looked down to find Leah looking up at her. Dear God, they were here too. She glanced over to where Hinda was standing, her son tucked into her side. For a moment their eyes locked. *Take her*, Hinda mouthed. Her eyes, fixed on her daughter, filled. *Please*.

Hinda's face blurred and reformed, until it seemed to Irena she was looking into the beseeching eyes of the Jewish woman with the baby.

She gave a slight nod and picked up Leah. The little girl

buried her head in the crook of Irena's neck. She began to move towards the exit.

'No,' the soldier whispered urgently, shaking his head. 'Just you.'

She couldn't leave Leah. She had missed the opportunity to save a child once and she wouldn't do so again. It was either both of them or neither of them. She lifted her chin and, holding the gaze of the soldier, took another step. She could read his indecision, feel his fear. She lowered her eyes and took one more step. Then another. Every moment she expected to hear the command to halt ring out or to feel a bullet in her back. Every step felt like a mile, but unbelievably no shout rang out. Then, just as she reached the exit, she felt a hand on her arm. It was the soldier again. But instead of dragging them back inside he propelled her roughly to the end of the queue and shoved her. 'Go,' he said. 'Don't look back. Just walk. If they catch you again, there is nothing I will be able to do for you.'

She held Leah tighter, trying to block out the sounds of machine-gunfire and, on legs that felt as if they wouldn't hold her upright, continued to walk. As soon as she reached a building she ducked inside, Leah heavy in her arms.

'Where's Mama?' Leah asked, wriggling to be put down. Her lower lip started quivering when she didn't see them behind her. 'Where's Mama?' she demanded again. 'Where's Jacob?'

Irena put her fingers to her lips. 'Ssh. We are playing a game of hide-and-seek. We will hide for as long as we can, and see if they can find us. Is that all right?'

Leah's brow knotted for a moment then she smiled timidly and nodded her head. It was the first time she'd been separated from her mother and brother and Irena prayed that if she'd learned one thing from hiding all these years, it was to do as she was told.

They stayed in the ruins of the building until long after it got dark. Irena knew she should leave the area – find a safe house or a bunker – but she couldn't. Not until she was sure that there was no one left alive. But as the sound of gunfire continued into the afternoon, it was followed by the smell of burning and the sweet, sickly smell of scorched human flesh. They were clearing up after themselves. She clenched her hands in to fists. She could do nothing for her countrymen and women, for Hinda and Jacob, but she would do whatever she had to, to keep this child alive.

When the soldiers finally left, and an eerie silence seeped through the street, Irena crept out of the building, tightly holding Leah's hand. She had to find whatever was left of the resistance. That was her only hope. They weaved their way through the burning buildings, stepping around the bodies that lay on the street. Leah said nothing, just sucked on her thumb harder than ever, eventually falling asleep, cradled in Irena's arms once more. It was dark before they managed to make it back to the building where the unit Anna and Antoni were with, had their base.

Anna hugged her for a long time, delighted to see her alive – news of the hospital massacre had already reached them – but less than happy to see Leah.

'We can't keep a child here,' she whispered. 'It's too dangerous. You must take her somewhere else.'

Irena glanced at the still-sleeping child on her bed of coats and sacks. 'Everywhere is dangerous! Where do you suggest I take her? All the Varsovians are either fighting or hiding in their houses and refusing to come out. I won't abandon her.'

'I know someone who might help,' Antoni said, leaving his position at the window. 'She took many children from the ghetto before it was liquidated and smuggled them overseas. She might be able to arrange something for the child – if you have a family that will sponsor her.'

Irena immediately thought of Isabel and Richard. 'I know a family in Britain. They will take her if I ask them. Where do I find this woman?'

Anna picked up her gun. 'Is she still in Warsaw, Antoni? I will have to make enquiries. Irena, you rest.'

One of the other freedom fighters looked up and frowned. 'We can't waste good soldiers on a fool's errand. We are fighting for the greater good of Poland, not for individuals.'

'What is Poland,' Anna countered, 'if not individuals? Tell me where I might find this woman, Antoni.'

'Anna, it's too risky right now,' Irena protested. 'I'll go later.'

'It's risky all the time and we need you, Renia, more than ever,' Anna said. 'Your hospital wasn't the only one where there were mass executions of staff and patients. With so many doctors and nurses murdered, we need all the medical help we can get.'

Irena closed her eyes as a wave of exhaustion swept over her. She didn't know if she had the strength or courage to continue. Today's events had drained her. But as an image of Hinda's eyes swam in front of her, she knew saving Leah was more important than anything or anyone.

Antoni chewed his lower lip. 'Go now, Anna,' he said urgently. 'But if you can't find this woman within the next twenty-four hours we'll have to think of another plan.'

'Thank you,' Irena breathed. Tomorrow she knew, when Hindi and Jacob failed to appear, Leah would begin asking questions and she had no idea what she going to say to her. In the meantime, there were men and women that needed medical attention.

After doing her best for the sick and injured, Irena lowered her weary body onto the bedding beside Leah. She removed her necklace and held it up to the flickering light of a candle, remembering her mother, the way her golden hair had fallen over Irena's face when she'd kissed her goodnight, her scent and her softness as she'd hugged her. She didn't need the necklace to remind her of her Mama. She had all these memories locked away inside her head. With a small pair of surgical scissors, she began unpicking the hem of Leah's coat.

Anna was true to her word. She returned the next morning with news that she'd found someone who was with the Żegota, the code name that was used for the Polish Council to Aid Jews, and who could take Leah to safety.

'You could go with her,' Anna said. 'I have a spare set of papers. But you'll have to go now.'

Irena looked down at the little girl. She was still sleeping, her cheeks flushed with tears. The child wouldn't be so frightened if Irena was with her.

But she couldn't leave. Not yet. Not when Poland needed every freedom fighter, every nurse and doctor, every builder, engineer and teacher, to stand together in this final onslaught. What mattered right now was Leah's survival.

She told Anna what she'd done with the necklace and pressed the remainder of the cash the SOE had given her into her hand. 'I think there's enough here.' She hesitated; the necklace was the only gift Irena had to leave Leah. 'But if you need to sell the necklace then do.'

Saying goodbye to Leah tore Irena's heart. Tiny as she was, it took Anna and another helper to wrench Hinda's clinging daughter from her arms. Irena's only consolation as she watched Anna carry her away, Leah's wide-spread flaying hands stretched out towards her, begging her with pleading, bewildered eyes not to let them take her, was that Richard's family would take good care of her until, God willing, Irena made it back to Britain.

Chapter 48

With no way any longer to get in touch with Britain or her contacts, Irena was drawn into Warsaw's battle for survival. Sometimes she had to take her medical bag and run across the street, ducking behind upturned tanks and cars to prevent herself from being fired on. With no longer any illusion that the sign of a red cross would protect anyone, Irena was as much a fighter in this final battle as the insurgents. The Russian army had reached the outskirts of Warsaw, but there they'd stopped. Supposedly their allies, they made no move to help the insurgents.

Sometimes in the evening, in a lull in the fighting, a group of them would meet in one of the bombed-out houses, either in the cellar or, if it was still useable, in the attic where, at least during the day, they could see the sky and feel the warmth of the sunlight through the broken windowpanes.

They were a mixed bunch – mainly young men who'd been part of the underground since war broke out, older men who'd managed to escape the round-ups, and young women, some still in their teens, who hadn't taken part in any fighting but were now determined to do what they could to help liberate their city in advance of the Russians.

Although they knew it was unlikely they would survive, or perhaps because they knew the chances of survival were negligible, they made the most of the evenings they had together.

Often someone would play a piano – there was usually one to be found in each ruined house – and they would sing Polish songs of liberation. At night, Irena would hear the muffled sounds of Antoni and Anna making love – they were separated from the rest with only a sheet hung from the ceiling to give them any pretence of privacy – and she would think of Richard, aching for the warmth and comfort of his arms around her, knowing it was unlikely she would see him again. It wasn't true to say that she wasn't scared; she was, but having faced death more than once she knew she could face it again with courage and there was a strange sense of companionship and comfort in being with the others. She hoped, however, that if she were to die, it would be quick. She still had her pill and would take it if necessary. She had no wish to be taken to a German prison, as many of the resistance had, only to be tortured before being executed.

When she wasn't tending to the wounded resistors she was treating patients in the basement of a makeshift hospital in what had been the Institute for the deaf, mute and blind near the Old Town, the only part of Warsaw held by the Poles. Sometimes she, along with a nurse or medical student, had to amputate an arm or a leg by candlelight with only vodka to dull the patient's agony.

They were almost out of all medical supplies, when it was agreed that Irena would accompany Antoni and Anna to the ruins of a hospital to try to recover any supplies that might have been left behind. They knew it was a high-risk endeavour – the bombed hospital was close to a part of Warsaw where the German soldiers had a clear view of the street, and it was possible – even likely – that anything worthwhile had been removed by them following the evacuation of the hospital. However, it was a chance they had to take. With almost no medicines left too many were dying needlessly.

They waited until it was dark. Germans prowled the streets at all hours, but it would at least give them some cover.

When the sound of gunfire was at its quietest, Antoni, Anna and Irena left the safety of their makeshift bunker and stepped onto the streets of their decimated city. The moon was hidden by clouds that would periodically drift away and light would illuminate the sky. When it did, they pressed themselves against a wall or hid behind a pile of rubble until the moon was once more obscured.

Irena's mouth was dry – and not simply because they were limited to a quarter litre of water every day. When Antoni called her forward, it took every ounce of willpower to make her legs move. In the distance they heard a cry followed by the rat-tat-tat of machine-gunfire. She wiped her perspiring hands on her dress and, crouching low, followed her two companions along the street, passing a pile of smouldering bodies on the way. They didn't look too closely, preferring not to see if a former patriot's face might still be recognisable amongst the ashes.

As they crept along, the sound of German voices and boots became louder.

'Are you still okay to do this?' Antoni whispered. 'You could stay behind. Leave it to Anna and me to get whatever we can.'

Irena shook her head. 'We won't have much time and two won't be able to carry much. More importantly, I'll be able to select what will be most useful.'

Antoni squeezed her shoulder. 'There might not be anything to salvage, then you will have risked your life for nothing.'

'We are all risking our lives all the time and mine is no more valuable than yours.' It was true. With so little medicine and no facilities, even if they found supplies, without the resistors holding onto Warsaw they'd all be doomed.

But her words didn't make her feel less scared. Although she'd long since given up believing in a God who could allow this to happen, she murmured a prayer. Not so much that she would live, but that if she died it would be with dignity and without betraying her friends.

It took them over an hour to traverse the streets, a journey that before the war would have taken them less than half the time. But to their dismay, the hospital, possibly only hours before, had been torched by the flame-throwers – or the mooing cows as they were known locally – and was burning, the wooden rafters falling into where once had been operating theatres and wards.

Anna swore. 'Shit. If we'd come yesterday, there would have been a chance.'

'There might still be something to salvage in the basement,' Irena whispered. 'If we can get in. That's where the pharmacy was. Perhaps the fire hasn't reached it yet?'

Antoni seemed indecisive for a moment, then he nodded. 'You two wait here while I have a look. If there's a way in, I'll come back for you.'

Before either woman could respond, he started running towards the building in a low crouch. As the moon came from behind a cloud once more, Irena saw that Anna was pale and shaking. She reached for her hand and squeezed it.

They waited for what seemed like an eternity but could have only been a few minutes. It was then they heard the sound of motorcycles. Anna looked at Irena in horror. 'I must warn Antoni.'

'There's no time,' Irena whispered. 'He might hear them and hide.' Just as the German motorcycles turned into the street, Anna shook herself free from Irena's grip and ran towards the hospital building. In the light of the flames she didn't stand a chance. The soldiers called out but when Anna didn't stop, they shot at her. She clutched her leg and hobbled on. They shot her again. This time she fell to her knees. At that moment, Antoni emerged from the building. He could have saved himself but when he saw his lover on the ground he ran towards her. Before he'd taken more than a couple of steps, he too was gunned down.

There was nothing Irena could do for them, but neither could she leave her hiding place. To do so would be to walk out into the bright lights of their motorcycles. She held her breath, trying not to move a muscle.

The soldiers drove up to the bodies to make sure their victims were dead. Just then something bit Irena's foot and before she could help herself she yelped. As a rat the size of a cat scurried away into the darkness, she prayed the Germans would think it had been the rodent who had made the noise. But it wasn't to be. The soldier in the sidecar brought his rifle to his shoulder and swivelled towards where Irena was hiding.

'You,' he shouted, 'come out.'

The driver swung his bike around until the full beam of his light fell upon her.

Irena raised her arms and stepped forward.

Chapter 49

Skye, 1989

'I'm so glad they've found Magdalena,' Katherine said. 'She's bound to know something about your mother. And she might also be able to tell us what happened to Irena – if she knew her.'

'*If* Magdalena comes. She might decide not to.'

'You could always go to Poland to see her,' Katherine suggested.

Sarah nodded. 'I plan to. Supposing she allows the solicitors to give me her address. Otherwise, I'll just have to search for her there.'

Katherine had arrived that evening for dinner as arranged. It had rained all afternoon so Sarah had stayed indoors, trying, but failing, to work on one of the manuscripts she'd brought with her. It wasn't thinking about Matthew, however, that had distracted her. It was Neil, those dammed photographs, and her reaction.

The dining room was cold and musty so she had set the table in the kitchen now nicely heated by the Rayburn. Sarah had prepared the salmon earlier, turning her nose up when the scales had stuck to her fingers. To go with it, she'd put potatoes on to boil and was planning to steam some broccoli later. It wasn't much of a meal, but then she wasn't much of a cook.

Katherine was wearing a soft blue sweater, clearly hand-knitted, and a tweed skirt. Her hair was tied back with a scarf and lipstick coloured her still attractive mouth. Once again,

Sarah thought she looked far younger than her years. Perhaps it had something to do with her relatively unlined skin and porcelain complexion. She must have been lovely when she was a young woman.

'Would it be okay if we eat in the kitchen?' Sarah asked.

Katherine grinned. 'If you'd seen some of the places I've eaten in you wouldn't be asking that. How was the crab?'

'Still in the fridge, I'm afraid. Neil helped me cook it but I don't have a clue what to do with it now.'

'Why don't you give it to me and I'll deal with it if you want to get on with whatever you need to do.'

Katherine found a small hammer and placing the crab on a breadboard began to crack open the claws, while Sarah put the salmon in the oven.

'I've been thinking about our chat,' Katherine said. 'It's brought back a lot of memories – especially of the war.'

'Was it terrible? I'm sorry, of course it was.'

'Well now, that's the thing. It wasn't terrible, at least not all of it.' Katherine had finished with the claws and had started on the body of the crab. 'Maybe time plays tricks and you look back and only remember the good times.' She paused. 'We did see some awful things, of course. Especially in Africa. Dreadful burns the men had – the flies and the heat and sand getting into everything – not having enough water to wash – I remember that too. Not that Johnny minded any of it. They were having too much fun blowing up German planes in their hangers. The SAS were a real thorn in the Nazis' flesh.

'Neil was brought up on stories of his grandfather's time with them. He worshipped him so it's hardly surprising he decided to do what he does.'

Sarah thought back to the photos and her reaction. She cringed.

'Was Johnny from Skye?' Sarah sipped her glass of wine, hoping Katherine would think that the flush creeping up her neck was from the heat of the fire.

'Johnny? No, he was from England. That's where we lived all our married life. I only came back here when I retired. He died about ten years ago.' Her eyes clouded. 'I still miss him. Donald never even came to the funeral. Those two never got on. I think that's why Donald became an artist. It was as far away from a war hero as he could get.'

'Neil told me about his father.'

Katherine's head jerked up. 'He told you about Donald? That's odd. Neil isn't usually one for talking. I'm afraid he doesn't have much time for his dad.'

Sarah pricked the potatoes with a fork and when the flesh gave way, she put the broccoli on to steam. 'I'm afraid I don't have a starter,' she apologised.

'But we do. We have crab. Do you have mayonnaise?'

Sarah shook her head. 'Sorry.'

'Oil?'

'Yes.'

'Right, pass me one of the eggs I brought for you and I'll whip some up.'

Katherine found a bowl, cracked an egg into it and started whipping.

'I often wondered why my mother married my father,' Sarah said. 'She was so quiet and reserved and he was, well, not quiet.'

'You take after your mother, then?'

'My friend Gilly says I inherited my Chicken-Licken attitude from her.'

'Chicken Licken?'

'It's from a story about a chicken who goes around scared the sky is going to fall on his head. My best friend – she's in PR but read psychology at university – says it's an analogy for free-floating anxiety.'

When Katherine looked baffled, Sarah continued. 'Some people feel anxious all the time. For no particular reason. That's me and I guess it is my mother too.'

'Do you look like her?'

'We share the same colouring. I'm a bit taller and she's skinnier.' She smiled wryly. 'We're both shy – and stubborn.' Perhaps she was more like her mother than she'd realised. For the first time the thought gave her pleasure.

'Neil's mother was only eighteen when she fell pregnant. Back then it was the done thing, the honourable thing, to get married. I thought they were too young but my husband insisted. Needless to say, it didn't last. I probably spoiled Donald, but he was never one for knuckling down.'

'I'm sorry.'

'Och, it's all right. I love my son, but we're not all made the same way, are we?' Katherine tipped a little more oil into the bowl and carried on whisking. 'Neil's mother couldn't really cope after Donald abandoned them, so I took Neil on. I had to stop nursing for a while but that was all right. I went back to it when he went to school. We were still in Kent then.'

'Does Neil still see his mother?'

'No. She married again and there was no place for Neil in her new family. I shouldn't be surprised if her second husband doesn't even know about her first marriage – or Neil.'

'Poor Neil.' It seemed she and Katherine's grandson had something else in common.

Katherine looked at her sharply. 'I doubt Neil thinks that way. He's always looked on me as his mother.' She dipped her finger into the mayonnaise and tasted. 'Perfect.'

When they were seated at the table, Sarah brought the topic back to Irena.

'Why do you think Irena went back to Poland?'

'I don't know. Patriotic spirit perhaps – a need to do something for her country? I didn't know her that well and she was very guarded. I suspect she'd become used to keeping herself to herself.'

'Yet going back meant leaving Richard. I thought you said she loved him?' Sarah took a mouthful of crab. It was delicious.

'He certainly loved her. His squadron was in Italy when I was there. After North Africa, I was posted to Bari near the end of the war, when the allies were making the final push into Germany. We bumped into each other at a dance. He drank too much and told me he and Irena had become lovers but that she'd gone back to Poland. I didn't see him again until after the war was over. When we were demobbed I went back to my mother's home in Edinburgh. Although Johnny and I had decided to settle in England, I was to be married from there. I heard Richard was in hospital so I went to visit him.' She pushed away her plate. 'He'd changed. The Richard I'd known had always been full of fun. The man in the hospital was almost unrecognisable.'

Sarah cleared their plates and put the salmon and vegetables on the table. Even to her eyes it didn't look very appetising. But although Katherine helped herself to a small portion, her mind didn't seem to be on the food.

'In what way?'

'Sad. Angry. He felt he'd let Irena down.' Sarah's heart started racing. She knew instinctively they were getting to the part of the story she most wanted to hear. 'War changes people. Especially men. My Johnny wasn't always easy to live with. Neither was my father when he returned from the first war. I think they both had their demons.' She sighed. 'Men, at least men like my father and my husband, didn't believe in talking about things that bothered them.'

'Why did Richard feel he'd let Irena down?' Sarah tried to get Katherine back on track again.

'Apparently Irena had arranged for a child – a little Polish girl – to be sent to him. But he'd been shot down over Italy and was in hospital there for months before they sent him home to convalesce.

'A child? Irena sent a child? From Poland?' Why hadn't Katherine mentioned this before?

'Yes. A little girl. About four or five. I'm not exactly sure. Didn't I say? Anyway, by the time he was told about the child, it was too late.'

Sarah's mind snagged on Katherine's last words. 'What do you mean *too late*?'

'The wee girl had been adopted by a couple. Friends of someone who knew the family, I think.'

Irena had sent a little girl from Poland who'd been adopted. The age was right. 'But that little girl must have been my mother!'

'How can you be sure? That child would be what, fifty? I assumed your mother was older. Didn't she have a stroke?'

'Mum was young to have a stroke. She was born in nineteen thirty-nine. It all fits.'

Katherine covered her mouth with her hands. 'Of course, then, she could be your mother! Oh my dear, I never thought . . . '

Katherine waited silently while Sarah absorbed what she'd told her. So Mum *was* Polish. If she'd been sent here as a child what had happened to her family? Had they been Jewish? If so, what had her mother gone through before she'd made it here?

'Did Richard know where she'd come from? Who she belonged to? Was she Irena's daughter? Irena's and Richard's, even – if they were lovers. Perhaps Irena didn't know she was pregnant when she went back to Poland.'

'I'm pretty certain they were lovers, but the wee girl wasn't Irena's and Richard's child. That I do know.'

'How can you be sure?'

'Richard would have told me. Anyway, the dates didn't match. The child was about six in nineteen forty-five, so she would have been born in nineteen thirty-nine or 'forty. That was before Irena and Richard met.'

Katherine was right. However, the little girl, Sarah's mother, must have meant *something* to Irena. 'Why didn't Richard's parents keep the child?'

'I think Irena assumed that they would. After all, they'd taken *her* in. She respected Richard's mother and trusted her. I'm sure that they did what they thought best for the wee girl at the time. She needed a stay-at-home mother, one who could devote all the time in the world to her. Richard was in hospital in Italy and Irena in Poland. I don't think anyone thought much of Irena's chances of surviving the war or, for a while at least, Richard's, either. Perhaps Richard's mother already had plans to leave. I don't really know.'

Isabel – the bolter! Sarah remembered what Lady Dorothea had told her about Richard's mother going to America at the end of the war. It was unlikely Irena would have known that. But who were Mum's parents? And how had Irena come to meet them? However it had happened, it seemed her mother owed her life to her. In which case so did Sarah.

They sat in silence for a while, each woman preoccupied with her thoughts.

'So Irena must have been alive in nineteen forty-four,' Sarah said eventually. 'Did Richard ever find out where the child had come from? Who she belonged to?'

'I don't think so.' Katherine stood and picked up their plates and put them on the counter. 'What will you do now?' she asked.

What indeed? 'I'm going back to Edinburgh tomorrow. Hopefully Magdalena will get in touch soon. I'm certain she'll be able to fill in the gaps.'

'You'll be looking forward to seeing your boyfriend.'

'Ex-boyfriend. You were right. Everyone's been right. I was just too scared to see it before. If Irena could fight in a war – I'm sure I can cope on my own.'

Katherine's lips twitched. 'Aye well, better now than when the dress is bought.'

Chapter 50

As soon as she was back in Edinburgh, Sarah went to see her mother.

She was in her chair but more upright, even without the cushions. Her hair was neatly combed and she was wearing all her own clothes.

When she saw Sarah walk into the ward, her face lit up.

'Sa ... rah!'

'Mum, a whole word! You'll be rattling away soon.' Sarah pulled over a chair and sat down next to her. On the drive back from Skye she'd thought very carefully about what to say to her mother and how to broach the subject of where her mother had been born. She knew she had to tread gently.

'Mum, the solicitors have found Magdalena!'

'Ma ... lena! Alive!'

'Yes, Mum. Hopefully she'll be coming to Scotland and we'll meet her.' She took her mother's hand. 'Mum, I think I've discovered where you came from – before you were adopted. I'm pretty sure it was Poland. Do you remember?'

Tears sprang to her mother's eyes.

'Don't cry, Mum. Please. We don't have to talk about it. Not now. Not ever if you don't want to.'

'Want – to – see – Ma ... leena.'

'So do I, Mum. So do I. I promise you, if she doesn't come soon I'll fetch her myself.'

As the solicitors refused to give Sarah Magdalena's address, there was little Sarah could do but wait - and hope – that Magdalena would get in touch with her.

She'd told her mother she'd broken up with Matthew and thought she'd caught a gleam of satisfaction in her eyes when she'd given her the news. She'd mentioned Neil, too. Come to think of it, having only met the man a couple of times, she managed to talk about him rather a lot. She'd written to him, care of Katherine, to tell him she'd seen his work and that she'd been wrong to accuse him of not caring.

She spent most of the week working and when she wasn't at the office or with her mother, she was at the library reading everything she could get her hands on about Poland and the war – dismayed by how little she'd really known about it. If Mum's parents were Polish then Sarah was part Polish too – perhaps even part Jewish. She read everything she could about the camps in Poland, down to the last sickening detail. They'd been taught about the holocaust in school but then it seemed too far in the past to seem real. Now it did. Heartbreakingly real. What about the rest of Mum's family? Had any of them survived?

While at the library, on impulse she'd looked up newspaper cuttings from the journals Neil had mentioned he worked for, searching through them until she found ones with his name on the byline.

His pictures were stunning in their simplicity. One photo depicted an old man, sitting outside the ruins of what must once have been his home. He was looking slightly to the left of the camera, yet somehow Neil had managed to capture the pain and despair in the eyes. There was another of Mrs Thatcher taken during an official trip to Africa. She was in the middle of a group of ragged children who had wide smiles on their faces. In their excitement they were pressing close to her and Neil had perfectly captured her discomfort. He seemed to have a canny instinct for catching people in their most unguarded moments, as if he could see into their very souls. Which is how she had felt when he had looked at her – as if he *knew* her better than she knew herself. And liked what he saw. Mostly.

There were other, more graphic, photos too. Ones that had been taken in China during the recent student protests – of young men and women, kneeling on the ground, their eyes blindfolded, their hands tied behind their backs.

The last ones she looked at had been taken somewhere in Africa – of children, their tiny bellies swollen, eyes covered in flies, a mother holding her baby to a breast that clearly no longer held any milk.

She sat back and closed her eyes. Neil was right. Someone had to bear witness, someone had to tell these people's story. And if not people like Neil, then who?

Today, she was back in the house in Charlotte Square. She'd already spent some time there, browsing Richard's extensive collection of books about the Second World War.

She brushed a stray wisp of hair from her face, sat back on her heels, adding one more book to the pile she'd made on the floor to take home with her to read. She'd lit the fire in the small sitting room and although the rest of the house was chilly, this room was warm and cosy.

Selecting a book she wanted to read, she went downstairs to make some coffee. She'd brought a small jar with her as well as milk, bread, salad and a few other essentials.

She took her coffee into the small sitting room and looked outside. An elderly lady was sitting on a bench, her handbag neatly placed on her lap. She appeared to be waiting for someone.

Sarah sat at the writing desk and started reading, taking notes as she went along. The first-hand accounts of what had happened to survivors of the war were harrowing and draining. Therefore when the doorbell rang, she was almost pleased.

Rubbing the small of her back, she went into the hall and opened the front door.

On the doorstep was a thin, elderly woman with short grey hair, clutching a cheap, vinyl bag. She'd been the one sitting on the bench opposite a short while ago.

'Can I help you?' Sarah asked.

'I believe this is Lord Glendale's house? At least it used to be.' Her English was perfect but accented. She peered past Sarah as if expecting someone to appear. 'I might have made a mistake. It's been so long and my memory isn't what it used to be.'

Immediately Sarah knew this was Magdalena. 'Yes this is Lord Glendale's house. Are you Miss Magdalena Drobnik, by any chance?'

The woman straightened. 'Dr Magdalena Drobnik, dear.'

'Please. Come in!'

Suddenly Magdalena seemed to deflate and she clutched the door jamb for support. Sarah caught her, putting her arm under the woman's shoulder, noting the fragility of her bird-like bones. She helped her inside and onto the sofa, lifting her legs so she was lying flat.

'Please don't fuss,' Magdalena protested. 'I'm a little light-headed, that's all.'

Sarah shook her head. Magdalena's lips had a bluish tinge to them. 'Stay put,' she said. 'I'll just get some water.'

By the time she returned from the kitchen a few moments later, Magdalena was sitting up and fumbling in her handbag.

She brought out a brown plastic bottle and tapped a blue pill into the palm of her hand. Sarah passed her the glass of water and Magdalena washed down the tablet with large noisy gulps.

'The beginnings of heart block, I'm afraid,' she said. 'I'm so sorry to have alarmed you.'

'It's all right. Take your time.'

Magdalena placed the glass carefully on the coffee table. 'I came as soon as I could, but it took a while to get my passport in order. My country might be a democracy again,' a smile flitted across her face, 'but it seems the bureaucrats still hold the power.'

'The solicitors didn't tell me you were already here.' Then she realised she hadn't introduced herself. 'I'm Sarah Davidson.'

Magdalena's face brightened. 'Sarah – I rather hoped you were.'

'I'm sorry if it looks as if I've taken up residence in what is, after all, your property, but you probably know that Lord Glendale appointed my mother as his executor in your absence.'

A look of unutterable sadness passed across her face. 'If I'd known Richard was ill ... I should have guessed when he stopped answering my letters. Not that it would have made any difference. I couldn't have come to him then. If only he had been able to hold on a little longer – I would have been able to see him one last time.'

'Would you excuse me? I'll be back in a moment.' Sarah ran upstairs and took the photograph of Magdalena from the mantelpiece before hurrying back downstairs.

'He has a painting of you like this – in his bedroom – opposite his bed. You were the last thing he saw when he closed his eyes, the first thing he saw in the morning.'

Magdalena took the photograph. 'Oh, Richard.' Her eyes

filled and she dabbed them with her handkerchief. 'I thought I had cried all the tears I was going to.'

Sarah sat down and waited for Magdalena to gather herself.

'I've been longing to meet you,' she said, when the older woman seemed composed again. 'My mother remembers you. She really wants to see you again.'

Magdalena's head snapped up. 'She remembers me?'

'Oh, yes. You meant – mean – a great deal to her.' She took the photo Richard had left her mother from her handbag and passed it across. 'That's her.'

Magdalena covered her mouth with her hand and when she looked up her eyes were luminous. 'So it is,' she murmured. 'Oh, and look, she's wearing my necklace.'

'*You* gave it to her? It's her most precious possession.' Sarah hesitated. 'What I don't understand is why Mum remembers you and not Irena Kraszewska. The woman who rescued her from Poland.'

Magdalena smiled. 'My dear, that's easy to explain. Magdalena is my assumed name. I had to change it when I went back to Poland and so I chose the name of a very dear friend of mine who died in the war. I couldn't take her last name, though – the Germans were very zealous record keepers. But Irena Kraszewska was the name I was born with and if you don't mind, now I'm here, it's the one I'd prefer to use.'

'You're Irena!' Suddenly it all made sense. Perfect sense. Magdalena and Irena were one and the same. Now she could see it. She had the same almond-shaped eyes as the woman in the photograph, the same full bottom lip, even the way her mouth turned up at the corners as if caught in a permanent smile. 'I can't wait to tell Mum.'

'How is Leah – I mean Lily? Is she here?' Irena looked around, her eyes shining. 'I've been so looking forward to seeing her again.'

'She's not well. She had a stroke a few months ago and is in hospital getting intensive rehab.'

Irena's face fell. 'But she's so young! How is she now?'

'She's improved quite a bit in the last few weeks. I think knowing Magdalena – you – were alive gave her something to look forward to.'

'Do you have a recent photograph of her?'

Sarah reached into her handbag and opened her purse. She had one that was taken when they were on holiday in Dorset and which she always kept with her. It was her favourite. In it, her mother looked so happy, so carefree.

Irena studied it. 'Leah,' she breathed.

'What can you tell me about her? How did you meet her? Who was she? Are any of her family still alive?'

Irena smiled. 'So many questions! Of course, I'll tell you everything – at least what I can.' She drew her hand across her face. Suddenly she looked exhausted. Of course it was bound to be emotionally draining for her to be here. Sarah also needed to give her time to recover from her journey.

'We'll leave that for later.' She glanced at her watch. It was after seven. 'Have you eaten?'

'Not since lunchtime. I don't eat very much, although I have to admit, I'm a little peckish.' She smiled in delight. 'There! I remembered one of your idioms.'

'Are you planning to stay here?' Sarah asked. 'I could easily make up a bed for you. Or you could come home with me, if you prefer? There's plenty of room. You'd be on your own tomorrow, but there are shops nearby and a bus stop if you wanted to go anywhere.'

'Thank you, you're very kind, but I would prefer to stay here.'

'Of course.' But Sarah wasn't sure she should, not on her own, not when she clearly wasn't well. However, it wasn't up to her.

'This house holds so many memories for me,' Irena contin-ued, looking around, and fingering the velvet tassel of one of the cushions. 'I never thought I'd see it again.'

'If it's all right with you, why don't we both stay? I've slept here myself, once or twice. It keeps it aired as well as making it easier for me to use the library. I'm sure there's enough in the fridge to throw together a sandwich.'

'I don't wish to put you to any trouble.'

'You won't. Now I've found you, I'm damned if I'm going to let you out of my sight – not until I know everything.'

Irena took off her spectacles and rubbed her eyes. 'I'm a little tired, but I'd love to see your mother again. Would it be possi-ble to visit her this evening, after we've had supper?'

'I'm afraid visiting hours are over for today. For some bizarre reason, they're restricted on Mondays – I guess they don't want hordes of people cramming into the ward and tiring the patients. But you must come with me tomorrow afternoon – Mum will be thrilled.'

'I'd like that very much.'

'How long are you in Scotland?'

'A month.'

'Then we have plenty of time for you to tell me everything.'

Sarah made Irena a cup of tea and left her while she made up some sandwiches and placed them on a tray. As an afterthought she added the remains of the bottle of wine she'd opened the other night. Even if Irena didn't need a drink, she did.

'Would you mind if we had supper on our laps?' Sarah asked when she returned with the tray. 'I'm afraid the dining room is a little chilly.'

'Of course not. I'm sorry to put you to all this trouble.'

'Believe me, it's no trouble. You can't imagine how much I've being hoping to meet you.' Sarah held up the bottle of wine and to her surprise, Irena nodded. 'Let's have our supper, then we can talk,' she said.

When they'd eaten, Irena leaned back in her chair and took a sip of wine. 'If you would indulge an old lady, I'd like to start at the beginning?'

Sarah nodded.

Irena closed her eyes. 'My – our, because it is your story too – story begins in Warsaw. I was about to begin the fourth year of my medical training, but all that changed when the Germans invaded my country.'

Sarah listened, fascinated, as Irena told her about her life in Warsaw, the typhus ruse and why she'd decided in the end to leave Poland.

'The boy, Dominik. Did he make it?'

'Then, yes. Although I'm not sure if he survived the war.'

'I couldn't have done what you did. I would have been terrified.'

'I was terrified. Almost all the time.'

'No, you were brave. Incredibly brave.'

A shadow crossed Irena's face. 'Oh my dear, I wasn't always as brave as I should have been.' She brushed a hand across her eyes. 'Would you mind if we left the rest of the story until tomorrow?' She looked utterly drained.

Sarah hid her disappointment behind a smile. 'Of course. I'll show you to your room. There's plenty of water if you'd like a bath before bed?'

She went to help her out of the low sofa but Irena brushed her away with an impatient hand. 'I might be old, but I'm not yet incapable of getting to my feet unaided.'

Sarah should have known from the little she had learned about her guest that she was made of stern stuff. All the women she'd met in the course of her search seemed made that way.

After Irena was settled in her room, Sarah went back downstairs and cleared away their dishes.

Irena and Magdalena were one and the same and she couldn't wait to tell Mum she was here.

Chapter 51

When Sarah went down to the kitchen the next morning she found Irena already at the kitchen table, dressed and with a lot more colour in her cheeks than she'd had the previous evening. In fact, she was almost buzzing with energy.

Irena pointed to the teapot on the table. 'I made some tea. I remember from when I lived here that you Scots like it in the morning.'

Sarah poured herself a cup and sat down at the table.

'I gather you lived here. I also know you completed your medical training at the Polish medical school. I hunted down a Dr Wilinski and he told me.'

'You've been looking into me?' Irena seemed less than pleased.

'I was curious. My mother seemed so desperate that I find Magdalena – I mean you.'

Irena joined her at the table and gave her a rueful smile. 'Sorry if I snapped. Comes from living more than half a lifetime under Communist rule. Until recently when someone looked into your past it was never for a good reason.'

'I understand.' But did she? Although the Cold War had been going on as long as she could remember, what could she possibly know about life behind the Iron Curtain?

'It's still difficult to talk about the past.' Irena sighed and rubbed her eyes. 'I made so many mistakes and yet there is so much I can't regret. Especially loving Richard and having him love me. I know it's not easy to tell, but behind this wrinkled face still beats the heart of the woman you saw in the photograph.' Once again there was glimmer of a smile. 'Sometimes I look in the mirror and wonder who the old lady staring back at me could possibly be. Perhaps it's for the best Richard and I only knew each other when we were young and beautiful. At least he was beautiful. As for me?' she shrugged. 'He persuaded me I was.'

'You loved him too,' Sarah stated.

'Oh, yes. Very much.'

'Why do you think Richard didn't leave me a letter with the photographs?'

Irena thought for a while. 'I suspect he wasn't sure if your mother knew she was adopted. Knowing him, he wanted to leave you just enough information for you or your mother to find out, if you really wanted to.'

The sun shone through the large sash window, illuminating the thousands of dust motes suspended in the air.

'Why don't I make us some breakfast while you carry on with your story?' Sarah suggested.

Irena inclined her head. 'A boiled egg would be lovely. Now where did I get to last night?'

'You'd decided you had to leave. How did you get out?'

'Henryk and Stanislaw arranged it all for me. They made sure it looked as if Irena Kraszewska had died, bought papers for me and found a guide prepared to take me. It wasn't an easy journey but I made it to London and Richard's father's house. That's how I met Richard . . . ' Irena let out a long sigh. 'But don't you have work?'

Sarah glanced down at her watch. 'Cripes. Yes, I'm afraid I'll have to abandon you to your own devices. Will you be all right?'

Irena's mouth twisted. 'I've survived this long on my own, my dear, I dare say I'll manage another day.'

When Sarah returned to Charlotte Square, after a quick detour to her flat to check for mail, she found Irena in the kitchen, up to her elbows in flour and a pot of stew on the stove.

'Something smells good.'

'I found a butcher's on George Street. I'm making dumplings, too,' Irena said. 'I bought bananas and apples for after.'

'Is there anything I can do?'

'You can pour me some vodka,' Irena said. 'I bought a bottle, seeing as there was none in the house.'

It took all Sarah's self-control not to raise her eyebrows. She rummaged in the kitchen cupboards. 'I can't find it, I'm afraid.'

'It's in the fridge. It's best when it's cold.'

'You drink it straight?'

Irena smiled impishly. 'Of course. There is no other way.'

Sarah poured a finger into a tumbler but when Irena raised an eyebrow she reluctantly added another one. 'What sort of doctor were you in Poland?' Sarah asked, placing the glass on the table.

'A paediatrician.'

'Can you tell me now how you came to know my mother?'

The sparkle in Irena's eyes dimmed. 'It's not a happy story.'

Sarah poured herself a glass of Chardonnay and took a long sip. 'Somehow I didn't think it would be.'

Sarah felt sick as Irena told her how she'd met her mother and what had happened later at the hospital. It was shocking, nauseating, almost unbelievable.

'To lose her mother and brother like that! Do you think she remembers what happened?'

'Yes. She might not have been aware of what was going on but she would have known it was something terrible.'

Sarah could have howled for the little girl her mother had been. It explained so much: her over-protectiveness, her fears, the constant sadness lurking behind her eyes. And why she hated being in hospital so much. 'I have to get her out of there.'

'My dear, are you sure?'

'I should have taken her home ages ago.' She jumped to her feet. 'I'm going to fetch her.'

'Would you like me to come with you?'

'I think it's something I need to do myself.' She pulled a hand through her hair. 'My God, if you could do what you did, I can do this.'

'Where will you take her?'

'Home. To my flat.'

'Is it suitable for someone who's had a stroke? Are there stairs?'

'Yes. Damn. I'll take her home, then – to St Abbs. We'll manage.'

'Why don't you bring her here? We could make up a bed for her in the drawing room. I could help you take care of her.'

'Mum's not your problem.'

'My dear, don't you think I owe something to her too? I should have gone with her – I knew how terrified she'd be without me. And if you do take her home, you're going to need help.'

'Let's go get her, then.'

Sarah's insides churned with anxiety and excitement as she led Irena towards her mother's bed. What if the shock was too much for her?

Her mother was sitting up in her chair, hair neatly brushed, staring out of the window. Irena stopped a short distance away and signalled Sarah with her hand to go forward.

'Mum,' Sarah said softly, and when she turned round she bent down and kissed her cheek. 'You're looking great today.' She sat down on the bed and took her hand in hers. 'Mum, I'm taking you home. At least, I will. Firstly, though, we're going to stay in the house in Charlotte Square.'

Her mother's eyes lit up.

'I should have got you out of here ages ago. But I'm going to take care of you now. Oh, Mum I know what happened to your birth family. I'm so very, very sorry.' She wrapped her arms around her mother's thin shoulders and held her close. To begin with her mother resisted but then she relaxed into Sarah's embrace. It was the first time in her adult life that Sarah had held her like this. Her mother's thin shoulder's started to shake. 'Oh, Mum. It's all right. I'm never going to let anything happen to you again. Not ever.'

She waited until her mother had stopped crying. 'Mum, there's more. I've brought someone to see you.'

She looked over at Irena and smiled. 'Mum,' she breathed, 'Magdalena is here.'

Irena stepped forward and Sarah jumped up, pulling a chair over for her. Her mother looked up at Irena, then back at Sarah, frowning.

'Leah,' Irena said softly, 'It's me, Magdalena.' She added something in Polish.

Sarah watched her mother's face closely, seeing puzzlement turn to realisation then joy. She stretched out her good hand and Irena clasped it, bringing it up to her own cheek. 'Oh Leah, it is so good to see you again.'

Tears were streaming down her mother's face as she gazed at Irena and then at Sarah. It was only then that Sarah realised she was crying too.

She heard the sound of a throat being cleared and looked up to find Sister Haggerty glaring down at her. 'What's going on here? I'm afraid you'll have to leave. It's not time for evening visiting yet.'

'Could you give me a few minutes with my mother, please?'

When Sister Haggerty hesitated, Sarah stood. 'Alone.'

She turned to her mother. 'You trust me to look after you, don't you?'

Her mother frowned. 'Ob?'

'Bugger work. I'll go freelance if I have to.' They were probably going to fire her anyway.

Her mother smiled. It was lopsided but it was a smile.

'Magdalena will stay with you, while I tell the doctors you're coming home,' Sarah said. 'I'll be back in a moment.'

She marched along the corridor and up to the nurses' station. Sister Haggerty was giving the report to the other nurses who were sitting around her in a semicircle, pens at the ready to take notes. She frowned when Sarah rapped on the desk.

'You really do have to leave,' Sister Haggerty said.

'I'd like to see my mother's doctor. I plan to take her home with me.'

The nurses looked aghast. Sister sighed and said a few words to her staff who scuttled off in different directions.

'Your mother isn't ready to go home.'

'Is she getting better?'

'There has been some improvement.'

'Yes, there has. And I'm grateful.' She noticed the small appeasing note that had crept into her voice and took a breath. Chicken Licken was gone for good. 'Is there anything you're doing for her that I couldn't do at home?'

Sister pursed her lips. Linda had come to stand by her side. 'No,' the staff nurse said quietly. 'And in my opinion your mother will benefit from being at home – as long as someone comes in to put her through her passive movements and give her her speech therapy.'

'I'll do her physio myself. I've seen them do her exercises with her often enough. And as for her speech therapy, I believe my mother's speech – if it's ever going to improve – will do so more quickly if I spend more time with her.'

'You can't just take your mother out of hospital,' Sister said. 'There are procedures.'

'So tell me what they are and I'll do them, but trust me, I'm not leaving here without my mother.'

It took several hours. The doctor had to be called. Forms had to be signed and medication ordered from the pharmacy but at last, Mum was in the front seat of Sarah's car, her stick held between her legs and her lopsided smile wider than ever. Irena was in the back.

'Okay, Mum?' Sarah asked, turning the key in the ignition.

She nodded. 'Hap-py … 'ank you, Sa-rah.'

Together she and Irena looked after Lily. They made her a bed on the downstairs sitting-room sofa. Then Irena and Lily talked long into the night. At least, Irena did the talking while Sarah's mother responded with taps of her stick, nods, smiles and tears. Many, many tears.

The next morning they packed their bags and left for Lily's house in the Borders.

Chapter 52

Three weeks after she'd taken her mother from the hospital, Sarah was sitting outside the house in St Abbs, her notepad in her lap, watching the sun slant across the hills. Overhead a nesting seagull's cry was like fingernails raked across tin. As expected, as soon as she'd told work she was taking more time off, they'd fired her. A few weeks ago she had a job and a boyfriend, now she had neither and yet she felt blissfully unconcerned.

She'd done the right thing by taking Mum home. She only regretted that she hadn't done it sooner. Her mother's speech was improving every day; now she managed a phrase or two, sometimes a whole sentence and even a little faltering Polish. She was able to dress and undress herself, even if it took a long time, and she could walk with just the aid of her stick. But it wasn't just the physical difference to Mum's health that made Sarah's heart sing, it was the way her dark moods and the sadness in her eyes appeared to have all but disappeared. Of course, this all might have happened anyway, Irena had told her that, but Sarah didn't think so. She was sure that being surrounded by love was what had made the difference.

The crunch of footsteps on gravel drew her from her reverie. Neil was loping towards her, a small rucksack draped over one shoulder. Her heart swelled until if felt as if it would burst through her ribcage. She'd known that eventually he'd come to find her.

He'd replied to her note of apology, and since then they'd exchanged letters and postcards. His made her laugh or cry, depending on where in the world he was and what he was covering.

'You took your time,' she said with a lift of her eyebrow.

'Been busy. Covering the fall of the Berlin Wall, amongst other things.' He crouched down beside her and lifted the notebook from her lap.

'Hey, that's private.' She tried to snatch it back but he held it out of her reach. 'Give it back.'

'Tell me what's in it, then.'

'It's just some scribblings.'

'You've started a book, haven't you?'

How did this man who knew her so little know her so well?

'No, not a book. Okay then, part of a book. But it's not going great.'

He sat down on the gravel and stretched his legs in front of him. 'What's it about?'

Sarah sighed. 'That's half the problem,' she admitted. 'It started off as a love story, but it's kind of dwindled into nothing.'

'Do you want a second opinion?'

'Not really.' The thought of him reading her work made her toes curl.

She studied him for a moment. Either he hadn't shaved or he was growing a beard. Whatever, the stubble suited him.

'Do you want to come in and say hello to Mum? You can stay the night if you like?'

'Thought you'd never ask.'

After dinner, Irena and Sarah's mother had their tea in the sitting room, while Neil and Sarah took their drinks outside.

She told him everything she'd learned and Neil listened in silence, interrupting only to ask the odd question.

'It's an amazing story,' he said when she'd come to the end. 'Why don't you write it?'

'Me?'

'Why not? You want to be a writer. It's a story that should be told.'

'Oh, I couldn't. I'd never do it justice.'

'Tell me something,' he said softly, 'could you write it from the heart?'

She thought a while. 'Yes.'

'Then you'll do it justice.'

Later, they rejoined the two women inside. Neil quizzed Irena gently and in return told her about his work and his childhood on Skye. 'I'm flying up there in a couple of days' time,' he said, 'once I've filed my story.'

'I would like to go back to Skye,' Irena said. 'It's where Richard and I were the happiest. When I die, I want be laid to rest next to him.'

'I hope that won't be for a very long time.' Sarah said. Over the last few weeks she'd come to love Irena and she wasn't ready to be parted from her – and she was sure her mother wasn't either. 'But of course you must go to Skye. It is your house, after all.'

'Oh, my dear, I have no intention of accepting either of the houses. I'm too old to leave Poland permanently now. How can I leave it after everything and just when it is becoming a democracy again? It is an exciting time and I want to be part of it. No, it is right that you and your children have them. So much was taken from your mother and her family, it would make me happy to know that her child at least was given something back.'

'You don't need to decide now,' Sarah protested. 'Anyway, it's us that owe you. If you hadn't rescued Mum, I wouldn't even be here. I owe my life to you.' And if it hadn't been for Irena she wouldn't have been able to wrap her arms around her mother and tell her that she understood. That she loved her and was proud of her.

'Now, can you tell me if there is still a train to Skye?' Irena asked.

'I want to go,' her mother said. Although her words were slightly slurred, most of what she said now was understandable.

'No need for trains.' Sarah glanced at Neil who gave her a thumbs-up. 'We could all go. Would you mind, Irena?'

Irena's mouth curved in a smile. 'There is nothing I would like better. I have been too much on my own over the years. It will be good to have company.'

'That's decided, then. We'll take my car. We can go whenever you want.'

'Soon,' Irena said, softly. 'Let's go soon.'

Neil grinned. 'Gran is going to love this.'

They set off on their trip less than a week later. Edinburgh was dark with rain but as they drove north the clouds cleared. It was promising to be a perfect day for the drive. Neil had left a couple of days before them and would be waiting for them in Skye. Sarah had packed the car with everything she could think of for Irena and her mother's comfort: hot-water bottles, wellington boots, two sets of waterproofs and some extra blankets. She'd also visited the supermarket and bought more vodka and some wine.

They made good progress until Glencoe when heavy traffic slowed their pace. 'We're not far from the Commando Monument,' Sarah said to Irena. 'In fact, we'll pass right by it. Shall we stop there and stretch our legs?'

'I would like to see it.'

Sarah glanced behind her. Mum was sleeping peacefully in the back seat.

'Is this the way you came when you came with Richard?'

'I think so. I remember taking a train, I think to a place called Kyle of Lochalsh and then a small passenger ferry. Richard wanted me to cycle the rest of the way, but I had to admit I didn't know how to ride a bicycle. So he taught me.'

'Did you know he was in love with you when you agreed to come here with him? I mean, wasn't it rather risqué coming away on your own?'

Irena's smile dimpled her cheeks. 'Are you scandalised?' she asked.

'Not at all.'

'The war changed everything a great deal. No one knew how much time they might have. People married without really knowing one another. Unless you've lived through it you can't really imagine the intensity of those days. Everything was multi-coloured. Every emotion magnified a hundred times. People wanted to grasp happiness while they could.'

'Do you think that's why Richard's mother left his father? It must have taken courage in those days.'

'I expect so.' Irena's eyes darted left and right as she spoke, as if she couldn't bear to miss a moment of the journey. 'I saw a photograph once. It was of a young man. He was wearing a leather jacket but he was clearly in a service of some kind. I knew Isabel must have been in love with him. Just because there was a war on didn't mean that people's domestic lives – their secret heartaches, their lives, their dramas – didn't continue, it just brought them into sharp relief.'

'Photographs,' Sarah murmured, thinking of the photos Neil had taken – the ones he'd shown her and the ones she'd seen in the magazines. She thought of the photograph of her mother as a child and the one of Irena and Richard that had started her on her quest. Photographs were the record of people's lives – their testament to their past and their present. And, as Neil had said, a way of bearing witness.

'Do you know they wouldn't let the Polish soldiers who had flown and fought alongside the British take part in the victory parades?' Irena said. 'So many people gave their lives, won so many victories, but somehow we were never considered a part of the victorious allies. I only learned the full role they played myself after the war, from Richard.'

Sarah almost swerved. 'From Richard! You mean you saw him again – after the war?'

A smile lit Irena's face. 'Oh yes. It took him ten years, but eventually he found me. I think I always knew he would.'

'He found you.' Sarah was delighted. She'd assumed that they'd never seen each other again.

'We would have met sooner if it hadn't been for Communism.' Irena's smile dimmed. 'If we thought we could get on with our lives after the Russians entered Poland we were mistaken. Warsaw was in ruins, but within days people started returning to the place they'd once lived. There was nothing left of their homes but they started rebuilding. I didn't know this at the time. After they liberated us from the concentration camp I was in hospital.'

'You were in a concentration camp!' Sarah said, horrified. Irena hadn't spoken about her time in Poland after she'd rescued Sarah's mother and Sarah hadn't liked to ask, sensing it was a no go area.

'Yes. For almost three months. They didn't know whether I would live. Like most of the survivors I was suffering from severe malnutrition. By the time I was fit to leave hospital, the Russians had imposed their rule. They were arresting all the Poles who had Western connections – particularly those who'd lived in the West and returned to work in the underground. I knew if I took back the name Irena Kraszewska they would arrest me too. So I didn't.'

'I had no job, nowhere to live, and the communists were hunting down anyone who had Western connections.' She looked out of the window. 'But I hadn't gone through everything that happened.'

'What about your father? And Aleksy?'

'Tata was still alive, but very frail. Aleksy . . . ' Her voice trembled. 'My darling brother was shot down in the last days of the war.'

'I'm so sorry, Irena,' She gave Irena a few moments to collect herself. 'Couldn't you have come back to Scotland? To Richard?'

'I wanted nothing more. But it was impossible. Even though I was going under a different name, I couldn't attract attention to myself. I didn't know if someone would give my real identity to the Russians. Eventually I made my way to people who'd been in the resistance and who hated the Communists. They kept me hidden until they could be sure the Russians weren't looking for me. They created documents showing that I had a medical degree, obtained in Poland. Only then could I go to Tata, not as his daughter of course, and look for a job.'

'You could have left then.'

'I couldn't. No one was allowed to leave. Besides, Poland needed me more than ever. More than half of the doctors in Poland had been killed. There were so many in need of medical attention, so many children sick and dying. How could I leave them? Or my father?'

'How did Richard find you?'

'As soon as I could I wrote to him. I asked him how our girl – Leah – was doing and signed it in my new name. I didn't know whether he still loved me – or forgave me for the way I left him. I didn't even know whether he was still alive.' Her voice splintered. 'All through the months when I was in prison, when I was in Bergen-Belsen, I kept his memory close to me. When I was freezing I imagined his arms around me; when I was hungry, I imagined him kissing me. I held the memories of our days in Skye and returned there in my head whenever I could. It's what kept me alive. Over the months after I was released from hospital I didn't know if I could go on if he was dead.'

'But you decided in the end to find out.'

'I had to. I also needed to know that Leah – your mother – was well and happy. Apart from knowing Richard was alive, it was that that kept me going during those long months.'

They had stopped by the side of the road.

Leaving Sarah's mother sleeping, they tramped their way along the path leading to the Commando Monument, which rose from the mist.

'I found a small apartment in Warsaw,' Irena continued. 'One that had been rebuilt but whose owners had long disappeared – probably to one of the death camps. It was small but enough for my needs. The Communists allocated homes and people took what they could get. But in the fifties, they gave me permission to attend a medical conference in East Berlin. I had just returned from a lecture and there was a knock on the door.' She smiled faintly. 'Even years later a knock on the door could still make me sweat.' Her face lit up with a joy Sarah had rarely seen. 'I opened the door and there he was: Richard.'

He was older and there was grey in his hair but it was him. Her knees buckled and he reached out for her, catching her in his arms, swinging her up and holding her close. He carried her over to the bed and laid her down.

'It's you,' she breathed, touching his face with her fingertips. 'It's really you.'

His eyes were filled with pain as he looked down at her. 'My darling, what did they do to you?'

She raised her hand in a futile attempt to smooth her hair. She was aware she had changed. She was thinner than she'd ever been and after her hair had grown back, she'd kept it in a short, easy-to-manage style. But she knew he wasn't talking about her hair.

She smiled. 'Is that the way to greet a woman you once loved?'

He lay down beside her and wrapped her in his arms. 'Once loved? My God.' He buried his face in her neck. 'Loved, still love, will always love ...'

They held each other for a long time before either of them spoke. 'Did Leah make it to you?' she asked eventually, terrified of the answer. The journey from Poland to Britain had to have been full of dangers. The Poles would never have betrayed those who had helped so many to flee, but she knew that not everyone had made it safely out of the country.

Richard sat up and his eyes clouded. 'She did. She's called Lily now.'

'She's with you?'

'Darling, I couldn't keep her.'

Irena sat up. 'What do you mean?'

'I was shot down over Italy in the last months of the war. I was in hospital there for a very long time. By the time I returned home, Leah had been adopted.'

'Why didn't your mother keep her? I would have bet my life she would never turn away a child in need of love and a home.'

'Mother wasn't there. My mother left my father after the war.' His voice cooled.

'Isabel left your father?'

'It's a long story. Apparently she was in love with someone else – Katherine's uncle – during the last first war. She thought he'd died, but towards the end of the last war, she discovered he hadn't. As soon as she knew he was still alive she had to go to him. Before she left, she told me that I was his child, not my father's. My father – because that's what he was to me – had always known, apparently, and yet I can't remember him ever treating me as anything but his only son. Perhaps my mother would have stayed if she'd known that a child needed her, who knows?' He traced her face with his fingertip. 'Do you remember Lady Fellows? Eleanor?'

'The beautiful wife of the pilot who'd died? Of course. I remember everything about that time, Richard.'

'She had a friend who couldn't have children. I'd met her before. She and her husband were decent people. Kind. And desperate to adopt. But one of the conditions they insisted on was that Leah should be allowed to forget her past life. They thought it was better if they adopted her and all ties with her previous life – including me – were severed. When I got out of hospital, I made them promise to send me letters about her once a year. She seems happy with them. They say she doesn't talk about Poland. They hope she's forgotten.'

'I think that's unlikely, Richard. I've been specialising in paediatrics these last two years and I've come to understand that children, even very small children, are more aware of what's going on around them than we can imagine. I think Leah will remember her family, she adored her brother, and I also think she'll remember what happened to them.'

He pulled a hand through his hair. 'She has good parents, Irena. I promise.'

He cupped her face with his hands. 'Are you ready to come

back with me? That's why I'm here. It took me this long to find you; I'm not going to let you go now.'

'Don't,' she said, reaching up and winding her hands around his neck. 'I can't go back with you. You know they won't let me. Besides, I have my work at the hospital and Tata. He's too old to leave and I can't go without him.'

'Then later, when he's gone, I'll use every connection I have to put pressure on the Polish government to let you go.'

'If you do that, you'll draw attention to me. It's too risky. No, my love, let's just enjoy whatever time we have together.'

Once a year until 1981 they'd met up in East Germany and had one glorious week together. Then the Communist government had imposed marshal law on its citizens and their meetings had stopped. She'd never given up hope that one day they would be together again for good, but when her last letters to Richard had gone unanswered, she'd known.

'That's so sad,' Sarah said when Irena finished speaking.

'Better a little of a great love than no love.' Irena smiled at her, a glint in her luminous eyes. 'I couldn't help but notice the way you and Katherine's grandson have been looking at each other.'

Sarah felt a blush creep up her neck. 'How can you know someone for such little time yet know that you will spend the rest of your lives together?' At last she was beginning to realise she could make a life for herself, one where there were risks and heartache and sorrow, but soaring heights of joy too. And if that meant loving a man who risked his life on a daily basis, so be it.

'We just know sometimes. Trust your feelings, Sarah. He's a good man.'

'I know, but I think I have to learn to be on my own first.'

They walked around the monument of the three men in commando uniform. '*United We Conquer. In memory of the officers and men of the Commandos who died in the Second World War 1939–1945. This country was their training ground,'* Sarah murmured, reading the inscription. 'You should be up there with them! Sometimes you'd think it was only men who fought.'

'None of us thought about how we'd be remembered – or cared,' Irena said. 'We were all in it together. Men, women, boys, girls, Poles, the French . . .'

'You haven't told me what happened after the soldiers arrested you.'

Irena looked into the distance. 'There are things I still find too painful to speak about but are still part of your story. One day I will tell you the rest.'

'You'd think we'd have learned that war only brings pain.'

'Sometimes wars have to be fought,' Irena said softly. 'No one has the right to decide who should live and who should die. No one has the right to make people into serfs. If your country and mine – and the rest of the world – hadn't fought the Nazis, we would be living in a different world. The Jews would have been completely wiped from the face of the earth and the Poles would be slaves. Sometimes the only thing we can do is fight.'

'I don't mean you shouldn't have fought. I can see you had no choice. I can't imagine the bravery it must have taken for you to do what you did. I couldn't have done it.'

'How can you be sure?' Irena slid her a look. 'I was an ordinary woman in an extraordinary situation. It is only when we find ourselves faced with exceptional circumstances that we can be sure of what we'll do. We all find courage deep within us when we need it most. And I didn't always do what I should have. When the Jews were being victimised in Warsaw before the war, a group of students protested. I wasn't among them. I thought it might reflect badly on my ambition to become a doctor. If we hadn't stood back then – if we had raised our voices in protest – perhaps what happened would never have happened.

'All I know now is that we must stand against oppression wherever we find it. We must raise our voices and shout whenever we see injustice. We must never think that just because it is not us who are being persecuted that we can turn our heads and avert our eyes. It's why we have to remember the past. Not to carry on hating, but to prevent the same thing happening again.'

Her words made Sarah think. If Neil stopped doing what he was doing, who would speak out for the unseen and the unheard?

Suddenly excited she turned to Irena. 'Did you ever think of writing your story?'

Irena smiled wryly. 'I swore that when the war was over I would tell the world what I had seen. So I wrote it down in a notebook. That's where I wrote everything I found too difficult to speak of, including my arrest and my time in the camp.'

'I'd like to read it. If you'd let me?'

'Yes, of course. When the time is right. But you'll see, I'm no writer.'

'But I could be. What if I wrote your story?'

'It's not *my* story. It's your mother's story, your story, Poland's story.'

'Then that's the one I will write.'

Chapter 53

Irena suppressed a groan as her stiff legs complained. She might feel twenty inside but her body knew better.

But she was here at last. Back at Borreraig house. An image of Richard standing next to the loch in light trousers and a thick fisherman's sweater came to her with such vividness she gasped.

Sarah was unpacking the car, while Lily waited next to it, giving Irena, she suspected, a few moments alone.

The house hadn't changed. Inside it was almost exactly the same as it had been when she and Richard had spent their ten days together. The same old sooty stove in the kitchen, the same table and chairs where they'd sat and drunk wine. Someone had placed a vase of wild flowers on the table and a plate of scones. There was a note, too – from Katherine. She welcomed Irena to Skye and said that she knew she'd be tired after her long journey so had lit the stove and left them something for dinner in the warming oven. She finished by saying that she was looking forward to seeing her again.

Irena moved through to the sitting room. Little here had been changed either. It had the same carpet on which they'd made love in front of the fire, the same drinks cabinet, even the same wind-up gramophone they'd used to play the records they'd danced to. She smiled. It had been a long time since she'd seen one of those.

She closed her eyes almost able to feel him, smell his particular scent, feel the hardness of his chest under her fingertips. She could hear his laugh, see his quirky grin, the way his eyes glittered when he looked at her. Her dear, precious love.

Irena left the house to walk around to the little boat house. It was musty and damp smelling but a fire would soon sort that out. A small boat was moored in the little bay, but Irena doubted that she'd be going out in it this time.

She thought about what Sarah had said about writing her story. It was right that Leah's daughter would be the one to tell it – supposing people wanted to read it. The war wasn't taught in school in Poland and most of the younger generation had little idea what had happened to their country during those dreadful years. Perhaps, if Sarah wrote it, it would be translated into Polish and that way people would learn what had happened to their grandparents?

Sarah and her mother were in the kitchen when she went back inside, fiddling with the old fashioned stove. 'I think I'll go upstairs for a rest before we eat,' Irena said.

'It'll be another hour,' Sarah replied. 'Supposing we get this stove going.' She grinned. 'I might have to go and fetch Neil to come and help.'

'If you don't manage, a sandwich will do me fine. I'm not really hungry.'

Irena left them to it and climbed the stairs to the bedroom she and Richard had shared. The bed was made and the house had clearly been aired in the years it had been empty. She crossed over to the window and looked outside. The loch glittered in the evening sunshine as it had done for centuries and as it would continue to do for centuries to come. Likewise Dunvegan Castle stood, a testament to life continuing. It had survived the Jacobite war and all the wars since and no doubt would survive more. With a sigh, she turned away and lay down on the bed.

As she closed her eyes a shadow moved in the room and she felt the bed sag.

She could smell pipe smoke and peat and feel the heat as he lay down next to her. Her love.

Chapter 54

December 1996

It was a journey Sarah had been meaning to take for a long time, but with her book accepted for publication, she knew she had to make it now. Since Irena's death, she hadn't been able to face coming back.

Over the years she'd visited Poland and in return Irena had come to stay with them in Edinburgh. The children had loved her. She'd never spoken much about the time after she'd been captured by the Germans, only given Sarah the barest details, but she'd entrusted her with her notebook. To be read only on her death.

Reading it had been the hardest thing Sarah had ever done. When she'd finished she'd immediately started writing. The title of her book was *The Silent and the Unseen*, the English translation of Cichociemni, the name given to the Polish SOE agents. It was Irena's story, but as Sarah had promised her, it was much more than one woman's story – it was the story of Poland, of those who could no longer speak for themselves, the story of every brave woman and man who had risked their lives for others. It was also Sarah's story.

She shivered, huddling deeper into her coat as the taxi swung into the hotel parking bay. Neil had offered to come with her but she'd said no. This was a journey she had to make alone. Besides, she didn't want to leave the children with anyone except their father and their grandmother. It was the first time she'd been away from them for more than a few nights and she forced away the images of all the disasters that could befall a four- and five-year-old. But what harm could possibly come to her children under the eagle eyes of their grandmother? Mum had almost completely regained her speech and was even painting a little again. Most of the time she lived alone, often coming to the house Sarah and Neil had bought to visit. Sarah's youngest daughter was the same age Lily had been when she'd been taken from her mother. As a mother herself she couldn't begin to imagine what courage it had taken for her grandmother to have let her child go.

She was here for six days and had it all planned: Warsaw for three days, a train to Krakow for the final three days and then flying home from there.

There wasn't much of the day left by the time she checked in and unpacked, but just enough to visit Pawiak prison.

She took a tram from outside the hotel to the nearest stop and walked the remainder of the way. It took her a while to find it, but there it was – an innocuous-looking building, more like the shell of a factory than a prison. She knew from her research that over a hundred thousand Poles had been brought here, most of them tortured before being taken away and shot. Irena had been taken to a similar prison in Germany.

Sarah paid for her ticket. The museum was empty, apart from the ticket collector and young couple with small rucksacks.

'Not many come here,' the ticket collector said.

She wandered amongst the exhibits, the whips the guards had used, the inscriptions on the wall, the old service revolvers.

The women had been blindfolded and their mouths filled with plaster before they'd been executed – to stop them shouting the Polish freedom slogan. How did these women feel knowing they were going to their deaths? What about those who were leaving children behind? On a board, behind some glass, were some of the farewell letters the women had written on scraps of paper, the handwriting so tiny it was impossible to read from where she was standing. The letters were to their children. What do you say to a child you know you'll never see again? How do you find the right words? What would she say to hers if she knew she was to die? She forced the thought away as well as the impulse to speak to them.

When she was finished, she took a taxi to the Gestapo headquarters. This was the same route that the women and men would have taken from Pawiak prison, in the back of a truck, knowing they were going to be tortured and probably wondering whether they'd have the strength not to betray their contacts.

Here was the office where they would have been interviewed by a Gestapo officer, some taken out into the courtyard and shot immediately; others, returned to Pawiak to await their sentence.

She was nauseous and frozen by the time she returned to the hotel. While she ran herself a bath she phoned Neil.

'How are the girls?' she asked.

'Irene is on a playdate and Annie is in the kitchen making figures out of Play-Doh. Considering it's approximately only eight hours since you've left me in charge, I haven't managed to lose one yet.'

'Don't joke,' she said, more sharply than she'd intended.

'Are you all right?'

'Hold on a moment.' She went to the bathroom and turned off the taps. 'I'm back,' she said. 'About to take a bath then get something to eat. I might order room service; I don't think I can face the hotel dining room tonight.'

'You should have let me come with you.' His voice was soft,

concerned. He still travelled all over the world as a photo journalist. How could she stop him? He was doing what needed to be done and she was proud of him. She'd learned to live with her terror that one day his luck would run out. She'd learned that courage from Irena.

'I had to do it on my own, you know that.'

'Say the word and I'll be there.'

Her throat tightened. Right now she wanted nothing more than to feel his arms around her. But she didn't want him to leave the children. Especially not now. She needed to know he was there, the only person, apart from Mum, she trusted completely to watch over them.

She lightened her voice. 'I know, but I'll be all right. I'm tired. You know I don't do well when I don't get my full eight hours.'

'I'll get Annie for you. Take care, honey. I'll speak to you tomorrow.'

She spoke to her youngest child for a while, feeling the tension drain from her as Annie explained she was making a farmyard from her Play-Doh. She loved her children with an intensity that frightened her sometimes. This was, she now knew, how her mother had felt about her, but tenfold.

The next day she walked to the street where her mother's family had been killed. This was perhaps the hardest bit of her journey. She walked under the archway, just as her grandmother, mother and Irena would have done. She could feel the sadness, the abject terror of the thousands as they were led to their deaths. Why didn't more try to run? From what Irena had told her it was clear that they'd known they were going to die.

In here, in this space, this piece of scrub ground with weeds, was where the patients and staff were shot and burned.

Although she couldn't believe in a God who could have let

this happen, she knelt and lit a candle for the dead. After that she visited the house where her mother had been hidden as a child.

Nothing about the streets of Warsaw hinted at the terrible events of the war.

She knew from her research that over 5,500 kilograms of ash, all that remained of most of the people killed in the Warsaw Uprising, had been collected and buried – 5,500 kilograms! How many people was that?

The pictures of Warsaw after the Germans had destroyed it made her think of a science fiction film about an apocalypse. Barely a building had remained intact. It must have been how Hiroshima had looked after the atomic bomb. In these ruins, Irena and others had fought and died, while the Red Army had waited and watched.

The next day she took the train to Krakow, buying a first-class ticket for a few extra zloty. The carriage was much the same as it must have been when Irena lived here. The same deep velvet seats, the same overhead rails for luggage where Irena had once placed her suitcase under the eyes of the Germans sharing her carriage. Was it on a train like this that her mother had been taken from Warsaw and to a place of safety?

She wrote up her notes, pausing periodically to stare out of the window as field upon field dotted with villages and farms, at this time of year barren and brown, rushed past.

Her hotel was close to the Jewish Quarter and not far from the Schindler Museum and the ghetto and she spent the next day visiting the museum, wandering the streets of the old Jewish Quarter. Just before darkness fell she found the townhouse where Irena had lived with her father as a child.

Tomorrow she was going to Auschwitz-Birkenau. She wasn't sure about the morality of visiting a place where so many had died; there was almost something ghoulish about it, but she owed it to the memory of her unmet grandmother's family – her great uncles and aunts who along with her great grandparents had lost their lives there – to go.

She had decided not to take a taxi, or one of the organised tours. Neither did she want to go by train. Instead, she took one of the regular buses.

It dropped her and her fellow tourists at the end of a long drive leading towards the museum. Auschwitz itself was a small nondescript village with nothing to suggest that it had once been the final stop for millions of Jews, Poles and other so-called *Untermenschen*.

It would have been a similar sort of day when Sarah's grand-mother's family had been brought here. Cold, so cold that even through her layers, Sarah could feel the biting wind. How did the internees survive with only the thin striped pyjamas they were given to wear? But of course they didn't. Most of those not sent to be gassed died of cold or starvation or other diseases within three months.

Although she'd read extensively about the camp, nothing – no book, no film – could have prepared her for the reality. She joined an English tour guide and trailed after him as he described the horrors as he must have done thousands of times: the places where the internees were made to stand for hours in the freezing wind for roll call, the place where they were hung, the cells where they were made to stand upright while slowly starving to death, the hospital block where the experiments were carried out – all of it.

But it was Birkenau that chilled her most. This is where the trains of prisoners were taken and selected. Right to survive; left to die.

Irena had been in Bergen-Belsen, which although not an extermination camp, was in every other way as horrific as this one. Like the inmates here, she had been billeted in a hut, where the women slept, four or five to a bed, the ones on top leaking pus from suppurating wounds as well as other body fluids onto those below as rats scuttled and gnawed at the corpses of those who had died in their sleep. Like the women here who hadn't been sent straight to the gas chambers, Irena had to endure unspeakable conditions. Had she not been taken to Bergen-Belsen just three months before the Red Army liberated the camp, she too would have almost certainly died.

They were shown the remains of the gas chambers, the tunnel where those condemned to death would take their final walk, the passage where the prisoners who'd been given privileged roles would come to collect the corpses to shave their hair and remove their gold fillings before taking their bodies to be burned.

There was one place of which Irena never talked, but had written about in her notebook. A fellow inmate – one who'd been marched from Auschwitz to Bergen-Belsen in the last weeks of the war, had told Irena about it. Sarah left the group and crossed over to an innocuous looking building, a little hut near the entrance of the camp. This was where the children – babies mainly – of the women who had been incarcerated were taken to be drowned in a bucket of water. The other women tried to hide them, tried to feed them with what little food they could scavenge, but it was hopeless. Not one baby survived.

When the tour had finished, Sarah felt drained. She walked away from the rest of the visitors. She needed to be on her own. Doubts were running through her head. Could her book really do justice to the horror that had happened? Could her book do justice to the courage of so many?

She smiled to herself. She was being Chicken Licken again. Hadn't Irena's story taught her anything? Hadn't being with Neil taught her anything? Life was filled with risks. Besides she'd promised Irena that she would tell her story.

She looked towards the sky where the setting sun painted it in shades of orange.

'At the going down of the sun and in the morning, I shall remember,' she said out loud. 'I promise you, Irena.'